More Praise for Beth

DOMESTIC PL

"Beth Gutcheon's marvelous novel tells the story of what happened to my generation in the 1980s better than any book I've ever read. . . . In her writing, she has perfect pitch. I would have been distraught if she had ended this book any other way."
—Pat Conroy

"Gutcheon observes New York as she observes her characters—affectionately and precisely, with a sharp and loving eye. The prose that results is often striking."
—*Chicago Tribune*

"The charms of *Domestic Pleasures*—its wit, its sharp dialogue, its perfectly tuned characters—tackle you early on and keep you pinned, turning pages, through the last, wonderfully satisfying scene."
—Michael Dorris

"An endearing urban fairy tale filled with surprises."
—*San Francisco Chronicle*

"Funny and romantic, Beth Gutcheon is brilliant with teenagers. I enjoyed *Domestic Pleasures* very much."
—Rosamunde Pilcher

"This engaging love story is more than it seems."
—*Los Angeles Tribune*

"One need not be domesticated to enjoy *Domestic Pleasures*."
—Rita Mae Brown

"If Rosamunde Pilcher lived in 1980s Manhattan, she might come up with a romantic novel like this one. . . . Gutcheon's gift for witty dialogue and her canny observations propel the generously proportioned story."
—*Publishers Weekly*

"An entertaining, discerning vision of the frenetic pace of the Big Apple and of the romantic pursuits of single parents in their forties."
—*New York Daily News*

"Well-crafted and absorbing. . . . An enjoyable, skillfully dedicated novel."
—*Cleveland Plain Dealer*

Robin Clements

About the Author

BETH GUTCHEON is the critically acclaimed author of six novels: *The New Girls, Still Missing, Domestic Pleasures, Saying Grace, Five Fortunes,* and *More Than You Know.* She has written several film scripts, including the Academy Award–nominated *The Children of Theatre Street.* She lives in New York City.

DOMESTIC
PLEASURES

Beth Gutcheon

Perennial

An Imprint of HarperCollinsPublishers

A hardcover edition of this book was published in 1991 by Villard, a division of Random House.

DOMESTIC PLEASURES. Copyright © 1991 by Beth Gutcheon. All rights reserved. Printed in the United States of America. No part of this book may be used or reproduced in any manner whatsoever without written permission except in the case of brief quotations embodied in critical articles and reviews. For information address Villard Books, a division of Random House, Inc., 201 East 50th Street, New York, NY 10022.

HarperCollins books may be purchased for educational, business, or sales promotional use. For information please write: Special Markets Department, HarperCollins Publishers Inc., 10 East 53rd Street, New York, NY 10022.

First Perennial edition published 2001.
Designed by Joseph Rutt

Library of Congress Cataloging-in-Publication Data
Gutcheon, Beth Richardson.
Domestic pleasures : a novel / Beth Gutcheon.
p.   cm.
ISBN 0-06-093476-X
1. Aircraft accident victims' families—Fiction. 2. Single-parent families—Fiction. 3. New York (N.Y.)—Fiction. 4. Divorced women—Fiction. 5. Women artists—Fiction. I. Title.
PS3557.U844 D66 2001b
813'.54—dc21
2001039193

01 02 03 04 05 [NK/RRD] 10 9 8 7 6 5 4 3 2 1

To David Gutcheon,
Wonderful Boy

For whom, and without whom

With thanks to Diane Reverand, Wendy Weil, and Tina Nides for their unfailing kindness and friendship, and especially for their patience. Thanks to Sandye Rosenzweig and Elayne Klasson for their time and skill in reading and reacting, and especially thanks to Robin Clements, for the golf game.

DOMESTIC

❦

PLEASURES

The last thing Raymond Gaver expected was that he would die with a key to the Beverly Hills Hotel in his pocket.

He was from New York. He didn't even like Southern California. And he hardly ever stayed at that hotel.

He expected to nail down the financing he needed before lunch, and that happened. He expected he could get to the airport in forty-five minutes, and he had. He expected the flight to be half-full, and it was. What he did not expect was that it would explode in midair halfway to San Francisco, nor that his body would lie in pieces, among the wreckage of the plane and of the other passengers, for more than a day in the silence of the Santa Cruz Mountains while rescuers tried to reach the crash site.

Sherry Zagar was vetting the Gaver-Zagar American Express bill when the phone rang. (You'd think with a specialty in tax law that Raymond could figure out for himself why it made her weary to find charges for his dates' pedicures and hair tinting larded into his hotel bills.)

"Good morning. Gaver-Zagar."

"Good morning. . . . Excuse me. Who have I reached?"

"Gaver-Zagar Partnership. This is Sherry Zagar, can I help you?"

"Is this the office of Raymond Charles Gaver?"

"Who is calling please?" And what fresh hell is this, said Dorothy Parker. Christ! Raymond *Charles* Gaver?

Pause. "My name is Frieda Mailman."

Oh. Who? "I'm sorry, Mr. Gaver is in California this week. Perhaps if you told me what this regards, I could help you."

Another pause. "Um. I'm trying to reach his next of kin."

Oh. Insurance. "Well that would be his son, Jack, who is probably in algebra class at the moment."

"Oh." Pause. "How old is Jack?"

"Sixteen. Are you sure I can't help you?"

"I need to reach Mr. Gaver's family."

"Why?"

"I'm afraid Mr. Gaver has been killed."

"What! By who?"

Sherry realized many hours later that this was an interesting response. She had seen a flashed image of a gun fired in a hotel room. A skull-crunching punch. A pair of hands around a jugular. The woman from the airline, whose name Sherry had already forgotten, replaced this with the true image, the one Sherry would have to live with for the rest of her life, of a man she had once loved, dying in fear and then lying in pieces on the side of a mountain he'd never heard of and never would.

For a while after she hung up, Sherry looked around the office as if she'd never seen it before, and tried to keep breathing. She was in shock. How many times in her life had she said "I'm in *shock*," when what she meant was, "I am crammed with outraged opinion and eager to jam a million words about it down your throat." Now she couldn't say anything. She just looked out the open door of the office to the reception desk and kept puzzling over the nearly empty jug of the office water cooler. Had the faucet handle on the cooler always been blue? She felt surrounded by a great colorless void, into which would occur spikes of thought, as if injected by syringe. Mostly random and amazingly off the point. She became aware that she was shaking her head in an odd way, as a dog does when it has an earache. And thinks there must be some mistake.

That kelim on the walls was Raymond's. From his den at home. The one time Sherry had been to their house (this was before Martha realized Raymond was sleeping with Sherry) she'd admired the rough masculine comfort of Raymond's den, as Martha had arranged it for him. It had kelims and an old leather sofa and a camel saddle from somewhere. And loads of plants. Sherry remembered the little boy, Jack, coming in in his pajamas to say goodnight. Jack was carrying an ancient stuffed beast, allegedly an elephant, that had once been his father's. He'd been sweet and warm and shiny from his bath.

On his own, Raymond was not so adept at creating comfort or effect. Sherry looked at the partners' desk Raymond had bought himself in London. Too good for this office, with a dingy expanse of West Fifty-sixth Street out the window. An antique partners' desk beside bunged-up file cabinets and an overflowing metal wastebasket. Raymond didn't take any meetings here. When he was romancing a backer he did it at breakfast at the Mayfair Regent. He used to take rolls of gorgeous architectural renderings with him. Well, he wouldn't do that anymore. Or sit at that desk.

Jesus. Raymond? What did she do now? What about the new hotel? What about his mother in Florida? What about his secretary? Could Sherry keep the business afloat at all? What about his tickets for *Miss Saigon* next week?

What about the early mornings here alone when they would drink coffee that tasted of cardboard from the Greek deli downstairs, and laugh about where life had brought them and where they meant to go? How, in the middle of your life, do you replace—get along without—a relationship of fifteen years, with someone you've loved and slept with and grown to hate and forgiven and trusted and been betrayed by and forgiven?

God, maybe it would be a relief.

Sherry hadn't spoken to Raymond's ex-wife in fourteen years. She could hardly call her now. But who was going to tell the boy?

∽

"*It looks like* a slam-dunk to me. They had a document in the file saying they couldn't honor checks for over five hundred dollars without a countersignature. The bank has to return the money. Period, full stop."

Charlie Leveque was in his partner Albert's office when his secretary buzzed.

"Mr. Leveque, can you take a call from Sherry Zagar?"

A pause. He tried to place the name. He succeeded.

"Take a number. I'll have to call her back."

"Is that the woman from Cap-Mack?" Albert asked.

"No, it's . . . you know my client Raymond Gaver?"

"The real estate guy . . ."

"Yes. His partner. I guess that's who it is. Look, I've got to go. I've got a squash game."

Charlie Leveque played squash that day with a Wick Brainard during his lunch hour. After that, he went to Cartier to get Sophie, his ladyfriend, a birthday present. He chose a silver fountain pen.

"This is a nice present. Isn't it?" he asked the salesgirl.

"I think your friend will love it." The salesgirl was one of those sleek blondes they grow in northern Europe. She had a beautiful accent. Danish? She smiled at him as she handed him his package. He could see himself in the mirror behind her and he wondered what he looked like to her. A handsome, rather formal man with a good tailor? A dull middle-aged midtown lawyer who couldn't stay up late enough to go out to discos? He took the package and left the store. He didn't know how Wick could bear asking women if they'd like to spend an evening with him, when he didn't know in advance what the answer would be. Wick seem to find it exciting. Charlie thought gamesmanship in matters of the heart was horrible. He hoped Sophie liked the pen.

When he got back to the office, he was a minute or two late for a closing, but fortunately it was a simple and nonadversarial matter, and opposing counsel was perfectly happy chatting up Charlie's secretary while he waited for him. After the closing, Charlie had another meeting, with a client with perennial tax problems. So it was late in the afternoon before he was able to start returning his phone calls. There were two more from Sherry Zagar by then.

⧜

Martha Gaver had taken divorce hard. She'd married young, a man who made more sense to her than he did to a lot of other people, but even after the marriage came apart she couldn't regret the attempt. It was less that she felt the marriage had failed, than she felt some evil genie had taken away the man she married and left behind a furious doppelgänger. When she met Raymond, he was riding a motorcycle down the Via Veneto with a basket of ripe cantaloupes strapped on behind him. The explanation was delicious, and so were the melons. The last time she saw him, he was wearing a suit that had cost two thousand dollars, and bitching because it had gotten impossible, just impossible, to use the subways in New York, and because of Martha he couldn't afford a car and driver.

She grieved for the loss of love and that young lover, and she had also hated the process of divorce in a way that, it seemed, Raymond hadn't. Raymond, through some curious alchemy of his own, had come really to think a divorce was something you could win, as opposed to a situation in which the wounded attempt to contain loss. She once said to her friend Annie, "It's like fighting over who gets the litterbox after the cat is dead. Raymond has forgotten we ever had a cat; he actually wants the litterbox. Full." She and Annie had laughed, and then Martha cried.

Martha, for her first official act when she found herself planning a life by herself, had decided to move to the strangest neighborhood in New York. It was downtown, a warren of huge odd spaces, about equally inhabited by sweatshops, which needed the big loft rooms for rows of sewing machines and illegal aliens, and by artists who needed the big loft rooms for large canvases, or big constructs of wood or glass or metal. She knew no one there, though she was an artist. Raymond, an original and a creator, whose major creation, however, was himself, had found SoHo appalling. They say that during bereavement you should make no major decisions, but Martha had no choice. She had to move. So she decided she wanted everything new.

Married, Martha had never been one to go to bars. But unmarried and working all day alone, she sometimes grew starved for the sound of conversation. She'd go to Fanelli's, supposedly the oldest tavern in the city, and sit in a window by herself drinking tea and reading a book, comforted by the hum of voices. One afternoon there, she met a man named Gillis who lived around the corner.

Gillis, she learned, was a composer who had been divorced for about five minutes. Martha too had been legally divorced for only five minutes but in her case it was a technicality; she'd been separated for three years, and the divorce had been bloody enough to cure her of Raymond Gaver once and for all.

Gillis, quiet, gentle, wearing soft ancient corduroys and a flannel shirt, had seemed about as unlike Raymond Gaver as you could get. And Martha, who had just that morning written in her journal that she was for the first time in years feeling truly at peace, wanting only not to be upset anymore, was deeply in love by the end of the week.

Annie said, "My rule of thumb is, don't go near them until they've been divorced half as long as they were married."

Martha said, "I'd have to wait seven years."

"I'm telling you."

"Annie, he's something very special, and he's had an awful time. He never really loved his wife; they were kids when they got married. He says he's in love for the first time in his life."

"Martha, I'm telling you."

But Martha hadn't listened, because of course nobody does listen.

Gillis was bright, Gillis was tender, Gillis was a gifted lover. Annie liked him, Martha's son Jack liked him; anyone would. For a brief couple of months Martha thought she'd finally got it right. Then she began to notice that for someone who was loved and in love, she was crying an awful lot.

And god knows, she was hearing a lot about Gillis's ex-wife. Valeria was frigid, Valeria was a child, Valeria was a narcissist, Valeria was sentimental. People fell in love with Valeria when she played the flute, Valeria was jealous of Martha. Gillis was obviously still very much in touch with Valeria. At last Martha conceded that no matter how often Gillis swore that he loved her, loved her, loved her, that their love was a starving beam of moonlight compared to the raging blaze in his heart, which was the drama of Gillis and Valeria. Unfortunately, by the time she fully understood this, she was four months' pregnant.

Annie was nice enough not to say I told you so.

Gillis and Valeria had never wanted children, and when they parted, Martha made it clear to Gillis that she didn't expect him to be a father to the baby. It was her choice to have it, not his. When her doctor told her she was pregnant, he had also told her what she already knew: that it was a class-B medical miracle. If she didn't complete this pregnancy, there would never be another. Martha discussed it with her son Jack, who thought a baby would be great, much more fun than breeding guppies, and she discussed it with Annie, who thought she was nuts, and she consulted her heart, and said yes. If success in life is in large part timing, Martha was not exactly on a winning streak.

When baby Fred was born, Martha was alone because Annie, her Lamaze coach, was on vacation with her husband. Jack came to the hospital and brought the baby a catcher's mitt he'd bought with his own money. And the next day, Raymond came to the hospital with Jack. "I wanted to see my son's brother," he had said. She had stared at him, holding flowers at the foot of her bed. Raymond did love children. He did love Jack. They had once hoped and hoped for more babies.

Almost two years had passed since then. Martha was often exhausted, and often lonely, but never sorry about the baby. She could work at home, and she had Annie for friendship, and Jack, and she had even managed to create, after a time of recovering from disappointment, a decent friendship with Gillis. Which is how she happened to be out at a recital of bewildering new music with him in a barnlike space that had once been a cheese factory, when Charlie Leveque was trying to reach her.

The building where Martha and her sons lived, on Crosby Street, had a hand-operated elevator. This meant that the last person who used it to ascend would have to bring the elevator to the ground floor if anyone rang for it. Martha and Jack usually used the stairs.

Martha and Gillis had said goodnight at the street door. As she trudged up the third flight of stairs, she could hear the Talking Heads carrying on in Jack's room. "This ain't no party! This ain't no disco! This ain't no foolin' around!" No. She smiled. This was in fact Jack's usual MO for getting through his homework. Jack was looking particularly hideous at the moment because his friend Pia had tried to give him a Mohawk with some clippers she'd bought with her Christmas money.

This had not worked out. "I look like I need the Lawn Doctor," Jack had said. So they had tried again, with the only blade on the clipper they could make work right, and now his whole head looked like a putting green, only blessedly not green. Martha kept pictures in her bedroom of Jack at six and eight and twelve, her beautiful shining-haired boy, to remind her that he had been a lovely child and would be a lovely man.

"I'm home, sweet pea!"

"This ain't no party! This ain't no disco!"

Martha smiled and went to hang up her coat. In the kitchen she and Jack kept a pad with running messages to each other. Tonight Jack had written in his angular script, surrounded by sketches of Batman and other superheroes of his own devising:

Maternal Unit.
8:15.
A Mr. Leveque called you. IMPORTANT.*** (he sez). Office
#555-8166. Home #555-8979.

Martha was pondering this as Jack emerged from his room and came to kiss her.

"Hi, sweet pea. How was your evening?"

"Fine. How was the music?"

"Very odd. Gillis liked it. How much do I owe you?"

"Four dollars. Freddie has the trots. I gave him a banana."

"Good boy. And no apple juice?"

Jack looked blank. He knew that by now, in bed with his bottle his baby brother would have put away about a pint of apple juice, his favorite substance.

"Oops."

Martha smiled. "He'll live. Thank you for remembering banana. It's bananas and rice for diarrhea, and no other fruit. Did you cook your lamb chops?"

"No, I ate a huge fried rice after school. I'll do it now."

"I'll do it, honey."

"Thanks," said Jack. "Who's this Leveque unit?"

Martha was rooting around in the refrigerator. "He's your father's divorce lawyer."

There was a silence. Nobody's favorite topic. She turned on the broiler and began trimming the lamb chops.

"He said it was very important," said Jack.

"I don't see how it could be," said Martha. She didn't see any reason she should have to talk to Charlie Leveque again in her life. She thought he was a cold-hearted snob, and he'd been all too adept at aiding Raymond in his campaign to become his worst self. The phone rang.

"Yes, hello?" Martha answered, with her knife in her hand.

"Hello, Martha?"

"Yes. This is she."

"Martha, this is Charlie Leveque."

Well, hell, Charlie, I knew that, but I don't see any reason to make anything easy for you. You sure never did for me.

"Yes, Charlie."

"I'm sorry . . . can you hear me all right? I'm in a pay phone . . . at the Met."

"Yes, I can hear you fine." Oh, a pay phone at the Met? Is this some new form of torture, Raymond's going to have his lawyer call me from the opera that I can't afford to see, and the ballet and the theater, just to tell me what's playing?

"I'm sorry . . . this is hardly ideal but I felt I should reach you as soon as . . . wait a minute . . . Martha, could you call me back here, I can't find another quarter. . . ."

"This really isn't very convenient for me. I'm cooking dinner for Jack. . . ." I'm a mother, remember? Asshole? Whatever your client may have told you about me.

"Please. The number is 555-1010." There was an electronic buzz, and a recorded voice requested another coin. Then the line went dead. Martha hung up. She stood for a moment, wondering if he would then go panhandling for quarters among his fellow patrons of the arts and liking the image. Then she looked at Jack, sitting with his back to her reading the paper, and pretending not to listen, and she called Charlie back.

"Thank you," said Charlie. Standing waiting, not panhandling. Oh no, that's right, there was a long line for those phones at intermission. Probably a line of cross mothers needing to reach the sitter to hear if little Nicole's fever was down and not at all pleased with some well-fed bozo refusing to relinquish it.

"You're welcome."

"Is Jack right there?"

"Yes." What is this?

"Oh." A pause. "I don't know how you're going to feel about this."

No of course you don't, because you don't know me. You may think you do, but believe me, you don't. Feel about what?

Charlie said, "Sorry. I'm not doing this very well. Martha, Raymond is dead."

There was a clap of silence in the room. And a buzzing in her ears. She felt her heart take a long irregular beat and wondered if it was going to stop.

"What?"

"He was killed in a plane crash in California yesterday afternoon."

The evening news last night. Aerial pictures of a PSA plane in pieces in the mountains, recordings of the last words of the pilots from the cockpit, then an explosion. Late-breaking news that a disgruntled ex-employee had claimed repeatedly that he'd planted bombs on the company's planes. . . .

"I didn't know he was *in* California," she said.

"I'm sorry. . . ."

"Thank you. I have to go now."

"I tried to reach you before, I knew you'd have to tell Jack. . . ."

"I have to go now." She hung up. Jack was looking at her. He knew something was coming, he didn't know what.

There was no funeral. Raymond was cremated in California and returned to the East Coast in a parcel wrapped in brown paper and tied with string. He was hand-delivered to the office of Carton, Leveque, and Humboldt by an employee of the airline who was on her way home to New Jersey to begin a maternity leave. He spent part of the morning in the drawer of the receptionist, until Mr. Leveque's secretary was sent to inquire if anything had arrived. Raymond was at last carried down the hall in the elaborately manicured hands of a girl he had once taken to Maxwell's Plum for drinks, and delivered to the office of his lawyer, Charles Leveque, now the executor of his will. He was still wrapped in brown paper because no one knew whose place it was to unwrap him.

Outside, drenching rain had begun to fall; the city had been on hurricane alert since morning. Some of the secretaries who lived on the Island were lobbying to go home early. Charlie Leveque, however, still had a long afternoon ahead. He was trying to reach Raymond's mother, Trudy Gaver Green, but this was not easy, as Mrs. Green was living on a sailboat in the Florida Keys with her new husband. Their only known telephone number, at least as far as Sherry Zager could find for him, seemed to ring in an establishment called the Coow Woow. His first call had gone like this.

"Coow Woow."

Pause.

"Hello?"

"Hello, Coow Woow."

"Yes, hello. I may have the wrong number. I'm calling from New York, trying to reach a Mrs. Roger Green. Can you tell me if I'm calling the right place?"

The voice on the other end was male, and relaxed. Very relaxed, in fact. "I don't know," it said pleasantly. "Hold on. *Hey Gordy!* Do we know anyone called Mrs. Green? Mrs. Richard Green?"

"Roger Green," said Charlie. In the distance he heard a voice answer, "Yo, that's Trude."

"Oh *Trude*," said Charlie's informant. "Yeah, Rog and Trude. You calling from New York?"

"Yes, I am, I'm trying to reach Mrs. Green. . . ."

"What's the weather like? It raining?"

Charlie hesitated. "Yes. It is. I tell you, it's quite important that I reach Mrs. Green. I don't suppose she's there at the moment?"

"No, man, they don't come in till four, five o'clock. They're working."

"I see. Is there another number, then, where they can be reached?"

"I don't think so."

"Oh," said Charlie. "Well, can you tell me, what is a Coow Woow?"

"Sure, I think it's like a bird or something. *Gordy!* What's a Coow Woow, a bird id'n it?" There was a rumble from, this time, a greater distance, as if Gordy had receded to a farther Key. "Uh huh . . . ," said

Charlie's informant. "Oh, yeah." Then to Charlie: "It's some rum drink, that like the pirates used to drink. You make it with lime juice."

"Thank you," said Charlie. "Well. My name is Charles Leveque. . . ."

"Mine's Ringo."

"Nice to meet you."

"You, too."

"You having a slow day down there?"

"Yeah," said Ringo.

"I see."

"Stopped raining, though."

"I'm glad. Anyway, my name is Charles Leveque, and it's quite important that I reach Mrs. Green as soon as possible. Can you give me advice on the best way to do that?"

"The best way to do that is to tell me, and I'll tell her whenever she comes in. What's it about?"

Charlie weighed his answer. "It's about her son."

"I didn't know Trude had a son," said Ringo pleasantly.

She doesn't, occurred to Charlie, but seemed the wrong way to break the news. "Could you take this number, please, and ask her to call me collect?" he said, and gave the number. Ringo swore he had a pencil and seemed to be taking careful dictation. "Please tell her that I'll wait in my office for her call. Will you do that?"

"Your office?" This seemed an exotic concept to Ringo.

"Yes. I'm an attorney. I'm her son's attorney."

"Oh. Okay."

"Please tell her I'll wait here for her call. You're pretty sure she'll be in today?"

"Yeah, well, they weren't in yesterday, so I'm pretty sure they will be."

"Perhaps I should give you my home number, too." Charlie did that, and Ringo promised that he had the message and its importance firmly planted, and in any case there was nothing more that Charlie could do.

In New York, the wind was beginning to rise and drift. The light outside was dim and yellowish; although it was three in the afternoon, it looked like sunset. One of the paralegals came to the door.

"Excuse me, Mr. Leveque. Jerilyn says the radio says the tunnels are starting to flood." Charlie looked out the window. Across the street in the Bigelow Building, he could see that office lights that often burned till dinnertime were being turned out, business over for the day. New Yorkers who had to face the L.I.E., or the Long Island Railroad, or the roads to Westchester and Connecticut, were going home while they still could.

"Is Mr. Carton still here?"

"No," said Karen, "he never came back after lunch."

"Oh. Well, I guess that whoever wants to go should go."

"Okay, thanks." She snapped off toward the reception area to spread the word. By the time the sun set, a little before five, Charlie was the only one in the office answering the phones. He took four calls for Jerilyn, the receptionist, and a dozen for the other attorneys before the call came through from Florida about six o'clock. From the careful, distinct way she spoke, Charlie suspected that Trudy had already sampled a few Coow Woows.

"Mr. Leveque?" she said. "This is Gertrude Gaver."

"Yes, Mrs. Gaver."

"Mrs. Green. I just meant this is Raymond Gaver's mother."

"Yes, Mrs. Green. I understand. Thank you for calling back."

"You're welcome."

"You're not easy to reach."

"No, I know that. We were out painting."

"Oh, you're a painter."

"Yes. I do watercolors. Rog does oils."

"I see."

Charlie wondered what to say next. How do you broach the subject of his call? He said, "Do you sell your work? Or is it just for . . . um . . ."

"Oh my, yes," said Trude. "Rog has a contract with the Wayside Lodge Motel chain; they only want seascapes though. I sell my work through a gallery in West Palm."

"Uh *huh*." A pause. Finally Charlie plunged in.

"Mrs. Green, I've been your son Raymond's attorney."

"I thought he used Mort Gelbwaks."

"He may for the business; I've handled his personal affairs. His divorce, for instance."

"Oh, yes," said Mrs. Green as if she didn't want to hear about it.

"I am also the executor of his will. Mrs. Green, I'm sorry to have to tell you, but Raymond was killed in a plane accident on Tuesday."

There was a silence.

"On *Tuesday*?"

"Yes. It took a day for the airline to . . . identify everyone and notify their families."

"Well *I'm* his next of kin, aren't I?"

"Yes, I guess you are, except for Jack. In any case, I've been trying to reach you, and I'm sorry to be the bearer of such unhappy news."

Through a muffled pause in which the receiver seemed to have been covered or stuffed into something, he heard "Ringo, give me another colada, will ya?"

"Mrs. Green?" he said, several times. After a bit, she answered him. She sounded like someone translating into a language she couldn't remember very well.

"Where was this plane crash?"

"California."

"Was it in the papers?"

"Yes, it was."

"Tuesday?"

"It was in the eastern papers Wednesday. Two days ago."

"Was Raymond's name in it?"

"I don't think so. They hadn't yet notified the next of kin."

"I'll say." The phone was muffled again. "Ringo," Charlie heard, "do you have any papers from this week?"

"I don't, prob'ly Gordy does."

Trudy came back on the line. "How do they know it was him?"

"I'm not sure. I gather identification wasn't a problem. . . . You could talk to his partner, Miss Zagar, if you want."

"No," said Raymond's mother. She didn't want. What did she want?

"Where is he?" she asked.

"Well . . ." Charlie's glance fell haplessly on the brown paper parcel now sitting on his couch. "That's partly why I'm calling."

"Is he still in California? Was there a funeral?"

"In his will, he made provisions for the event of his death. He didn't want a service, and he wanted to be cremated."

"Impossible. Against his religion."

"It's what he wanted."

"Who cares what he wanted. He's dead. Tell me where he is, and I'll figure out how to make the arrangements."

"I'm afraid his wishes have already been carried out. I'm afraid he's right here."

"What do you mean?"

"Here in my office."

"Oh, god." It sounded as if she were going to cry, but she didn't.

"Does Marty know about this?" she asked finally.

"Martha? Yes. She does."

"And she approved of it?"

"I don't know if she did or not. It wasn't up to her."

There was another silence.

"And Jack?"

"He wanted his father's wishes carried out."

"He's only fourteen."

"Sixteen."

Another silence.

"Mrs. Green. I know this is a shock for you. I wish there had been a more tactful way to let you know."

"I'm all right."

"Yes. Is your husband there?"

"Of course he's here," she said crossly, as if Charlie could see very well but was being stupid on purpose.

"Good. I wanted to ask you . . . do you have an idea about the disposition of the ashes?"

There was a sort of wail.

"Should he be buried near his father?"

"He can't. Not cremated."

"Perhaps you'd like to scatter him. In the sea down there." He knew he was sounding desperate.

"He was scared of water," she said at last, and broke down.

"I'm sorry. I'm really very sorry," said Charlie. He was thinking he'd probably never known a grown person before who was scared of water.

"I'll be in touch with you soon again, as we start to carry out the will . . . ," he said. But he was no longer in communication with the Coow Woow.

∞

"**H**ello? Jack?"

    "Yes?"

"This is Mr. Leveque."

"Hello."

"I need to go through your father's apartment."

"You do?"

"Yes, I have to look for papers, and I have to start making plans for his personal effects. You're the heir, and it's your house too. I thought you might want to be there."

When Raymond moved out of the apartment he and Martha had shared, he had chosen a high-rise in the West Eighties just off Columbus. He knew the older buildings along the park were more chic and that brownstones had more character, but he didn't really like old things, and he had had enough, living with Martha, of pretending to like things he didn't get the point of.

Martha came from a good family, and had gone to what Raymond's father described as fancy schools, so Raymond had expected Martha to be some help, socially speaking, to a man on the way up. Instead, she seemed to have no interest in impressing anybody or any particular talent for doing it. Take clothes alone; Raymond loved clothes and owned an immense number of them. He had pictured Martha, lovely Martha with her long neck and wide gray eyes, walking into parties on his arm looking drop-dead chic, so that other men would envy him and their wives would know he could afford to dress her in Geoffrey Beene. But instead of developing any taste in clothes, Martha had a tendency to go straight to her drafting board after breakfast, get lost in her work, and spend the whole day padding around in her pajamas. She had once admitted to him that she'd found herself in the bank at midday, her head full of the story she was illustrating, and suddenly realized she couldn't remember getting dressed. She had to say a little prayer before she looked down to see what she was wearing. Raymond could absolutely not understand why on earth she expected him to think that was funny.

The lobby of the building Raymond had moved to had a large mosaic mural in an abstract expressionist style that seemed to represent, if anything, jungle growth in lurid red and navy blue. At the base of these fronds was a pool with a fountain. Here Charlie Leveque stood with his hands in the pockets of his safari jacket as he waited for the building manager to take him up to Raymond's apartment. It was Saturday; the storm had passed and he'd walked across Central Park under a clear glittering sky.

There were pennies in the mosaic pool, and a slug the size of a subway token, and a chewed piece of blue gum. Charlie was studying these when he was joined by Mrs. Sears. They shook hands and entered the elevator.

"A lot of doctors in this building," Charlie observed. He'd noticed about eight brass plates screwed to the yellow brick outside the front entrance.

"Yes, we let them in when the market was soft. We want them out now. They're mostly shrinks, except the urologist on the ground floor. He has his own entrance."

The elevator labored up to the twentieth floor, where Charlie followed Mrs. Sears out and down the hall.

It was eerie to walk into an apartment you've never seen before, especially one where the occupant expected to be back in five days. Charlie had known Raymond Gaver fairly well, he thought, from the long and intimate process of handling his divorce. If he had tried to picture Raymond's digs, he wouldn't have pictured this.

He would have pictured surroundings like those in which he tended to meet Raymond. The deep leather chairs of men's clubs. Good, if dark, oil paintings. Of what? Scottish landscapes. And horses. Beautiful fabrics perhaps, like Raymond's shirts and suits. He'd have pictured flowers, like the handsome arrangements at the hotels where they met for breakfast.

Raymond's apartment was huge, but bare. The living room, a corner room with grand views and a tiny terrace, had in it a blond bookcase mostly filled with paperbacks, some cases of wine standing upright on the floor, two canvas sling chairs of the sort nobody can ever get out of, a sofa, a table holding a stereo system, and records in wire racks along the floor against the baseboard the length of one wall. The biggest and by far handsomest thing in the room was a huge pool table. The room was terribly hot, a parching, dry heat. There was the corpse of a potted plant on a windowsill that looked as if it had expired in a desert. Some girl must have brought it as a present; nothing about this apartment looked as if the occupant would have wanted the bother of caring for a live thing.

Charlie resisted a temptation to turn the wine on its side. It wasn't his business; it wasn't his wine, but still, he hated to see something valuable pointlessly mistreated. He wondered why, if Raymond didn't know even that much about it, he had bothered to buy it.

Mrs. Sears had her own concerns. After she'd gone through the rooms turning on the lights, she began to inspect the floors. This was the top floor (though there were penthouses above), and in several places the marquetry was white and buckled from leaks in the ceiling. In one place Raymond had put down a roasting pan lined with newspaper, but in others it appeared from the state of the floor that he had elected not to bother. The date on the newspaper in the roasting pan made it a year and a half old.

"Why didn't he call the super?" Mrs. Sears demanded.

Charlie shrugged. "Some people don't notice things."

"They do when they own. That's the trouble with rentals. Somebody's going to have to take care of this."

Mrs. Sears went into the kitchen to inspect; Charlie sought out the bedroom.

Walking into the bedroom made Charlie feel as if he'd walked into an occupied bathroom without knocking. There was a heap of shirts on the floor, apparently ready for the cleaner. There was a pair of undershorts in the wastebasket and one sock; its mate was on the floor nearby where Raymond's throw had missed. There was a suitcase open on the unmade bed, half-full. Charlie didn't know if it was still packed from a previous trip or whether Raymond had changed his mind about what bag to take in the middle of getting ready. There was a light burning in the bathroom, which had been left exactly as it was the moment Raymond finished his last shower before the plane west. There was a handsome cotton dressing gown on the hook of the door. A clothes hamper half-full. A number of toothbrushes in a glass, dental floss, a used-looking gum stimulator, all lying around the sink. A hairdryer, plugged in and lying on the counter. Charlie turned off the bathroom light and shut the door.

"How soon will you be moving out?" asked Mrs. Sears, coming to the door. She was carrying a Revere Ware double boiler in her hands.

"I don't know yet."

"The rent is due in ten days."

"Send the statement to my office."

"What about fixing those floors?"

"I don't know until I see the lease."

Mrs. Sears looked dissatisfied. At last she said, "Well, bring the keys back to me when you're finished. I'm in 2G."

"All right," said Charlie.

"This double boiler is mine," she added. "I lent it to Mr. Gaver when he was giving a dinner party." And she went out, clutching it.

When Mrs. Sears had gone, Charlie started opening drawers, looking for bank records and other things he would need to put Raymond's affairs in order, but all he found were clothes, in quite an array. He had just found a hanger full of wide ties from the sixties, which must have been left from Raymond's law school days, in a closet in the hall, when the doorbell rang. At the door Charlie found Martha. Her hair was loose and windblown, and she was thinner than he remembered. She looked sad, and older, with something deep and quiet in the expression about the eyes. She was carrying a baby Charlie judged to be about two. He was a beautiful child, with glossy platinum hair and long, dark eyelashes. With them was a horror wearing black jeans, thick black boots, and an old-fashioned overcoat. It had imperfect skin and was nearly bald.

"Mr. Leveque," said the horror, "how do you do? I'm Jack."

Charlie shook his offered hand and said, "Come in."

Jack shook hands and then walked past Charlie into the living room, where he stopped. His father's house. That it looked so exactly as it had the last time he saw it did not make this easier.

From the door, Martha watched her son.

"Hello, Martha," said Charlie. She nodded to him.

"I didn't think he should have to do this alone," she said, and went past Charlie into the living room. Jack, somber, took off his coat and then helped Martha with hers. Together, they extracted the baby from his jacket. Gravely, the host now, Jack took the clothes to the hall closet and hung them up. Then he went to the lounger and sat down.

"This is his chair," he said to his mother, and then stopped, to stop tears.

"The pool table's great," she said at last.

"Yes," and he smiled.

"When did you get it?"

"Christmas, a year ago."

"Who was better?"

"Oh, Dad was. He used to hustle in college."

She smiled. "I remember I knew that. But I never saw him play."

Jack got up and took a cue from the rack on the wall. He chalked it and moved one or two of the balls around the table, then walked around to the other side. Martha and Charlie both watched. He held for a nervous moment, and then tried for an elaborate double bank shot. He missed it.

"Damn," he said. He put his cue back.

"Where did you sleep?"

"This little room off the kitchen." Jack led the way. The room was little indeed, containing a battered desk, a Harvard chair, a tall file cabinet, and a couch that folded out into a bed. There was a bookcase with books and comics and cassettes belonging to Jack. It was bleak. Martha touched Jack on the shoulder and said nothing. It was very, very strange for both of them, to have Martha once again in the kingdom of her husband. One that she'd never seen. A place that was in some way her son's home.

"Well, Jack," said Charlie, "have you thought about what you would like to keep?"

"Sort of."

He walked out again to the living room, and stood in the middle of it, looking lost.

"Could I keep the records?" he was asking Charlie.

"You can keep anything you have room for. It belongs to you."

Jack moved suddenly, shifted and went to the window, as if this sentence were an unwelcome bird trying to perch on his shoulder.

"Do you want to sort the records, honey? Or take them all?" Martha asked.

"Take them all."

"Okay."

There was another silence, rather long. Jack seemed to want to say something, but couldn't bring it out. Martha watched him. Charlie was surprised at her sadness. It shouldn't surprise him, he supposed, but somehow it didn't . . . fit. He was, and he knew he was, perhaps the least appropriate person in the world to be witnessing this moment of her mourning, if that was what it was.

Charlie watched Martha, remembering. The first time he had met her was at a conference in her attorney's office. She had then, as she had today, a kind of composure that was very attractive. But as Raymond had read his terms for separation, prepared by him and Charlie, Martha had first looked amazed, then begun to shake, and finally in tears left the room. The last time he saw her, three years later, when they met to sign off on the separation, she had refused to shake Charlie's hand. (Raymond was pleased with Charlie, whose suggestion it had been to drag the settlement out. "The longer it takes, the longer you get to keep your money, the more it costs her.")

Charlie watched them both as Jack said lightly, as if he didn't care much at all, "The only thing I really want is the pool table."

Martha nodded. She stared at the pool table. She looked around the room. The pool table was massive, Victorian, with woven leather side pockets and great carved urn-shaped legs.

"Well, okay. Let's take that."

"Mom. We can't."

"Yeah, we can. We'll put it in the living room."

"Then we won't have a living room."

"So what?"

She knew her son. She knew if it wasn't truly important to him, he'd say no, and never mention it again. Instead, he gave her a look of boundless gratitude and smiled. Since it was the first time he'd smiled in four days, she smiled too.

The baby, who'd been in the kitchen, came in with a pencil and brought it to Jack.

"Thank you, Fred," said Jack, taking it. Fred beamed and waddled off.

"What about the books?"

"Do *you* want any of them?" asked Jack.

"Some may be mine, actually." Martha went over to the bookcase.

"What about the clothes, Jack?" said Charlie. Both Martha and Jack turned to him.

"I don't know," said Jack.

"Why don't you come look," said Charlie. Jack looked at his mother.

"Do you mind if I don't?" She had always loved Raymond's clothes. The way he dressed.

"No, fine." Jack and Charlie went into the bedroom.

"What size are you?" Charlie asked.

"Medium," said Jack.

"I mean, what shirt size?"

Jack looked bewildered.

"Let me look." Charlie moved the collar of Jack's shirt so he could read the label. It said The Gap. Medium. Jesus, didn't the kid *have* any real clothes?

Charlie put his hands on Jack's shoulders, assessed their width, the boy's height.

"You're not far off your father's size," he said, encouraging. The kid had beautiful teeth and beautiful eyes . . . if you could only put him in a proper suit and a wig, he might look almost human. "Take off your shirt. Let's see."

Jack took off his shirt, revealing a T-shirt underneath with a huge pair of lips on it, and the legend ROCKY HORROR PICTURE SHOW. Charlie went to the closet and chose a striped shirt with white collar and cuffs, London-made. He watched as the boy buttoned it. It was a little big in the neck but nearly a fit. Charlie began to feel excited. He felt like Professor Higgins. Take this guttersnipe from the flower market and set him loose at J. Press, and you could take him to the Century Club for lunch. Charlie chose a soft gray flannel jacket, impeccably cut, and walked around behind Jack. He held the coat for him. Jack slipped it on; the fit was nearly perfect except for the sleeves. They stood, Charlie behind Jack, looking into the full-length mirror at the boy in his father's clothes. Evidently they saw different things. Charlie was about to offer congratulations when Jack leaned against the closet door and started to sob.

Charlie sat down on the bed. He stared at the floor and wondered what would happen if Patsy were dead, and some asshole came and made Phoebe try on her clothes. He'd tear the guy's heart out.

The crying went on for a number of minutes. Martha's footsteps approached, in a hesitant, questioning pace. She stopped though when she heard the weeping, and waited. At last she came to the door.

"Let's see you, sweet pea."

Jack, amazingly, produced a clean handkerchief from his jeans and wiped his eyes and nose. Then he straightened, turned to his mother, and showed himself.

"You look wonderful." Very soft.

"I know."

"Would you like to take some of these things?"

Jack shook his head no. He couldn't risk more speech.

"Do you want to give them away?"

Jack didn't answer. He looked at the floor.

"I think," said Martha gently, "that Mr. Leveque would arrange to store them for a while, so you could decide later."

"I'd be glad to do that, Jack," said Charlie, wondering how soon he could get out of here. "Would you want that?"

Jack nodded. There was another pause.

Martha said, "What about choosing something for Grandma Trudy?" and Jack nodded and blew his nose and went out to the living room with her.

∞

"How *did you* like Mr. Leveque?" asked Martha.

"I liked him."

Martha and Jack stood in the living room, such as it was, and looked at the long leather sofa that had made the move with them from Gramercy Park, and at the long coffee table Gillis had made for them with walnut for a frame and bricks in grout as the top surface. They were measuring the area with a six-foot rule.

"We'll have to get rid of all of this," said Jack, worried.

"They're only things," said Martha, gently. The phone rang, and Martha ran for it to keep the ringing from waking the baby.

"Hello?"

"Hello, Martha, it's Charlie Leveque."

She turned her back to Jack.

"Yes."

"Is Jack right there?"

"Yes."

"You know, maybe we ought to . . . there are some things I should discuss with you. It might be better if we could meet."

"Oh, I doubt if that's necessary. I'd prefer the phone, really."

There was a pause.

"I wanted first to say I'm sorry."

"Yes? For what?"

"Oh. I take it you have a list."

Martha suddenly found that she was so angry that she could not say anything that sprang to mind as appropriate, not without shocking her son. So she said, "I think you're right, we should meet."

"Good. Do you have a place?"

"Well, I haven't spent a great deal of time in chic bistros lately, but there are some around here. If you don't mind coming downtown. I'd rather not leave the children too long."

"I can do that." He named a place he liked on Broome Street.

Martha kept him waiting. It had started raining again, and the bar glowing with oak and big green potted trees smelled slightly of damp wool and wet trench coats. Soaking umbrellas filled the umbrella stand and leaned against the walls, dripping. The floor was slick with water tracked in, and the few people who had ventured out in such a downpour were scattered around the room hunched over hot drinks, their eyes bright from steam.

Charlie stood when Martha came to the table. He'd have shaken hands, but she didn't offer. Her hair was wet, and it occurred to Charlie that the only time he ever saw his wife so unglossed was when she got out of the shower. It made Martha seem very real. She had very pale ivory skin and remarkable eyes, wide apart. Once she was settled, with her coat off, she met his gaze and there was a lot of pain and anger crackling.

"What would you like?" he asked.

"Something hot. Tea."

"They have nice mulled wine. And various hot rum things. Cinnamon sticks in them."

She shook her head. He ordered two cups of tea.

"Martha, I'm sorry about Saturday."

She nodded her head.

"What did Jack say?"

"He thought you were a nice man," she said. She stared at him.

Charlie had come from the office and was dressed like a midtown lawyer. He looked just like all those other fading jocks from Ivy League schools who staff the banks and law firms, she thought, who in college had thought it admirable to have parties where you drink till you puke, and had discussed girls in terms of synecdoche, anatomical parts sufficing to stand for the whole.

Charlie looked down at his napkin. He moved his fork from one side of the setting to the other.

"Well. I admit, this isn't an ideal situation."

Martha looked at the ceiling. Ideal situation. This guy spends four years dragging out a divorce that could have been settled in a month and then tops that by deciding the way to comfort a grieving boy is to dress him up in his father's clothes.

"Raymond has left the bulk of his estate to Jack. There's a small bequest to his mother, to Sherry Zagar, to a couple of charities. But the rest of it . . . and I don't know yet how much it is . . ."

"You're in for some surprises, then."

" . . . is in trust for Jack."

"And you are the executor?"

"Yes."

"What about trustees?"

"His mother—I don't gather she's in a position to be very active—and an officer at his bank called Howard Marshall. Do you know him?"

Martha shook her head.

"I don't either, but I guess we all should meet at some point."

"What's his function?"

"Mostly, to supervise the capital and be sure that we spend the interest on Jack and not Maseratis for ourselves and stuff."

"And what's yours?"

Charlie shifted, reluctant. "Until Jack's twenty-one, I try to function as Raymond would have."

Martha stared into her tea. "So every time Jack needs clothes, or an advance on his allowance, or tuition, or travel money, I have to come to you."

"Would you like more tea?"

Staring at him, she nodded. He killed a good two minutes hailing a waitress and ordering tea. Martha sat as if made of ice.

"I have to come to you."

"Or Jack does."

Martha put her fist to her mouth and leaned her face against it, hurting her lips. There was a long silence.

"What are you thinking?" Charlie said, softly.

"You'd do well not to ask me that." There was another pause.

"Sorry," said Charlie.

"But since you asked, I was thinking, who are you, and what do you know about my son? Or about children at all, after that last performance?"

"It wasn't my shining moment. I've said I'm sorry."

"I get really sick of I'm sorry sometimes. I'd prefer you keep the I'm sorry and let me raise my own son."

"I don't blame you." There was a pause. After a while Martha said, "I was also thinking about the pool table."

Charlie nodded. "I've been thinking about it, too. It seems . . . I mean, I understand the impulse but is it fair to *you* to rearrange your whole . . . I don't know how much space you have."

"He's lost enough. He needs to hold on to a piece of his father a lot more than I need a living room."

"Oh," said Charlie.

"But I don't see how we can do it."

"What do you mean?"

"I've been measuring. It won't fit in the elevator, and it's too long to turn the corner in the stairs."

"Is he very disappointed?"

"He doesn't know yet."

She started to cry. Charlie put his cup down and sat looking at his lap. After a while she stopped.

"What happens after he's twenty-one?"

"He gets a third of the estate outright. Then half of what's left at twenty-five, and the rest at thirty-five."

Martha nodded.

"It would help me, to use the proper judgment in Jack's interest and the interest of the estate, if I understand your situation. You have your trust fund. . . ."

"Oh, brother."

"Martha."

"Mr. Leveque, it's been four years. You have really not been listening."

"I've tried to," he said stiffly.

"I do not have a trust fund. When I was twenty-one, I had $100,000 my grandmother left me. And I've worked ever since I got out of school."

"So I understand."

She shot him a look, and he decided not to interrupt again.

"For three years, every dime I made went to our life. Rent, food, Raymond's tuition, Raymond's clothes, my clothes. Then I got pregnant and Raymond started his business. The famous trust fund was his seed money."

"He said his father put up the money."

"His dead father? Who conveniently can't be questioned? He asked his father for the money. His father said no. He said nobody gave him any handouts and he didn't see why he should give Raymond any."

"His father left his mother two million dollars," said Charlie, confused. "That's why Raymond didn't need to put her in his will."

"Yeah, well."

Charlie felt unhappy. This wasn't the way Raymond had told it. "If that *is* true, why don't you have any documentation? Why isn't there a loan agreement or a stock share in the company?"

Martha flared. "Look. I was in love. I was twenty-four. I was carrying his baby. It was us against the world. Are you married?"

"Divorced."

"Did you keep business records of every transaction that passed between you and your wife?"

"I never handed over $100,000."

"I'm sure you didn't. But I did, because I was very young and I adored my husband, and I thought I could make up to him for things that had hurt him when he was growing up. Would I do it again? No. But I wouldn't undo it either. It was the right thing to do at that time, for that marriage."

"Didn't you ask him to pay you back when the business was thriving?"

"Of course."

"What did he say?"

Martha stopped. She stared at Charlie steadily.

"Things had changed between us by then," she said eventually. "Could we change the subject?"

"Yes. So. Now you live on. . . ?"

"I live on what I make, which most months is not quite enough to pay for one of your suits. I enjoy my work very much, and I can do it at home and raise my children myself, which to me is worth a great deal. I can't give you an annual figure because it's different all the time. But most of the time I have more work than I can accept."

"What are you working on now?"

"A children's book for Random House."

"Who pays you? The author?"

"No, the publisher."

"I have a friend at Little, Brown . . . ," Charlie began.

"No, thank you," said Martha. Martha looked at him steadily. He felt that her eyes were pushing him away from her so hard that if he let go of the table, his chair would go over backward.

"I guess then, I need to know about your . . . about Jack's immediate needs."

"The tuition is paid. Raymond gave him a weekly allowance."

"How much?"

"Twenty dollars."

"Is that enough?"

"I don't know. He spends it all on food, I think. Feeding a teenage boy is like feeding a lion."

"So my mother tells me. My daughter gets thirty a week, but she's supposed to pay for some clothes."

Martha gave him a quick look.

"How old's your daughter?"

"Fifteen. She's at Replogle."

Martha nodded. She didn't approve of single-sex schools, and she didn't approve of schools where your child feels hard done by if you don't go to Gstaad for spring break. She'd have expected Charlie to choose Replogle.

She looked at her watch.

"I have to go. Fred will be up."

"If you'll wait a minute, I'll walk you home."

"Please," she said, getting up quickly. "Don't." She put on her coat, thanked him for the tea, and was gone. Afterward, she wondered why she thanked him. Thanks for the tea. Thanks for making me come out in a force five rainstorm to be told that I have to deal with you. . . . Oh, Raymond. Goddamn you, really.

When he had paid the check, Charlie did walk to Crosby Street and locate her building. It was a narrow building, not a cast-iron facade. In the wide, lighted windows of her floor, the third, he could see a stamped tin ceiling and lots of plants. The street itself was narrow and dark, but at least quiet. Charlie made his way back to Broadway in the wind and wet, to look for a cab.

"M*artha," said Madelaine* Forbes, "do you know a good magician?" Martha and her mother were having lunch at the Colony Club.

"I'm sorry," said Martha with a straight face. "I don't really think I do."

"I'm doing a party in Brookline for a dermatologist. A twenty-fifth wedding anniversary. I thought magic might be a good theme."

"Wouldn't magic be more for a plastic surgeon?"

"Oh, a plastic surgeon. I was thinking they were the same. Dermatologists do rashes and things, don't they?" She spoke as one who had never consulted such a person and never would, which was true, as she was a Christian Scientist. "Oh, that's a pretty girl, isn't it," her mother added. "She looks familiar. She may have been a model, don't you think?" Martha's mother had been, and in fact still was, a great natural beauty, although rather frighteningly well preserved, as if she slept in formaldehyde. It was her conviction that all pretty girls with good posture modeled when young, as she had herself. Martha looked at the woman her mother was watching.

"No, I'll tell you why she looks familiar. I think she was at school with me."

"Oh!" cried Mrs. Forbes happily. She loved everything about Martha's school days, which seemed to her to have been extremely recent. In fact little that had happened to Martha since seemed as real to her as the days her pretty daughter and her attractive friends used to giggle about boys in the library during vacation, or the day Martha in her white piqué dress had led the Daisy Chain at graduation. "What was her name?"

"I can't really remember. Connie, I think. Tell me, does the dermatologist have any hobbies?"

Her mother was easily distracted.

"Now that's what I asked his wife. You know it's so easy when you can festoon the place with golf clubs or fishing nets or something. She said that the only thing he really liked besides medicine were computers and wine. Computers aren't very gay. Or decorative."

"But wine is perfect, Mother." As Madelaine, both from religious conviction and vanity, had long since eschewed drink of any kind, this had not occurred to her. "You could cluster big purple balloons like grapes and hang them from the ceiling. You could set up tables for wine tastings. You could have all the serving people dressed like nymphs and satyrs at a bacchanal."

"I could?"

"Of course. Bacchus is the god of the grape."

"I love this idea," said her mother fervently, and fished in her bag for a pen to take notes.

"You could . . . I know, you could get someone to play glasses of wine, like a xylophone."

"Oh, how marvelous! I see the waitresses in flesh-colored body stockings, with grape leaves sewn to the private parts!" said Madelaine, excited. Martha decided not to point out it was fig leaves she was thinking of.

"It's so much more fun than another tired evening with chimps on roller skates," cried Madelaine. Madelaine's Party Service was the toast of suburban Boston, which really made great sense when you thought about it, since the two things she liked best in the world were parties and telling people how things ought to be done.

It wasn't until they were having their coffee that Madelaine asked about Jack.

"He's doing well," said Martha.

"Well of course it's easier for him, since his father was already gone in a way."

"Maybe."

"Has Raymond left him well provided for?"

"I think so. It all seems to take a while."

"Well I hope so, darling. You really have had enough hard times, that way. I'd like to see things ease up for you. But he hasn't left him anything outright, has he?"

"No."

"That's a relief. I don't know if you remember the—"

"Kelly Wainwright," murmured Martha.

"Wainwright girl. Her mother had her portfolio in trust, but of course she didn't expect to die young, although why not in her case, the way she drove. Anyway, she made her daughter direct beneficiary of one insurance policy so the girl suddenly had $200,000 in cash. Well, it ruined her life. She'd been accepted to Vassar but wouldn't go. She bought a fancy car and huge fur coat and no one could tell her a thing. She was married at nineteen to some *awful* creature . . . I'll never get over that fur coat. The worst-looking thing I ever saw. . . ."

"Well. I think that Jack would have better judgment than that, but no, Raymond hasn't left him anything difficult."

"It was huge and white and it *shed*, I remember. I think it was made of some sort of wolf . . . something canine. She looked like the cheapest sort of film tart. And her mother had such beautiful taste. Anyway, I'm glad. And who's the executor? You?"

"Well, no."

"Oh, that's right, you wouldn't be. George Wainwright was executor of Nan's estate, but—"

"That was different."

"Yes."

"The executor is Raymond's lawyer. He's called Charlie Leveque."

"His *divorce* lawyer? The one who called you a liar at the deposition?"

It was amazing what Madelaine did and did not remember.

"Yes," said Martha. This was not a conversation she wanted to have.

"Can't you appeal it or something? Have him changed?"

"I don't think so, Mother."

"I think it's always worth asking. I could call Carl Townsend."

"Thank you, but I think that would make matters worse. He's not evil or incompetent."

"But don't you hate him? I would."

"He didn't call me a liar. He implied it, but that was his job. The best thing I can do is forget about it and try to work with him as well as possible now. It's not forever."

"I'll discuss it with your father. And there's one good thing, at least Raymond didn't leave things so you'd suddenly have a major discipline problem."

"No."

"You just never know how children will act. I mean Jack was such an attractive little boy and now look what you've been through with his clothes, and his hair. . . ."

"Mother, I think all that is fine."

"You forget, he's really still a child. Just because he's grown so tall and his voice has changed. They are simply not ready for certain kinds of decisions."

"I agree. But one kind of decision he is ready for is what he wants to wear, and how to cut his hair."

"But he shows such terrible judgment."

"It's *his* hair. He didn't cut off *your* hair."

"But he looks like a thug."

"But he *isn't* one. He's a sterling character."

"*Much* too simple, Martha. It's important how you look."

"I know it, and you know it, and he'll learn it."

"Why does he want to look like . . ."

"I don't know why. I'm not Jack."

"I don't think we should talk about this anymore," said Madelaine fussily.

"I agree."

A silence. The pretty blond woman who had or had not been at school with Martha was leaving the dining room. Madelaine gave her a little wave. You could see the woman look blank as she, however, politely waved back.

"How is the baby?" asked Madelaine.

"He's fine, thanks."

"And where is he right now? With his sitter?"

"He's at day care."

"Oh, that's right. I forget how terribly young these children go."

Martha knew she didn't forget, she just didn't approve. "Little people need other little people."

"I suppose. I brought him a present."

Madelaine produced from her bag a package, gaily wrapped.

"Thank you, Mother, that's sweet of you." She knew better than to hope there was some token for Jack too. Her mother had always been better with people who couldn't yet talk.

"Be sure to tell him it's from Maddy."

"Of course I will."

"Do you ever see Gillis?"

"Yes," said Martha smoothly. "I had dinner with him last week."

"I see," said Madelaine, bravely folding her napkin. What she meant was, I don't see but I'm determined not to pry. Madelaine adored Gillis and thought her daughter's failure to marry him probably confirmed the character flaw Madelaine had suspected in her, ever since she had insisted on going to the Rhode Island School of Design instead of to Smith.

"Thank you for lunch, Mother."

"Oh you're welcome, darling. It was lovely to see you. Thank you for coming uptown. Now next time, I'll come to you." This was a lie. Madelaine thought that living in a loft was tantamount to living in a tree, and she was convinced that there were no taxis below Fourteenth Street, so if she ventured downtown she would never get home. She walked her daughter out to the street, hugged her and kissed her warmly, saw her into a cab, and pressed money into her hand to pay for it.

"I *hate my hair*," said Phoebe, staring at it in the mirror. It was blond and fine and hung down straight no matter what she did with it. Erica's was sleek and shaped in a swinging, shining bob that owed its deceptively simple effect to about $100 worth of haircut at her mother's stylist.

"It's fine," said Erica, making a kissing face at herself in the mirror so she could brush blusher into the hollows thus created in her cheeks, to emphasize the cheekbones. They were in the upper school girls' room at Replogle. "You just need styling mousse."

"It's so expensive." Phoebe was sulking. Erica's little brother was the star of a television show called *Two by Two,* and Erica herself had permission to cut school to go to auditions whenever she wanted. She had come *this close* to a part in *Les Misérables,* and she did a lot of commercials. She always had tons of pocket money.

"I don't want to go to art, do you? Mr. Arnstein is such a turd."

Phoebe was going to be on probation if she cut any more classes, but she didn't say this to Erica. She said instead, by way of agreement, "I really have to go to Bloomie's."

"I'll go with you."

Outside the school gates, they walked south on Lexington, smoking Virginia Slims. Erica had gotten smoking permission for her fifteenth birthday. On the corner of Lex and Seventy-second they met up with Serena and Kate. The day was brilliantly sunny, and although it was early October it was in the seventies.

"*Bonjour, chéries, ça va?*" said Erica kissing first Kate, then Serena, on both cheeks.

"*Très bien, très bien, mes petites choux-choux,*" said Serena. "Do you know yet if you're going on the French trip?" The school sponsored a three-week trip to France for the French language students every spring.

"I'm not. I told my mom that only nerds were going and she said I didn't have to."

"Good. I'm sure I can get out of it if you're not going."

"Kate, what is this fabulous garment?"

"Oh, it's Armani," said Kate. She opened the buttons of the jacket she was wearing and showed them the label.

"Oh it's so *cute,*" said Erica, her eyes wide.

"I couldn't believe they'd go for it when I brought it home, but Mom said sure, it's a good investment."

"Where'd you get it? Bloomie's?"

"Yes."

"That's where we're going," said Phoebe. She felt sullenly furious at her parents for making her go to school in a blue jean jacket.

"You'd look great in this jacket," said Kate to Erica, falling in with them.

"I know. I want to go try them on."

"Do you think I should have my hair streaked?" asked Phoebe.

"No, why?" said Serena.

"I don't know," said Kate. "It could be fabulous."

A girl in the sophomore class, Brett Byers, had had red and gold dyed into her hair strand by strand and it only took four hours, a ream of aluminum foil, and about $120. Phoebe though she might be able to boost it out of her grandmother as a birthday present.

They went to Bloomingdale's. They tried on slacks and jackets and skirts at Armani, and then Kate, the only one thin enough, tried on a $4,000 suit by Karl Lagerfeld that was to die for. After a while they went down to cruise the cosmetics counters. Serena bought a handbag for $400 for her mother's birthday, and paid with her American Express card. Phoebe bought a $7 can of imported hair mousse and paid with her lunch money. Then it was time for Phoebe to go meet her father at his office.

Phoebe never stopped at the secretary's desk at her father's office. She felt that Leveque was on the door, and that was her name, and she could do what she wanted there. She walked into Charlie's office, waved to him as he talked on the phone, and plopped down on the sofa. When he finished his call she went over to kiss him.

"Hi, sweetheart. You look wonderful. Is that a new skirt?"

"No," said Phoebe.

"How is it outside? Still warm?"

"Yes. I walked."

"Good. That's good. Listen, pumpkin, I have to make two more calls, then we can go."

"Okay."

Phoebe settled back down on the sofa, took her math homework out of her backpack, and went to work. Charlie watched her, lovingly, from the corner of his eye as he finished his calls.

"All done. Where do you want to eat?"

"Twenty-one."

"Get serious."

"I am serious. I'm the only girl in my class who's never been there."

"And I'm the queen of Romania," said Charlie.

"It's *true*," said Phoebe.

"You have a tough life."

"I do."

"Maybe we'll go there on your birthday. Now, where do you want to eat?"

"Slant or Wop."

"*What?*"

"Chinese or Italian."

"Phoebe, what did you say?"

"Sorry. It's a joke."

"There must be something wrong with my sense of humor."

You can carve that in stone, thought Phoebe.

They ate Japanese. "I don't have to eat anything raw, though, do I?" asked Phoebe.

"No."

"Because Mom's friend Aida? She got worms eating sushi. They were really big and white. I asked her how she knew she had them and she said—"

"Honey, please."

"Oh. Well anyway, she said she got them at a really good restaurant, too."

"You can have tempura. How is Aida?"

"She's fine. She's in Africa."

"Really?"

"Yes. She went with her boyfriend."

"Is this Jerry or someone new?"

"I don't know."

"How's your mom?"

"Okay."

They ate in silence for a while.

"How's José?" asked Phoebe. José was her father's parrot. José the parrot lived free in Charlie's living room, where he perched on the mantel or a lamp, or shit on the back of the club chair. Sometimes he would suddenly whistle and screech "Whatta paira legs!" Charlie didn't think that having a big green bird living on the back of the chair was any more annoying than cats that claw apart the furniture, and he loved it when José would swoop around the room. Sometimes José would settle himself carefully on a visitor's head and then lean far over until he was staring upside down into the person's eyes. Charlie and Phoebe found that marvelously funny. The visitors sometimes did and sometimes not. Phoebe's mother had never entirely warmed to José. She didn't really like animals, except for tropical fish.

"Are you coming to stay with us next weekend?" Charlie asked.

"Probably, except Serena's having a party Saturday night, and I might stay over at her house."

"Oh. What kind of party?"

"I don't know, Daddy . . . a party."

"I mean, with boys, and dancing, or girls watching a movie, or . . . what?"

"Well, of course, with boys."

"All right. But what will happen? Do you dance, or what?"

"There will be music."

"That's not exactly forthcoming, Phoebe."

"I'm not a witness, Daddy."

"Will Serena's parents be there?"

"I don't *know!*" Phoebe snapped, and began to push her food around her plate and roll her eyes. A couple at the next table stopped their talk to look at her.

"Please don't be rude to me, Phoebe. I have a perfect right to ask that question."

"Well, I don't *know*, okay?"

There was an unhappy silence. Charlie ate, Phoebe didn't. He had so little time with her, he hated to spend it in captiousness, let alone conflict.

After a while he said gently, "Honey. You are fifteen years old. You cannot go to parties with boys unless your mother and I know where you are, and who will chaperone."

"Chaperone. God, what a word. None of the other kids have to go through the third degree. . . ."

"That's lucky for them, isn't it. If true. But you do have to."

Phoebe was fuming. And sulking. And feeling extremely ill-used. The problem was, if her father called Serena's parents, he would find that they were planning to be out of town, and thought Serena was going to Kate's house. She wanted to cry, she wanted a hug, she wanted a hot bath, she wanted to tell him to fuck himself.

"Tell me," said Charlie, wanting to talk about something happy, "have you got the itinerary for the French trip?"

"Only nerds go on the French trip," she snarled.

Charlie felt his arm tense involuntarily, as if he were going to throw a punch. Do not say, When I was your age, do not say when I was your age, he chanted to himself, with jaw tight.

"Phoebe," he said with an effort at self-control, "when I was your age . . ."

"Oh stuff it, Daddy." Now she was staring at her fists in her lap, having put her napkin into her full plate of food. She knew her mother had forbidden him to say when I was your age. . . .

"Let me get this straight," he said at last. "You are fifteen years old. You have the opportunity to go to Paris, Tournus, Aix, Avignon, and Nice, in the company of your friends, all expenses paid, to speak French in France, and you say only nerds want to do that?"

A sullen pause. "Yes," said Phoebe, defiant.

"We should have spanked you," said her father, as if talking to himself. "We should have spanked your spoiled bottom while there was still time."

"Be my guest," said Phoebe, rudely, wishing she were dead. They sat together in miserable silence until the check was paid and they could get out of each other's company.

"*Oscar Wilde said*, 'When a woman remarries, it's because she detested her first husband. When a man remarries it's because he adored his first wife,'" said Patsy Leveque with a shrug that was supposed to be winning. Oscar Wilde was one of the stock gambits she used when things got desperate socially.

Patsy, who was fine boned, small, and pretty, was nursing a gin and tonic, although it was October. Her companion, who was called Bill, was not just a big man, as her friend had described him. He was a big, fat man. It was extremely unlikely that he knew who Oscar Wilde was;

entirely unlikely that he cared. Patsy kept trying, though. Because she considered herself a good sport. And because she was sure as hell not going to pay for half of this dinner, which she would feel obliged to do if she didn't go through with this whole charade exactly as if she hadn't known it was a wasted evening the minute she laid eyes on him. They were eating in a bistro in the Village in which all the food came with tomato sauce.

"You hate your husband?" Bill didn't really lift his eyes from his plate as he asked this. He still had some lasagna left.

"Oh no," said Patsy, embarrassed. "That's not why I said it."

Bill looked up. "Why'd you say it?" he asked. His great wide face was expressionless. She wondered whatever gave him the notion of having a beard with no mustache. The only man who ever had a beard with no mustache who didn't look obscene was Abraham Lincoln.

"It was just something to talk about, you know. Like, 'All happy families are alike, but unhappy families are all unhappy in their own ways.'"

"What?" Bill blinked.

"Do you believe that? All happy families are alike?"

There was a pause. "I don't get what you're talking about," said Bill.

"It's *Anna Karenina*, you know . . . everyone quotes it because it's Tolstoy, but no one stops to think if it's true or not," she said, like one trying to teach the rules of a not very complex parlor game.

Bill stared at her a bit more, as if trying to work out the puzzle of what she was on about, then gave up and said sullenly, "I hate *my* wife."

A pause. "What? Oh. You do?" Then, brightly, "And you haven't re-married. So, maybe the quote is true."

"I'm going to remarry," he said sullenly.

Patsy thought of asking whom he was planning to marry but decided not to bait him. She thought of asking why he hated his wife and decided she didn't care to know. She said, "I really wasn't unhappy with Charlie. He's a lovely man. We're very good friends. I just reached a point where . . . I needed to *be* somebody, I needed to learn to be alone. Even though Charlie loved me, I don't think I could really experience it because I didn't feel good enough about myself."

Bill was staring at her. This wasn't going over.

"So, I've come a long way since then," she rushed on. "I can change a tire or fix a leaky faucet by myself."

"Oh, do you have a car?" Bill sat up a little.

"No," she laughed charmingly, "I lost it in the divorce wars, but . . ."

"Then why do you have to know how to change a tire?"

She stopped.

"Sometimes," she said, finally, "when I need a car, I rent one."

Bill thought about this.

"What kind of car did you used to have?"

"A Volvo."

Bill nodded. He signaled for the check.

When Patsy finally locked the apartment door behind her, she leaned against it and started to laugh. She could hear the TV going in the living room. She went toward it, keeping the laugh going.

Her daughter, Phoebe, was sprawled on the sofa watching a *Star Trek* rerun. The windows were all wide open.

"You wouldn't *believe* what I've just been through," Patsy giggled, and she started to describe her date. Really, it was comic. That was the only way to look at it. She knew the business about "well . . . what kind of car did you used to have" would crack Phoebe up. But before she could get to it, the phone rang. Phoebe got up, but Patsy reached it first. She hoped it would be Aida, Aida would *love* this story.

It *was* Aida, and Patsy started the story over again. Phoebe seemed disappointed about the phone. Well . . . it was too late for her to be getting calls anyway. It was a school night.

As Patsy talked, she felt better. Presently Phoebe got up, turned off the TV, and closed the windows. She went down the hall to her room. Patsy called, "G'night, honey," and she thought she heard Phoebe answer.

Morning. Patsy was in tears. She'd had a dream about her lover. She dreamed he was there in bed with her, and when she woke the sense of loss was excruciating. She was overwhelmed by hot, bitter grief. George with his dry, sly humor. George's delighted laugh. George's body in bed. She couldn't remember, at this moment, why they parted. She knew only that she missed him. She thought of last night's comic date, not comic at all, but deeply an indignity, and felt so abandoned.

She was made of tears. The whole world was blotted out by this grief. She sobbed as quietly as she could.

In the kitchen, through the thin wall, she could hear Phoebe heating water for instant coffee. What time was it? Eight forty-five. Good. Phoebe would be out on time. Patsy would stay here quietly until she heard her daughter go out. She wouldn't want to upset her.

After a while she heard the door shut. She got up and went to the kitchen to make herself a pot of tea. She thought about calling George. Should she? No. She must not. Her grief made him angry. Anyway, his new girlfriend might be living in by now. It was hard to imagine that a man who had loved her so much wouldn't care anymore what she was feeling. . . .

No more blind dates. It was better to be alone. She opened the refrigerator and found there was no milk for tea. Damn. Phoebe liked milk in her coffee, too. Oh well. She'd live. Also there was no bread. So Phoebe had gone off without a sandwich. Did she have enough allowance money to buy a slice of pizza? Patsy couldn't remember.

Patsy took her teapot and her cup on a tray and got back into bed. She had no appointments before eleven. She got the notebook she kept by the bed and started to write down her dream.

Charlie and Wick Brainard sat in the steam room, recovering from an hour and a half of squash. Charlie had won, which surprised Wick a good deal. They had been friends a long time, and it didn't happen very often.

"So," said Wick, leaning against the tile walls, eyes closed. Perspiration stood out on his forehead. "What's going on?"

"I settled my bank fraud case," said Charlie.

"You did? When?"

"Monday."

"You happy with it?"

"Happy enough."

"That's a lot, in this world. How's Phoebe?"

"Maddening."

"She's getting awfully pretty," Wick said. "I saw her last week."

"Really? Where?"

"At Saks, in Ladies' Bathing Suits."

"What the hell were you doing in Ladies' Bathing Suits?"

"I was shopping for a friend," said Wick. Charlie laughed. Wick had such a parade of female companions that Charlie could rarely keep track of them.

"Did Phoebe behave?"

"Absolutely. She came right over and shook hands, and introduced her friends very properly."

"I think you're making this up."

"She was a perfect lady."

"I'm glad to hear it," said Charlie. Her mother's daughter, he thought. No matter what was going on at home, Patsy was perfect when it came to public appearances. Manipulative little beast, he thought, about Phoebe. And then, no. At least be grateful that she made an effort with those who hadn't earned her complete contempt. Like, apparently, her father.

Charlie asked, "Have you ever met a woman named Martha Forbes?"

Wick thought about it. "From Alewife?"

"You're amazing."

"I don't think I have met her. I know one of her brothers. Dick. We were on a board together."

"What's he like?"

"Nice guy. Very. A young lady I know mentioned he's a great two-stepper. He's bright. Has an awfully nice wife. He's a good tennis player. I think that's everything I know about him. I like him. Why do you ask?"

Charlie mopped sweat from his face and neck. He felt somewhat hard-put to answer.

"I met Martha Forbes about five years ago. She was Martha Gaver then; her husband, Raymond Gaver, asked me to handle his divorce."

"I remember." Charlie didn't doubt him. "That began just when you were getting your law firm up and running, yes?" Charlie nodded.

He *had* been very busy at the time the case started, and he hadn't paid a great deal of attention at first. For one thing, it had seemed routine. He didn't think Raymond was particularly acting in his own best interest, but Raymond had stories to tell about his marriage; he definitely had his version, and it wasn't Charlie's fault that Martha had married him. Charlie advised Raymond to use Martha's lack of appetite for the fight to his advantage. Wait. Drag it out. Demand that she negotiate face to face instead of through lawyers, which she didn't want to do. In the meantime, Charlie's own marriage had suddenly blown up in his face, and it wasn't the time in his life when he'd been most sympathetic to former wives.

Raymond came up with some twists of his own, notably a strategy he called the mindfuck. He would call or write his estranged wife, seeming to offer an olive branch. "I miss you, Martha. I find myself talking to you . . . I'll be talking to you in my head for the rest of my life . . ." would be a typical gambit, tacked onto the end of an unavoidable conversation about Jack, or enclosed with a check for his allowance, or some such. For a surprisingly long time, this sort of thing would actually fool Martha, and she would respond with gratitude and tenderness, wanting bygones to be gone. Raymond would follow this four days later by a letter full of venom and blame, and then four days later by another apparent change of heart, a sudden reappearance of the person Martha had married, who once had loved her and needed her love.

When Raymond heard that this strategy had her so devastated that she was refusing to open any mail from him, he laughed and laughed. And began addressing his letters to her lawyer. "Dear Bill, since you are now opening my wife's mail, will you please remind her that if it hadn't been for her . . ." on and on. Charlie knew it had been ugly. He had to admit though, it had worked. Martha had settled for an arrangement that was far more advantageous to Raymond than Charlie had thought she would.

Now that he had to think about how it must have felt to Martha, it did occur to him that as a man, if not as a lawyer, it wasn't the best piece of work he'd ever done. Her lawyer had been a family friend, kind of a dope, not up to Raymond's speed. Charlie liked to think of the law as a game—may the best man win. But for the last week or so, he had been troubled. He liked Martha. She didn't seem much—or at all—like the woman Raymond had described. He liked talking with her. He liked her friendship with her son. He liked her warmth and especially her smile. When she smiled she seemed lit from within, full of secret humor, a sense that the world is a hilarious place. He'd seen her smile like that at her children. He rather thought he'd like to see her smile at him.

"What's she like, Martha Forbes?" Wick asked.

"Much as you describe her brother. Although her husband complained she was a rotten tennis player."

"Can she dance?"

"I haven't asked her."

It *was the* last Saturday in October. The weather had held warm, as sometimes happens in New York in autumn. Martha would have liked to take baby Fred to the park, but she had to wait for the movers; this was the day Charlie Leveque had arranged to have Raymond's things delivered to Jack. Fred was watching a videotape of *Dumbo,* wearing earphones. Martha was working on a watercolor of a chambered nautilus, for a book about a little girl who digs for treasure on a beach, and finds it. Jack was in his room.

Jack was as sad as Martha had ever seen him. Not that there was much to see. He slept astonishing stretches of the time. For several days now, he'd hardly eaten. He'd say that pizza or shepherd's pie or steak sounded great, but when dinner was on the table he'd look at his plate and say "I'm sorry." She'd let him stay home from school the day before, and he'd stayed in bed most of the day. Late in the afternoon he'd gone to the library and come back with a stack of Oz books, which he hadn't read since they were read aloud to him ten years before.

Once, the summer when he was eleven, the last year she and Raymond were together, Jack had taken to sleeping like this. Raymond and Martha would look at each other, not knowing whether to laugh or scold. Was it depression? Was it African sleeping sickness? At last Raymond said, "I think I'll measure him." He stood him up against the doorjamb in his room where they'd marked his growth on the wall since he was three, and found he'd grown an inch and a half in two months.

So Martha let Jack sleep. She figured he was trying to regrow a piece of heart so he could go on in the world without his father. It was hard being a mother when things hurt her children and she couldn't help. With Fred, when something went wrong, she could give him a bath and cuddle him and read him a story. With a great hulking thing like Jack you just had to stay out of the way and let him mourn. And maybe learn to heal himself, a thing Martha wished she knew how to do, and certainly felt in no position to advise on.

It was a lonely feeling, like wind in an empty canyon that should make a whistling noise but makes none. The only person she wanted to talk to about her son was Raymond. If she felt that way about Raymond being gone, she who had hardly had a civil conversation with him in years, how must Jack feel? And the delay in his reaction scared her. The first week or two he was fine, and now this crash.

The doorbell rang.

"Who is it?" she asked the intercom.

"It's Charlie Leveque."

She buzzed to release the downstairs door. After a bit, she heard her upstairs neighbor descend with the elevator, and after a few minutes more the elevator creaked up to her floor and the door opened. It contained a stack of boxes, marked RECORDS, Martha's neighbor Karen, operating the car, and Charlie Leveque.

"Moving day?" said Karen.

"Seems so. Thanks." Meaning, thank you for interrupting yourself to take the elevator down.

"No problem," said Karen. "I'll leave it here for you."

She let herself out by the stairwell.

"I didn't expect you," said Martha to Charlie as the mover began carrying boxes into the house.

"I know. But I brought something for Jack."

"Oh."

"Is he here?"

"Yes."

"How's he doing?"

"Not good."

The two looked at each other. They were both parents, at least. They shared that.

"Want to see what I brought him?"

Martha shrugged. "Sure."

Charlie walked to the window and Martha followed him. She looked out. Directly in front of her building was a large red truck labeled GARY

MOVES. Leaning against the truck, minus its legs, was Raymond's pool table. Martha stared. Charlie smiled. He had a wonderful smile, she suddenly realized, and smiled back.

"But how are you going to get it up here?"

"I'm going to swing it through the window."

"You personally?"

"I've got a crane coming."

She just looked at him. She smiled again.

"Unless you changed your mind . . . ," he said. "You'll have to move all this. . . ."

She felt a rush of emotion. "I'll get Jack," she said.

Jack emerged from his room looking puffy eyed, as if he'd been sleeping, or crying. It was probably a measure of his misery that his hair was growing in, and he hadn't bothered to do anything weird to it. He shook hands with Charlie.

"What's up?"

"Look out the window, honey," said Martha.

By that time, the crane had appeared and was rolling down the narrow street. It took Jack a minute, like someone working out a puzzle (what's happening in this picture?) before he gave a whoop of joy.

Charlie, Jack, and the moving men loaded the living-room furniture into the elevator and took it down to the basement. As they reascended, Martha heard Jack and Charlie laughing. The crane fellow came up and measured things, and then took the big old double-hung window out of its frame altogether. Martha and baby Fred watched from the kitchen while Charlie and Jack supervised from the street, as the crane operator picked up the huge oak tabletop and majestically hoisted it into the air. It dangled three stories above the street, right outside the window, as the crane ground and snorted, repositioning itself for the next move. Martha could see her neighbors across the way put their heads out to watch, and the street began to be lined with people.

Outside she could hear Jack laughing. One of his neighborhood friends had appeared, and he was introducing him to Charlie and explaining with great animation. The two boys roared some chant of excitement at each other. Martha started toward the window to see what was happening, but just at that moment the table began to move, so that, carrying Fred and giggling, she had to run back out of the way to watch from the kitchen. Smoothly, silently, the table advanced through the window frame. Gently it descended to the floor and stopped, suspended on one side. There was a cheer from below. Two moving men, followed by Jack and Charlie, thumped up the stairs, and the movers detached the chains and lowered the table to the floor.

"Look at the crane, look at the crane," cried Jack, "it's like a big brontosaurus walked down the street and put its head in the window."

The crane deftly withdrew its head. Jack, glowing, took Fred in his arms and took him to the window.

"See the crane? See, like a dinosaur, it picked up the table in its mouth and put it through the window!" Baby Fred was thrilled. Jack galloped off with Fred to his room to show him a picture of a dinosaur. Charlie and Martha looked at each other.

"This is fun!" said Charlie.

"This is. This is really fun." Martha smiled, and her eyes glowed.

Jack and Fred were back.

"Is it going to have legs?" asked Jack.

"Oh. Yes. Let's go."

As they got into the elevator, Martha heard Charlie say, "Show me how to drive this." When they came back with the rest of the records, the cue rack, and four huge urn-shaped oak legs, the car stopped half a foot too high, with Charlie at the lever.

Charlie and Jack helped the movers put the window back into its frame. The original wood of the sashes had splintered badly and would have to be replaced. "I'll send a carpenter," said Charlie. "It will be all right till Monday."

The legs were bolted onto the pool table, and the movers and Charlie and Jack all together turned it over and set it up. They moved it around till they liked where it stood. They tested it with levels and had to put only a slight shim under one of the feet. Martha stood to the side and watched Jack's face. He was so happy. It made tears come to her eyes.

Even the movers felt the fun of the event, though they declined to stay and shoot a game. Charlie and Jack, with cues in their hands, paced around the table, testing sight lines, getting the feel of it, being pleased with themselves. Jack found the packing box that held the balls and chalks and rack. He racked.

"You break."

Charlie broke, and sunk two solids.

"Whoa!" cried Jack.

"Luck." But it wasn't. Charlie was good, and Jack was thrilled. They played for nearly two hours.

"I see two problems," said Martha at last.

"What?"

"One is, my sewing machine has disappeared."

"Oops."

"It went to the basement."

"I would like it to come back."

"We'll go get it."

"The other is, aren't you starving?"

"Yes!"

"I'll take us to lunch," said Charlie.

"The baby's asleep."

"I'll go out and get something."

So Jack and Charlie retrieved the sewing machine, which was repositioned in the corner Martha called her office, and then they went off in search of Chinese food and came back with cartons of ribs and fried dumplings and Peking duck.

When it was all served out in bowls Martha said, "There is not one piece of vegetable matter on this table."

"That's not true," said Charlie. "Look at this little green thing." He offered a scallion.

"I have a bean sprout in my spring roll," said Jack, eating.

"I don't think you two are going to be allowed to do this again unsupervised." She was watching Jack wolf down his food, and smiling. "What disgusting manners you have," she said to him.

"May I have all these noodles?"

"Yes," said Charlie. So Jack had them. When he had eaten an astonishing amount, he asked to be excused and went back to the pool table.

"It's more fun to feed a boy than a girl," said Charlie.

"Easier too. A chunk of raw meat on the end of a pitchfork will usually do it."

"Phoebe won't eat any meat at all, at the moment."

"Your daughter."

"Yes."

"I wish I had a daughter."

"You do?"

"Yes. I was very glad Jack was a boy when he was born, but now I wish I had one of each."

"Do you know many teenaged girls?" Charlie asked, dryly.

"I was one, of course. A really horrible one. My mother is still getting over it."

"We're not sure we'll ever get over Phoebe."

Martha took a sip from Charlie's beer bottle. "If it's any consolation, a psychiatrist once told me that people who go through no adolescent rebellion are rarely found in the helping professions. Doctors, nurses, teachers."

"I'm not sure what that means."

"No, I'm not either. I just find it comforting at times." She gestured subtly at Jack.

"I brought you your own beer, you know."

"Oh. Want to split it?"

"Sure."

Having undertaken such an intimacy, however, they both grew quiet. They drank the beer fairly quickly and in silence. Then Charlie allowed both Martha and Jack to thank him again, and he left.

"**H**ow's José?" Sophie asked, as her soup arrived.

"He's fine," said Charlie.

Charlie and Sophie had thought for a time of moving in together, but José had taken a bitter dislike to Sophie's cat. Sophie had tried to give her cat to her sister Connie in the country, but Connie's husband was allergic to it, so the cat came back and the moment passed.

"And Phoebe?"

Charlie shrugged. "At the moment we're pinning our hopes on menopause."

Sophie laughed. "I've missed you," she said warmly. Charlie stopped eating, and reached over to squeeze her hand. Sophie was one of the most forgiving souls he knew. He began thinking of this and other truths, went back to his lunch, and forgot that he still had barely spoken to her.

"Hey. Where are you?" she asked at last.

"Did you ever meet Raymond Gaver with me?" he asked finally.

"Sure. Remember, we had dinner down at Raoul's. He had the girl with him who worked at *Vogue*."

"Oh. Yes." Charlie remembered the evening, but he'd forgotten he'd been with Sophie.

"It wasn't that long ago," she added.

"I don't know why you still like me."

"I don't, very much," she said, and he smiled.

"What'd you think of Raymond?"

Sophie considered. "The girl was dumb as a post," she offered.

"Well, yes."

"I'm never too sure about people who date people so much dumber than they are. I don't get what the deal is."

"Don't you?"

"No."

"We'll let it pass. How did Raymond strike you?"

"You're not accepting my first answer?"

"I didn't understand that that was your answer. You mean, you hated him?"

Sophie paused.

"I found him very attractive."

"You did?"

"Yes."

"Would you have gone out with him?"

"No."

"Why not?"

"I hated him."

"Sophie. Why didn't you say something?"

"I try not to, if I can't say something nice."

"That's true of you. But you knew I represented him. I told you I liked him."

"That's the other reason."

"I'd have liked to know. I'd have valued your opinion." She could hear in Charlie's voice that he was distressed.

"No, you didn't want to know," she said gently. "If you had, you'd have asked me. He's probably terrific, you know him better than I do."

Charlie looked at her. "I don't think I knew him better than you did."

"Knew?"

"He's dead. Plane crash."

Sophie knew there was small point saying she was sorry, under the circumstances. She said, "I swear, I had nothing to do with it."

Charlie laughed.

"So it's a moot point now, if I liked him," said Sophie.

"Not exactly."

"Why not?"

"I'm the executor of his estate."

"So?"

Charlie hesitated. At last he said, "There are some things that make me uncomfortable. It's on my mind because I have to go over to his office this afternoon to see what there is to dispose of."

"Have you ever been there?"

"No."

"Where is it?"

"A couple blocks."

"Want me to go with you?"

"Don't you have to work?"

"It won't take all day, will it?"

"No."

"Then I'd like to. I like snooping."

"I don't."

"You'd like it better if you hadn't liked Raymond."

"I'd like it better if Raymond were seeming more to me like the person I thought he was."

"All through the divorce he told you who he was, and you believed him. That's good. That's your job."

The waiter arrived to clear their plates. "Can I bring you dessert menus?"

"No," said Charlie.

"Yes," said Sophie.

"You never have dessert," said Charlie, surprised.

"I'm trying to change the subject."

"Oh."

They shared a lemon tart and talked about Sophie's job, and her sister Connie in the suburbs with the screwed-up marriage, and all around the question of whether, if they were not growing closer, Charlie and Sophie were growing apart. Afterward, they walked the several blocks to Raymond's office. Sophie took Charlie's arm and thought about whether it would be a wrong move to ask him to escort her to her cousin's wedding. Charlie thought about Raymond, tall and powerfully built, resplendent in Turnbull and Asser, reporting with a certain effort at dignity, over breakfast at the Carlyle, that Martha had never supported his career, that she had refused for no reason to use contacts that would be helpful to him, that she became terribly upset when he used social occasions to do business. ("As if she didn't know how the world works. Everyone knows it's not what you know, it's who you know.") Now Charlie wondered what Raymond had meant, exactly. That Martha didn't like it if he tried to put the bite on old friends during dinner parties?

They arrived at the building they were seeking. It was dark, without architectural distinction, and none too clean. Sophie looked at Charlie. Charlie looked wary.

As they ascended in the dingy elevator, Charlie surprised himself by saying, "I learned how to operate one of those manual elevators with the lever this weekend." It was one of those inappropriate remarks you make when something is just on your mind, very much on your mind. Sophie heard it as such. She was surprised.

"Where?"

"In SoHo," he said, and wondered why he had spoken. She just looked at him, curious. She knew Charlie well enough to know that if he had a friend in SoHo, it was a new development.

They arrived at their floor, and then at the door marked THE GAVER-ZAGAR PARTNERSHIP. They went in.

Sherry was expecting them. From her phone calls Charlie had formed an image of someone small and tough and blond, with scarlet fingernails. But she was not that. She was tall and big boned with blue eyes that were almost green, and auburn hair going gray. Her voice was lower and warmer than on the phone.

"Mr. Leveque," she said, shaking hands.

"Charlie. This is my friend Sophie Curry." The women shook hands.

"I'm sorry, I haven't done much to get ready for you," said Sherry.

"It's all right," said Charlie. "I imagine you have enough on your hands."

"I'll drink to that," she said, heartfelt.

"How's it going?"

She hesitated. "It's touch and go."

"Really."

She nodded.

"Are you going to be okay?"

"If I can save the deal he was working on when he died, I will."

"Well. Good luck."

"Thank you. The sofa here is his . . . I'd like to buy it from you."

"I assume that's fine."

"What about the painting?" asked Sophie.

"Yes, that's his."

Charlie looked at Sophie.

"And the rug is his." Charlie looked at it. It was an oriental of some kind, worn but handsome, in faded colors of rose and blue that must once have been lush. Without it, the rather nasty office furniture would have given the room an air of bus station modern. Charlie saw the room, the separate components, quite differently than he would have if Sophie were not there.

"His office is this way," said Sherry, and they followed her.

Raymond's office was separated from Sherry's by a plasterboard wall with a fixed window and a hollow-core door, the bottom-of-the-line lumberyard fixtures. Inside was a nice-looking desk, another carpet, a pair of tall, army green file cabinets, and stacks of cardboard cartons in the corners.

"This is not what I expected," said Charlie when Sherry had left them.

"The more I see, the more it's just what I did expect," said Sophie.

Charlie gave her a questioning look.

He opened a drawer of a cabinet and found it jammed. Half seemed to consist of unsorted correspondence waiting for filing. Beside the cabinet was an oak coatrack, and on it hung a raincoat. Charlie looked at it, thinking of the coatrack in the corner of his office, where hung a similar raincoat, and where also he kept a pair of rubbers. Sophie put her hands into the coat pockets and came out with two ticket stubs from

Carnegie Hall, a couple of business cards, some with notes and numbers on them, and a set of keys. She handed all these to Charlie.

"Charlie, what does this carpet remind you of?"

"The dean's room at law school. He'd invite the 1L's for sherry."

Sophie nodded.

"Check out the computer," said Charlie. "Oh god, a Victor. What's a Victor? Do any computers use disks this size?"

"Not anymore."

"He must have felt like the poor dolts who bought the Alphamax. You ever see one of those?"

Sophie shook her head.

"Check out this desk," she said. Sophie was kneeling, opening drawers. In the top drawer, Charlie spotted a tiny portable TV.

"A watchperson," he said, taking it out.

"This is real," said Sophie.

"I always wanted one of these," said Charlie.

"This desk is real, Charlie, it's not a reproduction."

"Oh," said Charlie, turning on the television. It worked beautifully. "This is neat, the screen has a magnifying lens."

"The rugs are, too."

"What, real?"

She took the TV and turned it off.

"Yes."

"So what, are they worth something?"

"This rug is small, but it's perfect. The one outside is worn, but if it's what I think it is . . . and the painting, too . . ."

"Yes? The painting, too, what?"

"I'll bet you dinner this desk is worth fifty thousand dollars."

"*What?*"

"Didn't it ever occur to you that sweetheart was the type to hide his assets?"

Charlie had a vision of Martha in tears, in the conference room at his office. Raymond, with Charlie at his side, explaining, with becoming humility, that he *had* no assets. He had pending deals, he had income from one loft conversion in Chelsea and from a small apartment house on Fifteenth Street. Everything else he'd been lent or given had gone into the business and up in smoke. Raymond and Charlie, side by side, in their fifteen-hundred-dollar suits, had firmly and sorrowfully held the position that love was for better or for worse, that Martha had paid her money and taken her choice. "I'd have made it big in another two years. I still will," Raymond had said. "But she wouldn't wait. Nothing I ever did was going to be good enough for her."

"I think this carpet is a Star Ushak. If it is and it's as old as it looks, it's worth about twenty-five."

"Thousand," said Charlie.

"Yes."

"And the painting?"

"A Jasper Cropsey. It was bright of him not to have it cleaned."

"I feel like a nickel waiting for change," said Charlie.

"I think you better call Sotheby's. Get an appraiser in here. Was there anything valuable at the apartment?"

"There was kind of a big pool table."

"*Kind* of a big one? How big?"

Charlie, thinking about it, realized it was pretty fucking big.

"What was it like, Charlie?" He described it.

"Tell me you didn't give it to Goodwill."

"I didn't. I gave it to his son. Well, gave it to him. It's his."

"What's he going to do with it?"

"Play pool on it."

"Perfect. And if he gets tired of that, he can probably pay his way through college with it."

"I see."

"Are you the widow's favorite person? What's her name?"

Charlie thought about that. In fact, in the last week he'd thought about it more and more, with a sense of . . . sadness. Something like that.

"Martha. No. I can't say I am."

"I can't say I blame her, asshole."

"Give me a break. I don't know anything about furniture."

She rolled her eyes. "I have to go. But tell me something. If you had known what he was doing, would you have acted differently? It was your job to do the best job you could for him, wasn't it?"

"If I had known, I wouldn't have represented him."

She thought about it, then nodded. "Ain't life grand." She gave him a kiss. "Thank you for lunch."

"You're welcome."

"I'll send the estate my consulting fee."

"Oh, great."

She left before she found out whether he meant to make another date with her soon. When she had gone, Charlie went to Sherry's office and asked her, trying not to sound as if it were important, if she would mind walking through the offices and pointing out exactly which objects had belonged to Raymond. Sherry, who also didn't know much about furniture, was glad of an excuse to postpone the next phone call she had to make. There were three more paintings, dingy little pictures of sailing ships, and in some boxes in the hall closet, they were both surprised to find a collection of snuff bottles, and a set of very old-looking lead soldiers in uniforms that looked like pictures from the Battle of Waterloo. Somehow, Charlie didn't think Raymond had bought them to play with.

Sophie and her sister Connie had had lunch together about two hundred times since Sophie moved to New York. Once a month at least, even when Connie was nursing the twins. Especially when she was nursing the twins. Connie would leave Mrs. Tsatch a batch of Enfamil and drive off with her heart hard as Bluebeard's, knowing the babies wouldn't take bottles and they'd be screaming their little brains out by one o'clock. And thirty miles away in some midtown bistro with her pretty sister, Connie would know that her babies were crying and she'd take a slug of wine and swear not to talk about it.

Connie's pretty sister Sophie hadn't married. She had an apartment in Yorkville all to herself. (Connie had never had anyplace all to herself except the one year in college she'd had a single. As children she and Sophie shared a bedroom, and Connie had moved from her college dorm straight to Dave's double bed.) But Sophie had a closet all to herself and in it were espadrilles in seven colors to mach her summer dresses. Connie had a drawerful of bras and underpants that didn't match, and shoes that were all worn down at the outside of the heels. Sophie went out on dates and had a stack of *Playbills.*

When the twins were born, Connie's husband, Dave, went around calling himself Supersperm. His big laugh boomed around the house and across the golf course on weekends. Dave was, even then, fleshy and competitive, and it didn't do you any harm at all in the locker room to have your wife popping the old progeny out two at a time.

The twins were not identical, and tense, tiny, nervous Ruth had to eat about twice as often as Molly, so there was never a time that one or the other was not weeping with hunger and waking the other. There was no problem about waking Connie because she never got to sleep at all. She had felt throughout that time as if she hadn't slept in years.

The first time Connie had left the babies to go into town to see Sophie—this was fifteen years ago, now—her milk had let down at the table, drenching her blouse, and Connie had begun to cry. Sophie had been distressed but Connie smiled, with tears pouring down her face, and said there was really nothing wrong, she was just so tired. It was rather fun, actually, like being on mind-altering drugs, she said, to be so tired.

"Are you sure you don't want to talk?" Sophie had asked. Connie said god no, she wanted to hear about life in the real world.

The real world. Well. Sophie had a boss who wished to hug her and kiss her, while she preferred that he not. She was studying French at night at the Alliance Française, and planning a trip to Bordeaux. She took ballet classes for exercise. To Connie it sounded terribly glamorous and lonely.

Connie and Sophie were different. They always had been. Even as children Sophie had been lean and wary and self-contained, while Connie was like a ripe peach inside. Connie had always been pretty, she had always been popular. She was the kind of girl other girls' boyfriends told their troubles to. She was the kind of girl even the rough, tough drink-'em-up guys like Dave referred to as "good people." Connie was responsive; Sophie was cooler, and hard to read.

Even after all these years, it took Connie some time to settle down and think of what to talk to Sophie about. Should she ask her about Charlie? Sophie gave her so few clues. In fact, her younger sister's reserve tended to rattle her. Connie began, "I decided to drive because I had to bring the vacuum cleaner hose to be fixed. Gladys said she was going to quit if I didn't. I don't know why, it's perfectly easy to put more duct tape around it. The thing is I brought the station wagon because the transmission fell out of Dave's car so now I'm wondering if anyone would steal a fifty-foot vacuum hose from a car I mean, it's not in a trunk or anything."

Connie knew her attention was bouncing around. Driving in traffic made her nervous, as did New York, that bastion of ambition and achievement, none of it hers. She noticed they were surrounded by rose-colored walls and gray upholstery. On the wall was a mural of Venice. Connie had never been to Venice, though Sophie had. In fact, Sophie was in Italy when the twins were born, and she brought Connie a pair of tiny blue linen dresses trimmed with lace that could be starched and ironed in just under an hour apiece. Connie wanted to weep when she saw them. Sohpie had come straight to her from the airport, and Dave was out playing golf, and Ruth had been crying all afternoon and wouldn't eat.

"How could the hose be fifty feet long, Connie?" Sophie asked.

"It's one of those central systems with the machine in the basement. Don't you know? I can't believe it. I can't believe we've never discussed vacuum cleaners, it's the only appliance I'm really interested in. How about laundry presoaks. Have we talked about those?"

Sophie laughed. The waiter brought them red wine in glasses with stems like pencils and bowls like bathtubs. They raised the glasses to each other.

Mrs. Colonna, head of the lower school at Hudson Country Day, had been trying to reach Connie Justice for twenty minutes but there was no answer at the house. Dave's secretary said Mr. Justice was out of the office. She had no idea where Mrs. Justice was. Across her desk in big leather chairs sat William Justice and his art teacher in a smock dotted with clay and slip stains. Mrs. Colonna put down the receiver and turned to them. The little girl whose clay circus William had destroyed had been comforted, but William had not explained himself or apologized. William had not in fact said a word since he took the rolling pin with which he was flattening clay for a slab pot and squashed and smashed every one of the horses and giraffes and lions and bears that Karen Scully had been building since the term began. He himself had been making a series of ashtrays for his mother, although she didn't smoke.

"Karen was teasing him," said Barbara, the art teacher. She had a problem because she knew that William's behavior was inexcusable, and yet she loved William and didn't like Karen.

"We do *not* deal with that by smashing people's belongings," said Mrs. Colonna.

"No," said Barbara. She glanced at William. He had been looking at her, but now he looked down. They had each tried several times to get William to explain himself, but he wouldn't.

Barbara looked at her watch. She had her sixth-graders coming any minute and had to get back to the art room. Mrs. Colonna's notion for situations like this was that a parent, suitably alarmed and ashamed, should rush to school in a station wagon and remove the wild spore from Mrs. Colonna's environment. This was not the sort of school where the enrollment forms had spaces for the mothers' and fathers' separate addresses or for a mother's office location or daytime telephone number.

"Maybe his sisters will have an idea," said Barbara, rising. Mrs. Colonna nodded, and Barbara, with a last glance at William, beat a retreat. Mrs. Colonna telephoned the middle school office to find out where Molly and Ruth were. Molly was down at hockey practice, but Ruth was taken out of French class, and she finally arrived.

Ruth Justice stood at the door of Mrs. Colonna's office. She didn't know what this was about and she was frightened. She knew that Mrs. Colonna had never liked her, and she lived in dread of being sent to her office the whole time she was in the lower school. To be hauled out of class in eighth grade and sent down here had filled her with an irrational panic that something awful was about to happen, like being expelled for something you did five years ago, or being blamed for something you didn't do at all.

Ruth had grown almost five inches in the last year, and she seemed to be all arms and legs and neck. Mrs. Colonna had never cared for that age much. From first grade to sixth, children were like little trees; they grew at a sort of even rate, all their parts keeping pace with each other from year to year. Their heads were round, their noses small, their skin clear and glowing, and they smelled good. Now Ruth Justice stood in her doorway looking like a hooved animal—a colt or a deer. Her skirt was shorter than Mrs. Colonna liked them and she had breasts. Even as a little girl Ruth always had a kind of unchildish gravity, a thin-skinned quality of taking herself seriously that Mrs. Colonna never cared for. Ruth's teachers liked her, and she got good grades even in citizenship, but Mrs. Colonna always thought she needed taking down a peg. Of course, Mrs. Colonna was a professional and treated all the children with perfect evenhandedness, so she knew Ruth had never suspected that she wasn't a favorite here.

Ruth saw William, sitting in a big chair, gazing at her. She forgot herself for a moment. Was he hurt? Was he sick? She waited in the doorway for a clue.

"I've been trying to reach your mother, Ruth."

"I think she's in New York."

Well. That was no help. What now? Mrs. Colonna turned her high beams on William.

"William, perhaps you should tell your sister what has happened."

Ruth looked at him; yes, tell me. What was this?

He looked back at her. His eyes were wide and deep. Ruth could see some mute appeal there, and whatever he'd done, she didn't want Mrs. Colonna to get him. She went to him and stood beside his chair. Now, for heavens sake, Mrs. Colonna had two of them staring at her.

Ruth was thinking that William had never done a mean or destructive thing in his life, that she knew of.

"I'll take him home."

"Do you have more classes this afternoon?"

"Just chorus."

"All right, Ruth. I'll have you excused. Will your parents be home this evening?"

"I don't know. Yes. I'm sure they will."

"Please tell them I would like to talk to them tomorrow at nine. Right after assembly." Ruth nodded and took William away.

As the door closed behind them, William took his sister's hand.

The hallway was silent. "Do you have homework?" she asked William. He nodded. They walked together to his classroom, and Ruth watched as William the criminal walked through the thicket of stares to get his books from his desk and then his jacket and backpack from the closet.

They went upstairs to get Ruth's books. These halls were quiet, too. The upper walls here were painted a dull yellow. Lower school kids hardly ever came up here; William studied it all intently. Ruth got what she needed from her locker and they went out by the side stairs.

The afternoon was clear and quiet.

"Did you get any lunch?" Ruth asked, as they walked. William shook his head.

"Are you hungry?"

He nodded. He looked up at her. Ruth suddenly, briefly, felt like crying.

She took off her backpack and took out her brown bag. Only the lower schoolers had to take hot lunch at Hudson. In seventh grade she could choose to make her own lunch, and she took the same thing every day: a tomato and cheese sandwich, and an orange. Now she unwrapped the sandwich and gave half to William. They walked along, eating. When they finished, she peeled the orange and gave him half of that. She glanced at him from time to time and wondered what he was thinking.

"Mr. *Leveque, can* you take a call from Martha Forbes?"
"What line?"

"Four."

He punched the button angrily and picked up.

"Martha."

"Hello, Charlie."

"What can I do for you?"

"I want to talk about Jack's allowance."

"Okay."

"I'd like you to raise it five dollars."

"To twenty-five a week?"

"Yes. He's in a play at school this term, and he often has to travel home late after rehearsals, when he can't use his subway pass."

"So that's another buck a pop."

"Yes."

"What else is he using his money for?"

His voice was testy.

"I told you, Charlie, he eats it. He eats about five meals a day. There's only so much food I can send to school with him."

"It seems to me like an awful lot of cash. We pay for all his books and school supplies."

"You know what? I really don't want to discuss this with you. I don't know what he spends every dime on, but I know this request makes sense to me."

She stopped. Her voice had been hot with resentment.

Charlie said, "Could we start this conversation over?"

"I think we better."

There was a silence. Charlie said, formally, "Martha. I'm glad you called. I need some advice."

"Oh?"

"My daughter was kicked out of school an hour ago. She told the headmistress to fuck herself."

"Oh."

"So I think I should tell you how to raise your child, because I'm doing such a good job with mine."

"Got it." Pause. "I'm sorry."

"No, I'm sorry."

"I meant, I'm sorry that happened to you."

"I'm sitting here staring at the walls, wondering who to talk to. I don't know what the fuck to do." Pause. "At least we know where she learned her language."

There was another silence.

"Where is she now? Your daughter."

"Her mother is on her way to get her."

"What's her name?"

"My daughter? Phoebe."

"I knew that. Her mother."

"Oh. Her mother's name is Patsy."

After a bit he asked, "What would you do?"

"Me? If it were Jack?"

There was another silence.

"I've got to get out of here," said Charlie. "I'm going to start screaming. Do you have any idea how hard it was to get her *into* that goddamn place?"

"Some."

"ERB's, interviews, letters . . . getting approved by my co-op was easier. Getting into law school was *much* easier."

"How will your wife handle it?"

"Ex-wife."

"I know."

"Could I come see you?"

"You mean right now?"

"Yes. I've got to get out of here."

For a moment Martha didn't answer.

"I've got to figure out what to do. I don't know whether to comfort her or punch her lights out."

"I guess so."

Charlie was leaning on Martha's buzzer twenty minutes later. He walked in and said, "My ex-wife will handle it by making it be all about *her*. 'How could you do this to me, you make me feel like such a failure, how am I going to tell your grandmother?' Weeping and wailing, rending of clothing."

Martha nodded. "I've had friends like that."

"I hate it," said Charlie. "I hate it. I've seen more self-control in the monkey house than when Phoebe and Patsy get each other going. Is the baby here?"

"No, he's at day care."

"Can I buy you a drink?"

"It's two in the afternoon."

"So what."

"I really have to work, later. . . ." What she meant was, she really should be working now. She resisted looking, longing, at her drafting table.

"Well, could we take a walk? Isn't that what you usually do with your friends?"

Martha paused a minute. How do you know that? Oh yes. Hours of conversations with Raymond. She nodded. "Yes. That's what I usually do." She went to put on her shoes and get a jacket.

They set off walking down Broadway. Trucks rumbled past them heading for Broome Street and the Holland Tunnel. Broadway was a gray canyon heading straight to the Battery; trash skittered in the gutters. They crossed Canal Street, where even the signs at McDonald's are in Chinese.

"It's something that's been building for a long time," said Charlie suddenly, "that I just didn't want to see. She's been rude, self-centered, hostile . . . it isn't normal teenage stuff. It's been horrible to live with."

"Does she live with you?"

"No. I see her as much as I can, evenings and weekends."

"Whose choice was it? The custody?"

"Patsy's, I guess."

"How long have you been apart?"

"Almost four years."

"So Phoebe was . . ."

"Turning twelve."

They walked in silence for a block.

"Four years ago," said Martha, "one of the things that really hurt me was walking into your office and seeing those pictures of you and your perfect blond wife and daughter all over the place."

"When were you in my office?"

Negotiations in cases like the Gavers were always held in the conference room.

"After Raymond and I signed the settlement. You asked us to come in so you could use your calculator for something."

Charlie remembered.

"It was already such a painful, confusing experience, I thought, Well fuck you and the horse you came in on. There we were with our lives in rubble around our ankles, and who were you to be advising and negotiating for us, you who had no idea what we were going through." The pain in her voice surprised them both.

Another silent block. "It was a good question," said Charlie.

They walked. In the distance, where the buildings fell back from the street at the park around City Hall, they could see an arch of sky, surprising blue in a world of black and white.

"I've been so proud of being a good father. Vain, really. I've always thought you teach by example, you show her what kind of person you want her to be, and you trust her and love her, and bingo. I don't understand where this monster came from. She says horrible things to me, she seems bigoted and shallow." He paused. "She's spoiled, is what my mother would call it."

"Was she like that when she was little?"

"No. She always had a streak of something . . . but, no. She was giving, she was loving."

"When did she change?"

"I don't know! It's as if it's been right in front of me for months, years, I don't know, and I just kept ignoring it. I thought if I just kept treating her the way I always have, the Phoebe I love would come back."

Martha nodded.

"Have you ever walked across the Brooklyn Bridge?" she asked.

"No," said Charlie, surprised.

"Let's go this way." They had reached City Hall Park, and she pointed across it to the bridge.

Charlie said, "Fine." He walked beside her, only half seeing. They passed the great Gothic stone pile of the Municipal Building. Under the groined vault, a bride in full regalia and hugely pregnant was in tears, surrounded by bridesmaids in green taffeta. They were throwing rice.

"Are drugs involved?" Martha asked.

"I certainly never thought so."

"But?"

"But she was caught smoking a joint in the bathroom this morning."

"This is before she told the headmistress to fuck herself."

"Yes."

Before them hulked the modernist monolith of One Police Plaza, and now they could see a whole dome of open sky above the river.

"You don't know if that's the symptom or the illness, though."

"No. She's never seemed druggy to me, but . . . would I know? Would you? She could probably walk around on heroin and I wouldn't get it."

"Jack tells me a chronically runny nose is a bad sign. Or long sleeves in summer." She meant it as a joke.

Charlie nodded. He knew that much, he'd been to the movies.

They reached the bridge.

"She's angry at you?" Martha asked.

"Furious. She seems to be trying to make me hate her."

"Is it about the divorce?"

"It didn't seem so. She knows it wasn't my idea, she knows Patsy left me."

Martha glanced at him quickly. He was looking out over the river. They were ascending the curve of the footpath above the water.

"This is *wonderful*," said Charlie.

Martha nodded. She loved the bridge and walked it or rode her bike over it about once a week.

"Is she angry at her mother, too?"

"They've always fought a lot. Patsy's a little volatile."

"But not you."

"I hate confrontation."

"The law is an interesting choice for you, isn't it?"

Charlie laughed, rueful.

Martha said, "Maybe she's not trying to make you hate her. Phoebe. Maybe she's trying to make you see her."

"What do you mean?"

"I was just thinking about when I was her age. For some reason, I suddenly refused to set my hair or wear lipstick. I wanted to look like Joan Baez. My mother went critical; it took years to repair the damage. At the time it just seemed like two egos galloping at each other a hundred miles an hour for no reason. Blam! But now . . ."

"Now, what?"

"Now I think I was trying to say, 'Look, I'm a separate person from you, I have qualities you haven't seen, I want you to look harder.' And to my mother, that was very provocative. She really didn't want me to be different from her. Or separate."

"Yes, but . . . Phoebe seems to want me to approve of her unconditionally. She blows sky high if I even hint that I find her behavior or judgment lacking. If she wants me to *see* her, I see a person I can't approve of. She's selfish, she's prejudiced, she's—that's different from what you were saying, isn't it?"

"Yes. Although, I'm not sure my behavior at home was all that wonderful. I can't remember."

"But what do I do with a child who's rude and horrible to me if I don't find her perfect, and then behaves so badly she gets kicked out of school?"

* * *

They had reached the middle of the span. As if by agreement, they stopped to look down the river to the mouth of New York Harbor. There were sailboats fighting their way upstream against an ebbing tide. There were barges, there were tugboats. They could see the Statue of Liberty. They stood on an arc of bridge under a gorgeous wide arc of cloudless sky.

"What do I do now?" Charlie asked.

"I haven't the faintest idea."

"Boarding school?"

"You could try that, I guess. Did you go to boarding school?"

"No. Did you?"

"Yes. I hated it. Do you want her to go away?"

"I want to choke her. But, no, I don't really want her to go. I've never thought boarding schools could pay as much attention as parents can."

"They can't."

"And it doesn't seem like the right thing for a kid in trouble. I'd solve *my* problems with her by getting rid of her. But if I don't know what's going on with her, how can I expect a school in Connecticut to?"

Martha nodded.

"Does that sound right to you?" Charlie asked.

"Yes, it does."

They resumed walking toward Brooklyn.

"What do you think of Jack's school?"

"It's great for him. Great faculty, high academic standards. A lot of sense of humor about kids. I like what it's done for Jack, and I like his friends."

"Do they like kids who tell them to fuck themselves?"

"I imagine they've heard it before."

Charlie nodded. Thoughtful.

Martha said, "I learned a very important thing from Jack once. He'd lost his first serious girlfriend and he was a wreck . . . not sleeping, screwing up in school. . . . One day he came home with his eyes all red and I was furious because I thought he'd been smoking pot, and then I realized he'd been crying. He wasn't doing homework, he wasn't snapping out of it, and I couldn't stand it. I asked him if he wanted to see a shrink, and he said absolutely not. I asked him if he wanted to change schools or live with his father. He said no. I said, 'Okay, you tell me. I don't know what to do for you. What would being a good parent consist of here?' And he said, 'I think you should let me have a problem.'"

Charlie was listening intently. He was thinking of Phoebe's sullen anger and Patsy's histrionics. He was thinking of his own mother, who was always, always smiling and whose hair was always so curled and sprayed it looked like a hat. He nodded.

Connie was watching the news while she made dinner. She had gotten over the shock, herself, of what Ruth had told her when she got home. She was bracing now for telling Dave. She was thinking that this would be a sort of test, a test of the marriage, of the strength of the partnership. Could she and Dave pull together on this, to stand by William?

Connie heard Dave's car. She turned off the TV and listened for his step on the porch. (Hi, honey. Listen, something happened to William today—no. How about, honey, I'm sorry to hit you with this right away but—no. Honey, get a drink and come back and talk to me. I'm afraid we have a problem.)

It was after midnight. Ruth and Molly were both awake, but they stayed in bed. Their parents had been fighting for two hours.

Their mother murmured.

Their father roared. "NO I WON'T FUCKING LOWER MY VOICE! WHO DO YOU THINK YOU ARE TO BE TELLING ME THE CHILDREN, THE CHILDREN!"

Their mother murmured.

Their father yelled, "Oh they do not, they're asleep! If they're so fucking close to you, how come Ruth didn't tell you she made honor roll last spring? Who did she tell, Connie?"

Their mother answered, a little more agitated and at length, until their father interrupted her.

"You know what? That's *bullshit! You* don't want him to grow up! He's got the mental age of a five-year-old!"

Their mother interrupted angrily and without success.

"He's like a five-year-old, afraid of *bugs,* afraid of *turtles.* . . ."

Angry murmurs.

"Because you like it that way!! You want him weird, so he'll stay home and be your little pet!"

Then the door slammed and their mother's footsteps marched angrily downstairs, and the house fell silent.

At nine-fifteen, Mrs. Colonna was waiting in her office for the Justices to arrive.

William's parents were a handsome couple. Connie was pretty and blond, with her hair in a breezy cut like Princess Di's. She wore tidy bright girlish clothes. Dave was big and bearlike, with thick honey-colored hair and warm hazel eyes. He was dressed for work and carrying a briefcase. Mrs. Colonna had wrecked his morning, she knew, calling him in here; he wouldn't get to New York till noon. Not all fathers would have come, either. Mrs. Colonna watched carefully for the body language that tells so much when people are under stress. The Justices chose to sit together on the couch. They looked composed, deeply concerned, as they should. Interesting.

"I presume you know by now what happened yesterday? Both of you?"

Connie and Dave nodded.

"Well, I'm sure you're very concerned, as I am. I'd like to hear what you make of it." Pause. "I hope you agree with me that we have a rather serious situation here."

Connie and Dave looked at each other, reassuring, worried. Actually, they hadn't thought about it as all that serious. Weird, of course. Out of character. But nothing to make a federal case of. Connie had been so mad at Dave that she had had very little sleep. Then when she crept back up to the bedroom at dawn so that the children wouldn't think anything was wrong, Dave, contrite and basically asleep, nuzzled her so sweetly like a lost little boy that they had ended up making love. Typical.

"He seems terribly sorry, Mrs. Colonna," said Connie softly.

"*Is* he sorry?" asked Mrs. Colonna.

Connie bristled, "Mrs. Colonna, he's one of your babies. You've had him at Hudson since he was four. You *know* he's the gentlest . . ." Her voice was mild but she had to stop because she was too angry to finish the sentence.

"Tell me, what explanation does he give?"

There was a pause.

"William?" asked Connie.

"Well, yes. William."

"Ruth tells us he broke some things another child was working on in art class," said Connie. Connie and Dave glanced at each other. That *was* what this was all about, wasn't it?

"Yes, he did. My concern was, why? Why did he do that? What has he said about it? The little girl, Karen Scully, swears she wasn't doing anything to him."

"Who is Karen Scully?" asked Dave.

"She's new this year." Mrs. Colonna had not been deflected. She waited.

"He hasn't really said anything," said Connie. "He didn't want to talk about it."

"Mrs. Justice," said Mrs. Colonna sharply, "we all have to do things we don't want to do. I'm afraid that when children begin smashing things with rolling pins, they really have to give some account of their behavior, whether they feel like it or not."

Connie and Dave looked at Mrs. Colonna. They were both distressed. But somehow surprised, thought Mrs. Colonna. She bore down.

"Was he angry at Karen? Was she annoying him? Was he frustrated by something we could help him with?"

Pause. "He didn't say."

"Well, what *did* he say?"

"Nothing," Connie glanced at Dave.

Mrs. Colonna said, "You mean, he hasn't spoken at all?"

Well, no. He hadn't. He'd been in his room. He didn't want any dinner. Connie couldn't figure out why it didn't really seem so strange to her until this moment, until she heard how strange Mrs. Colonna thought it was.

"Has this ever happened before?"

"What?"

"Has he ever stopped talking before?"

Dave said, "No." Connie shook her head. Was that what had happened? He'd stopped talking?

"He didn't say a word to any of us yesterday," said Mrs. Colonna sternly. There was a silence. "I really think that you must get William professional help immediately."

This landed like a bomb lobbed onto the carpet at Connie and Dave's feet. It lay there, ticking.

Professional help?

"Maybe we should try public school," said Dave. Connie slowly turned to look at him. What? What the hell are you talking about, Dave? What does that have to do with the price of eggs?

"Why do you say that, Mr. Justice?" asked Mrs. Colonna, coolly. Dave was charming. Ingenuous.

"Just a question," he explained. "Maybe things are too precious for William. I don't mean your school, of course, Mrs. Colonna. But maybe it would toughen him up."

Mrs. Colonna considered. Connie was still looking at Dave thoughtfully. Her thoughts were: Jesus, you are an asshole.

"Well. That might be a thought for the future, Mr. Justice. But at the moment, I think we have to attend to the immediate situation. Your son has had a violent episode, and he has stopped speaking."

A violent episode! Come *on,* the kid got pissed off and broke something.

"Mrs. Colonna, it's so unlike William . . . don't you think you might be overreacting?"

"No," said Mrs. Colonna smoothly, and suddenly Connie wanted to kill her. She didn't move, of course, since an attempted homicide in the family after yesterday's events would do William no good.

"I can recommend a therapist, if you like. There's a woman in Tarrytown who did wonderful work with a student of ours in a similar situation."

Similar situation? thought Connie. What do you imagine the situation to be? How dare you imagine William's "situation" at all, you don't know him. . . .

"What if we decide against therapy?" asked Dave pleasantly.

"I hope you won't," Mrs. Colonna replied, equally pleasantly.

"Does that mean you wouldn't take William back?" asked Connie. That's a little high-handed, isn't it? You bitch?

"I have to do what's best for each child, Mrs. Justice, and what's best for my school. In this case, I think they're the same. Would you like me to get you the name of the therapist?"

"I *want to* go to the Tutoring School," said Phoebe, kicking the leg of her chair under the table. Her mother, who had spent two days in her room on the phone, in tears, retailing the latest crisis, had finally heard of a charming French family transferred to New York in midyear, whose children had been very happy there until they could start the Lycée in the fall.

"Phoebe, it costs twenty thousand a year!"

"So what?"

"So . . . I'm already out half a year's tuition at Replogle, that's four thousand dollars, and these tests have cost a mint, and application fees . . ."

"Gosh, Daad," Phoebe drawled. "What a bummer. I didn't know getting kicked out was so expeeensive. It's only my *life,* you know."

Charlie counted to ten. Then he did it again.

"Phoebe," he said softly, "this is not the moment to play chicken with me. You are very close to being sent to public school."

"Fine," said Phoebe. "That's what I want." Phoebe knew perfectly well that her parents had had a screaming fight the night before, because Patsy contended that all the talented kids at the high school level in the New York system attended the special competitive schools like Stuyvesant and Music and Art. If they dumped her into a neighborhood school, she'd be there with boneheads and junkies and dope dealers.

"On the Upper East Side?" asked Charlie.

"You'd take that chance with her, wouldn't you?" screamed Patsy. "She's much too fragile now. We should call Marie Elise at St. Bart's and you know it."

"St. Bart's had two students arrested for cocaine smuggling last year!" roared Charlie.

"Oh, stop it. It's a very fine school and we have an in there."

"First of all it's a country club, and this isn't the moment for rewarding her. Second, I don't want her to go away."

"Why not!" Patsy was screaming again. "Just because I went to boarding school?"

"Patsy, she's not you! And boarding schools have changed!"

"How do you know? Since when are you the expert?"

"Could we get back to the subject? Which is, Phoebe." Charlie whispered.

They glared at each other. Then Patsy burst into tears. Charlie counted to twenty.

"I don't think any boarding school can pay as careful attention to a single child as parents can," said Charlie, measured.

"Then let's send her to the Tutoring School and try to get her back into Replogle in the fall."

"No."

"No?"

"No! Actions have consequences, Patsy. She's got to learn something. Right now."

"Well then, what's your bright idea?"

"She should apply to Turley, and to the York School, and I'd like to look at Cropp and Thatcher."

"What's Cropp and Thatcher?"

"It's a school in Brooklyn Heights where a friend of mine sends her son."

"Oh, a *friend* of yours."

"Yes, Patsy."

"Now we're going to have your new girlfriend choosing where Phoebe should go to school?"

"Patsy, for christsake!"

"Well I never even *heard* of this place!"

"No, because it's not on the Upper East Side."

"Well, *Brooklyn!* Get serious!"

Charlie was having some trouble with his temper. And sometimes he had trouble remembering why he ever liked this woman.

"Listen. Phoebe has been kicked out of school, and it wasn't a mistake. She deserved it. She did something *wrong*, Patsy. And, she was barely passing math at the time, and she cannot pick and choose. She would be luckier than she deserves if she got into Cropp and Thatcher, and I would be overjoyed to have her in an entirely different borough from Bloomingdale's."

"She'd be utterly miserable."

"Have you ever even *been* to Brooklyn Heights, Patsy?"

She had not, of course, but for heaven's sake.

"Phoebe, this is Ms. Forbes."

"Martha," said Martha to Phoebe. Phoebe shook her offered hand and called her nothing.

Martha had watched Charlie and his daughter coming toward her through the restaurant, and suddenly heard her own mother saying to her teenage self, "You'd be so pretty if you'd smile, dear. And stand up straight." Phoebe looked like someone determined to show the world how ugly she felt inside, but she couldn't completely hide her beautiful eyes.

"So. You liked the school," she said to Phoebe. Phoebe shrugged.

"I did, very much," said Charlie.

"Did Jack take you around?"

Again she addressed Phoebe.

Phoebe shook her head. "A girl called Jenny."

"Jack was having a test or something."

"Oh." Martha sipped her coffee and sat quietly for a while, glancing now and then at Phoebe. Charlie had asked her to write a letter recommending Phoebe, and Martha said she would, but she'd have to meet her.

"They don't have much sports," said Phoebe, finally.

"Probably not what you're used to. Are sports very important to you?"

After a while Phoebe said, "Not really."

Martha looked surprised.

"I understand you did well on your ERB tests."

"Pretty well."

"And you've had your psych tests, to see if you're a hardened sociopath?"

Phoebe looked surprised. Nobody had been taking anything about her situation lightly, lately. She nodded.

"Were they interesting?"

"No."

Martha laughed, and Phoebe looked at her, curious. Was she funny? That would be nice.

"The inkblot part was fun. They all looked like butterflies to me, but I said they looked like a wolf's face."

Martha smiled. "You'll be lucky if you don't end up in reform school."

Phoebe nodded. And smiled briefly.

"How are your friends being? About what happened to you?"

"The girls are being nice. Except Serena, who's a dick."

"How?"

Phoebe shifted in her seat. She said, bitterly, with an entirely different kind of pressure behind her speech, "I called her to come have a coffee or something and she said she was grounded, which is a lie, and she told my other friend she didn't know I was that stupid." Phoebe's lower lip was jutting, and she stared at the table. A waitress brought coffee for Charlie and a Coke for Phoebe. Phoebe paid no attention.

"That seems . . . unnecessary."

"She's a dick," said Phoebe. Her voice was so full of anger and pain that Charlie turned to look at her.

"What will you miss the most? About your old school?"

"Everything," said Phoebe. She was very near tears. Charlie and Martha looked at each other. Charlie looked pretty sad himself. Something about his way of being with Phoebe had kept her raw pain at bay, and he was finding this hard to bear.

"Do you think you would like Cropp and Thatcher?" asked Martha.

"It's better than the other ones," Phoebe said with vehemence.

Charlie looked surprised. "I thought you liked the Turley School."

"It's for *retards,* Dad!"

A silence. It was true, Charlie knew, that Turley had done very well with children with learning disabilities.

"But you told your mother you liked it."

Phoebe shrugged.

∞

Connie and Dave sat in the office of Tina, the child psychiatrist. Dave had pictured that she would be a person about four feet tall, dwarfed by her big grown-up chair and oversized glasses. The fact that she appeared before him, a normal-sized adult with no glasses and a warm smile, didn't really erase the image from his mind or his essential scorn for her profession. Tina was a Jew, of course.

Nor was she in fact a psychiatrist. Dave had asked her about her training and she had admitted, smiling pleasantly, that she held only a master's in social work from a city college. Dave had a roommate at U.Va. who once dated a girl from that school. Skip swore that the girl could be brought to orgasm just by having her nipples touched. So many of the guys had heard this boast and disbelieved it that finally Skip hid a microphone in his room and ran the wire down the outside wall to the bedroom below where six guys listened and one put it on tape. It took fourteen and a half minutes from the time Skip dropped his second shoe. Of course, they had to take his word for it where he touched her, but Skip was a real honorable guy. Anyway that was the only girl Dave ever met who went to that school.

William had come in with them for the first part of this meeting, but since he wouldn't say anything he'd been asked to wait outside. Tina then began by asking Connie and Dave in turn to describe each other when they first fell in love.

"Every girl in my dorm was in love with him," said Connie, and Dave blushed. "When I first arrived, I heard about him. He was going out with the nicest girl at school: Sally Berry, president of the dorm. They were this golden couple. We used to hang out the window and watch him drive up in his MG to pick her up."

"You didn't," said Dave, glowing.

"We did! And his fraternity was the best. The nicest guys . . ."

"Buncha wildmen," Dave smiled.

"We used to laugh till our sides hurt, on party weekends."

"Connie was the one that made that happen. She was the den mother. All the guys told her their troubles. I had to marry her quick, there were half a dozen waiting in line if I hadn't."

Connie denied this, beaming. Watching them, Tina could see a glow of deep remembered happiness.

"And if you had to say now one thing about how you each may disappoint the other?" This changed the mood quickly. Connie seemed unwilling to answer.

Dave said, "I have a temper. So did my father; maybe it just runs in the family."

Tina nodded. "Can you give me an example?"

"Sure. For instance, one time at Sunday dinner . . ."

Tina was taking notes.

"My dad would stand up in his blue suit, after church, and carve. One Sunday I finally had my plate and I was working away with my knife and fork"—he smiled and pantomimed a little kid struggling—"when suddenly Dad said, 'I've been watching David cut that piece of chicken for five minutes. He finally cut off a little bite-sized piece, and then he left it on his plate and put the great big piece in his mouth!' Well, Dad laughed, and everyone at the table looked at me and roared. So I thought I had done something funny and while they were all looking at me, I took another big piece and stuffed that in my mouth. And whew, just like lightning, my dad dragged me out of the chair and turned me over his knee and walloped the daylights out of me!" Dave told this with brio, as if it was a hell of a good joke. Tina was listening with a sympathetic look.

"You didn't realize they were laughing at you, not with you?"

"Well, not till he started to pound me."

"That sounds terrifying," she said gently, after Dave stopped laughing.

"Oh, Christ, no. That was just the way he was. I mean the point is, my old man changed gears so fast you never saw it coming. Pow, zero to sixty in nothing flat!" Dave laughed again, as if it was rather a trait to be proud of.

"You were how old?"

"Seven. Eight."

"Is 'walloping the daylights out of you' your dad's expression?"

Dave looked puzzled.

"Because, if it were my story," said Tina, "I'd probably say 'he beat the shit out of me,' or something."

Dave was surprised. He appreciated this. "Yeah, so would I. I guess you're right, that *is* what my father would say."

There was a silence. Tina let the silence stretch. Finally Dave said, "My mom and dad never fought, though. *She* just let it all roll off her back."

Connie shot Dave a surprised look. The Child Psychiatrist made a note.

"And what about your parents?" Tina turned to Connie.

"Oh, my father was very gentle."

Pause. "You say was . . . is he not living?"

"Oh, yes, he's . . ."

Dave announced, "Connie's old man is going to bury us all. He lives on herb tea and green slime."

Pause. "Yes?" Tina smiled and waited.

Finally, Connie said, a little embarrassed, "He's become sort of a . . ."

"He's a full-bore hypochondriac," Dave announced.

Connie looked as if she would have liked to finish the sentence herself, but she didn't say anything.

"My mother's very outgoing."

Dave added, "The first conversation I ever had with her old man, he spent five minutes talking about how many times he chews each mouthful of food!" Dave laughed. It was kind of nice, having this babe take notes every time he opened his mouth.

Soon Tina said she'd like to see William alone for a few minutes. Connie and Dave went out, and William came in. He was a beautiful boy with soft dark hair and eyes and long black eyelashes.

William found the woman sitting on the floor this time. After a bit he sat down on the floor, too. They just sat quietly for a while. Then the woman reached into a cabinet behind her and got out some action figures. There was a Batman and a Robin, a GI Joe, a Superwoman, and some of the toys the kids called transformers, because they can be taken apart and transformed from, say, a robot to a hovercraft. The woman took the Batman and walked him over to William's knee. He stood staring at William. William took a transformer and walked it over to Batman.

In a deep theatrical voice Batman said, "My name is Bruce Wayne." Silence. The Batman doll moved a little closer to the transformer and stared at it quizzically.

The transformer said in a voice like C3PO's, "I-am-a-robot. I-am-a-robot."

Batman said, dramatically, to the robot, "By day, I seem to be a mild-mannered businessman. I eat Rice Krispies for breakfast. I wear a big suit. But at night, I have secret powers. I can scale walls. I can fly. . . ."

The robot said, "No-you-can't. You-can-drive-your-Batmobile."

"Oh," said Batman.

The robot moved around Batman a little, sizing him up. He said, "I-have-secret-powers-too. I-can-fly. I-can-ride—my silver-stallion. I-can-make-dead-people-get-well-again."

"Well!" said Batman. "I'm impressed. Perhaps you could be my new sidekick."

"What-about-Robin?"

"He grew up and went to college."

"Oh."

"Do you want to be my sidekick?"

"I-have-more-secret-powers-than-you. You-can-be-my-sidekick."

Batman laughed. "What kind of things will we do?"

"We-will-beat-up-bad-guys. We-will-save-babies-that-fall-out-of-air-planes. We-will-eat-a-car."

Batman laughed again. "Why will we do that?"

"To-show-bad-guys-how-tough-we-are."

"Will we hurt people?"

"Some-times."

"When?"

"When-they-make-us-mad."

"How will they make us mad?"

"By-being-crybabies."

"We hate crybabies?"

"Yes. We-hate-them. We-hate-them."

"What else do we hate?"

"Rhubarb."

Batman laughed, and said, "Well, robot, I am glad we met. I look forward to seeing you again."

"O-kay."

She made Batman go shake hands with the robot. Then she put Batman on her chair, sitting, and she stood. William stood, too. The robot went into his pocket.

When Tina opened the door to the outer office, she found Dave and Connie reading magazines in silence.

She said to them, "William and I would like to see each other next week."

Connie and Dave seemed surprised to hear that she knew anything about what William would or would not like, but they agreed and scheduled another appointment.

M*artha was laughing.* Her friend Annie was describing a new idea she had for a show. "Cemetery art. I'm going to build big tombstones and paint them, faux marble don't you think, so you walk through the gallery as if you were at Forest Lawn. And the tombstones will all say things like, SHE HAD A GREAT BODY. Or, SHE SUFFERED TERRIBLY FROM PREMENSTRUAL SYNDROME WHEN SHE WAS ALIVE."

They were walking on upper Madison one Saturday afternoon in early November, and they had a serious case of the giggles, when Martha realized she saw a familiar figure walking toward them. It was Charlie, carrying a bag of groceries. He smiled broadly as he recognized her. He was wearing a tweed jacket and loafers. Martha was wearing tights and a sweatshirt that came nearly to her knees. Annie, as always, was wearing retro punk.

"Hello, Martha." He stopped before them. "You're a long way from home."

"This is our constitutional. Annie, this is Charlie Leveque." Annie greeted this news with intense interest. She shook the fingers Charlie offered her as he clutched his groceries.

"Did you really walk all the way up here?"

"Yes, we do it twice a week."

"We'd go to aerobics class but we can't stand the music," said Annie. She mimed a few lines of "Material Girl," while doing jumping jacks.

"I thought you got nosebleeds above Fourteenth Street," said Charlie to Martha.

"Hives," said Martha. "But only if I eat something, or spend the night." There was an edge to her tone. "What are you doing in town on such a nice weekend?"

"It's Phoebe's birthday. I'm taking her to the theater."

"That's nice," said Martha, thinking she would like to be able to afford to take Jack to the theater.

"This was her second week of school," said Charlie, shifting his groceries.

"Oh. How does she like it?"

"I can't tell. It's obviously very different. You wouldn't like a cup of coffee, or something?"

"No, thanks. We have to keep moving."

"Like sharks or we die," said Annie.

"Oh. Well." He looked disappointed. "Nice to see you in this neighborhood. Say hi to Jack." Martha had the feeling he didn't want them to go.

"I will. Enjoy the theater."

"Oh, Martha . . ." He stopped them. "I should know this but . . . is Jack his real name? It's not John or something? It's in the will like that. I'm his lawyer," he added, to Annie.

"I know," said Annie. She'd been all through the divorce with Martha.

"It's just Jack."

"Is that a family name?"

"No," said Martha, smiling. "Raymond and I really wanted to call him Solid Jackson, but we chickened out." Annie laughed. Charlie looked blank.

"I don't get it."

"You know. Solid, Jackson. You say, 'Solid, Jackson.'"

Evidently, Charlie didn't.

"Jazz musicians used to say it. It means good."

"Oh," said Charlie. He guessed if you lived in places like SoHo you knew things like that. "Well, I won't keep you." Suddenly very formal, he waved them good-bye and marched off. Annie and Martha resumed their pace.

"He was trying to be nice," said Annie.

"I know. He has been trying. But he doesn't have much choice, we have to get along with each other."

"I think he likes you."

"He should like me, I'm very nice. Too bad he didn't notice that four years ago."

"Well," said Annie.

"No wonder Raymond chose him," said Martha, looking around at the neighborhood. They had rounded a corner and were now headed south on Park Avenue. "He's just what Raymond wanted to grow up to be."

"I guess that's true."

"How sad," said Martha. "Raymond was such a wildman when I met him. Who could tell he wanted to be another Wall Street Presbyterian."

"Watch it," said Annie. Her husband was an investment banker and an Episcopalian.

"Sorry."

Annie said. "You're very prejudiced, you know. I thought Charlie was very nice." She said it in a prim way that made Martha roar, it seemed so wonderful coming from this creature in black tights, a miniskirt, a leopard-skin belt, and black Reeboks. "You and Raymond. The proud and the prejudiced."

"I can't help it," said Martha. She gestured at the wide avenue, the beautifully tended pots of flowers down the middle of it, the manicured door-manned apartment buildings. "I look at this, and it feels like a ghetto."

"I think it's nice," said Annie. "There's no garbage. There's a park." They walked in silence for several blocks.

"You know who he reminded me of?"

"Who?" said Martha.

"Charlie. He reminded me of your brother. Is he married?"

"Divorced."

"Good," said Annie.

It was eleven-ten. Phoebe had missed the start of French class. Oops. She sat at a window table at Blimpie's two blocks from Crapp and Thrasher and lit another Chesterfield. She was wearing a pair of Calvin

Klein blue jeans she had once borrowed from Serena, and now would never give back, and the pisser was nobody at this school cared. The hip kids were more likely to wear camouflage pants you could fit three people into, than designer jeans.

Or they wore hippie shit, like the two Jennies, McKinney and Krass. Serena would put her finger down her throat, but here everyone seemed to love them. Phoebe couldn't figure out what was going on.

Jenny McKinney drifted around school in long gingham dresses and granny glasses. Jenny Krass wore miniskirts and layers and layers of tie-dyed tank tops. The joke in the lounge was, how many skirts can Jenny Krass put on and still be naked? The Jennies both knew every word to every Beatles song ever made. They seemed to speak a code language such that you could listen to every word and still not know what they were on about unless they wanted you to know. The two Jennies were in favor of peace and love and marijuana, and opposed to beer. Phoebe was drawn to them because they were so daffy and sunny, and because she envied their communion, though frankly at Replogle the hip kids did cocaine. She was drawn to the Jennies and their group, but she wasn't one of them. Where she wanted to belong was in the opposite camp, with the "lounge crew."

A principal difference, Phoebe had noticed right away, between Crapp and Thrasher and Replogle was that Crapp and Thrasher had boys in it. The lounge crew, so called because they spent their free periods smoking cigarettes in the senior lounge, definitely had boys in it and was definitely in favor of beer. They had (with permission) painted the lounge walls with a hideous Day-Glo mural. They all had graffiti tags and most had strange haircuts and a lot of safety pins on their clothes. They all talked about cutting classes and tossing brews and getting burners up in the subway and tags up inside the school (the penalty for which was expulsion). The smart ones, who planned to grow their hair out and go on to Yale, sat around and talked about cutting classes and tossing brews, and the dumb ones actually did it. Actually, nobody at this school was dumb, but as with many teenagers some were seriously confused about the difference between style and substance.

Phoebe had discovered that whereas at Replogle it was hip to disdain the arts, or hard work of any kind, and to favor spending money, doing coke, or going to the Island Club and getting fucked up, here the hip thing was to *do* things. The lounge crew was made up of kids who worked on the school plays, or actually worked on Broadway, or made video art, or invented new typefaces, or played classical music at the professional level. It had taken Phoebe about five minutes to develop a crush on the one called Jaywalk. He was about six feet eight and weighed perhaps a hundred pounds. Jaywalk was unfortunately in love with a beautiful skinhead called Valerie. Jaywalk was the only kid in school ever to flunk driver's ed, owing to poor motivation.

Phoebe had been sitting in Blimpie's since assembly, drinking coffee and smoking. She had $1.30 left and had had no breakfast, because Patsy had again forgotten to buy any milk, or to leave her any allowance. She'd been grounded, except to go to school, since she was kicked out of Replogle, and Patsy seemed to think that because Phoebe didn't go out her metabolism had slowed, like an alligator's, so that she only had to breathe once an hour and eat once a week.

Assessing her situation, Phoebe figured she could get a small box of fried rice later if she didn't have another cup of coffee. However, they weren't going to let her sit here forever if she didn't order anything, and since she'd already blown the whole morning, she might as well stick around to see if Jaywalk and Valerie and Nick came in. She was pretty sure Jaywalk had two frees on Thursday starting at ten-thirty.

She stared at the pale milky line beginning to dry in a circle at the bottom of her coffee cup. Once her mom had gone to this psychic who told your future by giving you a cup of Turkish coffee to drink and then reading the grounds that were left in the bottom of your little brass cup. The woman was completely amazing, Patsy had reported. This was right after the separation, because Patsy and Phoebe were living up near Columbia in that apartment her mother shared for a year with Sylvia the oldest living undergraduate. (She wasn't really the oldest, but she had gray hair and had left a husband and four teenage children to go to Barnard.) This was in her mom's academic phase, after the piano phase, and the ballet phase, and before the phase she was in now, which was being a free-lance editor.

Sylvia, the oldest living undergraduate, had made a huge deal of loving Phoebe because she missed her own children so much, but Phoebe wondered if she missed them so much why she had left them and why they didn't come to see her. And also if she was such a great mother, why she hadn't noticed that Phoebe didn't like *her*.

Anyway, the coffee grounds woman had told Patsy that she had a daughter whose name began with P. She told her that there was a Sagittarius in her life who thought she was the best thing that ever happened to him. (That's George! Patsy had glowed. Isn't it *incredible,* I didn't even know his sign, but I asked him and he *is* a Sagittarius!) And she told Patsy that she was going to Paris in the summer with a person whose name began with G, and that she had been married to a man who still loved her and that she would be married again within two years. Also that she was enormously concerned about a piece of music she was composing. Patsy had in fact been a music major in college! In point of fact, what she was then struggling with was a paper on economic problems of Caribbean women. But it kind of had a structure like a sonata, if you thought about it.

Patsy had thought that was the best forty dollars she ever spent, that hour with the coffee grounds woman. She had promptly launched herself into an affair with George, who had her in tears at least once a week even from the beginning, and who most certainly did not go with her to Paris and frequently would cancel at the last minute plans to go to the corner deli for a beer and a sandwich, and about whom Patsy still wept a year after the last time she threw him out.

Phoebe stopped staring at the coffee cup. Oh, dip, was that boring. She was about to get up, when she saw Jaywalk coming in with his friend Dime. So she resumed her coolest fuck-you pose and went on sitting.

The boys came and sat down with just five seconds before the moment her heart would have stopped, had they passed her.

"Yo," said Jaywalk.

"That your breakfast?" asked Dime. He was a nice guy. A real person. In fact he had particularly tried to look after Phoebe when she was first dropped into the school, but she had refused to let him because she was particularly suspicious of the kindness of strangers at the moment. It took her a while to realize that although he sometimes liked to look as if he would knife you on the subway, he was really the class nurse. If anyone was sad and went to Dime, Dime would say, "Oh, bummer" with real sympathy, never mocking, and administer hugs. Once when a new girl in school who'd been freaking for about a week began to cry and say, "They're yelling at me again," when the lounge was more or less silent, it was Dime who held her and rocked her and kept the whole lounge crew after school for an hour stroking her and hugging her until she had cried it out.

Dime actually cared if Phoebe hadn't had anything but coffee for breakfast.

"It's cool. I'm addicted to coffee," said Phoebe.

"Substance abuse!"

"Truly," said Phoebe. "It all started with instant Nescafé, but soon I went on to electro perk. I was soon up to five . . . six . . . ten cups a day. Then . . . the hard stuff. Until one day, my mother found my works in my room. My papers. My Chemex . . ."

The boys were amused. Phoebe was not used to getting attention from the crew. She was used to being grateful to hang around. She spilled some sugar onto the table, shaped it into a line of white powder, and made as if to snort it with an invisible straw. The boys laughed.

Dime picked up Phoebe's coffee cup and then put it down. "I read this amazing story once," he said to Jaywalk. "This guy is married to this wife he really loves. But he has an accident and goes blind. And then, his brother comes to live with him, you know, to help out or something. And every night the wife cooks dinner and then she serves coffee in the living room in these beautiful demitasse cups. Each one is a different color. So, after a while, even though they both really love the husband, the wife and the brother start to fall in love. They feel shitty about it but they just can't help it. So now at night they'll all go into the living room and the husband will sit in his chair, and the wife and the brother will sit on the couch. And they cuddle up in each other's arms but they go on carrying on this casual conversation with the husband. And this goes on for a while, and it seems as if it's actually all right. You know, like it isn't hurting anybody or anything. And then one night, the wife hands her husband his coffee and then goes and sits down with the brother, and the husband says in this gentle voice, 'Tonight I'd rather have the green cup.'"

Big pause. "Oh, *whoa*," said Jaywalk.

"Selective blindness," announced Dime.

"Who *wrote* it?" Jaywalk read comics more than anything else, but he *could* read. Mostly he was a genius techie on the theater crew.

"Don't know. I read it in an anthology. I'm sure it's from the Spanish but I don't know if it's Borges or what."

Phoebe didn't know what they were talking about, but she was glad to be included.

"I told it to my father and he went nuts," said Dime. Meaning, liked it. Phoebe looked at him. She was surprised he had mentioned his father, since she happened to know Dime's father was dead. Dime mentioned him as if it was a comfort just to do that, to speak of him as if he were alive. Interesting. He was interesting, Dime.

The boys stood. Phoebe stood with them. Apparently they expected this. They sauntered out into the sunlight and Phoebe sauntered with them. Apparently this was okay with them. The boys didn't have another class until two, so they suggested going across to the park to hang out with some homeboys they knew. The three of them ambled off to the park together. Phoebe, of course, didn't mention that she had algebra starting in seven minutes. Fuck it.

A*ll during the* drive north, the snow had been drifting down in huge soft flakes. Jack was excited.

"When Dad and I came last year, there were big bare mud patches all over the slopes."

"It looks like we're going to get some deep powder this time." Martha wasn't so sure how she felt about that. She hadn't been skiing since she and Raymond parted, and since her last pregnancy her knees had been feeling their age. That, however, was less on her mind at this moment as dusk began to fall than getting them to the mountains alive.

Martha wanted to take Jack skiing this vacation, as Raymond had planned to do, and they had tried to get an early start. But the problem was renting a car in New York on a holiday weekend, Martha explained to Jack. You call weeks ahead, you give your credit card, your blood type, and the name of your personal banker, you explain in short, simple words how important it is that you have a car with snow tires, and a charming young lady in Houston, or wherever the 800 number rings, assures you that there is "no problem." Then you arrive at the agency office at the appointed hour, and not only do they have no cars with snow tires, they have no cars at all. And there are fourteen people ahead of you, all with confirmed reservations, whose patience is growing threadbare in a variety of languages.

On this particular Wednesday of Thanksgiving weekend, after the harassed young lady behind the desk had ascertained in a series of grim phone calls that her company not only had no cars in the garage on Twenty-fourth Street, it had no cars in Manhattan, Martha with baby Fred in tow had finally agreed with several other desperate souls to be driven to the company's location at LaGuardia.

The man beside her in the backseat demanded, as they pulled into the Midtown Tunnel, "What happens if they don't have any cars at the airport?"

"They do, sir. I called ahead."

"We all called ahead, too, we were told there were cars at Twenty-fourth Street."

"Sir, I promise, there will be cars."

Baby Fred was staring up at the man who had spoken first; he'd never seen such a large black mustache. The man shrank away a bit and stared aggressively ahead, as if he were afraid a baby was a fragile vessel, likely to explode in drool or effluent if he so much as returned Fred's gaze.

"Why didn't you rent one of us this car?" asked a man on the front seat.

"I can't. It's not registered."

"Why not?" asked several voices.

"It hasn't got an inspection sticker."

"Why not?"

The girl shrugged. "Something about the lights, I think." Oh good. As long as it's the lights, not the brakes, and we get there by nightfall.

They did have cars at LaGuardia, but not many, and none with snow tires. Martha finally was awarded a compact that reeked of cigar smoke and new upholstery, and was told her rate would be reduced. She thanked them, not very heartily, and drove back to Manhattan where she and Jack strapped on the ski rack and loaded the car. It was already snowing then and they were two hours late getting away.

There had been little problem on the highway; the plows and salt spreaders were out. But the last hour in darkness on country roads in deepening snow had been exhausting.

They reached the lodge in time for the second supper seating. Fred, who had slept in the car, was wide awake and full of beans. Jack was so happy to be there, showing them this place where he'd been before with his father, that he made Martha smile. They all had some soup and bread and cheese, and Jack ate tons of lamb stew and apple cake as well.

After supper Martha was shown to a room under the eaves with a big four-poster bed. The room smelled of pine; its walls were of rough boards, and the windows were frosted with ice and snow. Martha's bed had a huge feather duvet on it and Ulla Tjensvold, the daughter of the family that ran the lodge, showed Martha how to turn the little sofa into a bed for Fred. There was a stack of linen and blankets in the armoire for him. Jack, a familiar of the operation, had found himself a bunk in the boys' dormitory room and met up with a boy he knew from previous winters, named Carl.

Jack and Carl, with eyes glowing and cheeks red, had come to Martha's door to say goodnight. They were going outside to throw snow-balls in the moonlight and later to play pinball and drink cocoa in the dining room, while the Tjensvolds finished getting the kitchen ready for early breakfast. Martha, after solving a crisis in which Fred's mangy stuffed elephant had apparently gotten into Jack's duffel bag and been carried off into the dorm with the big boys, and explaining four hundred times how soon it would be that baby Fred would be allowed to sleep in the dorm with the big boys and throw snowballs at them, got him set-tled down, and herself crept into the soft big bed to sleep the sleep of the just.

By morning, which came very early in a room shared with Fred, the snow was drifted deep and the world glittered. The big boys, dressed in layers and layers of clothes over long johns, were down by the fire wait-ing for the first breakfast seating when Martha and Fred came in from a journey out to the barn to visit the moo-cows. The boys ate masses of

French toast, and Martha watched them—her hands warming around a huge mug of coffee—smiling. Jack wanted to get to the slopes as soon as the lifts started running.

The new snow was not yet packed or plowed, and it took both boys and one of the Tjensvold brothers pushing to get the rental car out of the parking space and turned around facing the road.

"Does this car have front-wheel drive?" asked Ivor or Paul, whichever brother it was.

"No such luck," said Martha.

"Sandbags?"

She shook her head. Ivor looked concerned about letting her go; he took Jack to the barn, and they returned with two enormous sacks of cattle feed, which he loaded into their trunk for weight.

"If you have to, pour it under the wheels for traction."

"Right," said Martha. With one bag containing an array of ski gloves, goggles, sun cream, scarves, and hats, and another with diapers, books and toys, juice bottles, bananas and oranges, the three of them set off. The worst part of the trip was the driveway out of the lodge, which was steep and unplowed. Martha made it by driving very slowly and evenly and never leaving first gear. The main road, when they achieved it, had already been cleared.

At the slopes, they installed baby Fred in the day-care group at the main lodge and went out to the mountain. The day was clear and intensely bright, and Martha and Jack spent an ecstatic morning skiing together. Martha had forgotten the exhilaration of the heated body, the brilliant cold on her cheeks and in her lungs, and the great wide sky. She skied cautiously but with a returning grace, a memory of how to do it apparently stored in the muscles. Jack skied like a wildman, fearlessly. He would shoot off down a trail ahead of her, but usually she would catch up with him backing out of a stand of trees, or picking himself up off the back side of a mogul. One time she found him face down in powder, having lost his skis, his poles, one glove, and his goggles.

"This," he said, as she came to a stop beside him, "is called 'staging a yard sale.'"

At lunch they met up with Carl, and rescued baby Fred from where he had been impounded. The big boys ate vast amounts, and then Martha sent them off to ski together. From somewhere, high gray clouds were gliding in, and a wind had come up. By two o'clock it had started to snow again. When Fred went back to the nursery for his nap, Martha went out to the mountain by herself for an hour or two. It was beginning to be bitter, high in the air on the lift in the wind, but to be swinging down the mountain between fragrant black pines in the silence and the veils of snow was a gorgeous pleasure.

In a lodge at the top of the mountain, where she stopped to get warm by the fire and to have a glass of mulled wine, she heard the girls in the kitchen talking about a blizzard. They seemed thoroughly pleased at the idea.

Martha met Jack and Carl at the main lodge at four, by agreement. Carl had patches of white in his reddened cheeks.

"I'm afraid that's frostbite, kiddo. What have you louts been doing with yourselves?"

The boys looked at each other and began to giggle.

"Yard sale," said Carl.

"You should have seen him! All the stuff from his pockets was lying around on the snow, in this crater where he fell!" This seemed to them hilarious. Martha rubbed some Nivea cream from Fred's bag onto Carl's cheeks.

"The water in your cheeks can freeze. It won't feel good when it thaws."

"I had ChapStick and cream and stuff, but I lost it," said Carl, submitting to this.

"He lost everything. He skied thirty feet on his nose."

"They'll find my stuff in the spring. All frozen and mummified."

"They're lucky they won't find him in the spring." More laughter.

Martha got all three boys, with equipment, back to the little car. The boys loaded all the skis and poles onto the rack, and then piled into the backseat with Fred, where they told him fabulous lies about their adventures on the mountain, and raided his bag to eat his oranges. Fred, as best he could, told them with eyes wide with wonder about the huge cascade of icicles he had seen suspended from the rainspout at the roof of the lodge.

Martha, in the front seat with an array of wet scarves and mittens and hats and gloves with ice balls clinging, began to wonder how deep the steady snow was going to get. She discovered that the blades on her windshield wipers were not the best, and visibility was becoming a problem. She lost traction once and only barely kept the car on the road. When it happened a second time she began to wonder if there would be a garage open anywhere on the weekend so she could have chains put on.

That night the inhabitants of the lodge shared Thanksgiving dinner, and afterward Carl's mother played "We Gather Together" and "Come, Ye Thankful People, Come" on the piano in the living room, and many people sang.

The cold intensified sharply during the night and the wind grew fiercer. By morning, the question of chains was moot, for when Martha went out to try to start the car, she found that the engine block had frozen. Snow was still falling, but lightly, though more was promised for afternoon.

Jack and Carl wanted to ski, despite the cold; Carl's father was willing to go on the slopes with them, so with thanks Martha saw them off. Then she set about trying to figure out what to do about the car.

She called the emergency service number of the rental car. She explained she was in the mountains of Vermont in a blizzard with two children and a frozen engine block. They asked why the car hadn't enough antifreeze, and she said she was fairly certain that knowing the answer to that was not among her responsibilities.

They said they would find out the nearest towing station in their network and have the car taken away as soon as the roads were cleared.

"Taken away to be fixed?"

"If possible."

"How long would that take?"

"Oh, probably a couple of weeks."

Martha asked how she was supposed to get home and they said they would be glad to replace the car. All she had to do was get herself, her children, her luggage, and a ski rack to any of their rental locations. Where was the nearest of these locations? The clerk thought Boston.

By lunchtime, the boys were back from the slopes. It was fifteen below on the thermometer, but with the wind chill the temperature on the mountain was more like eighty below. And snow was falling again; the wind whipped it so that it seemed to be falling sideways, in sheets, wrapping around and around them. Even after they took off their ski boots, the boys walked as if they were hobbled, their feet were so cold.

"What are we going to do?" Jack asked. Carl's family had offered to take them to Boston the next day, but that wasn't exactly the right direction, nor was there really room in their car.

"There's a bus from White River to New York, but Ivor called and it isn't running. Not today and probably not tomorrow."

"How far is White River?"

"Forty miles. Paul said we could call a taxi to take us there but it would cost eighty dollars. Or he could try to find someone in the village to drive us. . . ."

They sat in the dining room after everyone else had left. Martha felt miserable, and Jack didn't want to go off and hang out, even though sitting glumly with her didn't help.

"I'm sorry," he said.

"For what?"

"You were just doing this for me."

"Don't be silly, honey. I was having a wonderful time, I'm delighted we came. Someday we'll remember this as a great adventure." She looked to Jack as if she was about to cry.

After a while, he said, "I'm going to call Charlie."

"What?"

"I'm going to call Charlie."

"Why?"

"Because we need help. Maybe he'll help us. Isn't that what he's supposed to do?"

"Not with things like this, honey."

"Why not?"

"Because you can't ask favors of people who aren't responsible for you. That's what family and friends are for. Besides, you don't even know where he is. He's probably having a gay old time in Central Park or something, thinking weather is fun."

She'd already thought of calling her brother, who would be on Long Island, or her parents. But what could they do?

"I do know how to reach him. He gave me all his numbers. If he's not in New York, I'll try him in the country." Jack made her give him all her quarters and padded off in his thick socks to the pay phone. Martha went on sitting at the table, watching the snow.

Jack came back. "He's coming for us."

"What?"

"He's at his country house. He said it should be about a two-hour drive, and he's on his way."

The drive took six.

As the afternoon drew on to evening, and the weather worsened, all the brave souls who had left the lodge in the morning arrived back in ones and pairs, and the stories of how they did it began to be harrowing. People laughed, of course, but there was a story on the radio about two twelve-year-old girls who had gone up the mountain at noon, and not come down. Rescue teams were out looking for them.

At eight o'clock Martha and Fred were in a chair by the fire. They had had their supper. Martha was reading to Fred, softly, but increasingly distracted, especially each time the Tjensvolds' phone rang. Jack, tense, was playing chess with Carl when the front door opened, and along with a gust of cold, Charlie, with snow on his boots and hair, stepped in and stood still, as if he couldn't believe he was there, or as if he was dazzled by the light. He looked gray. Jack, who had nearly jumped at the first sound of the latch, went to him and gave him a bear hug. Charlie hugged him back.

"Who do you have to know to get a drink around here?" were his first words.

Paul Tjensvold came out of the kitchen, saw it was the man Jack had been waiting for, and boomed a welcome. He opened the cupboard of the self-serve bar, and Charlie, shaking, poured himself a lot of bourbon.

"I thought you'd be like dead in a snowdrift, man," said Jack, "and it would be all my fault, like what a bummer."

Charlie laughed. "I thought I might be, too. God, that was boring!" He was shaking.

Jack, thrilled now with relief, drew Charlie to the fire. Martha had stood to greet him; she didn't realize how broadly she was smiling. She put out her hand to him, but he kissed her on the cheek. He had never done that before. Then he moved as close to the fire as he could, and as they watched him, anxious, color began to come back to his face, and his arms and shoulders relaxed. They lost that trembling constriction of someone completely tensed against the cold.

"I thought I'd be here by four, and take you back to my house for a nice hot supper."

"But nooo," said Jack.

"But nooo. I have four-wheel drive, but the problem was, I couldn't see. There were times when I didn't even know if I was on the highway. There were no other cars, you couldn't see the median fence. . . . I could have drifted off into somebody's cow pasture and thought I was still on my way. Oh, and then I began to run out of gas."

"Uh-oh."

By now quite a few of the guests were listening to the war story.

"Wasn't anything open in White River?"

"There was a Mobil station, all lit up, but no one was there. But my needle was on the big red *E,* so acting as an officer of the court I declared a state of emergency and helped myself."

"Thank god they left the pump unlocked."

"They weren't even closed. For all I know the guy was frozen stiff in the men's room. I'll stop on my way back through and pay them."

And then, speaking of states of emergency, the lights went out.

"If this had happened fifteen minutes ago," said Charlie in the darkness, "I'd have driven right past. I'd have gone on driving till I ran out of gas again and froze to death."

This was so nearly plausible that it wasn't really funny, though they all laughed. In the darkness Charlie felt a hand briefly touch his arm.

The room buzzed with questions and jokes about what would happen next. Paul Tjensvold soon emerged from the kitchen with a lighted candle in his hand and boxes more under his arm. Soon the room glowed with fire and candlelight; it was in fact very beautiful. Some people, laughing and rather enjoying it, went back to their games of Scrabble and backgammon. Paul stoked the woodstove at the end of the living room and added logs to the open fire. Ivor, carrying wood, led some of the boys upstairs to crank up the stoves in the dormitory rooms.

"Your furnace is oil, isn't it?" asked Carl's mother.

"Yes," said Paul.

"So we're all right for heat."

"Well, not exactly. The thermostat's electric."

"What does that mean?"

"The furnace puts out heat, but the fan system that sends the heat through the house won't work."

There was a worried silence.

"So we better all sleep in the basement," said Carl's mother.

"Or in the barn with the cows. And at midnight maybe they'll talk," said Carl.

"That's only Christmas Eve," said Jack.

"Oh."

"I think we'll be all right," said Paul. "With the woodstoves and the fireplaces and heat upstairs from the chimneys. I've never known the power to stay off more than eight hours."

"You should have a backup generator."

"We should, of course," he agreed.

There was another pause.

Carl's father said, "Wouldn't it be a good idea to stoke up the fires and all go to bed before we get tired and the cold starts to settle?"

"It would," said Paul.

"And shouldn't someone stay up to keep the fires going?"

"Ivor and I will do that, of course."

"And everyone sleep in all the dry clothes they have."

Charlie took Paul aside and spoke low to him. Paul looked worried, then brightened, and said he was sure everything would be fine. He gestured him to come upstairs, and Charlie followed him. Jack, feeling responsible, went along.

"Here is the boys' dormitory," Paul showed him. The woodstove was humming, but the beds nearest the door were not going to get much heat.

"Where are you?" Charlie asked Jack.

Jack showed him. "I'll be okay, I've got my long johns and a sleeping bag. I'll show you Mom's room."

"You see," said Paul. "It has the chimney from the kitchen fire. Warm, see?" They put their hands against the brick, and indeed, it was throwing some heat. Paul then led them down the hall to a tiny dormered room at the back of the house. It was privy to no heat source of any kind; in one corner stood an electric heater.

Jack and Charlie looked at each other and started to laugh. "Good luck, man," said Jack.

"Yeah, thanks. Isn't there any more room in the dorm?"

"No, I'm sorry. There is in the girls' dorm. . . ."

"That seems extreme," said Charlie. "I'll be fine."

"Gosh, Uncle Charlie, I'll sleep in the girls' dorm for you."

"Thanks a lot, sport."

"I'll bring you some more blankets," said Paul. "And what about food?"

"I could use some of that."

So Charlie went down to the kitchen to have some stew, left to warm on the woodstove, and a glass of wine, while the young people piled up to bed by candlelight. When Charlie went up to his room again, it was absolutely frigid.

Somewhere in the darkened lodge, a clock chimed the hours. The moon had risen, and outside the black night was suddenly silver. Martha heard the three o'clock chime, and she lay on her side with her knees pulled up to her chest for warmth. If she opened her eyes she could see her breath freeze in the air. Suddenly she heard her door open and close, and in another moment a tall, dark, very cold figure slipped under the covers with her.

"Sorry, toots, I'm fucking freezing to death. It's you or the little girls."

"Aach!" Martha jumped. Charlie's bare feet had touched hers and they were ice.

"Feel your pulse," she whispered, "you may already be dead. Oh God, you're shaking all over." She turned and wrapped her arms around him and rubbed his back and arms.

"I thank you, my mom thanks you . . . ," he whispered. He had to clench his teeth to keep them from chattering.

"Do you suppose the children are all right?"

"I think so. Freezing is much more dangerous for old people."

"You didn't have to risk death, you know," she said.

"I did. Gallantry is part of my nature."

His shivering was becoming less. Martha was feeling warmer, too, and happier. It took nearly a half hour though before he was warm enough to relax completely, and perhaps to sleep.

"You okay now?" she whispered.

He nodded in the dark, against her shoulder.

"Goodnight, then."

"Goodnight." She turned on her side, away from him, and he fitted himself against her and wrapped his arms around her. As she was sliding into sleep he felt her sigh.

The baby began to cry. Before she was even awake again, Charlie was out of bed. He scooped up the baby and leaped back under the covers.

"Is he wet?"

"No, amazingly. He's just cold."

"Hush, little bunny," Martha whispered to Fred and warmed his hands by holding them between her own and blowing on them. The baby fell back to sleep almost immediately, and Martha and Charlie settled back down with the baby between them.

In the darkness, Martha began to giggle.

"What's so funny?"

"Nothing," she said, smiling.

When Martha woke, the blizzard was over. She lay on her side with her arm around Fred. Across the baby, Charlie, already awake, had his arm around both of them. Martha touched one of Fred's little warm paws, and in his sleep he closed his hand around her finger. She kissed the top of his head. Charlie smiled. There was a knock at the door.

It was Jack. "Mom? Can I come in? I need my other shirt."

Charlie and Martha looked at each other.

"Sure, honey."

Jack slipped in and took in the scene. "Oh, a game of everybody into a pile?"

Martha laughed. "How'd you do?"

"Okay, but I'm cold now."

"Well, stoke up the stove before you change your shirt."

"I will."

"Are the others up?"

"They're getting up. Why are all the faucets running?"

"So the pipes won't freeze," said Charlie.

"Oh. I'm leaving, it's warmer in the dorm."

After he left, Martha said, "He just wanted to see if we were still alive."

Charlie smiled and nodded. "He's a nice person."

"He is, isn't he?" said Martha.

"You're lucky you have two."

Martha nodded.

"It's amazing if the pipes haven't frozen," said Charlie, getting up.

But most of them had. Water for breakfast was being melted from snow, and everyone was asked not to flush the toilets. Martha and Charlie left as soon as they could get the car packed and the boys organized. They drove without difficulty to White River, where they stopped to pay for last night's gas and to use the john. The man at the gas station seemed to think the whole story a great joke on the Tjensvolds, those thrifty Swedes who wouldn't put in a generator.

"Someday we'll look on this as a great adventure," said Jack.

"I will as soon as I've had a hot bath," said Martha.

They reached Charlie's house a little after ten.

"Yo, this is great," said Jack.

"It is, it's lovely," said Martha. Charlie was pleased. After they'd all had hot baths and changed their clothes, Charlie gave them a tour. Martha most liked the huge, sunny kitchen; Jack liked the stereo and the broad porches and the snow-covered meadow. Fred like Phoebe's room because it had posters of monkeys and koala bears on the walls. Charlie produced some chili from the freezer for lunch and introduced Jack to the miracle of the microwave. After lunch Charlie and Jack went cross-country skiing, while Fred had his nap and Martha read. When they came in, Charlie found her curled up by the fire, a picture of contentment.

"I'm glad you got to see my house," he said.

"Although there must have been an easier way," said Martha.

"Jack and I are going to have a sauna. Do you want one?"

"No, thanks. I'm very happy here. Who plays the piano?" She gestured to the baby grand in the corner.

"Patsy did, for about six months."

Martha nodded and went back to her book.

By the time they reached the interstate at four that afternoon, it was not only clear but dry. Except for the mounds of snow at the sides of the roads, you could hardly believe a blizzard had happened.

When he pulled up in front of Martha's building on Crosby Street and they unloaded the car, Charlie offered Jack his hand, but Jack gave him a hug.

"That was great," Jack said.

Charlie laughed, because it was so ridiculous.

"We must do this again sometime," said Martha. "Fred, say thank you, Charlie."

"Thank you, Charlie," said Fred.

"Can I have a kiss, Fred?"

Fred was glad to give him a kiss.

Then he gave Martha a kiss on the cheek. He got back in the car and was off.

"Well," said Martha to Jack. "That was unusual."

"A blizzard! Dangerous emergency! I can't wait to tell my friends," said Jack.

I*t weighed on* Martha that she hadn't been able in so many words to say thank you to Charlie. She sent him flowers.

"The most beautiful flowers I've ever seen," he said, when he called.

"I hope they're what I ordered. It makes me mad when you send French tulips and get thanked for daisies."

"These aren't tulips, are they?"

"They aren't supposed to be. What do they look like?"

Charlie paused. "Well, let's see. There are some big white things and then some bunchy blue things that smell wonderful and then this one round one like a ball. . . ."

"Are the bunchy blue things on branches instead of stems?"

"Yes, and then there's this one amazing thing that's mostly sort of violet colored but with streaks in it . . . like a sunset."

"Why do I have the feeling you're going to put them in a jelly jar?"

"I have a vase," he said, stoutly.

"I'm glad you like them."

"I love them. How are the boys?"

"Fine, thank you for asking. Jack is planning a career in polar exploration now; he's got a taste for crisis."

"He can have it."

"How's Phoebe?"

"Oh, all ticked off. She's convinced that she got left out of some great drama on purpose."

"Did you tell her how much baby Fred liked her koala bears?"

Pause. "Yes." In fact, he had told Phoebe, and she had responded with a bad-tempered shriek that he better not have touched any of her toys. Charlie was finding his daughter's sullen selfishness nearly intolerable, and as a result he'd had less contact with her than he might have, which of course made her more sullen.

"When does her imprisonment end?"

"Friday."

"What does she say about school?"

"Not much. I get the impression she doesn't know what to make of it. At Replogle, whatever Serena and Kate said was cool, was cool. I think she's trying to fit in and isn't quite sure how to do it."

"She'll figure it out."

"Yes. Do we know if she and Jack have crossed paths?"

"Jack said he'd keep an eye on her. I haven't heard any more from him, though; I figure the worst thing you can do is push it."

Privately, both Martha and Charlie thought their children so unlikely to be each other's cup of tea that they had very much avoided the subject.

With Phoebe, Charlie had gotten as far as "Did you like Martha?"

Phoebe had nodded angrily, as if this liking constituted another unwelcome trick that had been played on her.

"Martha's son is at Cropp and Thatcher," Charlie had said, and Phoebe had nodded again, with a sneer. Phoebe remembered too many afternoons, delivered into bondage to play with some strange child Patsy said she was going to love, and the hours of misery or fury following their dislike on first sight, while Patsy happily talked and laughed with the mother of whichever little beast it was.

Charlie had said, "It was nice of Martha to speak to the headmaster for you."

Phoebe had answered, "Is she your girlfriend?"

Hesitation. "She's a friend."

Phoebe had turned away, as if she hadn't expected an honest answer anyway. And if Martha wasn't his girlfriend, Phoebe didn't have any further interest. She was sick of getting to like people like Sophie and having them disappear, let alone getting to hate people like George and having him keep coming back.

"Maybe you should come see these flowers. We could have dinner," said Charlie to Martha.

There was a pause.

"You could see my bird," he added.

"Your what?"

"My parrot. He's called José."

"I don't think I can pass that up."

"Tomorrow?"

"I'll have to see if Jack can baby-sit."

"Tell him I'll pay him double the going rate."

"I certainly will not." She hung up, smiling.

It took Martha—standing barefoot in a huge football jersey that she used as a dressing gown—a surprisingly long time to decide what to wear. She found herself wondering what Charlie's wife had been like. Very beautiful, presumably, with no runs in her stockings or spots on her clothes, and a drawerful of brand-new underwear in scented lingerie bags. In the end Martha decided that in Rome it was best to dress as a Roman. She wore a slim black dress and high-heeled shoes for which some reptile gave its life. Charlie opened the door wearing blue jeans.

"You look wonderful," he said.

She was intensely nervous; it suddenly struck her that she didn't know this man at all, that he probably hated women who dressed like this, and that he was very attractive.

"I was admiring your wallpaper," she said, simultaneously wishing someone would bind and gag her and put her in a cab downtown. I've been admiring your wallpaper? What? She'd just been standing here in this dumb foyer waiting for him to answer his bell; she hadn't even noticed the wallpaper.

Charlie looked at it himself, an excessive little pattern in white against a dark blue background. Laura Ashley or something.

"My neighbor chose it," he said, indicating the other door. "The table's mine. And the umbrella stand." Martha looked at these, and said they were nice, which they were. She was relieved about the wallpaper.

"Please, come in."

"Oh, thank you." She stepped into his front hall, a wide, bare room. Her heels clacked on the floor.

"I'm overdressed."

But he was very touched that she had dressed. "Let me take your coat." He moved to help her, and somehow it occurred to both simultaneously that they were very close together and that helping someone out of a coat, or being helped, was an embarrassingly intimate act, such that they botched the job and took what seemed hours to accomplish it. Finally Charlie carried the coat off to the closet and shut it up inside, leaving it in the dark to ponder its iniquities.

She followed Charlie to the living room.

"The flowers," said Charlie. They stood in a vase on the piano, beautifully arranged. The room was warm and handsome, lined with books and softly lit. There was a fire burning. There were photographs in silver and leather and wood frames everywhere, giving Martha the feeling she'd come to a house where a family lived. She liked that better than the dreaded bachelor pad of magazine fantasy, filled with fancy drinking equipment and eight-foot televisions, but again, here was a man who already had parents and a wife and child and friends and vacations and sailboats and beaches in his life, and she was no part of it. She wanted to walk the room examining each image, but knew she would discover that everyone in the pictures was handsomer, happier, more loved, and more fun than she was and that they all were masters of games they played perfectly. Everyone in the pictures on the piano would be wearing tennis whites, for example.

"This is José," said Charlie. He held out his arm to a large green bird that sat on the back of a tall leather chair, and the bird, after thinking it over, deigned to step onto his wrist and be carried to Martha. José cocked his head very slightly and studied her with bright black beads of eyes.

"Say, 'Martha,'" said Charlie. Nothing happened.

"Say, 'Martha.'"

"Krak! Birds can't talk," said José. Martha laughed.

"Say, 'Hello, Martha.'"

The bird gave a shrill whistle and cried, "Whatta paira legs!"

"Okay, back you go." Charlie carried José to his chair and José stepped off onto his perch. "I have a birdbrain!" he screamed, pleased with himself.

"The horror is, birds live forever."

Martha was entranced. "Where did you get him?"

"A girl gave him to me. A long time ago."

"This is a wonderful room."

Charlie smiled. "Can I give you a glass of wine?"

"I think you better."

"Come."

She followed him to the kitchen, which was small but warm and bright.

"What smells so good?"

"This is my date dinner. I don't have many dates, so I only know how to cook one dinner. I hope you eat meat."

"I love meat."

"My date dinner involves steak. I admit I once served it to a young lady who hadn't told me she was a vegetarian. She ate it all, but then she had to go home to throw up."

"Oh, dear."

"Yes. What color wine would you like?"

"Do we have red?"

"We do. Unless you'd like something stronger?"

"No."

"We could eat fairly soon if you'd like to. Or, we could sit in the living room awhile and make each other nervous. That's what I usually do."

"I think eating is a good idea."

"Good. Do you mind standing around talking to me? As opposed to sitting in the living room by yourself, I guess? I could lend you a book."

"I could help."

"No, you don't understand, I'm trying to show off."

"Oh. Then I'll watch." She stood first here and then there, watching as he set about his tasks. She found the best place to be out of the way was to sit on the counter by the refrigerator.

"You look nice there," he said suddenly.

"Thanks."

He took an impressive dish of potatoes out of the oven. They were thin sliced and bubbly hot, with a lovely crust. He put the dish down quickly on the stovetop and turned and kissed her. Surprised, she kissed him back. Afterward, he turned away and made a lot of noise putting the steak under the broiler and getting glasses out of the cupboards. Martha slipped down from where she sat and helped set the little table that stood in the corner of the living room. They didn't look at each other again until they were at the table, and then the conversation was warm and bright, a relieved retreat to friendship. When they finished eating, they cleared and washed up in the kitchen together, so aware of each other and of the domestic intimacy of the task that once again their talk became shy and full of pauses.

When everything was put away, they stood in the middle of the kitchen. The apartment was silent. Frightened to death, they moved back to each other and finally once again kissed.

"What time is it?"

Charlie looked at his bedside clock. "Almost ten-thirty." He kissed her bare shoulder. "Do you have to go?"

"Soon."

"Not yet."

"No."

"I don't want you to go."

She turned over and nuzzled against him. He smelled like warm hay.

"I feel deliquescent."

"What does that mean?"

"I think it means I'm melting."

He stroked her hair.

"You came and rescued me. In the blizzard."

"That's right, I did."

He sighed happily, as she nuzzled closer to him.

"What's your wife like?"

"Ex," he said.

"I know. Sorry. But it seems only fair. . . ." He certainly knew more than enough about the man she married.

"Patsy is charming," he said, judiciously.

There was a pause.

"You're not helping me out much here."

"It's not my favorite subject."

"Give me an example of her."

Charlie said, "When she first left me, she'd call up and chat for hours about who I was seeing and whether I'd slept with her yet."

"What?"

"It doesn't sound very good, does it? I got so used to everybody loving Patsy that sometimes I have to tell something like that, for a reality check. It was as if she cared so little about me she thought we could be girlfriends."

"And yet if she cared so little, why monitor your life? Why not let you go?"

"There was that."

Charlie was thoughtful.

Martha said, "You really don't want to talk about her."

"It's more that I'm afraid you'll find out for yourself." Martha smiled, though it seemed inappropriate. "There's something I have to tell you," he added.

"What?"

He told her.

She laughed and said, "Antiques! That's so like him. Poor Raymond."

"Poor Raymond?"

"Sorry. I don't know why I'm laughing. I guess because it's sad and there's nothing to do about it."

"I thought you'd be furious with me."

"Why? It took me fourteen years to figure him out, why should you be any quicker?"

"I wasn't in love with him," said Charlie.

"No, but Raymond was not a simple system. Sometimes it was like putting a quarter in a slot and hearing it fall straight through and hit the sidewalk. He just didn't engage. I'm sure you told him he had to reveal his assets."

"Thank you."

They fell silent again. Finally, Charlie said, "So. Where are you from?" and they both laughed. Then they fell silent again, and shy, because from somewhere each felt a wave of desire. But it was getting late, and there were children waiting.

"I'm from a town outside Boston," said Martha. "I have two brothers, one in New York and one in Wyoming. My parents are living, and married to each other, and still in the house I grew up in. What about you?"

"I lived in Boston once. And in Richmond and White Plains and Hawaii. I have a sister much younger than I am . . . almost like Jack and Fred. She lives in Irvington."

"A full sister?"

"Half."

"And your parents?"

"My father's dead. My mother lives with my auntie now, in Rye."

There was another silence.

"I was going to make you crème brûlée tonight," said Charlie, "but I just wanted you so much I couldn't."

Martha smiled and stroked him.

"It's too bad, too, because I make the best crème brûlée in New York."

"I'm quite sure that you do not," said Martha, "because I do."

"Want to bet?"

"Certainly."

"We'll have a contest."

"Perfect."

"When?"

"Tomorrow."

She laughed. "I can't. Wednesday?"

"I can't."

"Thursday."

"Your place or mine?"

"Mine. The boys can act as our panel of impartial judges."

"Oh, *that* sounds very fair."

Martha kissed him and got up. She began looking for her clothes; Charlie watched her for a bit without moving. Then he got up and quickly dressed.

She said, "You don't have to . . ."

"Oh, hush."

On Park Avenue he put her in a cab and then stood in the frigid air watching until its taillights disappeared. Then he walked around the block, although he was wearing only a light jacket, and when a hunched old woman walking a schnauzer said, "Good evening," he realized he must be smiling.

∽

Phoebe *was hanging* out on Montague Street waiting for Dime. School got out at noon because the faculty was being given a workshop on "Exploring the Right Brain." Very few of the students had mentioned this fact at home, so very few of their parents knew that their children were ambling loose through Brooklyn Heights. They would see them at the usual time this evening.

The two Jennies drifted up the street and stopped to hang out with her awhile. The air had the fragrant raw chill of early winter. Jenny Krass wore leg warmers with her denim miniskirt, but still her thighs were goosebumped and blue. This was sexy as hell, and she knew it.

Phoebe was wearing a big denim jacket with crossed hammers carefully painted on the back. It was an emblem from Pink Floyd's movie *The Wall.* Everyone in school knew Dime's jacket.

Jenny McKinney touched it as she greeted Phoebe. "Cool," she said. Everyone was glad Dime had a sort of girlfriend or whatever.

"So whassup?"

"Nada."

"You finish your story for Mr. Kelley?"

"Nope."

"You start it?"

"I *started* it . . . ," said Phoebe, but it wasn't true. "What about you?" The two Jennies always turned work in on time. They were done.

"You know what? Mr. Kelley was telling us about what he did when he got back from Vietnam. He went home to his father's farm in Vermont and lived in a cabin on alfalfa sprouts and homemade yogurt for seven years."

"He said the only place he liked to be besides the cabin was at the shopping mall."

Phoebe laughed.

"He liked to just go there and stand around looking at stuff. He'd follow people around and listen to them talk and after a while he'd feel like he'd been at a party and it was time to go home."

"He did a *major* amount of dope, too."

"Did he tell you that?"

"Yes."

They considered this. The two Jennies and their crowd felt that Vietnam, the "Rock and Roll War," was their war. They had read *Dispatches*. Jenny McKinney had an uncle who went to Canada in 1969 and basically never came back.

"So how did he get normal again?"

"After about five years he decided he wanted to raise tropical fish. And he couldn't do that in the cabin because you need electricity for their little heaters and aerators. So he showed up at his dad's house and set up all these aquariums."

"Vermont's cool," said the other Jenny.

These kids loved Mr. Kelley. He swore and made them laugh and knew more about rock and roll than even Ben the DJ. Maybe they also sensed that like them, he knew about being broken. There was nothing fragile about him now, but he understood their fragility. And he liked them. Really liked them. He seemed to like the brilliant fuck-ups among them best. And they worked their tails off for him.

The two Jennies drifted off to the health food store, planning to replicate Mr. Kelley's sprout and yogurt diet to see if they would get a macrobiotic high. They hoped it wouldn't take more than two weeks because Jenny Krass's parents would be home by then and they'd stop her. Anyway, they'd promised to stop before that if their gums started to bleed or they fainted.

Phoebe wished Mr. Kelley liked her as much as he liked the two Jennies. They were in his honors class. Phoebe wasn't too good at English, unfortunately. And because Mr. Kelley wasn't interested in busting anyone's hump, you could turn in your work for him or not. If you didn't turn anything in, he just ignored you. Phoebe didn't know if he passed you at the end of the year. So far, she hadn't turned in much work for him. She did read *Brave New World* with everyone else though. She had to find out what it meant when Jaywalk called her a Delta Minus Moron.

For her first month at this school, Phoebe had thought that there was always a party going on and she wasn't invited. Now she had discovered that nobody was invited. You just had to hang out until you heard the plan form and then you joined if you wanted to. Nobody was going to throw food at you or yell eeeuuuw if you showed up. But if you didn't show, nobody was going to call you. It was all an exercise in being at the right place at the right time. It made life seem pretty hazardous. You couldn't just be at all the right places all the time, if only because then you looked desperate, which did make people say eeeuuuw. But if you didn't seem to care if you hung out or not, you could hang out. Of course, that wasn't friendship or falling in love. That was not a party you got invited to either. Phoebe had no idea how you got those things.

The plan this afternoon, it developed, was to go UTB, which means Under The Bridge. There was an open-air den in the shelter of the Brooklyn Bridge on the Brooklyn side, where hours disappeared. The cops knew it was there, but they left the kids alone. This afternoon the lounge crew was having a *Beach Blanket Bingo* party here. In the dank shadow of the bridge in view of the skyscraping tip of Manhattan, which gleamed in full sun, on an asphalt riverbank littered with broken bottles, butts of all kinds of smokes, and the odd used condom (which the crew called Coney Island whitefish) they had a tiny bonfire. They sat around it in black jeans and leather jackets, torn T-shirts, black glasses, and hair that stuck straight up, trying to keep warm.

Someone had scored some brew. As Dime and Phoebe picked their way toward the group, Jaywalk and Valerie were roasting marshmallows. Sarah Shapiro, whose tag was Disney, was singing with her boyfriend, "Feed the birds, tuppence a bag, tuppence, tuppence, tuppence a bag" from the movie *Mary Poppins*. Valerie was trying to feed bits of a chocolate chip granola bar to a pigeon. Some more of the crowd joined in the song, singing with sweet cracking voices and deep seriousness. Sarah and her boyfriend Nick, who looked like a member of a Nazi youth group, liked to baby-sit for Sarah's friends, the Cutlers, because they liked kids and because the Cutlers had every Disney film on videotape. Sarah and Nick watched *Snow White* and *Dumbo* with the little ones, and *Pinocchio* after the children were in bed because Nick said it was too scary for them, and then they watched *Midnight Blue* on cable.

Phoebe and Dime settled down at the edge of the group. Somebody lit a joint and passed it around. Somebody else sent around a quart of Old English Malt Beverage. Jaywalk started to talk about Mr. Kelley, about the story he told this morning about when he came back from Nam.

"You know what it's like, man?" said Dime, suddenly. "It's like 'Bearskin,' the fairy tale. You remember that?"

"I do, sort of."

"I don't."

"It's just like Mr. Kelley. In the story this soldier comes home from the war and he doesn't know what to do with himself. His whole family is dead. So he goes to the woods where he meets the devil. The devil gives him a bearskin coat and says that if he doesn't wash or cut his nails or comb his hair for seven years he can be free and happy and rich for the rest of his life."

"It *is* the same."

"What happens to him?"

The crew liked stories, and songs. They could talk all afternoon, like adults at a cocktail party, but they didn't really know anything. Instinctively they tried to understand things by figuring out what things were like. Even when they didn't intend allusion or metaphor, their speech was filled with the word "like."

"Well, he's allowed to have money. The devil says there will always be gold in his pocket. He's a hero, and he's rich, man, he's just going to look strange. Things aren't too bad for the first year or two, but by the third year he's getting pretty rank, and by the fourth year," said Dime, "he is *high*. He is *Gorgonzola,* man, and there's flies all around him.

"He wants to spend the night at this inn, but the guy doesn't even want him in the stable, because he'll scare the horses. But finally the guy gives him a room at the back, and he hears this other old guy back there crying. The old guy is broke and can't pay his bill. Bearskin says, 'Really, no problem,' and gives him handfuls of money. So the old guy stops crying and goes and gets out of debt. Then he comes back and says, 'I have three beautiful daughters, why don't you come marry one of them,' So Bearskin says, 'Okay, I'll give it a shot' and goes with him.

"The first daughter says, 'Yuck and peeuw,' and the second one says, 'Double yuck and peeuw, bad idea, Dad.' But the third one looks at him and says, 'Who cares what he looks like, he must be a good man.' So Bearskin gives her a ring. He breaks it in half and she takes one part and he keeps the other, and then he says, 'I have to keep traveling for three years, but then I'll be back.'

"Then all he has to do is not die, because if he dies before seven years the devil gets his soul."

"Why doesn't he just stay there where he is?" asked Valerie.

"Because he's Gorgonzola," giggled Nick, and everyone else laughs.

"No," said Dime, "it's because that's part of his deal. He has to keep traveling this whole seven years. And he is so disgusting that he can't get anywhere inside to sleep anymore, so it's, like, a little bleak, but he gets through it. So the devil shows up and takes back the bearskin coat and gives the soldier back his own coat and he washes his hair for him and cuts his nails and shaves him and everything."

"He must have looked like Howard Hughes," said someone.

"Foot-long nails," said someone else.

"And the soldier keeps thinking there's a hitch, that the devil is still going to get him. But anyway, he goes back to the three daughters, and he's tall and handsome—he looks like this warrior again—and the old guy gives a party and the oldest two daughters are all over him. But the youngest one just sits there in black like a widow, because she's waiting for Bearskin. So the soldier gives her a glass of wine with his half of the ring in it, and when she finds it she's very excited, and when the older sisters realize who he is, they're so pissed off they fucking kill themselves." Laughter.

"They do," said Dime. "One hangs herself, and the other throws herself down a well. And then the devil comes to the door and says to the soldier, 'See? I got two souls instead of your one.'"

There was silence around this circle of kids in armor and costumes, spikes and rags, wild hair and fur and leather.

"Did Mr. Kelley stay Gorgonzola for seven years?"

Jaywalk said, "The seventh year after he got back, he got married."

Silence. "Far out," said someone.

"He met his wife at the tropical fish store," said Jaywalk, and everyone laughed. "No shit. He did," he added, smiling.

A fresh joint went around. Phoebe was beginning to feel loose. She lay back against Dime and thought about what the shapes of the clouds reminded her of.

"Gorgonzola," said Nick and started to laugh, and the whole circle laughed, too, a happy aimless noise that made them a tribe, at least for the afternoon.

"I wrote a great story for Mr. Kelley," said Jaywalk.

"Tell it," said Valerie.

"This guy goes into the Museum of Modern Art," said Jaywalk. "He walks through all the galleries looking at the paintings but he keeps coming back to the Monets. Finally when no one else is looking he takes out a razor and slashes a great big X in the *Water Lilies*. Then he glides out. As he strolls down the stairs he can hear people start to yell.

"He gets outside and takes a deep breath. Then he rolls up his sleeve and there, on his arm, he's got a tattoo of Monet's *Water Lilies*."

Appreciative hoots and grunts.

"He takes the razor and slashes an X across his tattoo, and then he strolls off down the street, with blood pouring down his arm."

"Whoa!"

"That's fresh. . . ."

"You didn't make that up!"

"Yes I did."

"No you didn't."

"Yes I did!"

"You never did!"

"I wanted an argument! This isn't an argument, it's just contradiction!"

Pause. "No it isn't!"

"Yes it is!"

They were off on their Monty Python imitations. Dime, the class actor, could do a variety of accents. He and Jaywalk once convinced a roomful of fairly threatening people in an East Village bar called Downtown Beirut that they were punks from Manfred, and kept it up for an entire evening.

"Yo, Dime, are you doing the play this term?" asked Sarah. She was now lying facedown across Nick's lap, having her back rubbed.

"Yeah, why not, luv." He was into one of his new dialects, Australian. Pronounced. *Straiyun.*

"What *is* the play?"

"*The Three Musketeers.*"

"That's not a play, it's a book."

"No it isn't."

"Yes it is, I read the Classic comic."

"You did not."

"Yes I did."

"What are their names, then?"

"The three musketeers? There are four, actually," said Nick.

"I know . . . what are their names?"

Nick looked blank.

"Athos . . . ," said someone.

"Asshole," said Phoebe. "Asshole, Porthole, Pyramus, and Thisbe." Jaywalk and Dime went nuts. Everyone laughed.

Dime had been fiddling with a yellow paperclip he found in his pocket, twisting it into a ring. Now, he slipped it onto Phoebe's finger. "Someday, years from now, I'll come back for you," he said. "You won't recognize me . . . I'll be wearing a three-piece suit . . . I'll have a briefcase . . . I'll reek of Canoe cologne. . . ."

"It's pronounced *Can-oo-ay*, asshole," said Jaywalk.

"Your sister will fall madly in love with me. . . ."

"I don't have a sister," said Phoebe.

"Your mother, then," said Dime, "but you alone will recognize me, for I will be wearing a ring exactly like this rare and lovely one I give you today. . . ."

"And she'll say, god, I liked you better when you smelled like Gorgonzola," said Nick.

"I'll say, 'Eeeuuuw, a suit, gag me with a spoon,'" said Phoebe.

"But your mother will still throw herself down a well," said Dime.

"Thank god," said Phoebe viciously, and everyone laughed.

One thing Patsy really hated was meeting Charlie's girlfriends. The last time it happened was exactly a year ago, at the Birdsalls' Christmas party. Poppy Birdsall was kind of an airhead, and she just forgot that maybe she should have told Patsy that Charlie and Sophie were coming. Instead she said only that she wanted to introduce Patsy to a Dear Friend of theirs, recently widowed.

Patsy had been with a group in the den eating Poppy's ever-evolving Christmas pâté, when Poppy came in with a small, handsome woman in a red dress. The fire was crackling, tiny white lights twinkled all around the molding and in among the green boughs on the mantel. Poppy gave a nervous giggle and said, "Oh! Well I guess *you* two know each other" and left them. The woman in the red dress, who had lovely pale blue eyes and could have used a little makeup, smiled and said to Patsy,

"Hello. I'm Sophie Curry." Patsy was set back only a moment. She laughed gracefully and said, "I'm Patsy."

The shook hands. Sophie said, "Of course. Phoebe is so like you."

Patsy had liked Sophie's face, actually. She was small and good looking, though not as good looking as Patsy.

Patsy had found Charlie by the bar, where he was talking football with Tom Birdsall. He had given Patsy a kiss on the cheek, and then ordered a Dubonnet for her from the bartender without having to ask what she was drinking. He had asked about her Christmas plans; she had asked about his. Then she said she had to be rushing off, in a way that strongly suggested a crowded evening of festivities waiting. Poppy was just leading toward her a man of about sixty with a kind, sad face and a tattersall vest, but Patsy gave Poppy a kiss and said she'd had a perfect time but must be going. She tripped off home to eat a macaroni and cheese from the freezer, and watch television. She was hell going to have a blind date in the same room with her ex-husband and his new squeeze.

Tonight, a year later, Patsy and Charlie sat side by side on folding chairs in the gymnasium of Cropp and Thatcher in Brooklyn Heights. Patsy was looking very pretty, she felt, but she also felt annoyed to have been dragged to a completely unknown neighborhood where the taxi almost got lost. She had always enjoyed parent meetings at Replogle, especially since the divorce. She enjoyed running into old friends with Charlie at her side, knowing everyone was thinking, Ah, what a handsome couple, both still single, and still such good friends. She wasn't going to know anybody in this place.

Phoebe's interim reports, to Patsy's surprise, which she invited Charlie to share, were fairly good. Phoebe seemed to be working intermittently, not being an asshole in class, and she only owed homework in English and French. She might be falling behind a little now that she was working on the tech crew for *The Three Musketeers,* but Patsy was pleased that she was doing that. Patsy was pleased because she thought working in the theater would help Phoebe make friends.

Patsy and Charlie were each wearing paper name tags stuck on their clothes. Patsy's said Patsy Leveque (Phoebe). Charlie's said Charlie Leveque (Phoebe).

A woman labeled Peggy Fish (John Walker) stopped and exclaimed, "You're Phoebe's parents!"

"Yes," said Patsy brightly.

"She was just up at our house. I'm Jaywalk's mother."

Patsy was drawing a complete blank. "Where do you live?" she asked, irrelevantly, because she'd never heard of Jaywalk.

"Well, my husband and I live on Central Park West. But you know Gary, his father, lives in Tribeca. The kids spend time at Gary's because it's closer to school but of course I'd been hearing about Phoebe. Dime is Johnny's best friend."

Peggy might as well have been speaking in tongues for all Patsy could make of this. So she said, "Oh. Tribeca. That's that rather odd neighborhood downtown, isn't it?"

Peggy Fish laughed and rolled her eyes.

"Sort of the urban equivalent of living in barns," said Patsy, and Peggy laughed again. Actually, it was George's bon mot, and he had said it about SoHo, but it didn't matter. Phoebe had been forgotten, and Patsy was making another new friend. Charlie knew they were about to find out why Peggy's ex-husband lived in such an odd place, or else what it was that Peggy liked so much about the West Side, or else what it was that Peggy's new husband did for a living or how much they paid in rent. Charlie sometimes wondered why no one ever said to Patsy, It's none of your damn business, but no one ever seemed to. Fortunately, just then, the headmaster got up to speak. He told them that the fall term had been a great success and that they must follow their schedules carefully from conference to conference or they would all be here all night. As the parents rose and shuffled out, Charlie said, "Phoebe has a friend called Jaywalk?"

"I haven't met him yet. We're supposed to go to her math teacher first. That's the eighth floor," said Patsy, leading the way.

They found the room and stood in line. Charlie was wondering how it happened that Patsy didn't know Phoebe's friends, when the friends' parents knew Phoebe. Patsy was calculating that it had been four years plus four months ago since the last time she and Charlie slept together.

It had been Thanksgiving weekend. They were in the country. Phoebe was eleven. Patsy had been cooking all weekend, first an elaborate holiday meal with goose instead of turkey and chestnut dressing and fried oysters, all of which his family had hated. In fact his sister Juney threw up the oysters, not at the table, though.

After his family went back to Rye, and Patsy's mother went back to New Canaan, Patsy had kept cooking. She had made a thick aromatic turkey soup with wild rice and mushrooms and homemade bread, and invited some neighbors in. On Saturday she made couscous, and Charlie and the neighborhood played touch football. Charlie told Patsy to come play, they could order pizza, but she wouldn't. Couldn't. She was on some sort of homemaking bender, as if her psyche was running amok trying to express how trapped she felt, how desperately she wanted to do something or be something that only she could do or be. Desperately she grated fresh ginger for the homemade ice cream.

Charlie didn't really like odd food. He liked turkey, and liver with onions, and steak, and creamed chipped beef. Once when she was, on the spur of the moment, whipping up a special salad for some friends who had dropped in, he said wistfully, "Honey . . . are you going to put those things in that you used last time?"

"What things?" she said, remembering crumbled bacon and chives and a long list of special touches.

"I think they were Raisinets," he said.

Charlie had been very quiet all that Thanksgiving, four years plus four months ago, the last time they ever made love. She had known she was making him miserable. In the middle of Friday night, Patsy had gotten up and telephoned to San Diego to an old boyfriend she hadn't seen in fourteen years, and talked for an hour. When she came back to bed, Charlie was lying awake. He didn't say a word, he just put his arms around her, and she burst into tears. On the Saturday night, after the couscous, they made love, but this time it was Charlie who got out of bed afterward and sat at the window, wrapped in a blanket, looking out at the meadow till dawn. Patsy lay awake in the bed, unable to care about anybody's suffering but her own.

They had presided four hours later over a noisy brunch with their next-door neighbors. They talked and smiled to their guests but never looked at or touched each other, as they passed each other going in and out of the kitchen. Then, as Patsy packed up the house and Phoebe watched television, Charlie went downtown and filled up the new diesel Volvo with gasoline instead of diesel fuel and then drove it back to the house, completely destroying the engine.

"How is your mother?" asked Patsy now, as they climbed the stairs to locate Phoebe's English teacher. They had learned that Phoebe was having no trouble in math at all. She was rather good at geometry, a first in their experience.

"She's fine," said Charlie.

"Is she coming to the country for Christmas?"

"Yes, if Aunt Rita's back gets better."

"Juney told me she'd thrown it out again. Poor thing."

A pause. "You talked to Juney?"

"I had lunch with her last week. Now, we want room seven-three."

Patsy had lunch with Juney? Why? They never had lunch together in all the years he and Patsy were married.

The English teacher, a Mr. Kelley, told them that Phoebe had turned in an exceptional short story in the last week. However, she had missed several classes this term. Patsy was concerned. Why didn't she know about these missed classes? Mr. Kelley didn't know. Either he forgot to report them, or the school forgot to send the warning notice, or Patsy forgot she got it.

"I'm not *at all* happy about that," said Patsy on the stairwell afterward. She also wasn't absolutely positive she *didn't* get it, so she thought she better take the offensive.

"They don't go in for much nursemaiding here," said Charlie.

"They're supposed to do more than *that,*" Patsy said tartly, meaning Mr. Kelley. She wasn't nearly as sold on this school as Charlie was.

"I guess. You'd have loved a high school like this, wouldn't you?"

"Yes, I would have. But I never did anything wrong. I was always Miss Perfect."

"I think it's good to let kids make a few mistakes. They learn the consequences that way."

Patsy was exasperated. Where was this coming from? This didn't sound like Charlie. "*You* would have. *I* would have. But Phoebe isn't *like* us."

"What is Phoebe like?"

Patsy suspected he was baiting her. "She just isn't driven by anything. She drifts! There's nothing she loves enough to really throw herself into it!"

They achieved the floor they sought and paused in the hall to figure out which way to go.

"She seems quite involved with this play," said Charlie.

Shit, thought Patsy. All she wanted was an innocent game of us against her, and Charlie wouldn't play.

"Good evening, Mrs. Leveque," said the French teacher, and she and Charlie took seats in desks with broad writing arms. The French teacher admitted that Phoebe had been late with assignments. "But never mind," she said, "she will do well in life—her excuse is always so charming."

Patsy tried to picture what Phoebe these people knew. Several of them seemed truly to like and enjoy her. Why weren't these people nailing Phoebe for every imperfection, teaching her to fear failure till she woke up with cold sweats in the night? What would become of Phoebe if she didn't feel every day that she was skating across disaster?

"I'm confused," said Patsy, as Charlie led the way to the science teacher. "I can't tell how she's doing."

"If she wasn't doing fine, I think they'd make it clear," said Charlie calmly.

"How do we know?"

"I think she's doing fine." They walked in silence. All around them were parents, now weary and overheated in their overcoats, consulting their schedules and looking lost.

"What are you doing for Christmas?" asked Charlie. "Are you having your mother?"

"I don't know yet."

"I guess you'll want Phoebe."

Actually, she didn't want Phoebe, and especially she didn't want some miserable roast turkey breast in her little apartment with her bitch of a mother in her Adolfo and pearls. She wanted romance. She wanted adventure. She wanted something else from what she had.

"I was sort of thinking of going out of town with friends," she said. A pause.

"Does it matter?" she asked, challenging.

"No. But let me know as soon as you can."

Why? Patsy thought, but didn't say. You've got a big house in the country. You have family you like. You can just wait until I decide. You can worry about me for once, instead of me worrying about your convenience.

"Martha," said Charlie suddenly, looking over Patsy's head. A handsome woman with reddish hair and a dancer's posture was coming toward them, smiling. The woman had one of those faces that even if they aren't beautiful, remind you of Audrey Hepburn. It was the delicate nose and the wide-apart eyes. Patsy's own mother, in Patsy's hearing, had once said to a friend that her daughter was pretty in spite of her little pig eyes.

"Martha, this is Patsy."

"I'm very glad to meet you," said the woman, offering her hand. Patsy shook it. But the way Charlie had suddenly begun to smile made her want to tear Martha's heart out.

"I'm Martha Forbes," said the woman. "I'm one of Charlie's clients."

Sure you are, honey. So you dumped that nice Sophie Curry, Charlie. I wondered why Phoebe hadn't mentioned her in a while. And here you are with another girlfriend, when I'm better looking than you are, Charlie, I'm the one with the famous way with people. Jesus, you have no idea what a seller's market you're in.

Patsy couldn't figure out what Martha's figure was like, in that loose wool jumper, but she was willing to bet it was less than perfect.

"It was Martha who recommended Cropp and Thatcher," said Charlie to Patsy, but he was looking at Martha, and he was looking happy.

"Oh, yes, you have a son here," said Patsy with a charming smile.

"That's right."

"Ah. What's his name?"

"Jack Gaver."

"I must ask Phoebe if they're friends."

"I think they're getting to be quite good friends," said Martha.

"How lovely. We can't thank you enough for your help," said Patsy. "Do you know where the music room is?"

"Second floor."

Patsy could feel Martha and Charlie tearing their eyes from each other the way you would tear in half a piece of paper, as she led Charlie away.

∞

Molly and Ruth Justice barely looked like sisters, let alone twins. Ruth was blond with brown eyes and hair straight as a pin. She had slim hips and a sizable bust, giving the lie to her father's dictum that big boobs are the Lord's way of letting you know which girls are the dumb ones. Ruth had rarely gotten lower than an *A* minus on any subject except phys ed or citizenship.

Molly had curly auburn hair, a wide mouth, and more hips than chest. She was a half a head shy of Ruth in height, and in other ways as well. She had rarely gotten above a *C* plus in any subject except phys ed. So Molly was the only one in the Justice household who did not immediately think it was good news, when it was learned that their brother William, who had consented to talk long enough to go through a battery of cognitive and psychological tests his child psychiatrist recommended, apparently had an IQ of 190.

Molly played center forward on the hockey team. Ruth played left back. Ruth would be happy not to play at all, but at Hudson you had to. Molly in her red pinny today scrimmaged fiercely for the ball.

Hudson rarely beat Garrison Forest but they did today, and the reason was that Molly Justice had been flashing her fierce little buns up and down the field like a tiger. The bleachers were wild with joy as the Hudson team came off the field, dripping, and the Garrison JV, shamed by its defeat by fourteen-year-olds, followed them to the showers.

As she walked up the hill toward the locker room door, Molly was astonished to hear an upper schooler, Scott Boatner (Scott Boatner! The Hunk!) call from the sidelines, "Way to go, Justice."

Their eyes met for a moment. She was so surprised that he knew her name that she could hardly react. She called, "Thanks," and went on, chattering with her teammates. As if with eyes in the back of her head, as if with super X-ray hearing, she knew (without doing anything so uncool as turning around) that Scott Boatner had walked off toward the upper field just after she passed. Meaning, he was there waiting for her to pass, so he could say "Way to go" to her.

By the time she reached her locker, her childhood had ended. She stripped off her sweaty blouse and tunic and walked to the big tiled room ringed with shower heads, all pumping hot water onto a score of naked pubescent hockey players. She joined the Garrison goalie under a stream of hot water, and instead of darting in and out, just to show the PE teacher that her shoulders were wet, she stood there feeling the water course over her, and instead of hearing and seeing a roomful of foreign female bodies, she was alone in the warm, amazing, protecting embrace of Scott Boatner's attention.

"I wonder if William will have to go to a special school," said Ruth, as she and Molly walked home through the near-darkness.

"Why would he?"

"Because he's a braintrust. His brain's so big, the next size is the box."

Molly thought about the hockey ball. How great it felt to thwack it and whack it and thwack it and follow it racing down the field and watch it slam home into the goal net.

"Will we have to move?" Molly asked.

"Move where?"

"Like, New York or something. Where they have special schools." Ruth didn't know.

"If we do, I'm going to boarding school," said Molly. She pictured her family moving to an apartment in New York with only a bedroom for William, and herself and Ruth shipped off somewhere to live in a dorm for the rest of their lives.

When they got home, the house was empty and dark. Connie and Dave and William were all at the child psychiatrist's. William had not been told the results of the tests he took. He had however gotten into a fight with the only black child in the class because the boy refused to believe that William had his own stallion in the backyard.

Ruth thought William's stallion was great. She wondered if he mentioned at school that the stallion could fly. Last night William and Ruth had locked themselves in the bathroom, and while William took his bath Ruth sat on the floor in the steam playing with a Playskool bath toy while William told her all about his stallion and his spaceship.

William had finished telling his story just as they heard their father's car peel angrily out of the driveway. That meant Mom and Dad had stopped yelling at each other for the moment, so William washed his face and neck and Ruth held a towel for him to get out of the tub. Then they had unlocked the door and come out of the bathroom.

*   *   *

Molly got a pizza out of the freezer to heat in the microwave. It wouldn't be very good; there were special microwave pizzas you could buy but Mom never got the right kind. This one would be like biting into a dish towel. Also, it would spoil Molly's dinner, but that was a good excuse not to come to the table. Molly turned on the tube, sat down and stared at the screen, and thought about Scott Boatner.

Scott Boatner was really cute. He had amazing blue eyes. She remembered a lacrosse game last year when he got hit in the face with a stick and had blood streaming down the side of his face. He had kept playing, even though he was half-blinded, until the coach pulled him off the field, and in the end he had to be taken to the emergency room and given seven stitches. Molly had hoarded, as one does a pressed corsage from her first dance, the image of Scott tearing down the field with blood in his eye, thinking only of fighting the point. They scored, too, before the coach could make him stop.

The house was dark except for the kitchen. Ruth had gone off somewhere. She was probably in their room doing her homework. Molly wished she had her own room. She used the television as her room. She turned it on and went into the box formed by the noise it made, and then people left her alone.

Right now, though, she would sort of like to be with Ruth. But she didn't really want to walk through the dark downstairs to get to her. She'd always been afraid of the dark, but since Ruth wasn't, her mother never saw a reason to take her fear seriously. ("Oh, nonsense. See, Ruth isn't scared. . . . It's a bathrobe, honey, on the closet hook, not a witch. . . . Now, come on. I don't have time for this. Be a big girl.")

Headlights raked across the lawn as a car pulled into the driveway. This would either be an escaped murderer from the insane asylum come to drive a knife into her heart and write swear words in her blood across the harvest gold refrigerator, or else it would be her family.

It was the latter. Connie, Dave, and William all stumped into the kitchen, and suddenly the room that had seemed huge and bright and empty like a hospital operating room seemed cramped and crammed with people all taking off steaming dampish overcoats and staring about themselves. They brought the smell of the cold inside for just a minute.

At first no one spoke. They were all three charged, her parents and

William, with some experience from which she was excluded. Then her mother said, exasperated, "Well, honey . . . didn't you read my note?"

Pause. "No. What note?" But as the words were coming out of her mouth, she saw that there was a big pad of foolscap with a note in her mother's writing addressed to her and Ruth in plain view on the breakfast table. Beside her backpack, in fact. Not at all sure how she happened to miss it, she got up quickly to show how willing she was and went to read it now.

"Well, that's a lot of help! I asked you to preheat the oven and put the roast in." Connie was crossly bustling about the kitchen as she spoke. "Now we won't be ready to eat for hours. And I told you not to spoil your dinner!" she snapped as she caught sight of the pizza package left on the counter. "Goddammit, Molly!"

William was making his escape. Dave was getting a beer for himself.

"How'd your game go?" he asked.

"Great . . . we won," she said gratefully.

"Did you play the whole game?"

"Yes."

"Did you score?"

"Yes."

"How many times?"

"Two. Me two, the team five."

"Whoa!" He grinned and held out his hand to her. She slapped it, grinning.

"Way to go!" he said, proudly.

She glanced at her mother. Her mother's back was turned; she was furiously scouring carrots at the sink. Everything about the pitch of her shoulders and the way her hands moved expressed annoyance.

It was mid-January. Charlie had dropped down after work for a late supper with Martha. After the baby went to sleep they would have some time alone; Jack was spending the night with Jaywalk because they were building an incubator together for a science project. Martha had made spaghetti and put on Mozart and lit candles, but Charlie didn't eat much. While she made coffee he excused himself for a moment to lie down, and when she went in to check on him, she found he was running a fever of 103. Two days later he was still there.

Charlie had been in and out of sleep all day. Martha was a patient nurse, but Charlie hated having people around when he was sick. And Martha's bedroom, such as it was, was separated from the rest of the loft by tall art deco folding screens. Thus, as the realtor would explain if she ever tried to sell the place, "You have visual separation," neglecting to mention that acoustically, a loft is all one room. How the hell Martha had raised two children here without tearing their heads off, Charlie had no idea.

Baby Fred had been fussing; he was probably getting sick, too. Martha had not been able to get out of the house or get any work done, and she was getting short-fused. She had ducked out finally to the corner bodega to buy milk and Pampers and apple juice and Pepto-Bismol. The baby was watching *The Electric Company*. Charlie was supposed to be watching the baby, but events of the day suggested that he couldn't get out of bed without throwing up.

The buzzer rang. Charlie opened his eyes and stared at the molded tin ceiling, thick with ancient coats of paint.

"There is no God," Charlie whispered. He didn't move.

The buzzer rang again. The buzzer made a horrible noise, intolerable if your head ached, and Charlie's did. He lifted his head and groaned. He sat up. By the time the buzzer went the third time, he was on his feet shuffling toward the door. From the kitchen came baby Fred, nose running and blanket trailing, to see if everyone had died and left *him* to answer the door.

Charlie pushed the talk button on the intercom and yelled, "Go away!" Then he pushed the button to listen to the street. He heard a bleat: "Daddy, it's me." Puzzled, he pushed the button that unlocked the downstairs door.

Charlie sank into a slightly broken chair by the door to wait while Phoebe climbed the stairs. He wrapped both arms around his stomach. Inside, his intestines were being clamped in four hundred places by hot pincers. He sincerely wondered if he was going to shit in his shorts or if he could make it to the bathroom. Baby Fred came over and stared up at him, concerned. Charlie reached out to him, and Fred came close and leaned his head against Charlie's lap.

Phoebe arrived. She had never been here before, and Charlie wondered what she was doing here now. He stared at her. Then he said, "Go with Phoebe, honey," and detached Fred's hand from his knee. Phoebe took it. Somehow she dropped her backpack with a crash doing it, though.

Charlie was already on his way to the bathroom. He employed a crablike movement, as if he could fool his innards into believing he was still sitting down.

Martha could hear a howl from Fred while she was still on the stairs. Lugging an armful of groceries, a purse, and an umbrella, she started to run. The front door was open. As she burst in, she saw Fred on the floor yelling, his face red, and Phoebe of all people trying to pick him up. Charlie had apparently disappeared and been replaced by his daughter. Fred stretched his arms to his mother and kicked his legs on the floor and cried harder. To whatever injury he had sustained was added the worse injury of remembering at the sight of her that his mother had left him in his hour of need, the bitch.

Phoebe was starting an explanation, but Martha, running, dropped her groceries into Phoebe's arms and stopped to scoop up Fred. He wrapped himself around her like a baboon child, howling. She could feel that he'd have liked to have a prehensile tail to hold her with, too. He wailed. But as she danced with him, crooning, he calmed down slowly.

"There honey. Poor baby . . . there baby, there now, you're all right. Maxwell Edison, majoring in medicine, calls him on the phone. Can I take you out to the picture . . . show oh oh ooooh. . . ." She danced as she sang and her warmth and breathing and motion began to get his attention. "Bang, bang, Maxwell's silver hammer came down, upon her head doo dedoodoo. . . ." Her reassuring calmness was stronger than his pain and fear and it swam through the membrane between him and her. Fred's anguish began to ebb away; his sobs declined and turned to soft gasps as he snuggled against her. He reached with his flat-open little hand to touch the side of his head, whimpered, and turned his head back and forth against Martha, shuddering and sniffling.

Phoebe watched every move. She felt terrible. She felt something black and bad.

"What happened? Where's Charlie?"

"In the bathroom."

"Oh." Pause. "What happened?"

"Nothing!" Her voice was hostile, daring Martha to find fault. "I just put him on the counter where he could see the TV, and he asked for apple juice. . . ." Phoebe stopped. Martha, still dancing gently and crooning under her breath to the baby, looked at her, intent.

"You put the baby on the counter, and then you turned your back and walked across the kitchen to the refrigerator." Her voice was steady. Fred continued to calm down.

"He fell off the counter," Martha said. Phoebe shrugged. The two stared at each other. Martha, without taking her eyes from Phoebe, began gently to walk testing fingers over Fred's head till she found a lump. It was huge. When she touched it Fred began to cry again. Phoebe suddenly turned her back and started putting away the groceries.

The bathroom door opened and Charlie came out. He was an interesting gray-green color as if he'd been dead for some days. He looked at Martha, then at Phoebe. His face expressed no curiosity at all. He began to shuffle off toward the bedroom. After a moment Martha followed him, carrying the baby. Phoebe was left alone in the kitchen. When she heard the bed creak and a soft murmur of voices begin, she changed channels on the TV and sat down on a stool staring at the screen.

The phone rang at last. Phoebe, now watching a game show, didn't look up. Martha reached the phone before it rang a second time. She had left a message with her pediatrician's service.

Now she said, "Hello?" and smiled. "Oh, Shirley. Thank you for calling back. Listen, Fred's had a fall and he's got a giant lump on his head . . . about four feet. Four and a half. He's awake . . . he ate a little supper, and he's playing." Pause. "Well, he's flushed . . . Fred, come here a minute, honey." Fred crawled over and Martha bent over to press her lips against his forehead. "No. No fever . . . oh, dammit, Shirley, I'm sorry, that's the other line. Hold on one second." She pushed the button. "Hello?"

"It's Patsy. Is Charlie there?"

"Patsy, he's asleep. Look, I'll have to . . ."

"It's important, Martha. Will you please wake him up?"

Martha, in spite of herself, raised her voice.

"I'm on the other line with Fred's doctor, Patsy. I'm hanging up now." She jabbed the button. "Shirley? Sorry. Anyway. No, I don't think he lost consciousness. He cried a lot, and he's very clingy. Dammit . . . that's the other line again. Just ignore it."

Shirley explained that the main danger was that he could slip from normal sleep into a coma. There was no way to know, and nothing to do except put him in a hospital and watch him all night. Shirley thought that as long as he wasn't knocked out that he needed to be home with his mommy a lot more than he needed that.

The call waiting beep interrupted the conversation a third time. Shirley said, "Go ahead and take it. The service can reach me any time all night if you run into problems." She hung up, and Martha took the other call.

Patsy was beside herself.

"Martha," she stormed, "you have no right to keep me from talking with Charlie! As a matter of fact, it is URGENT that I reach him. Phoebe has disappeared. . . ."

"Phoebe is here," said Martha.

"What! *Why* didn't you call me! You must have known I'd be wild, Martha."

"I didn't know that. I didn't know if you were home, or if you sent her here, or what was going on, and frankly I didn't think of it."

"You didn't think of it. Well that is the limit."

"I didn't think of it because Charlie's ghastly sick, and I walked in the door to find Fred screaming and I had to reach the doctor."

"Well, you have call waiting, don't you?"

"Patsy . . . I didn't know it was a problem. Forgive me."

"I want to speak to Charlie."

"I'm sorry, he's asleep. He's been very sick and I'm not going to wake him."

A pause.

"Martha."

"Yes."

Another pause.

"You're not going to steal my daughter."

There was a silence, except for the drone of the TV. Martha lifted her eyes to meet Phoebe's sullen stare from across the room.

"Phoebe, dear," she said evenly, "it's your mother. She's been worried about you." She laid the phone down and went to sit on the floor by Fred, who climbed into her lap and laid his head against her.

Phoebe was ordered home at once but she dawdled excruciatingly, getting her things together.

"Can I say good-bye to Daddy?"

"Please don't, Phoebe. He's sleeping. I'll tell him you said good-bye."

"Oh. Okay." She hoisted her backpack on and finally started for the door. She stopped and said, "Would you tell Daddy I got a part in the school play?"

"I'll tell him."

Phoebe waited another beat, as if there were something more she wanted to say. At last she turned and went to the door. Now there were footsteps pounding up the stairs, and as Jack burst in her sullen expression was transformed. Martha, looking at the baby, missed the bright flash of her smile. Phoebe and Jack met at the door.

"Yo, Dime," said Phoebe, elaborately casual.

"Hey!" He smiled at Phoebe and they slapped palms. "What's up?"

"I came by to see Daddy. But I have to go home now."

"You do?"

"Yeah. Good-bye."

"'Bye. See you tomorrow." And Phoebe trotted off. Her voice and smile, as far as Martha could tell, in the last thirty seconds of her visit belonged to a completely different person than the sulker who'd been hanging around for an hour.

"Hello, Momski," said Jack, dropping his backpack in a corner. "How is the invalid?" He headed for the kitchen.

"Awful. How was your day?"

"Good. Did you know Phoebe got a part in *The Three Musketeers?*" Jack was playing Athos.

"She just told me."

"It's a big part. Natasha Richman had it but then she got on academic pro and had to drop out, so we made Phoebe audition." He was staring hopefully into the open refrigerator. "Is there anything for dinner?"

"Not much. I haven't been able to leave for more than ten minutes."

"Want me to go to the Grand Union?"

"I do, honey. Do you mind?"

"Nope."

"Take money from my wallet and get a roasting chicken. And honey, put your books in your room."

Jack took his backpack to his room and came back wearing a Walkman. Martha could hear some Chinese water torture noise like Run DMC blasting into his ears through the headphones, but she couldn't bring herself to shout at him to turn it down. He went out, and Martha, with Fred in her arms, turned her attention to *Mr. Rogers' Neighborhood*.

When *Charlie finally* let himself into his own apartment he was dead pale and four pounds lighter; he felt as if he'd been away at war. He wondered if there would be cobwebs on everything and yellowing copies of *LIFE* magazine lying around, so much did it seem as if the last time he was here belonged to another era. He was surprised his key still turned in the lock. He carried himself as if his bones were made of glass as he went inside and turned on the lights.

José, on hearing him come in, took off from his chair and flew a fierce silent circuit several times around the still-dark living room, to express what he felt about being left alone so long. Then as Charlie watched from the doorway, he pounced back onto his chair and screamed, "Birds can't talk!" and refused to speak again for two days.

Charlie refilled José's water bowl. He still had plenty of seed. The plants in the window and in the bathroom appeared to have been watered, and the coffee mug Charlie had left in the sink a hundred years ago or whenever he last slept here, had been washed and put in the drying rack.

There was a note on the refrigerator.

Your office told me you were out sick. I brought you some chicken soup, but . . . the stone was moved, the body gone. ¿Qué pasa, muchacho? XXX, S.

Sophie. He looked into the refrigerator; there in a Tupperware container was the homemade soup, beautifully gelled and flecked with parsley.

Charlie tottered into the bedroom. His answering machine light was showing steady red, meaning there had been more messages than the machine could count. He sat down to listen. There was one from Sophie: "Hello, old friend, old friend. It's been quite some time. I'm home from Mexico . . . did you know I was going? Anyway . . . I miss you. I'll try you at the office. Big hugs." Very cheery.

There were five from Patsy, at an increasing pitch of hysteria, culminating in a two-minute fulmination against "that bitch your friend Martha" and a demand that he call at once. Interspersed were a dozen calls from the office, and finally an utterly different one from Patsy, warm and affectionate, saying she hoped he felt better and asking that he give her a ring.

Charlie went back into the bedroom, lay down on the bed, and turned on the news. He watched Tom Brokaw, then an hour more of the same news on the educational network. After that he went back to the kitchen and heated Sophie's soup and brought a bowl of it back to bed with him. For several hours he watched his cable sports channel, which that evening brought him an auto-wrecking derby, and a college basketball game that was won by Brigham Young University at Hawaii. After he had been eight solid hours without hearing a live human voice including his own, he telephoned Sophie, thanked her for the soup, and made a date to have dinner.

Two nights later, he waited for Sophie in a booth at a quiet restaurant called Turino that had always been a favorite of theirs. Charlie had ordered champagne, and sat looking at a huge globe of lilacs on the bar. Where did they get lilacs in January?

Sophie slipped into the booth beside him before he could stand, and kissed him on the cheek.

"Penny for your thoughts."

"You look *wonderful*," he said, so earnestly it made her laugh with pleasure. He looked at her as if he hadn't seen her before.

"Thank you. I guess I still have some tan."

"You do. And I like this frock or whatever we call it."

"Do you? Thank you again." She smiled happily, glancing down at the dress she had bought that morning, knowing it cost too much, but hoping. "You have a rather fascinating gauntness yourself," she said.

"Let us draw a veil over the whole subject," he said.

"What was it? Flu?"

"The flu from hell. It must have come back from space with the astronauts. I've never been so sick. Humans couldn't have survived so long if they'd had to go through that."

She smiled.

"Tell me about Mexico."

Yes, change the subject, thought Sophie, before I ask you the next logical question, Where were you all that time? I promised myself I wouldn't ask, and I'm not going to, I'm not going to. "I wanted to go to Belize, as I think I told you, but four strong men finally convinced me it was too dangerous."

"Is it?"

"I wish I'd tried it, but my friend Henry said he wouldn't let a woman go there alone. . . ."

"Do I know Henry?"

"Don't you? I've told you about him, I thought. My friend the ornithologist. With the Smithsonian."

Charlie didn't believe he knew about Henry, and he wondered why not. Sophie hoped he was a little jealous, although there was unfortunately no need for him to be. "I went through the Yucatán and then up to Zihuatanejo. It was lovely, especially after they found my luggage."

A waiter came and took their order. Charlie tried to figure out if she had been traveling alone. Sometimes she said "I," sometimes "we," but perhaps she meant simply fellow passengers, or fellow hotel guests. As she told him about some friends of hers who had been caught in a coup in South America on their honeymoon, he thought again about how very attractive she was looking. They clicked glasses and drank their champagne, and the happier she was, the prettier she looked.

Charlie reported that his sister Juney had had her baby, and that Phoebe was settling in to her new school.

"Se seems to have sustained a complete style transplant. Four months ago it was all designer clothes and Cinandre haircuts; now she wears black jeans and talks about the ballet."

"Sounds all right to me," said Sophie.

"And god knows who cuts their hair. They seem to cut each other's."

"Well, the price is right."

"I'll drink to that. She's completely stopped dropping hints about coming-out parties."

Their food arrived. Sophie took a craftsman's interest in what they were eating and how it had been prepared.

"I think this chicken is rather brilliant," said Sophie. "We could do this. You know what we should do? We should have Mason and Sandra to dinner. I could do the risotto we liked at Umberto as a first course. . . ." She wound down a little, waiting for him to chime in.

But there was a long pause, during which Sophie realized she wasn't hungry anymore, and in fact what she had eaten was sitting in her stomach like a live brick. She put down her fork and waited. She knew they were not going to be giving any dinner parties together anymore.

Charlie said, "There's something I should tell you . . . I probably should have told you before. . . ." Then he fell dumb, unable to tell her.

She said, "You've met someone." He moved to touch her hand, but she withdrew it. She was sitting very still, waiting, almost as if she'd stopped breathing. Waiting for what, he didn't know, because he didn't know what more to say. He could hardly expect her to want to know details. Or would she? What was he supposed to do now?

"I didn't say anything sooner because I didn't know. . . ."

"Are you in love with her?"

"Yes."

Sophie flinched almost imperceptibly. There was another silence.

"But what's the matter with me?" she asked at last.

"Nothing! Nothing, Sophie, you're wonderful!"

"Well, then, why not me?" The pain in her voice was palpable, although her demeanor was dignified.

"I don't know."

"I was here. . . ."

"I know. Sophie, I know you were. You've been a wonderful friend, and I love you, you know that. I'll always love you. . . ." Her tears started to fall. Shit, if that wasn't the right thing to say, what was? Nothing. He felt wretched. But not, he knew, as wretched as she did.

"Are you going to marry her?"

"I don't know. We're just at the beginning."

"Tell me what she has that I don't."

"Nothing!"

"I don't want to hear that! Explain this to me! I'm thirty-eight years old!"

"Well . . . she makes me laugh, she's bright and kind. . . ."

"So am I!"

"I know! You are, why are you making me do this?"

"I just want you to explain it to me."

A waiter approached, caught the tone and saw the tears, and sheered off.

Charlie said, "I feel . . . as if we're made out of the same skin or something. She makes me feel loved, we talk for hours, she's brave . . . she's funny . . . she's a wonderful mother. . . ."

Sophie flung her napkin onto the table, and pressed her mouth into her hand to keep from sobbing aloud as she shook and the tears fell onto the tablecloth. Charlie didn't ask—he knew. It was that Martha had children and could share that with Charlie, and Sophie who desperately wanted to share it could not. Now, because she had less than Martha to begin with, Sophie would get nothing.

Charlie wanted to touch her, but he was afraid she would strike him. Not that he'd mind, but he didn't want to make her lose control any more than she had, because she would hate that later. He sat very still.

"May one ask who it is?" she managed to say, after a bit. And took some deep breaths, and was calmer.

"Martha Gaver."

Sophie nodded, as if it made prefect sense.

"The sorrowing widow."

"Yes."

"And she lives in SoHo."

"Yes. Did I tell you that?"

"Sort of." She laughed a little and wiped her nose. "Her son is sixteen?"

"She has two. Jack is sixteen and Fred is two and a half."

"Two."

"Yes."

"Did she and Raymond? . . ."

"The baby's father was a man named Gillis. She and Raymond had lost several babies after Jack. She had always wanted more. So she went ahead."

"And Gillis didn't want her to?"

"I'm not sure what happened there."

"And what does this Gillis do?"

"He's a composer."

"Is he still single?"

"Yes."

"Maybe *he'd* like me." It was said with a laugh, but then the tears started again.

"Honey. Don't."

"The pathetic thing is, I'm not really kidding."

Charlie reached for her hand, and this time she gave it to him.

"It'll be all right," she said. "I'm jealous, but I'm happy for you. "It's hard to meet someone you fit with . . ."

"It's hard to meet *anyone*," said Charlie.

Sophie was looking in her bag for something. It took a long time, and she had to stop once to dry her eyes, and it seemed to annoy her that she couldn't instantly find what she wanted. Finally, with a forceful gesture, she handed to him the key to his apartment. Charlie looked at it, dismayed.

"You don't have to do that."

"Yes, let's be clear. At *least,* let's be clear."

He looked at the key and felt very sad. He put it into his pocket.

"*I'm trying to* comfort this friend of mine . . . she's having trouble with her kid," said George.

(What friend, Patsy asked herself. Does friend mean friend or does friend mean lover? Oh shut up, Patsy, she said to herself.) Patsy was smiling at George with a glow as if she'd been lit from inside.

"The kid's left home, he doesn't talk to her . . . it'll pass, but she's upset, right? So I decide to tell her a joke. I say, 'There's a minister, a priest, and a rabbi, and they're arguing about when life begins. The minister says, life begins at birth. And the priest says, no, no, life begins at conception. And the rabbi says, no, life begins when the kids leave home and the dog dies.'"

Patsy laughed heartily, but George held up his hand. "Wait! Wait till you hear what she said to me! There's this long silence and then she says solemnly, 'Did you know our dog died?'"

Both Patsy and George roared. Of course, this doesn't sound at all like a lover or ex-lover. She said our dog . . . she's married.

"It's too good, you're making it up!" Patsy laughed.

"I couldn't make it up, I'm not that funny. Jesus, I couldn't believe it."

"Comforter may not be your long suit. You're a Job's comforter."

"I felt like Job." George signaled for another round of beers. George looked as handsome as Patsy had ever seen him. He was tanned and fit. He'd been off by himself, hiking the Appalachian Trail. She didn't know what that meant, except that he hadn't been living with his girlfriend, and that being alone, he missed her. She felt giddy. She'd have liked to talk until dawn about all that she'd felt and thought since they were last together. Nobody was more fun to talk to than George.

"Speaking of kids, how's Phoebe?" George lit a cigarette.

"*There's* a can of worms," said Patsy.

"What's up?" George lounged back in the booth. The jukebox was playing "Twilight Time." Student hangouts always seemed to have the best jukeboxes. And onion rings.

"Well . . . my damn ex-husband."

George always enjoyed a conversation that began "My damn ex-husband," because it meant the story would reflect well on present company.

"Last Tuesday I had an appointment for Phoebe to have her hair cut after school at Bruno Dessange. She used to beg me to let her when she was at Replogle, and I finally decided I would—it cost the goddamn moon, by the way, pardon my French. But, I couldn't stand the way she's been getting herself up lately. She's taken to going around with no makeup except this black stuff around her eyes and she stopped setting her hair or combing it, as far as I could tell."

"This is Phoebe we're talking about?"

"Well that's another story, this unbelievable school Charlie picked out for her. Anyway, I *rushed* to meet her at the salon at three, and she didn't show up, and she didn't call. . . . I called home and she wasn't there, and I called the school and they said no one had seen her since about one-thirty. . . . I called Serena and Katie both and they hadn't heard from her and they couldn't *believe* she'd miss a haircut at Dessange. So naturally I panicked, and thought she must be dead."

"Has she been upset or anything?"

"No! She's been . . . well, I'll tell you in a minute. Anyway, I was wild. It was about five. I thought she's been kidnapped, she's run away, she's been run over. . . . Finally, I decided to call Charlie; I mean if I'm going to call the police, her father ought to know. So I call his office, and they tell me he's at his girlfriend's house. So I call there, and this Martha woman answers and won't let me speak to Charlie."

"What? Why?"

"Who knows?"

"Is she jealous of you?"

"I don't know. Maybe . . . no really, she was on the other line or something, but she wouldn't call Charlie to the phone and in fact she hung up on me once."

"No!"

"Yes, and then when I finally got through to her, and got tough with her she says—get this—she says, 'Oh, Phoebe is here'!"

"You're kidding!"

"Phoebe had been there for hours, and Martha hadn't even thought to call me. When I asked her, that was just what she said, 'I didn't think of it.'"

"What about Phoebe's appointment?"

"She forgot, apparently. She went to some audition or something instead. Can you imagine? So *that's* how Phoebe is."

Patsy took a long pull on her beer. War stories. George's ex-wife once set fire to his clothes; fortunately, they didn't have any children. Right now, his thick, glossy hair was falling into his eyes in a way that made Patsy want to smooth it back for him. She'd forgotten how he listened, how he made her feel smart and funny. It would be some time before she remembered that the reason he could listen, so accepting, to so much data, was that basically he didn't give a shit about any of it.

"What was Phoebe doing at the girlfriend's?"

"I don't know. I don't even know where she'd been all day."

George reached across the table and took her hand. "Poor baby," he said softly and Patsy felt such a jolt of desire that she forgot what they were talking about. George stroked her fingers.

"You've tried so hard with her." Patsy nodded. She didn't ever want him to stop touching her.

"I've missed her, you know," added George.

"Have you?" Patsy was very touched. Actually, they used to quarrel about Phoebe all the time. When they first met, Phoebe was twelve and just getting pubic hair and things, and somehow her mother's sex life must have been a very hot topic with her . . . in any case, she was alternately very clingy with Patsy when George was around and rather rude and distant, withdrawing to her room as soon as he arrived. Patsy seemed to George paranoid that Phoebe would hear them making love. I mean, so what if she did? She couldn't expect her mother to live like a nun. He'd made a lot of effort with Phoebe. He'd take her and Patsy to the movies, and then Phoebe would insist on sitting between them. He took them ice skating at Sky Rink and Phoebe began running a fever and had to be taken home. He was sorry he wasn't her father, but he wasn't and there wasn't much he could do about it, and he thought she was a controlling little bitch.

Patsy, their fight went, seemed only to see the needy child in this hulking creature with breasts and pimples. She was guilty about having broken up the putative happy home, so she couldn't recognize that Phoebe was tough as nails and had her own ways of getting exactly what she wanted, thank you very much.

"I don't think she gets anything she wants," said Patsy, in a rare moment of perception.

"Well, I know I don't get what I want," yelled George, which had made Patsy feel a shattering fear that she didn't even know what adequate lovemaking was, since she had just finished performing oral sex on him for twenty-five minutes by the clock, and rather well she had thought.

That particular fight was about Patsy not wanting to take a bath with George while Phoebe was in the house even though she was asleep.

In the end they had, at two in the morning, crept into the bathroom and taken a long, hot bubble bath by candlelight, whispering and suppressing giggles. Except for George's one whoop of laughter when he squeezed too hard on the soap and it shot across the room. They never knew if Phoebe had woken up or not, and they never would.

"So, how will Phoebe feel now, when she hears we're back together?" murmured George. He was still holding Patsy's hand, but now his fingers caressed the tender flesh of her inner forearm. She could barely speak she was so hypnotized with desire.

"Is that what's happened?" she whispered. "We're back together?"

They gazed at each other across the table. The jukebox played "Yesterday." George whispered, by way of answer, "Right now, I want you so much I doubt if I can walk across the room."

Patsy giggled. They sat holding hands, eyes locked, breathing heavily and fantasizing.

Finally Patsy whispered, "Try." And George, smiling, signaled for the check.

When they got up to cross the room George pretended to hobble. "They say a hard man is good to find," he said, and Patsy laughed, giddy with happiness.

"So, you're a lawyer, Mr. Leveque," said Madelaine Forbes. She had been introduced to him as Charlie, but she continued to call him Mr. Leveque, to indicate what she thought of his savaging her daughter during the divorce proceedings.

It was a warm night for February, one of those strange early tastes of spring that come sometimes after a cold snap. There were patches of gray snow everywhere, and bigger patches of brown mud and bare yellow lawn. Martha's parents preferred to dine early; the sky was just streaked with the last light of sunset. Tall ivory candles were burning on the table in spite of the evening sun, so that pools of day- and candlelight were reflected in the mahogany.

"Yes," said Charlie. They were having leg of lamb, cooked to fork-soft grayness. Bessie passed vinegar mint sauce in a silver gravy boat, and Martha watched a little nervously to see if Jack would serve himself in a way that suggested he knew how to be served. When the mint sauce came to her, she said, a little louder than necessary, "Thank you, Bessie." When Bessie next came around with the roasted potatoes, Jack took his and said, "Thank you, Bessie," and his mother smiled at him, though he pretended not to notice.

"Is divorce law your specialty?" asked Madelaine.

"No, ma'am," said Charlie. "I don't like it and I'm not very good at it."

"I see," she said. Fred, in the battered white high chair that had been Dick's and then Matthew's and then Martha's, dropped his fork on the carpet and looked over sadly at it, leagues below him on the floor. Charlie retrieved it and cut some meat for him. Fred hadn't slept much in the car and he was tired; Martha hoped they would get through dinner without major incident.

"Do you play golf?" Martha's father asked Charlie.

"I don't get much chance, but I love to."

"Well, maybe we'll play in the morning. Supposed to be nice weather." This, Martha knew, was a good sign. Martha didn't bring home a new man in her life lightly. Martha's four grandparents had been childhood friends, and at Thanksgiving and at Christmas Robert Forbes said grace, thanking his Lord for the gift of "a fabric of family affection." And after dinner on each of these days and on Easter and family birthdays, he went to the cemetery overlooking the sea to visit his mother and father, his brother Freddy who'd been killed in a riding accident as a child, Madelaine's mother and father, and a baby girl he and Madelaine had lost in infancy. At Christmas he brought their graves pine wreaths, and at Easter altar flowers after church.

So Martha did not bring home a new man casually, because her parents didn't like change, and they were not the easiest people in the world. But Charlie had clearly hit it off at once with her father.

"People ask me," said Dr. Forbes to him over their cocktails, "how did you get such a beautiful daughter? I say, 'Why, I married a beautiful woman.'"

"You did, indeed, sir," said Charlie. He had smiled to see his host enjoying the sight of Martha, with her bright smooth hair and warm smile, sitting in a big chair with Fred, and nearby his wife, with her ramrod-straight backbone and elaborate coif, who seemed to delight and amuse him, although many might have considered her more formidable than amusing.

"And it's very beautiful here," said Charlie. He and Martha had walked out toward the sea before dinner. "It must be wonderful in the spring when the forsythia blooms. And the rhododendron."

"And you should see my daffodils," Dr. Forbes added, pleased.

"I'd like to," said Charlie.

Madelaine thumped around under the table for the buzzer under the carpet that would ring in the kitchen and indicate they were ready for dessert. Jack asked his mother if he should take Fred off to play.

"Don't you want dessert?"

"What is it?"

"Floating island," said Madelaine. Baby Fred, who was at the end of his tether, started to cry.

"I'll get mine later," said Jack, and he scooped his brother out of the high chair. "May I be excused?"

"Yes, dear," said his grandmother. Jack galloped out of the room and down the hall, and in the distance they could hear Fred's weeping turn to happy gurgles.

"He'll get him overexcited," said Madelaine.

"No, he won't, Mother. He's going to read him *Uncle Wiggily*. They talked about it in the car."

"Fred is terribly bright for his age, isn't he? I don't think Jack liked *Uncle Wiggily* till he was four." This was untrue; Jack had read everything early and in fact could read *Uncle Wiggily* to himself when he was four.

"They both have sweet tempers," said Charlie.

"They do, don't they. Do you have children, Mr. Leveque?"

Martha looked at her mother, who ignored her.

"I have a daughter named Phoebe. She's sixteen."

"I see. And she lives with your wife?"

"My former wife. Yes."

"And where is she in school?"

"She was at Replogle. . . ."

"Oh, Replogle, that's a *fine* school. My roommate at Westover went to Replogle, you remember Aunt Honey, Martha. She had the most beautiful posture, Mr. Leveque, and she always said it was because they spent the first ten minutes of every gym class walking around the gym with books on their heads. They probably don't still do that. Aunt Honey's father was the one who was so famous he invented some new stuff that he thought would revolutionize the tire industry, but it turned out that it froze and broke in pieces below ten degrees. But I believe then it made a fortune being used inside golf balls. He killed himself some awful way. Robert, wasn't Honey's father the one who jumped out the window and landed on the doorman?"

Dr. Forbes took a while to answer this, as he had not been paying close attention. He had to finish chewing his lamb while he thought, and then swallowing seemed to be an extensive operation as well.

"Yes, I think it was. Or, no . . . it wasn't, that was old Jock Alderdice who landed on the doorman."

"Oh yes, you're right. Honey's building didn't have a doorman. Does your daughter like Replogle? She must love it."

"She's left it now. She goes to Cropp and Thatcher."

A pause.

"Cropp and Thatcher . . . where Jack goes," Charlie explained.

"Oh. Yes. You did tell me, didn't you, Martha. A daughter, Phoebe, and she goes to that school where Jack goes."

"Yes," said Martha. Her tone was a little terse.

"This is wonderful floating island," said Charlie. "I love floating island."

"Do they get along? Phoebe and Jack?"

"They seem to."

"You know that reminds me of what happened to the Pursegloves. Martha knows this story but you'll be interested, Mr. Leveque. The Pursegloves' daughter Laura was divorced several years ago, and she re-married a man who had a very attractive son, about three years older than her own daughter. Apparently the son and the daughter fell madly in love, and there wasn't a thing the parents could do, I mean they were right down the hall from each other, comings and goings at all hours of the night. Everyone was sick. Of course, that wasn't the worst of it. The boy, who was terribly attractive and quite a bit older, got tired of little Pammy after a while, well that's what you would expect. But then there they still were under the same roof. And he'd bring home new girl-friends and Pammy was just undone. She cried all the time. This went on for months, the boy was sorry, but what was he supposed to do. . . . I think Pammy actually had to go to a sanitarium for a while."

Martha and Charlie looked at each other. Madelaine's gaze blanketed both of them, like the headlights of a hunter jacking deer.

Madelaine said, "I suppose as a divorce lawyer you hear that sort of thing all the time."

Charlie said, "Not really."

Madelaine thumped around and found the buzzer under her feet, and Bessie tottered in.

"Dr. Forbes is finished, Bessie, you may clear. Thank you so much. We'll have coffee in the living room."

The four rose. "Please save some dessert for Jack, Bessie. He loves floating island."

"Oh does he," said Bessie. Usually what food returned to the kitchen from the table was never seen again, as Bessie wrapped it up and took it home to her pig.

As they walked into the living room, Madelaine took Martha's arm and said, "Tell me now, what do you hear from Gillis?"

At nine-thirty, Dr. and Mrs. Forbes said their goodnights. "You have everything you want, Mr. Leveque?"

"Yes, thank you."

"There's an extra comforter in the closet in your room. It does get chilly at that end of the house. And the shower in the boys' bathroom has been fixed. I hope you don't mind all of Dick's horse show ribbons."

"Not at all."

"I'm sure Martha will be up early with the children, but is there any special time you'd like to be called?"

"No, thank you, I'll be fine."

When they were alone, Martha and Charlie looked at each other. "Well," he said, "I certainly snowed her." They both laughed.

"I'm sorry," said Martha.

"Don't be silly. She was fond of Gillis, I gather."

"I guess. Well, he did do a good imitation of a charming son-in-law."

"Sometime describe to me how he did it."

"Oh, honey."

They held hands for a while in silence. Then Jack wandered in, with his dessert in a cracked plastic bowl. He reported that baby Fred was sleeping with a nearly bald stuffed bear that had belonged to Great-

Uncle Fred seventy years ago; Dr. Forbes had gone up and found it in the attic for him, and baby Fred was allowed to take it home. When Jack finished eating, they turned off the downstairs lights and all went up to bed.

"*H*ave at you!" cried Jaywalk from behind dark glasses at an overburdened lady making her way up the aisle of a swaying subway car. The car rattled and shook, so that anyone walking had to move hand over hand from pole to handle to keep from being thrown against other passengers. Jaywalk and Phoebe and Dime were slumped together on the seat, giggling. They had come from a late rehearsal of *The Three Musketeers*. The Four Muscatels, Jaywalk called them. Ernest and Julio, Bartels and Jaymes. Jaywalk was D'Artagnan, and all the musketeers were taking fencing lessons. Jaywalk was for some reason convulsed at the phrase "Have at you!" He said it in class when asked a question he couldn't answer. He said it in the hall, starting brief duels, so the high school was filled between classes with youths fencing their way down the hall with pencils.

"Have at you!" he greeted the overburdened woman again, and then hopped up to give her his seat. She looked up, surprised. She had not noticed him till this moment, and she was not used to having six-feet-five-inch boys in black leather give up their seats to her. She sank down beside Dime, settling a large bag between her feet and wrestling with a purse and an umbrella. "That's nice of you. Thank you," she said in a voice that sounded a bit as if it were a 45 rpm played at 33. To her astonishment, and Phoebe's, Jaywalk replied with his hands in rapid sign language. The woman smiled, as if she had just remembered that life was not merely made up of cold and silence and rude crowded subway cars, but in fact of mystical transformation and hilarious surprises.

"Are you deaf, too?" The woman signed back.

"No," he signed, "my friend is."

"Him?" She indicated Dime.

"No, I have two friends," signed Jaywalk, and he and the woman both laughed.

"You sign well," she said with her hands.

"Thank you." The train pulled into the Astor Place Station and Dime and Phoebe got up. "Don't take any wooden nickels," Jaywalk's hands said to the woman. She smiled and signed back, "I take anything I can get."

The three kids darted off the train, Jaywalk laughing.

Phoebe asked, "How the hell did you learn that?"

"Bernie."

Bernie was a deaf boy in the freshman class who was also in a wheel-chair.

"How do you know Bernie?"

"I asked him to teach me to sign. I like languages."

Phoebe was mesmerized. She didn't care much about languages, but she loved secrets. She loved the idea of being able to carry on a conversation right in front of people and not have them know what she was saying.

"Bernie's cool," said Dime.

"He *is?*" Phoebe had always assumed he was a nerd.

"Yeah. He's a funny little dude."

"Can you sign, too?"

"No," said Dime, "I'm too stupid."

"It's really easy, man. I can teach you."

"I doubt it."

"Can you teach me?" asked Phoebe.

"Sure."

They started up Eighth Street to the park, where they were going to hang out until time for *The Rocky Horror Picture Show.*

The kids who hung out in Washington Square Park could map it into territories, like the land of Oz, with the central fountain for the Emerald City. In the East, behind the statue of Garibaldi, lay the Land of the Hippies . . . people in patched jeans with long hair and colorful beads and bandanas. None too clean, nor necessarily kindly, but pacific. Even if you knew hippies, the way Crapp and Thrasher knew the two Jennies, you didn't know them. They had friends you didn't know. They did things like get into vans and go to Rhode Island for a Grateful Dead concert and not come back for a week. Their underworld occupied a slightly different plane in time and space than the rest of the territories. You never quite knew, when they got in a van and went to Rhode Island and didn't come back for a week, whether the Dead concert they went to took place in the 1980s or the 1960s.

West of Garibaldi, in what used to be the volleyball court (and sometimes still was used for volleyball, if someone brought a net) lay the land of the Skaters. Skating could involve roller skates, but mostly it meant skateboards. The skaters whipped back and forth, around and through the pedestrians who passed over the park without belonging to any of its nations. They threw their boards in the air, leaped up, and landed on the boards, rolling. They did, or attempted, a variety of other surprising variations, almost all of them noisy. Normally dressed skaters were just Skaters. Skaters in punk regalia were called Thrashers. They were very loud. Skaters were rarely older than fifteen. Mostly they'd been using their boards for serious transportation for years.

In the center, around the fountain, was a free zone. There were panhandlers, there were tourists, there were children. There were homeless men and women here; there was one guy who liked to sit facing the arch with his leg extended and his shoe off, revealing that he had only half a foot. It could be sort of a sport to watch tourists catch sight of him, to see who stared, and who flinched and looked away. The half-foot guy himself didn't seem to care. There was a woman with a lot of things in a baby carriage. She usually wore several sweaters and a rather good polo coat. She walked slowly around the fountain looking at the ground, and when she found a butt of any type unsquashed, she picked it up and lit it and smoked it.

There were homeboys with huge boxes, playing rap music. Homeboys wore sweatpants or jeans in colors like royal blue or purple. They wore sneakers with jumbo laces, or no laces at all. They liked little round seamen's caps, and gold teeth and gold chains like ropes with their names on a gold plate. Homeboys lived, a Crapp and Thrasher kid would tell you, in the outer boroughs or in Alphabet City. They had jobs like delivery boy. They were not going to take off their colorful clothes and go on to Amherst in a few years, and there was no affinity and no love lost between them and the white part-time street kids, no matter how alienated the demeanor of the latter. But they occupied adjacent turf—evenings and weekends, the homeboys and the part-time street kids—with plenty of potential for kindling and combustion.

The whole park, day and night, was a floating drug boutique. The sales representatives for this product were mostly large, mostly black, mostly predatory. They lounged alone or in groups, or paced the park chanting softly, so that only as they passed very close could you hear that they were offering "smoke . . . sense . . . smoke. . . ."

Sense was sinsimilla, seed-free female marijuana plants that become intensely resinous in their hopeless attempt to attract male plants. All street dealers claimed to have it; few or none of them did, though they'd be glad to charge you plenty for ordinary pot that they called sense. Jaywalk knew this because his father, Gary, an ex-drummer turned recording engineer, tended a tiny marijuana farm in boxes on the sunny south window ledge in Tribeca. He sang to his plants and tenderly watered them, and pottered about gazing at them and giving them little dramas and personalities in his mind. He had taught Jaywalk everything he knew about plant husbandry and harvest. Gary, in his purple-tinted granny glasses, who rose at two in the afternoon and retired at six in the morning, was never going to be the kind of daddy who played softball with his little one. Gary was glad that agriculture was a hobby he and his son could share.

When tourists from out of town passed through the park, they looked at the hippies and the homeboys and the hip-hop kids and the punks and they thought, Who *are* these people? Where are their parents? This was normally a rhetorical question, but for the record this is where a few of their parents were.

Dime's father was dead.

Gary Walker, Jaywalk's father, was at a recording session for a soft drink commercial. He had a girl group singing a fifties-style jingle, and he was on his feet dancing as he ran the thirty-two track board. He hadn't seen or talked to Jaywalk in a week.

Jaywalk's mother, Peggy, was at home with her husband watching the *MacNeil-Lehrer Report* and thinking about finger paint. Peggy taught kindergarten. She thought Jaywalk was spending the night with Dime.

Phoebe's mother, Patsy, was at the movies with her on-again off-again on-again boyfriend George. She was giddy with happiness, bubbling with laughter, and horny as hell. She hoped Phoebe wouldn't come home too early.

Phoebe's father, Charlie, was watching Dime's mother, Martha, cut baby Fred's hair. The baby tried to sit still, but it was hard for him. Martha kept telling him what a good boy he was. Suddenly she exclaimed, "Okay! Jump down, run all the way to the kitchen, and then run back!" Fred, flooded with purpose, clambered down, rushed to the kitchen, and thundered back on short fat legs, smiling proudly. He climbed back onto the stool and sat quite still while Martha finished. Charlie thought suddenly of Phoebe at two, whose silky straight blond hair had never been cut. He remembered her sitting for a portrait, and that when she fidgeted her mother snapped at her and made her cry.

He couldn't hug Phoebe at the moment, so when the haircut was over, he hugged Fred.

Phoebe and Jaywalk and Dime were pacing, three abreast, down Fifty Avenue toward the huge arch at the north edge of the park. They had their arms around each other, three musketeers, and they cleared the sidewalk as they went. The streets of Greenwich Village were brightly lit, and before them the center of the park had an aura of being an island of weird daylight under a dome of night.

Both boys were dressed in black jackets and jackboots, and it had been Phoebe's fancy, preparatory to seeing *Rocky Horror,* to use the stage makeup during rehearsal to get herself up as a Goth. (A Goth was a gothic punk, a girl with heavy eye makeup and lots of chains. Phoebe's chains were made of safety pins from the wardrobe department and her hair had been made to stand up straight from the top of her head. The boys thought she looked beautiful.)

"I've always been afraid of the park at night," said Phoebe.

"George Washington addressed his troops here! Henry James walked here! Delmore Schwartz sat here on a bench staring into space. . . ."

"Who's Delmore Schwartz?"

"Exactly!" Jaywalk exclaimed. "Delmore Schwartz sat here on benches, staring into space and wondering, Who's Delmore Schwartz?"

"Listen, finish this sentence. 'I've always been afraid of . . .'"

"Being seen," said Jaywalk. Phoebe and Dime looked at him and he looked surprised himself.

"I've always been afraid of . . ." Phoebe poked Dime.

"Chickens," he said.

"Chickens?"

"Yeah."

"You mean, like Kentucky Fried?"

"No. Chickens, with feathers. In flocks. I just think they're *horrible,* man. I think they're going to peck me all over and bite out my eyes."

"Do you know any chickens?"

"I don't think so. I don't know for sure that I've ever seen one."

"Except Big Bird."

"Is he a chicken?"

A small family was coming toward them, also three abreast. The man and the woman wore matching Chesterfield coats. Between them, holding their hands, was a girl of perhaps eight. In about four seconds there would have been a confrontation for control of the sidewalk, but before it happened, Jaywalk stopped and swung his end of the line backward as if playing crack the whip. He cleared the sidewalk for the little family as if opening a gate and finished the move with a grin and D'Artagnan's bow. The family hurried past. The mother looked back, staring at Phoebe.

"You're welcome," called Jaywalk.

"And how are things in New Jersey?" Dime added.

"My grandmother brought me here once," said Phoebe. "She brought me here in a taxi and let me walk once around the outside of the park to see the beatniks. Then she put me into another taxi and took me away."

The boys hooted with laughter. "Beatniks!"

They stood under the arch and watched a group of little hip-hop boys do a rap. It was straight out of Run DMC, but they did it well and they were very small. Dime put some money in the hat they had left on the ground, and the three went on.

"I used to come here after school," said Jaywalk. "I spent my whole life here. This is *mine,* man. I love the park."

"Rock . . . trips . . ." offered a ragged-looking Rasta as they passed.

"I had a little plastic motorcycle, and I used to ride it up and down the hills."

"What hills?"

"I'm taking you."

Phoebe noticed something. She was not afraid of the park tonight. She was armored like a triceratops in her stand-up hair and her black Goth eyes, and she felt she couldn't be hurt.

The hills were in the southwest quadrant of the park.

They were artificial mounds covered with some rubbery compound, so that if you fell down while running or biking or skating you wouldn't be scraped to ribbons. There was a flat grassless expanse adjoining where children could play catch or Frisbee on a small scale while mothers watched from the bench, and next to that there was a sort of jungle gym construction made of timbers bolted together, that Jaywalk and Dime called the Thing. They were taking Phoebe to the Thing.

The Thing was like a playhouse inside. A structure, a safe house. You could see out of it, but it was hard in the dark for outsiders to see in. Phoebe and Dime and Jaywalk climbed up to the top and sat astride the walls.

"Have at you!" shouted Jaywalk.

"I'm hungry," added Dime.

"How much money do we have?"

They took out all their money and counted. The total was $24.70. They needed $5.00 apiece for the movie and $1.00 apiece for the subway. That left $6.70 for food or beers or popcorn or dope. They decided on three hot dogs and a joint to share. Dime was elected to do the shopping. When he had gone, Jaywalk lit a cigarette and gave one to Phoebe. They sat on the ground and leaned against the timbers looking at the stars, talking until Dime came back.

Jaywalk saw a figure approach the Thing. "Have at you!"

"*C'est moi,*" said Dime. "There's a kid out there on the hills doing crack." He handed the food in to them and clambered in himself, and they settled down to eat. "He looks about forty but I asked him how old he was and he said twelve."

"But hey, he's fresh."

When they finished the hot dogs, Phoebe wiped her hands on Dime's jeans.

"I didn't want juice on my clothes," she said.

"Makes sense," said Dime. They lit their joint and passed it around until it was burning their lips. Then they went out to float around the park.

The Rocky Horror Picture Show didn't start till midnight. Phoebe would miss her curfew and be grounded but she was going to do it anyway because she was a Virgin, the only kid in the crew who had never been to *Rocky.* Anyway her mother was with George tonight and Phoebe didn't want to be around him.

They were thinking of walking over to B. Dalton to read cartoon books, when a girl sitting on the ground under a tree asked Phoebe what time it was.

The girl was maybe fourteen. Her guy was older, bigger. They were both very clean and scrubbed. They were leaning together under this tree on the cold ground, and there seemed to be something wrong with them. For instance, the girl who wanted to know what time it was was wearing a big chronograph.

"It's nine-fifteen," said Phoebe.

"Oooooooohhhh," said the girl, wisely. She and the boy looked at each other. They nodded a few times and then looked back at Dime and Phoebe and Jaywalk, a hedge of punks towering over them.

"What's wrong with your hair?" the boy asked Phoebe, suddenly.

"What do you mean?"

"It's all . . ." He was not apparently in a highly verbal mode. He finished the sentence by indicating, with his hand pulling at his own hair, that hers was standing up all over her head.

"Yes," said Phoebe.

"What's wrong with your watch?" Dime asked the girl.

"*My* watch?" The two on the ground looked at each other. Then they both looked at the girl's wrist. She held it up, revealing her watch. They appeared amazed. After a while she said, "Oh. There it is." And the two began to laugh. When they finished, the boy looked up, suddenly worried, and said, "We don't know where we put our car, either."

"Your *car?*"

"Yes. Our car."

"You're not planning to drive tonight."

The two looked at each other again. Apparently they were.

"Where are you from?"

"Arden Forest," said the boy.

"You can't go home tonight," said Jaywalk.

There was a silence.

"No?" asked the boy.

"You're tripping, man. What were you going to say? Mom! Dad! I'm home! Where's the door?"

Molly and Scott looked at each other. It appeared that this thought had, in fact, occurred to them independently, if too late.

"When did you drop it?"

"I think . . . I think . . . an hour ago."

"You're not going to make any sense at all until tomorrow."

"Oh," said the boy. "Oh dear," said the girl and they both started to laugh.

"Didn't you *know* that?"

Molly and Scott looked at each other. Of course, they seemed to have known it, but seemed not to have taken it into account.

"Where did you get it?"

"Well," said Scott, marshaling some coherence, for here was a subject on which he felt vehement. "Well *first,* we gave a large Negro twenty dollars. And he told us to wait right here and then he went away and came back with these squares of paper, and we swallowed them. Then we went and sat in the car for fucking hours."

"The car!" Molly exclaimed. She had remembered about the car. Not where it was, just how it was to sit in it. Like having your own house on wheels that you can go sit in.

"And when you came back to the park he was gone," said Jaywalk. Scott nodded. "Then we went over there." He gestured toward Garibaldi. The hippies.

"A guy asked us how much money we had and we told him and he said, 'Okay, give me all of it.'"

Scott and Molly were looking up anxiously into the three faces. They were beginning to get upset. These nice young people, their new friends with whom they seemed to have been chatting for several hours, seemed concerned about something. Maybe things weren't going to work out well.

"Well," said Jaywalk after a time, "good luck . . ." and they drifted off. Dime and Jaywalk talked a little about how unfuckingbelievably naïve those two must be. Or something. And about how long it was going to be before they figured out what kind of trouble they were in.

"What will happen to them?"

"They don't have any money. They can't stay in the park; they'll be arrested. They can sit in their car if they can find it, but they'll be very cold by morning."

"Unless they run the engine, then they'll run out of gas and they don't have any money."

"They can sit in coffee shops."

"If they have money for coffee."

"They must."

"Can you imagine the scene in Arden Forest in the morning?"

"How old do you think that girl was?"

"Probably fourteen."

"Jesus."

The three walked on to the bookstore in silence. They went in and spent some time getting warm in the magazine section. Then Phoebe said, "Let's go at least make sure they have money for coffee," and they all put back what they were reading and started back to the park.

Molly and Scott had disappeared. They weren't under the tree, they weren't near the arch, they weren't anywhere near the fountain. They weren't with the hippies. Not that the hippies would let two such obvious trippers hang there.

Dime finally spotted Scott behind the stinking brick bunker that housed the men's toilets. He had fallen into rapt contemplation of the pattern made by the bricks in the wall. When he looked up to see his three new friends he seemed very pleased.

"Oh, wow," he said. Phoebe was amazed. She'd never seen anyone tripping before and she didn't expect it to be so much like a parody of a movie from the sixties.

Jaywalk introduced himself and Dime and Phoebe. Scott told them his name.

"And the girl?"

"Her name is . . . Molly."

"Where is she?"

"I don't know."

"You don't know?"

"No. She started to cry and told me to go away."

"Why?"

"She was upset because the fountain was empty. She wanted to walk on water."

"Why did she tell you to go away?"

"She said she doesn't know me."

"*Does* she know you?"

Scott considered. "Not very well."

Phoebe reported that the girl was not in the bathroom. They told Scott to stay where he was and they separated to search the park. It was Phoebe who found Molly in the opposite corner of the park, in the playground. She had crawled under a large steel geodesic dome where children climb in the daytime. She was shaking with terror and her eyes stared wildly. She wouldn't come out, so Phoebe crawled in to where she was and found that Molly was so frightened her neck and jaws were clamped rigid.

"It's all right," Phoebe whispered, but Molly shook her head.

"You see something?" And Molly nodded wildly.

"There's nothing out there. It's only me. It's all right." She was wrong that it was all right; what was out there was the dark, but Molly couldn't say that. Phoebe had to hug her and rock her for a long time before she could get her to come out to find the boys.

Neither Scott nor Molly would tell their last names. They would not call home and they would not let anyone else call. They did have enough money to buy four cups of coffee, but that would not rent them stools for the rest of the night. Besides, Molly was clearly way underage and she couldn't stop crying. Sooner or later, someone would call the cops.

"Let's take them to Gary's," said Jaywalk. They stopped at a phone booth; there was no answer at Gary's. They hailed a cab. It took four tries to find a driver who would take them, but they finally hit a Rastafarian in a Checker.

The country club dining room was all green. The carpet was the limey color of a putting green in spring. The upholstery of the dining chairs was kelly green with a white bamboo pattern boldly printed on it. The arms and backs of the chairs were wood, fashioned to look like bamboo and painted a gray-brown putty color. The heavy draperies at the windows were a forest green, like the blackish pine trees that hedged the golf course. Outside the French windows, which were open to the terrace all summer but now were locked against the chill spring night, the black outlines of trees were stark against the fence of the tennis courts.

Connie and Dave were having a candlelight dinner. This morning, Dave had come closer to actually hitting Connie than he ever had before. In the moment of barely, just barely, deflecting himself he had picked up the expensive camera her parents had sent her for her birthday and smashed it against the wall.

Fortunately, the kids were downstairs having breakfast. In the silence in the master bedroom that followed this event, Connie backed away from Dave, her angry terrified eyes fixed on his face, and locked herself in the bathroom. After a while she heard Dave's voice in the kitchen, and then his car starting in the driveway.

Early in the afternoon, Connie had called Dave at his office. He had sounded like a frightened little boy when he answered the phone. She said, "Honey . . . we can't go on like this." He said, "No," in a guarded tone. Then he waited. "I think we better try to mend some fences," she had said. "Okay," he said. He'd expected her to say she was going home to her mother's.

Feeling a rush of maternal tenderness for him, Connie had hung up and called a sitter for William, and made a reservation at the club.

Dave had been unfaithful to her for years; Connie knew that. He had actually been unfaithful even while they were courting, but Connie assumed it would stop when they were married. And then for years, she had thought every time it happened that he was so sorry, so shocked at himself when he realized the damage he had done, that it would never happen again. They had had a couple of good years after the twins were born—after they started nursery school, to be exact—when Connie had more time for herself again, and got the house back in order and started cooking again and going to exercise classes twice a week. But then something odd happened. Suddenly Dave had developed a problem. Often he couldn't have an erection at all, and when he could he couldn't maintain it past penetration. This was so bewildering and so unlike Dave, who was given to referring to the contents of his briefs as Old Eveready, that neither of them said a word about it.

Connie thought if she mentioned it she would make it worse. Instead she asked delicate offhand questions about how thing were going at work, seeking the source of his stress, and read books like *Passages* about midlife crises (for which he was, however, still too young) and magazine articles about "The New Impotence" (which laid the blame on the terrifying phenomenon of feminism and the new woman, neither of which had much to do with a full-time housewife and mother of twins).

Then one evening when they had a date to go to the movies with the Rathbuns (and Connie hadn't been out after dark with grown-ups to talk to for ten days), Dave had called to say he had to work all night because his secretary had fouled up the leases for an important closing. Connie went to the movies with the Rathbuns anyway but felt uncomfortable because they were golfing friends of Dave's and she really didn't know them very well. And when Dave came home at two in the morning, he had his socks on inside out.

They'd had a blistering battle that had lasted six days and cured Dave's impotence for the time being. Violent anger excited him greatly and for a while he was a hell of a guy in bed. Things seemed to settle back into a pattern they both could live with after that. In fact, things went so smoothly they both sort of felt at a loss, so they had another baby.

Twice in the nine years since William's birth, the impotence had returned. The first time, the situation came to a head because the girlfriend, who couldn't have been very bright, actually started calling him at the house and leaving coy messages with Connie.

The second time, Connie just ignored it and the affair must have ended of its own accord, because in time their sex life resumed, but in the manner of tracer rounds—there'd be a series of blanks, and then occasionally a live bullet. But Dave was distant and belligerent to her and to William almost all the time now when the family was alone. He'd never taken to William, who just wasn't his kind of guy, but he wouldn't acknowledge anything difficult or provocative in his behavior—either the infidelity, or the hostility to his own son. He was fine. He was Dave.

Oddly, this attitude was so illogical, in the manner of a child with chocolate all over his face who howls fiercely, "I did not either eat any candy" and truly grieves that he is not believed, that Connie found herself weirdly touched by it. When he hurt her, part of her—the mother in her—wanted to comfort him, as she would comfort an actual child overwhelmed by real life who resorts to fantasy to comfort himself or explain the unbearable. I'm not lonely and powerless, I have a magic stallion in my backyard. I didn't forget my homework, the baby-sitter accidentally took it home with her.

So instead of packing his bags and putting them out in the driveway, Connie had arranged a date with Dave, to try again to talk about their mutual frustration. She had told him she loved him and he had gotten tears in his eyes and told her he loved her, too. "You're a lot to live up to, you know," he had said.

She took his hand in the candlelight. She was just about to tell him that she admired the courage with which he battled his demons, when the Peabodys stopped by their table and they all had a noisy recap of last Sunday morning's paddle tennis tournament. Then their prime rib arrived, and the Peabodys left, and sometime over coffee they got back to the subject. It was amazing how warm and affectionate Dave could be, right up to the moment she mentioned William.

"Sweetheart . . . you have to pay more attention to him. You don't have to do anything special, just listen to him. Spend time with him."

Silence.

"I spend plenty of time with him."

"Oh, David! Be real!"

"Oh, Constance! Who says *you* know what real is?"

"Dr. Green says he needs—"

"Oh, fuck Dr. Green . . . she isn't even a doctor. . . ."

"She's a Ph.D. Oh, is not! Is too! Could we please talk like adults?"

"I am. I said, fuck her."

There was another silence.

"I'll pay more attention to him," said Dave finally, "when you start paying the kind of attention I want, to me." Meaning, you don't come on to me in bed.

Another silence.

"Dave," said Connie between clenched teeth, "it's very hard for me to feel turned on to a man who behaves like a four-year-old to his own son. It's just not very sexy."

"I feel like I'm talking to Nurse Jane Fuzzywuzzy. I try to talk to you about our sex life and all you talk about is the children."

"You can't separate them! You can't take a system apart! This is a marriage!"

"Oh, bullshit. The children have nothing to do with you in bed!"

"Dave . . . our son starts smashing things and stops talking for three weeks! He gets in fights with other children! Something's *wrong*, this is serious!"

"Something's wrong with *him*, I'll give you that."

"Oh, for chrissake. Just tell me one thing, Dave. Why don't we talk about our sex life at the shrink, where it might do some good?"

"Oh, that's a *good* idea. You'd enjoy that, wouldn't you? You don't want to get it on, but you'd like to talk about it. . . ."

They were now at a complete stalemate. They had at least had a bit of a cry, and a good piece of rare roast beef, so it was time to go home. In silence they retrieved their coats, and did so.

The baby-sitter had finished watching *Dallas* when they came in. She reported that William went to bed quietly at nine-thirty, and that Ruth and her little friend Jeanie, who was spending the night, had just finished making popcorn, (As the oil was uncapped on the counter, the unwrapped remains of a stick of butter was half melted on its paper in the middle of the stove, and the unwashed pots were on the kitchen table, Connie could have deduced that they had made popcorn.)

"And what's Molly doing?"

"Molly?" asked the sitter, as if she never heard of her. Connie waited.

"Molly isn't here," the sitter explained, as if Connie must be deficient. Imagine her not knowing where her own daughter wasn't.

"She has an eleven o'clock curfew," Connie explained back, rather tartly. Imagine the sitter not knowing that Molly must have come home by now.

"I'll ask Ruth," said Connie, and left Dave to pay the sitter, a lumpish student from the local business college.

Ruth and Jeanie were lying on Ruth's bed on their stomachs with a comforter over them, giving a dramatic reading of a *True Romance* comic.

"Oh, Brad, I thought . . . I thought I had lost you!" cried Jeanie, and they both giggled helplessly. "But then I moved the couch to vacuum, and there you were with the other furballs. . . ."

Connie smiled at them from the doorway, and knocked on the frame to let them know she was there.

The twins had the biggest bedroom in the house. It had a separate alcove that was probably once a dressing room but which the girls had used as a playroom. It was still piled with toys they hadn't used for years but wouldn't let go of. Games of Candyland and Chutes and Ladders, pick-up sticks and Stratego and Clue. Dolls and stuffed animals and checkers and chess and Chinese checkers and Ruth's collection of trading cards and Molly's millions of jacks. One thing about being a twin, you always had someone around who was the right age for the games you wanted to play. There must have been five hundred playing cards here from pooched decks, destroyed in endless games of Spit and War.

"Hi, Mom."

"Hi, Mrs. Justice."

"Hi. Did you have a good evening?"

"Yes."

"Yes."

"Where's Molly?"

Pause.

"Why? What time is it?" Ruth sat up and craned to see the clock radio on the bedside table. Clearly, it was after eleven. Ruth and Jeanie looked at each other.

Martha *woke in* the darkness, knowing something was wrong. A moment later the phone rang. She slipped out of bed and ran, barefoot in the dark, to the kitchen phone. Her heart was in her mouth; a call in the middle of the night had to be the worst kind of news. She'd gone to sleep early. Where was Jack?

"Hello?"

"Mom."

"Oh, *honey.* Where are you?"

"I'm at Jaywalk's dad's."

"Are you all right?"

"Yes."

"What time is it?"

"About three."

Now Charlie, naked and warm, was beside her in the dark. He put a hand on her bare shoulder and she moved against him. She could feel his skin and his warm rough hair against her back.

"Why the hell aren't you home? Is Jaywalk all right?"

"Yes, but we have a problem." Now she could hear the fear in Jack's voice.

"What is it? You promised to be home at one-thirty, Jack. Isn't that when the movie ends?" She was beginning to feel cross that he had frightened her.

"We need help."

"Where's John's father?"

"I don't know. Look, we didn't go to the movie. We met these kids in the park who were tripping and we brought them here."

"Why?"

"Because they were in trouble. The girl is about ten. First she was crying because she was scared of the dark. Now she's shaking and blithering and not making any sense at all, and we don't know what to do. She feels all cold and we can't get her warm."

"Who are they? Are they friends of yours?"

"No! Mom, we need help. Can you come?"

Martha, thoroughly upset, stood silent.

"Give me the address." She took it, then she hung up and explained the situation to Charlie, although neither of them understood it very clearly.

"Have they been doing drugs too? Jack and Jaywalk?"

"I don't think so."

"What time is it?"

Martha turned on a light over the counter and they looked at the clock. 3:20.

"I can't bear raising children in this town. It's too frightening."

"In this town. In this decade," he said. "I'll go."

Martha nodded. Charlie went to pull on his clothes, and Martha, after putting on a robe, put a kettle on for tea and then went to check the baby to be reassured that he was there, that he was breathing.

Charlie, hurriedly dressed, came to put his arms around her. She said, "Thank you."

"You're welcome. I'll call you."

She nodded and Charlie found his coat and his keys and went out.

The loft of Jaywalk's father was on a deserted street above a meat wholesaler. The streets ran at odd angles in this part of town, and at this time of night, they were utterly deserted. Once sure of the address and in the door, Charlie ran up the two flights of stairs, and Jack met him on the landing. He looked drawn and frightened. Charlie could see for himself that Jack was sober in every sense of the word; he put a hand on the boy's shoulder and together they went inside.

In the loft was a wall of state-of-the-art sound equipment, two mattresses on the floor, and Gary's clothes on a galvanized-pipe rack and in boxes. This was not the home of a man finely attuned to domestic pleasures. The kitchen consisted of a narrow stove and some open plywood shelves with fabric thumbtacked on to act as curtains. The bathroom had a flush and a stall shower, which you could see because it had no door.

On the larger of the mattresses Molly lay curled into a ball. Her eyes were open as if staring at something. She was stiff and still. Jack's friend John Walker, who was incredibly tall, was sitting beside Molly on the bed, but when Charlie came in he got up and went to stand near him as if to express his relief at Charlie's presence.

"She was yelling and talking and not making sense before," said Jack.

"What did she take?"

"Acid."

"When?"

"Six hours ago."

"Is there such a thing as bad acid?"

"I think there's bad anything."

Charlie felt Molly's pulse and her forehead. "I don't know what I'm feeling for," he said.

"Do you think she should go to a hospital?"

"Yes," said Charlie.

"So do we."

"How do we do that?"

"We'll get a taxi."

"What about him?" The boys indicated a figure Charlie hadn't noticed before. Scott was sitting at the other end of the loft, staring out the window. He rocked and swayed a little, as if he were listening to music.

"He took the same stuff?"

Jack and Jaywalk nodded.

"Do your parents know where you are?" Charlie asked Jaywalk.

"They think I'm at Jack's."

"You'll have to stay with that one, I guess. Please call your parents and tell them where you are, and then call Martha and tell her we've gone to St. Vincent's." Charlie picked up Molly, who didn't seem to notice, and Jack hurried to open the door for him.

On the deserted street, they debated where they might find a cab. Their footsteps seemed to echo as if in a canyon. They decided to go to West Broadway, where once in a while, in fog and stillness, a taxi cruised downtown toward the Odeon, looking for revelers. After a few minutes, a lone cab appeared like a salmon rising in an empty river. Jack stepped into the street and waved. The cab slowed, but when it got near enough for the driver to see Jack well, in his black clothes and boots, it speeded up again and passed them.

"Shit," said Charlie.

"Let me take her, you hail the next one," said Jack. Charlie transferred Molly into the boy's arms, and Jack stayed on the sidewalk in shadow until the next car stopped for them.

But this driver, an Arab in a yachting cap, would have stopped for them if they'd been wielding Uzis. The door was barely closed before he jammed his foot on the gas, and on the excuse of their errand, he drove like a madman, zooming up Sixth Avenue, crashing on the brakes as they came to a red light. He seemed to speak no English when they asked him to slow down.

"The operative word here is 'speed,'" said Jack, bracing himself. Charlie nodded, grim.

Jack asked, "Do you think she's going to die?"

"I have no fucking idea. I hope *we* aren't. Do you know her name?"

"Molly."

"That's all?"

Jack explained how they came to be involved. He didn't mention that Phoebe had been with them. The driver slammed on the brakes at the emergency entrance to St. Vincent's, throwing them against the front seat.

Inside, as they were trying to explain who they thought Molly was, and what they thought was wrong with her, the room, dazzlingly bright, exploded into activity as a boy of fourteen, unconscious and covered with blood, was wheeled in on the run, strapped to a gurney. Finally, taking Charlie's name and address and Martha's number, the admitting nurse gave up trying to do further paperwork on Molly, and a very young woman who looked as if she'd had five minutes' sleep in the last week came to examine her. She took Molly's pulse, listened to her heartbeat, pulled back her eyelids to look at her eyes, and briskly gave her a shot.

"Is she going to be all right?" asked Jack.

"I have no idea," said the doctor, who seemed to resent the question. And she gave the signal for Molly to be rolled away.

Patsy *wasn't sure* what woke her. It was a moonless night and would have been black as pitch, except that in New York all nights have a yellowish glow from electric lights trapped under a dome of atmosphere. The apartment was still except for the occasional snore from George, whose breath smelled of beer and the Bangladesh curry they had eaten for dinner. Patsy hadn't liked to tell George that hot food gave her fever dreams.

She lay awake with a feeling of unease, afraid to turn over too often for fear of waking George, wishing she could put on a light and read for a bit. The window was open and a breeze moved the curtains; a bolt of panic shot through her as, at first, she thought there was an animal moving.

She lay still, hoping that sleep would return, and growing instead more tense as the minutes ticked past. The clock by the bed said it was 3:30. An hour later, it was still only 3:37. Patsy felt sweat begin to prickle beneath her arms, and the sheets beneath her seemed to burn. After another hour, which registered on the clock as twelve minutes, she slipped carefully out of bed and felt her way across the black room. At the door, she kicked her toes painfully against the leg of a chair where George had draped his clothes. Sucking air between her teeth to keep from swearing, she slipped out.

The living room was not as deep black as the bedroom; there was light there from a streetlamp below. Patsy moved silently to the cabinet where she kept her liquor; she didn't want George to wake up and find her having a snort by herself in the middle of the night. She opened the cabinet door. She squatted and felt the bottles till she located by shape the brandy. She had gotten it partway out without so much as clinking it against another bottle, when she realized she wasn't alone in the room. She had sensed, and then distinctly heard, a footstep.

She turned. She saw the black spiky figure in the doorway; she screamed. Simultaneously the creature screamed too, and Patsy leaped up in terror as bottles crashed to the slate floor. She staggered and stepped on a slice of broken glass and screamed again with pain.

The lights flared on, and there, stiff with fear and blinded by the light, but staring at Patsy, was her daughter.

"Phoebe!" yelled Patsy.

"I thought you were a burglar!" howled Phoebe.

"What the hell have you done to your hair?"

Phoebe put her hand to her head. She had forgotten what she looked like.

"And what the *hell* are you doing up at four in the morning?"

At this point, George, dressed in his shorts, appeared at the door from the bedroom. Both turned to stare at him.

"Why, Phoebe. Don't you look pretty."

"Answer me, Phoebe! What the *hell* are you doing prowling around at this hour?"

"She's trying to sneak in," said George, as if stating the obvious.

"You mean you're just coming in *now?*" bellowed Patsy.

"Glad you didn't wait up," said Phoebe.

"What *do* you have in your hair, Phoebe?" asked George, feigning amusement.

"It's called gel, George." Everyone was talking at high volume.

"Jell-O?"

"Goddammit, Phoebe, I'm *ashamed* of you!"

"I'm pretty proud of *you,* too, Mom, up to your ankles in booze."

Patsy leaped across the room and slapped her hard, and yelled with pain at the same time, for the cut in her foot was quite deep and she left a bloody footprint on the pale straw rug. Phoebe slapped her back.

"Bitch!" yelled Patsy.

"Takes one to know one!" yelled Phoebe.

George began to laugh. "Oh god, this is wonderful!"

"Shut up, asshole!" Patsy turned on him. Her rage was towering.

"Oh, okay, okay," said George, backing away, still laughing. "I'll shut up. I'll shut up and I'll get out of here, and you and your attractive daughter can stand here and scream at each other like cats in heat."

"Good riddance," snarled Phoebe.

"*You* shut up!" Patsy turned on her.

"Make me!"

"George, what are you doing!"

He was back from the bedroom, having pulled on his pants and shirt. He sat down and hurriedly put on his socks and shoes.

"Maybe everyone else you know likes to be told to shut up, since you do it so often." He stood up, strapping on his watch.

"Oh come *on*, George! Stop it!"

"I am going to stop it," he said, laughing as if it were all very droll. "I don't like screamers, I don't like being called an asshole, and I've got pleasanter ways of getting laid. Hope you can say the same." He was heading for the door.

"Well, *fuck* you!" Patsy couldn't believe this was happening.

"Thank you for your interest," he said, still laughing. And then he was gone.

Patsy stood for a minute. She glared at Phoebe with a burning red heat. Then she picked up an ashtray and threw it at the door, where it thudded disappointingly to the floor. Then Patsy burst into tears, and sobbing, rushed to her bedroom and slammed the door with a violence that seemed to shake the building.

Phoebe stood still in the sudden silence. Then, soundlessly she too began to cry. Leaving the lights burning, she turned and went to her room.

I*t was nearly* five when Charlie and Jack got home from the hospital. Martha was sitting in the kitchen, drinking her second pot of tea.

Jack, so tired from strain as well as sleeplessness that he could barely speak, went straight to bed. Charlie and Martha put their arms around each other.

"It's hard to raise children by yourself," said Martha. Meaning, I'm glad you were here, I'm so glad you were here. Charlie understood her.

"You're doing a good job. He's a nice person, your son."

"Thank you."

"I'm exhausted," said Charlie after a bit.

"Come to bed. I'll rub your back."

"The baby will be up in about a half hour."

"Probably."

At six-thirty the phone rang. It was Jaywalk.

"I'm sorry. . . ."

"It's okay," said Martha. "Are you all right?"

"Yes, my dad's on his way home. But Scott remembered the rest of Molly's name. And her address and stuff."

"Let me get a pencil."

Jaywalk told her the name and address, and Martha in turn telephoned the hospital. Then she called information for the Justices' number in Arden Forest. A woman answered on the first ring, in a voice that was full of terror, and when Martha gave her the message, Connie burst into tears and the phone went dead. As Martha too hung up, longing desperately to go back to sleep, the baby started to cry; her day had begun.

Charlie and Jack slept into the late morning. Martha was reading to the baby, trying to keep the house quiet, when the phone rang.

"Martie, this is Patsy Leveque. Is Charlie there?"

Martha took a deep breath. "Hello, Patsy."

"Hello. I've been calling his apartment since seven and he's obviously not calling back. Will you tell him I'm on the line please?"

After a moment of hesitation, Martha said, "Could he possibly call you a little later, Patsy? He's had kind of a rough night, and he's not up yet."

"Martie, *I* have had a rough night, and I need to speak to the father of my child. Will you get him please?"

Her voice was tense and shrill, as if she might become, or had recently been, hysterical. Martha, who wasn't feeling too sharp herself, said wearily, "All right, Patty."

"It's Patsy."

"And it's Martha," she said, and went in a snit to wake Charlie. He was deeply asleep and it took him a moment to orient himself, but then he smiled and kissed Martha, and went to the phone.

"Jesus, your girlfriend's a bitch," said Patsy.

"Excuse me?"

"Oh, forget it."

"Patsy . . . will you tell me what you want?"

"Yes, I will. I will tell you. Charlie," she said, speaking now with the tone of someone accepting an Academy Award, "I have given this matter a great deal of thought in the last few hours, and I've made up my mind. I cannot live with Phoebe anymore. You will have to take her."

Charlie stared into space, scratched himself, and finally said, "I take it something has happened."

"Yes," said Patsy in a flutey voice one note away from chalk on a blackboard, "something has happened, but frankly, it was simply the last straw. It is not working out, and it's time you took some responsibility."

"Why don't you tell me what's happened."

"No, no. I'll tell you some other time when I have your full attention and you're prepared to listen seriously. You go back to whatever you were doing and we'll talk later. But I felt you should know, and I promise you, Charlie, I won't change my mind." And she hung up.

Charlie hung up the dead receiver. He looked at Martha, who was watching him. He said, "I'm going back to bed."

Martha nodded.

Charlie caught sight of the pad that said "Molly Justice, Bathgate Road, Arden Forest."

"What's this?"

"The name of the girl you took to the hospital."

"You're kidding."

"Why?"

Charlie shook his head and padded off back to bed, and neither he nor Jack reappeared until after noon.

∞

"They *want to* sue Jack or have him arrested or something, at least Dave does," said Sophie fiercely. She hadn't seen Charlie in weeks, and it was hard to tell now if she had come as friend or foe. She was like an electrical thing plugged into the wrong current, something that was working, but overheated and snapping dangerously. Charlie got up to ask his secretary to hold his calls, then shut the door to his office.

"Oh," said Sophie. "That's how to rate with you. You never held your calls before when I came to see you. Maybe I should have yelled more."

"Sophie, please. Please."

She went to his desk and stood looking at the things he had placed above his blotter. He still had there a pretty blank book with marbled endpapers given him by Sophie. Beside it, along with the assortment of ragtag coffee mugs that collected wherever he was, he now had a sterling silver pig with an inkwell on its back and nib-cleaning brushes at the sides. A copy of the *Belles Heures of Jean, Duke of Berry* she hadn't known him to own before, and with it an edition of Maimonides' *The Guide for the Perplexed*.

"Joke," said Charlie.

"I got it," said Sophie.

Beside those was a photograph of a woman about the same age as Sophie, with wide grave eyes, smiling. Charlie watched Sophie stare at Martha and saw Martha, with her steady warmth, look back at Sophie, hurting her by existing.

"Great pig," said Sophie, finally. She went back to the chair and sat down.

"Yes."

"Valuable."

"I guess . . . if quill pens come back."

"A gift."

"Yes."

"You gave me a pen once."

A painful pause.

"Yes," said Charlie.

"Why am I doing this?"

Charlie let it go.

"Sophie. Jack rescued Molly. She was already tripping when they found her."

"It's interesting. Even the nicest people can cause the most grievous hurt, without meaning to. They just don't mean not to."

"You don't mean Jack."

"No."

"Do you mean to hurt me now?" Charlie asked.

"Yes. Oh, yes. I may not be lovable but I'm not dumb."

And she started to cry. She said, again, "Who is *doing* this? God, I hate the woman who's doing this."

Charlie was sitting with his head in his hands. Sophie grew calmer and said, "Connie and Dave can't believe that somehow a kid who'd never even been to New York by herself suddenly decided to go to Greenwich Village and get herself poisoned. Somebody had to tell her where to go, what to take, where to get it. What do kids from Arden Forest know about that? You told me yourself Jack horrified you when you met him."

"I'm learning about what things look like and what they really are."

"What does that mean?"

"He's a fine boy and he didn't hurt Molly. He helped her. How is she, anyway?"

"She's still full of whatever the hospital gave her. She's mostly been asleep since they brought her home."

"Is she going to be all right?"

"No one knows. When she's got all the sedative out of her system, she's supposed to go for tests. Connie's a wreck."

"I don't blame her."

"Neither do I."

"There could be brain damage. Flashbacks. They don't know what all."

"Please tell Connie . . . tell her, you know. If there's anything I can do."

"I don't think you'd be the person she'd call, Charlie."

They sat in silence for a moment.

"It's funny, after all the times we talked about going out to Arden for the night. To meet the kids, see the house. Well, not that funny. But I can't remember why we never did it."

Except she did, really. It was the kind of thing you do if you're really family, not if you're not, considering that Charlie found Dave resistible.

"Who was the girl with Jack?" Sophie asked.

Charlie looked blank.

"Molly says there were three. Two boys and a girl who hugged her when she was scared of the dark."

"I have no idea."

"Charlie."

"Sophie."

"I miss you," she said, choking on it. And she began to cry again. This time he really couldn't bear it; he went to her and held her.

"I'm sorry, you know, it's such a simple thing," she said through tears. "We're both grown-ups. It didn't work out. I understand. But you were my lover and my friend. I lost my lover and my friend at once and . . . we had fun, Charlie. It's hard . . . I miss my friend." Charlie held her and stroked her back.

"I'm still your friend, Sophie. Dear Sophie."

"I know but . . . you know." And she sobbed.

"Would you like us still to see each other?" he asked, wondering why this seemed like such a bad idea. He felt swamped by her emotion and unable to feel his own. Was there something wrong with this? He wanted her grief to stop.

"I don't know," said Sophie, sobbing less. "See each other as what?"

"As friends," he said, feeling confused.

"I don't know. You'd want me to meet Martha."

"No. Of course not."

She began fumbling for a handkerchief. She took some deep stuttering breaths.

"God, I've worn myself out. It's exhausting to be so sad."

She smiled a little. And his phone buzzed.

"I'm sorry," said the voice on the intercom, "but it's Mr. Misirlian."

Charlie made a face, looked an apology at Sophie, swore silently. "Tell him I'll call him in two minutes. One and a half."

He and Sophie both rose. She said, "I didn't mean to do this. I really came to talk about Molly. It seemed so bizarre, you being involved, and that somehow she'd gotten mixed up with this famous Jack. . . ."

"I understand."

"It's been such a rough two days. First she disappeared, and Connie was wild . . . what an awful night. And now, they don't know what to do about her, they don't even know if she'll be all right."

"Please let me know. I want to know how she is, and Jack will want to know, too."

She flinched at the mention of Jack. The buzzer sounded again.

"Sophie . . . I'll call you. I'll call you in a day or two to find out how she is. And how *you* are. I miss you, too."

"Okay," she said. She was calmer. He picked up the phone, and she picked up herself, and went out.

Tina, *the child* psychiatrist, was not surprised when Connie Justice appeared for the family counseling session by herself. She welcomed Connie and sat smiling pleasantly in silence, until Connie burst into tears.

"I haven't done anything in my life except be a wife and mother," Connie wept. "If I've failed at that, I want to die. I should die, I shouldn't be taking up space on the planet." She cried some more and Tina sat, thoughtful, until the storm of grief had lessened.

"Children of suicides often have a very hard struggle," Tina remarked.

Connie, still weeping, began to take an interest in her hem, which was coming unsewn. She tore viciously at the loose thread. She *had* thought all night about killing herself, but it was still annoying to have such an extreme suggestion treated seriously.

"Where is Dave?" asked Tina.

"He's home with Molly. We felt one of us ought to be there."

"And why is it he?"

"Because he wouldn't have come here by himself."

"And it was important that one of you come here?"

"I don't know what to do!" Connie was suddenly yelling. And then crying again. "Where is it coming from? Why is it happening?"

"What *is* happening?" Tina asked.

"It's *Molly* who ought to be here!" And Connie described the long night of excruciating fear, her sense of failure, her rage at the police who would do nothing, not even consider Molly a missing person until she'd been gone twenty-four hours. Then she fell silent, waiting for sympathy, craving relief, wanting an explanation that didn't put her, the child's mother, squarely at fault.

"The person who ought to be here is the person who wants to be."

"No, it isn't, it's the fucking coward who won't change anything, who won't look at anything."

"And that's Dave."

"Of course, Dave!" Connie yelled.

"But he's not here."

"That's what makes me so mad!"

"*That's* what makes you mad?"

"Stop making everything a question!"

"All right."

And they sat in silence for several minutes.

"I don't usually yell," said Connie. "Dave yells."

"I know."

Another silence.

"Suppose you tell me why you're here," said Tina.

"I'm here," said Connie rudely, "because one of my children stopped talking for three weeks and the next one put herself in the emergency room." She sat with her ankles neatly crossed, as she had been taught to do at dancing school.

"A case of the tail wagging the dog," said Tina.

"I don't understand you."

"Don't you?"

"Stop doing that!"

"Sorry."

All the way home, Connie felt terrible, because she was still in pain, and now angry at the child psychiatrist on top of it. But even that anger paled when she pulled into her driveway and saw that Dave's car was gone. Molly was sitting outside on the lawn in her pajamas, looking at grass. She didn't seem to notice her mother's arrival.

Connie calmed herself down, putting it aside so Molly wouldn't know anything was wrong (And where, dear, oh by the way, oh by the way do you happen to know where your fucking father has gone when he's supposed to be taking care of you!). But Molly never even looked up. She had as long as she wanted to study her daughter. (Take deep breaths. Count. She's too fragile. She couldn't cope with anger.) And what she saw was something so familiar, and at the same time so strange, that she felt as if she'd gone to sleep and awakened years later. She could see in Molly's face a little girl of three, of five, of nine. This was the girl who'd been jacks champion of her cabin group two years in a row. Her baby, who'd brought a kitten home in her pocket and kept it in secret in her room for six days before her mother found it. (She had sobbed terribly when they made her give it away, although they explained that Dave was allergic.)

When she was very little, Molly had a doll's tea party on the very spot where she now sat, at which she and her sister served tiny painted cookies. This little girl, with her soft round cheeks and glowing eyes, won a swimming race when she was six (water churning, little chin held high above the water, eyes clamped shut) and could do five cartwheels (to the right, not to the left) when she was seven. This little girl was sitting utterly still staring at grass, and her hair was stringy and her eyes were dull, and Connie barely knew her.

Connie, moving softly, came to Molly and sat down beside her. She put out her hand to stroke her, but Molly flinched.

"What's wrong, honey?"

"You're always so mad."

(Me? ME? Connie wanted to shout. *I'm* not mad it's your FUCKING FATHER who's always mad!)

"That's not true, honey," she said gently.

Molly shrugged. Time passed.

"What are you looking at?"

Molly put her finger into the grass, and took it out. Then she did it again. "If you were the size of an ant, the grass would be like a forest." Her speech had a slightly, very slightly, strange rhythm.

"Do you feel very small?"

Molly didn't answer. Instead she said suddenly, her face alive and speaking fast, "It's like living inside a drum. Boom, boom, boom, it's all around you, but you can't tell where it's coming from!"

"Noise?" asked Connie.

Molly shook her head hard. But she didn't say anything more, as if that burst had exhausted her. And Connie felt like someone who knows she's had a dream and can almost, but not quite, remember what it was. She knew what Molly meant . . . she almost knew . . . she kept losing it. Connie had had a dream, but only Molly knew what it was. Boom, boom boom. Everywhere, but you can't tell where it's coming from.

Charlie *opened the* door to his apartment and Patsy strode in. Charlie had dreaded this meeting, feeling that he could not bear to deal with one more weeping woman today. But he could see at once that Patsy was not in the mood to weep. This was her Eleanor Roosevelt mode, or was it Nancy Reagan. Life was simple for Patsy tonight. She was right; everyone else was wrong, and if she didn't get exactly the answers she had in mind, she would Just Say No.

Patsy swept into his living room and plopped down in the overstuffed velvet chair. This had once been "her" chair, where she did needlepoint in lamplight while Charlie read the paper, in the study they had shared on Eighty-sixth Street, another life. Charlie followed her into the room and asked if she wanted a drink.

Oh, what an idea. Just like Charlie to try to make it a social call. She pulled from behind her back the green pillow Charlie now used in "her" chair, stared at it, and put it back behind her back with a gesture that said Oh, well if *you* like it. It took Charlie about twenty-five minutes in Patsy's company, tops, to get to feeling as if he couldn't tie his own shoes.

"Charlie," Patsy trumpeted, as if speaking from a pulpit, "you have had it all your way with that child for the last four years. You pick her up when you feel like it, then dump her at home to ruin *my* life, while you go on your merry way. It simply isn't fair."

"If I recall, I thought it wasn't fair to me, to have her with you full time, and you said fairness didn't matter, what mattered was what was best for Phoebe."

"Oh *fuck* you," said Patsy. Her smooth pageboy haircut gleamed in the lamplight.

"Well, we're off to a pleasant start."

"Well you piss me off, you really do. Would you mind just listening for once?"

"Please," said Charlie. "Go ahead."

"I thought she ought to go to boarding school, and I still do. But you said no, you chose this place in Brooklyn, and I'm the one taking the consequences."

"Which are?"

"Which are, that I'm starting to hate my own child! She's whiny, deceitful, and hideous! She comes and goes at all hours! I give her curfews, she ignores them! She lies about where she's been. She's insulting. Really, Charlie. You've got everything you want, and I'm stuck with *her*."

She folded her arms and stared at him. Charlie counted to ten.

"I understand you're upset, but could you be more specific?"

"You've got your career, you've got your girlfriend, you've—"

"I meant about Phoebe. I assume something more has happened than you got on each other's nerves."

"As far as I'm concerned, this romance with your girlfriend's son is the last straw. I give up. *You* can handle it. She came home at three in the morning on Friday, looking like a ghoul and crashing around the place. . . . If that's what you sent her to Brooklyn to learn, you can have it. God bless you. If that's the kind of friends you want her to have, fine. I can't talk to her. How can I tell her anything when *you're* shacked up with this boy's mother?"

"Patsy, time out. Would you stop for a minute?"

Patsy paused. She hated to do it, close on to overdrive, but she did. Charlie said, "What do you mean, 'romance with my girlfriend's son'?"

Bingo! Oh the pleasure! She thought he didn't know, and he didn't! Oh, if only he could see his own face at this second!

"Oh, I see," she said. "I thought you and your new little family were so close. What I mean is she's gaga about this appalling boy in case you hadn't noticed, although I don't see how you could miss it. She's off with him more than she's home, as far as I can see. And this wonderful son of your wonderful new friend seems to have undertaken to introduce her to the joys of I don't know what all. . . ."

"Why don't you try to tell me what you do know, instead of being snide."

"Oh sorry. I'd hate to be snide at a time like this."

"Where was Phoebe Friday night?"

"She was in the park with your friend Jack. Dime, she calls him, heaven knows what that means. She told me she'd gone to see a movie that didn't start till midnight if you believe that. But they didn't see any movie, and she wouldn't say what they did do but she came bashing in at the most ungodly hour, waking me up, and I won't even tell you what she looked like. That child used to have the most beautiful hair, and such a sense of style. . . ."

"Patsy, could we stick to the point?"

"Fine. Oh, fine. So there she is with the house in an uproar, and *then* she wouldn't tell me who she'd been with, but I found out, because he called the next day and I got it out of him. And in case you hadn't noticed she's got a huge crush on this creature."

There was a pause.

"I see you're surprised," said Patsy.

"Yes. I must say I am."

"Well, I don't know what you're going to do about it. I've explained to her that she's coming here to live, and I told her to start packing."

"I thought your shrink friend said it wasn't a good idea, a teenaged girl with her father instead of her mother."

"I don't care anymore. I'm being frank with you. All I know is, I've done all I can. I've got to be true to myself, Charlie. It's your turn to deal with Phoebe."

"If she's with me, won't we be throwing her and Jack even more together?"

"I have no idea. That's your problem. From now on."

"Patsy. I leave for work at seven-thirty in the morning. Half the time I'm not home until nine or ten. A child needs a parent who's home when she gets home. I thought that's what all those checks I write are for, so you could work part-time and be there for her."

"She's had that, and I don't see that it's worked. We're going to try something else now."

And Patsy, before she gave herself time to think that if Phoebe lived with Charlie he *would* stop the support checks, before she started doing the math and thinking what it would do to her day to work full time, decided to savor what was about as complete a satisfaction as she'd experienced since she discovered she hated being single, and quit the field.

*C*harlie and Martha had decided to go to the dress rehearsal of *The Three Musketeers*, because Patsy wanted to go to the official opening performance the next night. Patsy felt that she should be the one to applaud her daughter on the day, the more so because Phoebe had just the weekend before moved to her father's apartment to live, and she and Patsy had not parted on the warmest of terms. Patsy planned to bring Phoebe beautiful roses, although she thought it unlikely her daughter could act her way out of a paper bag. After the performance she would amuse Phoebe with the story of how Patsy's own grandmother, a teenaged girl in Cleveland at the turn of the century, had held up an amateur theatrical performance of *The Cricket on the Hearth*, in which she had a crucial role, weeping on the fire escape because she thought it so wicked to be acting on the stage before strangers.

The dress rehearsal was on Thursday night, attended by half the school, and by many relatives who couldn't come Friday or Saturday. Charlie said Phoebe was nervous as a cat about it. Martha said Jack had been working so late at rehearsals in the past week that practically their sole communication had been an exchange of notes on the pad in the kitchen.

On the night of the dress rehearsal, Charlie drove downtown to pick Martha up, so they could talk in the car as they drove through the empty evening streets of downtown Manhattan and over the Brooklyn Bridge. They had barely seen each other since Phoebe's move.

"I came early so we'd have time to neck," said Charlie, as Martha climbed into the car.

"Thank heaven," she said, and slid into his arms.

After a few minutes, he asked, "Are we shocking the neighbors? I could find someplace deserted."

"I don't think they're shocked by anything that involves consenting adults of the same species."

Presently, Martha added, "We probably ought to go, though."

Charlie started the car, but he looked regretful.

"This has seemed like the longest week of my life, away from you."

"Fasten your seat belts. It's going to get worse."

"I know." He turned onto Broadway, downtown toward City Hall.

Charlie said, "Have you had any chance to talk to Jack?"

"Not much. He said he didn't tell us Phoebe was with them in the park because he didn't want to get her in trouble."

"But what about the rest of it? Is it true, they . . . I don't even know how to say it. Are they involved with each other? God, there's no way to say it that doesn't sound disgusting. Involved. I get this image of arms and legs all spinning around in a Waring blender."

Martha laughed. "I get the impression that when she first arrived at school he was just trying to help her out, as much as a favor to you as anything. But he seems to think she's something very special, now."

"He does? Why?"

"Bite your tongue."

"I thought that was a good question. I know why I love you."

"You do? Tell me."

They swung onto the Brooklyn Bridge.

"Look," said Charlie, "here we are on our bridge. This is the first place I realized I loved you."

"Here? You mean the day we walked here? The day Phoebe got kicked out? You lie."

"No. I looked at you, standing under the sky, looking down toward the harbor, talking about wanting to look like Joan Baez when you were sixteen, and I realized I was completely hooked. I wanted to go on walking forever, I just wanted you to keep talking to me, and listening to me."

"But I was still mad at you."

"I know, but I thought you might like me if you got to know me."

Martha was giggling. It seemed so funny to remember a time when they didn't know each other, or didn't know they were in love.

"I think you're lying. You didn't let on for a minute. You didn't lay a hand on me for weeks."

"That's because I had too much respect for you," said Charlie, formally. "But the desire for union was very great."

Martha roared with delight. "No one but you, no one in the world would put it like that."

Charlie was trying not to smile.

"Anyway," said Martha, "you were going to tell me why you love me."

"I love you," said Charlie, "because you're beautiful and smart and you make me laugh, and because I trust you completely and because even when I'm asleep I can feel you loving me, and because you're the most exciting lover in New York. New England. The world."

"Gee," said Martha, "it doesn't *sound* like much."

"Ask me again later and I'll think of more things. Why do you love me?"

"I love you because you're kind and incredibly handsome and because you look so sexy in those glasses, and because you love animals and children and because you call Jack's boom box a record player. And because you say things like 'the desire for union was very great.'"

"If you don't move your hand I'm going to drive off the road."

"Oh. Damn."

Charlie negotiated the turn off the bridge and into Brooklyn Heights.

"Phoebe and I have had several interesting father-daughter moments this week."

"You asked her about Jack? What does she say?"

Charlie shrugged. "She just sort of stares at me with her lip stuck out like this"—he demonstrated—"and then informs me that I wouldn't understand and stomps off to her room."

Martha laughed and held his hand. They drove on in silence while Charlie looked for a place to park.

"Is this play going to be any fun, by the way?" Charlie asked.

"You'll be surprised, I think. The kids do everything, lights, makeup, sound, costumes. And the acting is usually wonderful."

"The thing that surprises me is that Phoebe wants anything to do with it. At Replogle, she used to inform me, it was only the dweebs who tried out for the plays or for orchestra, or anything that might mean staying late or working weekends. The cool kids were the ones who spent all their time lying around somebody's fancy apartment while the parents were in Europe."

"That's what my school was like," said Martha, "and I hated it. I was one of the cool ones, though. All the right clothes. All the right moves."

"Thank god we didn't meet when we were eighteen. You'd have scared me to death."

"No. You'd have known right away that I was completely lost and looking for you."

"Martha, *no* one was looking for me when I was eighteen. I'll show you pictures. I was the one with the Adam's apple and the ears out to here."

They walked up the stairs of Cropp and Thatcher. There was a poster announcing *The Three Musketeers!* in the lobby. Martha showed Charlie the way to the theater, which was in the back building.

"Maybe Gillis would like to have custody of Fred *and* Jack," said Charlie, when they found themselves alone on the stairs. "Then you could come live with me and Phoebe."

"Gillis doesn't want custody of a hamster." She paused, thinking of the joy of waking up with Charlie's sweet warm weight beside her. "If they *are* sleeping together, then we have to . . . it changes everything. Shit."

Charlie said, "I don't think they could be. Phoebe's only sixteen. When I was sixteen I thought people could tell if you were a virgin by the way you walked."

Martha laughed.

"I mean, I'm not sure she knows where babies come from. I never told her. I thought I'd tell her on her wedding day. You don't think they are, do you? God, I can't even think about it." Martha laughed. "Besides, *where* would they?" said Charlie earnestly. "This is New York, they don't have backseats of cars."

A freshman at the door of the theater checked her reservation list for their names, and gave them programs. They went in and found seats. Then each of them read the program and smiled with pride at seeing their children's names.

Backstage, where the cast and crew were waiting, there were not exactly dressing rooms. Far from the new $2 million theater Replogle had built the previous year, Cropp and Thatcher's theater was an ex-gymnasium with the stage in the three-quarters round. There was no curtain, but the sets and lighting were extraordinarily sophisticated; C and T had a tradition of producing genius tech crews. The techies had long hair and pasty faces and spoke a strange language of wiring and gels, electricity and art. Their parents were all here tonight, proud and mystified; the dress was as much for the light and sound as it was for the actors.

On the floor, behind the scenes, there was a suppressed babble, as young actors struggled with costumes, and stretched and vocalized and posed and teased; anything to let off steam. Phoebe and Pia were doing their makeup at a table in the corner with a couple of portable plug-in makeup mirrors. There were pots of greasepaint and cold cream and rows of lipsticks and jars of makeup brushes on the table. Pia, a veteran who had starred in *South Pacific,* the fall musical, was showing Phoebe how to put on a false beauty mark.

"Where do you want it?"

"How about . . . here."

Pia painted a black spot on Phoebe's cheekbone with eyeliner, then covered it with eyebrow gel.

"That sets it."

"Is it hard to get it off?"

"No. Cold cream will do it."

"Maybe it should be in a different place for each act." Pia laughed.

"Hi, Pie. Hi, Phoebe B. Beebe Baby," said Jack and Jaywalk. They appeared in the mirrors behind the girls.

"Look at you!" The girls turned to admire the musketeers. They were wearing frock coats and lace, and three-cornered hats.

"We look quite dashing, I think," said Jack. "I was hoping we got those pants with codpieces, but the wardrobe mistress said I had the wrong century."

Just then they were joined by the wardrobe mistress: Bernie, in his wheelchair. Phoebe greeted him with a smile and the sentence she had mastered so far in sign language: "Greetings, earthling."

Bernie signed rapidly to Jaywalk, who said to Phoebe, "He says the dress is *you.*"

Phoebe was playing the beautiful and sinister Milady, and she was wedged into a dress with a killer corset that made her waist the size of a normal person's thigh; above, her décolletage was quite dramatic.

"If my boobs fall out when I bend over I'll know who to thank," she said, and Bernie laughed.

"So will we all," said Jack.

"Gimme a break."

"Are you still nervous?"

Phoebe had been in tears at the rehearsal last night.

"Of course I am. You shouldn't have talked me into this. I can't act."

"Oh, I don't think that matters," said Jack.

"Of course it matters!"

"If you screw up, we'll love you anyway."

"Oh, fuck you."

Jack laughed.

"Guess who's in front," said Jenny Krass, arriving on the run. Jenny didn't like to be onstage, but she was assisting the wardrobe mistress and hanging out.

"Who?"

She named an actor who was having a stupendous success that season in a new Lanford Wilson play.

"Oh great," said Phoebe. "Now I'm going to die."

"Why?"

"Because I'm in love with him! I'm completely in love. I've forgotten all my lines. I've forgotten my name."

"What's he doing here?"

"Is he cute?"

"The eyes are pretty amazing," said Jenny. "Mrs. Delaney was trying not to stare at him as she walked past and she tripped and fell down in the aisle."

"What's he doing here?"

"Delia Blodgett is his niece." Delia was a freshman, playing a serving wench. Well, it wasn't that surprising. New York is full of famous people, particularly famous people working in the arts, and their relatives had to go to school somewhere.

"Settle down, everyone," said Carol Boyd, the stage manager. "We're ready. Places, please." She went past to the next group, giving her message.

Bernie rolled off to the wardrobe department with Jenny Krass, to be ready to help with costume changes and unforeseen emergencies.

Pia went to find her boyfriend, since she was playing the queen and wasn't on until the second act. Jaywalk went to prepare for his entrance.

Phoebe and Jack looked at each other. She touched his hair, now grown out and curling from beneath his hat.

"Too bad you didn't get a wig," said Phoebe.

"Too bad you didn't get the top half of a dress."

"Oh, thank you so very much."

Jack put his arms around her. "You're going to be just great. Break a leg."

"I should break yours."

Jack laughed and kissed her.

"I gotta go."

"You break a leg, too."

"Thanks, Beebe."

Phoebe, left alone, sat down to do the centering exercises that the drama teacher gave them to counteract stage fright. Breathe, count. Picture a place where everything is serene and you're always at peace. Phoebe pictured the meadow, in summer, at her father's house in the country. Breathe, count. She had blanked on her lines two days ago in rehearsal, and now she was completely terrified.

There were a few glitches in the performance. One of Richelieu's soldiers lost his wig during a sword fight, and Louis le Roi, elaborately costumed and bewigged, went up in his lines, though he claimed it was fine, he was just playing the monarch in the style of Ronald Reagan. But the musketeers were full of fun, and Phoebe, the wicked seductress, gave a lustrous, confident performance full of sly wit, and at the curtain calls there were cheers and whistles for her until she blushed.

"Who *is* that child?" asked Charlie, clapping for his glowing daughter until his hands hurt. "I feel as if I've never seen her before in my life."

The only person who got a greater round of applause was Bernie, who was wheeled out by the musketeers to take a bow after his triumph as wardrobe mistress was explained by the play's director. (Bernie had written eloquent letters to costume houses, theater companies, and drama schools describing the school's pathetic costume collection. He'd scored a major windfall from the Light Opera Company of New Jersey, which was getting rid of its costumes from an old production of *Così fan tutte*.) Some of the cast saved some roses they had brought for the director and threw them at Bernie, who laughed and bowed. He couldn't hear the noise, but looking out from the stage he could see it being made, and he could read the lips.

As they walked together down the stairs hand in hand afterward, Charlie and Martha could hear people talking all around them.

"That lovely little blonde playing the villainess has a real presence," said an extraordinarily handsome man right behind them. When they were outside, Martha said, "Do you know who that was?"

"Who?"

"The man who was talking about Phoebe. That's whatsisname, the actor who's starring in the Lanford Wilson play! Phoebe's going to faint when you tell her."

"I may faint myself. She was wonderful. They were both wonderful. They were all wonderful. Shouldn't we wait for them?" Charlie stopped outside the school and turned to look up at it, as if to understand what kind of place this was that had turned his daughter from a Bloomingdale's brat into the marvelous girl he had seen tonight.

"No, they'll want to be together and scream and yell. There's always a cast party when the dress goes well. Jack said Jaywalk would see Phoebe home. His mother lives near you uptown."

"I can't get over it. It was like seeing a different person."

Martha smiled, very happy too, amazed and proud of both children and utterly happy to be holding Charlie's hand.

"Do you want to go somewhere for a drink?"

"I'd rather walk, if that's all right."

"Yes. Much better. Let's walk. They must have had great fun doing those sword fights."

"I think they did. Jack and Jaywalk were fencing all over the loft for weeks."

"So they're not coming home for hours?"

"I doubt it."

"Well then," he said eagerly, "we can go home and fuck."

Martha laughed. "Achieve union, you mean."

"Exactly."

"It will have to be at my house. I have a twelve-year-old baby-sitter who needs to go home."

Charlie suddenly took Martha by both arms and stopped her in her tracks. Then he knelt down on the sidewalk in front of her and said, "I have never been happier in my life and I love you. I will love you for the rest of my life, and probably after I'm dead. Will you marry me?"

Martha began to laugh. All she could think was that no one except Charlie would get down on his knees to propose. A couple walking a tiny poodle was rapidly approaching them under the streetlamps, looking curious.

"This is very serious," said Charlie. "Will you marry me? Answer quickly, I'm kneeling on a pebble."

"Yes," said Martha. Charlie sprang up and lifted her in the air, kissing her. When he put her down, he said, "See? Wasn't that simple?"

"No. But I adore you."

"Oh, good. Oh, do. Do adore me, it feels wonderful." And he stopped again to kiss her. "Let's go home."

"Yes," she said.

"I *want a* divorce," said Connie.

She was sitting by herself in the middle of her king-sized bed. The bedclothes were all on the floor because Dave had gotten up in the middle of the night and stripped them all off her and thrown them there. Then he had wrapped himself in his ratty bathrobe and a big towel, and crashed off downstairs to sleep. For all she knew, the children had found him like that this morning—huge, disheveled, and blotchy, sleeping in a towel in the living room.

She herself had lain on the bed, awake, chilled to the bone, staring at the dark. She didn't get up and get the covers back because she wanted to feel what had happened. This was her real marriage. The big handsome house and the three attractive children and the Jeep wagon and the jolly friends at the country club were what it looked like. Not what it was. And she herself, she herself, she most of all, had lived her life as if it were what it looked like.

She wanted to feel something she had never felt before. Since the occasion offered, she decided to start with being cold. All night long. With all comfort and protection stripped away, to see if that clarified things.

In the daylight at the end of that long night, when her children had washed and dressed themselves and whoever wanted breakfast had eaten whatever there was to eat, and hoisted briefcases and backpacks and the door closed behind the last of them, and she knew she was alone in the house, she said out loud, "I want a divorce."

Then she waited for tears, but they didn't come. She felt quite calm. The tail had wagged the dog. She could finally see it. What was showing in this family was the strain of tolerating the intolerable. So she said it out loud once more, the unthinkable phrase, and then got up and went to the bathroom for a long, hot shower.

When the girls got home, she gave them money and told them to take William downtown for supper. They probably all had a ton of homework and Molly had a horrible cold, but Connie didn't care. She had something to do that required all her attention, and she wanted to do it at home where she and the man she had married could be as loud and as ugly as they really were.

The bed was still as Dave had left it, with the sheets and blankets heaved on the floor. Downstairs, the breakfast dishes everyone had left in the sink were still in the sink. Connie had washed only her own. She spent the day in silence. She walked around the house saying good-bye to things. Good-bye, teapot. Good-bye, piano that no one played. Good-bye, records, not that *anyone* played records anymore. There must have been hundreds from their college days. Judy Collins, Kingston Trio. Ella Fitzgerald sings Cole Porter. Elephant Gerald, Dave called her. They always danced to Ella in Dave's living room at college, and forever after when they felt romantic. After they won the paddle tennis doubles, for instance. Or on their anniversary. Or when Dave just had a snootful.

Good-bye, framed *New Yorker* cartoons in the downstairs bathroom, good-bye, Dave's hideous lounger that he sat in to watch football games. Good-bye, embroidered tablecloth that they bought in Saint Martin, good-bye, monogrammed glasses that said C&DJ in the English style. Good-bye, garden tools, good-bye, bicycle she gave Dave for Christmas, good-bye, grandfather clock from Dave's grandfather's house, good-bye, vase, good-bye, Dave's Time-Life series on World War II. Good-bye, toaster, good-bye, microwave, good-bye, dining-room rug, good-bye, photograph albums. She didn't know what he would take or leave but she didn't care if he took it all.

When Dave came home he was carrying flowers—an armload of roses—and a half gallon of rum.

"I thought I'd make us some daiquiris," he said.

"I want a separation," she said.

Dave stared at her for a moment, then went past her into the kitchen.

She stood in the twilight looking out at the lawn, expecting him to put his things down and come back. But he didn't, and after a while, she heard the whir of the blender. She waited a little longer and then went to the kitchen.

Dave was sitting in bright light at the kitchen table, drinking a daiquiri and reading the paper. The flowers were lying on the drainboard. Dave didn't look up.

Connie went to the sink and began cleaning the roses. They were beautiful ones, long stemmed, deep red. She stripped the lower leaves, recut the stems, put the flowers one by one into warm water in a crystal vase.

"Want a daiquiri?" said Dave.

"Sure," said Connie.

He poured her a drink and went back to his paper. She sat down and picked up another section of the paper and settled down to wait him out.

When he'd read the want ads, the real estate listings, and the car ads, he put down his paper. She put down hers. They looked at each other.

"Where are the kids?"

"Out." (Oh, it only took you an hour and a quarter to think of them? Good, Dave.)

"What, did you send them into the woods with a trail of bread crumbs?

"Something like that. I want a divorce, Dave."

"I thought you said separation."

"Take your pick."

"Why?"

This wasn't a question she'd expected.

"Because you seem to hate me."

"I hate *you*? You're the one who doesn't want to screw. . . ."

"You hate William."

"I don't hate him. I think you've made him into a twerp and a momma's boy."

"So you hate me."

"I don't know what you expect in life, Connie. This is how it is. Things aren't perfect. You want everything to be sweet and nice like the mausoleum you grew up in. This is real life. People have problems, they deal with them, they get on with it."

"I want a divorce."

"You don't know how lucky you are. You don't know how spoiled you are."

Connie didn't say anything. She was frightened to death that he was right. Think of all the women in the world whose husbands beat them black and blue, who didn't have a nice house and food on the table. Besides, maybe their marriage was this way because of her. Maybe the same thing would happen next time. Maybe there wouldn't be a next time and she'd be alone for the rest of her life. How many things were there about living in the world that she didn't know? Maybe the car would blow up because nobody had ever told her that you had to have the something-or-other changed every winter, or the something-else checked every so many miles. She'd never owned her own car. She didn't know how the furnace worked. She didn't know if the chimneys ever needed sweeping or how to relight the pilot on the water heater. She was afraid of mice and sometimes they appeared in the kitchen.

Dave poured himself another drink.

She said, "William is suffering, and Molly nearly died. . . ."

"Molly's fine."

"As far as we can tell. And no thanks to us. They can't stand this anymore, and we shouldn't either. I think you should move out tonight."

"I move out? Why me? It's my house. You're the one who wants a divorce." Dave looked at her hard now, and she recognized the glaze in his eye as he began to look forward to a fight, like a schoolyard bully who doesn't care what it's about, he's just excited by the action.

"Why don't *you* move out? Go to New York. Live with your sister," said Dave.

"And you'll take care of the children? Shop, cook, pick them up at school?"

He shrugged. "I'll hire a nanny."

"Oh, bullshit, Dave. You know that's the worst thing we could do to them now, they come home and find me gone. . . ."

Dave picked up a section of newspaper. "Well then you'll have that on your conscience, won't you?"

Connie wondered what the hell to do. This wasn't the way she pictured this working.

"David."

"Constance."

"Oh cut it out!"

He turned a page of his paper.

"Please go," she said softly. "Please. If you ever loved me. Please let's end this with some dignity. Go to the club. Go to Bob's house. I'll pack your clothes and send them to you. But please, go, before we hurt each other more."

Dave turned another page of the paper.

"Dave, I don't want to live with you anymore. This marriage is over. I want you to go."

"You on the rag?" he asked, without looking up.

She picked up the vase of roses and hurled it at him. But full of water it was heavy, and it fell short and fell on the floor, spilling flowers and water everywhere. "OH SHIT!" she yelled. The vase hadn't even broken. "Leave! Get up off your fat ass, and leave this house!"

Without looking up he said, "I'm not going anywhere, Constance."

"Yes you are!"

"What are you going to do, call the police?" He looked at her calmly. "Oh, good evening, officer. My wife wants you to take me away because she had a couple of drinks and threw a fifty-pound vase at me." He turned another page of the paper. Connie stood, paralyzed, and then walked to the table, stepping over the roses, and sat down beside him. She turned to Dave, her eyes full of tears, and touched him.

"Dave," she whispered. "Look at me. Listen to me. Think about what's happened to us."

"Jesus!" he said. "Here's a 450 SL with only 15,000 miles on it for sale for 32K!"

So she stepped over the roses again and left the house. And all the way to New York she drove as if in a pounding rain because of her tears. She couldn't stop picturing the children coming home, asking where Mommy was.

K*ate and Serena* sat at a table at the back of the room. The Beach Club was crowded and noisy and dim with smoke. They were drinking Surfers, big blue drinks with parasols in them. Nobody knew what was in a Surfer besides pineapples and parasols, but they were sweet and sour and potent.

The Beach Club was a bar on upper Lexington that would take a fake ID printed by a chimpanzee, as long as it was laminated. Nobody knew how the place stayed open, since drunk sixteen-year-olds with trademark chains of parasols around their necks were constantly being busted after an evening at the Beach Club for various misbehaviors, from disturbing the peace to frolicsome bits of housebreaking. But the only time the Beach Club had ever closed was over one Thanksgiving weekend, after an underaged son of a state congressman, full of Surfers, wrecked his father's new Saab Turbo on his way home to Scarsdale.

Replogle girls made the Beach Club their home away from home. It was like a party you didn't have to plan, only better because there were blender drinks, and you might meet new people in addition to all the same old ones you'd been going to school and dancing school and the Hamptons with for*ever*. Girls at all-girl schools needed a place to meet boys. Kids away at school needed a place to go when they came home, to hang out with their friends who had stayed in New York.

Girls entering the Beach Club were like their mothers arriving at a holiday party. There were cries of joy, embraces, kisses on both cheeks in the French manner. People hopped from table to table, collecting the news, telling tales, sharing drinks, cadging drinks, spilling drinks, planning parties at someone's house when someone had parents out of town. And after a while it became a love fest, because these celebrants were young and a small amount of drink made them sentimental. ("Alison, you are my best friend forever, I swear. If you don't write me every week at school I'll die.") A large amount of drink made them licentious or argumentative or teary, and there were passes made and received, fights, and crying jags every night. The Beach Club was better than the movies, because it was full of surprise and passion and drama, and all about *them,* and more sophisticated than the movies because plotless, just like real life.

Kate and Serena hadn't seen Phoebe since winter break. One of the sophomores had seen her though, in the Village, and reported that her hair was all like punk or something. So they were greatly looking forward to her arrival.

Phoebe, for her part, wasn't quite sure what had moved her to call them. She missed Jack terribly when she couldn't be with him, and she wanted to talk to friends. She hoped they were her friends. But it also seemed to be time. It was as if she'd been away in foreign territory, proving herself. Proving something. It was time to find out what would happen now if she came back. The same, but changed.

She stood at the door of the Beach Club feeling pushed back by a wave of smoke and sound; voices, laughter, shouts, glasses. A boy she'd known since kindergarten was sitting at the bar drinking beer. He turned to look at her, and looked with interest, then turned away. He didn't know her.

Serena looked up through the smoke, looked up from the tale Kate was telling her about ordering a dress for the Gold and Silver Ball from Victoria's Secret. "They didn't have it in black, they only had it in like, fuchsia, and it wasn't even the right size. I look horrible in fuchsia. But it was right before our math test and I was like so bored, so I ordered it. . . ."

"Phoebe!" Serena called, and then stood. Phoebe, grateful, saw them at last. She made her way toward them, squeezing between tables for four where eight were seated. She smiled, remembering something Jack had said about issuing citations to people who use the word "party" as a verb. Jack and Jaywalk, the grammar police. What would Serena say if she tried to explain Jaywalk?

"You look *great!*" cried Serena, kissing her. Kate kissed her next, and Phoebe smiled and kissed them back. She squeezed into a chair beside them.

"Where'd you get that jacket?"

"From a boy."

"That's really neat. It's like Marlon Brando or something. You know in *Streetcar* or something."

"I think your hair looks great."

"You do?"

"Yeah. You never had it short before, did you? It's like that girl in the Calvin Klein ad, you know that girl?" said Kate.

"Isabella Rosellini," said Serena.

"Right. She's so beautiful. What's in it?"

"Is it that Wet goop? Where'd you have it cut?"

"My boyfriend cut it," said Phoebe.

"You're kidding."

"No."

"Whoa, is he like a hairdresser or something?"

Phoebe laughed. "No. But I wanted it short one night so he said he'd try it."

"Stand up. Turn around."

They admired her from all angles.

"I thought you might say 'ach, phooey' because it wasn't Bruno Dessange or something."

"Are you kidding? It's terrific!" They went on picking over each other, like baboons grooming for fleas, until they'd renewed the feeling of closeness they once had shared. The surprise was, it was so easy and the warmth so genuine. They all had a round of Surfers.

"You really have a boyfriend?" Kate asked again.

"Did you hear Camilla Kennedy was raped?"

"You're kidding!" Phoebe cried.

"Well, Serena, come on. Date rape."

"Well, Kate, come on. She was *raped*. Who cares what you call it?"

"By who? When?"

Kate and Serena kept interrupting each other.

"You know that crowd that got kicked out of Buckley?"

"Allan Black and whatsisname Kenny—"

"Renny—"

"Yes, them. Remember the blond one, Phil or Paul or something who played rugby, who was at Rochelle's party that time—"

"Phoebe wasn't at that party—"

"Oh. Well he was with them at the Valentine dance at The World, oh come on, I know you know—"

"With the glasses? Like, John Lennon glasses?"

"Yes!" two voices exclaimed.

"He was so cute. . . ."

Phoebe certainly did remember Paul. She had danced with him twice and been disappointed when he moved on to a girl from Spence with enormous breasts. The World was a club, in the lower bowel of the East Village; inside the music was loud and all the walls were painted black. Outside the streets were filthy, lined with graffiti and overflowing garbage cans, and prowled by strays, quadrupedal and human. Phoebe remembered someone saying as their taxi pulled up that it was too bad the poor couldn't at least keep their streets clean. It had occurred to her then that there was a puzzle there: it was true that the streets were clean and the garbage cans neatly emptied in their own nice, neat, rich neighborhood, but that was not because the nice, neat people who lived there swept the streets or hauled the garbage off themselves. Still, the puzzle had been quickly forgotten in the fabulousness of having a friend whose parents would give their daughter a party in such a mad, avant-garde urbanoid hangout as this. (The father was in the music business.) Though the party girl's mother, who wasn't in the music business, did keep saying, "I can see now why people stick to the Colony Club. We even had to bring hand towels for the ladies' room."

"So where did she meet him? What did he do?" (The raper. Rapist. Paul.)

"She knew him from around."

"She knew him from *here*," Serena said to Kate. Serena was the one who remembered all the gory details. Serena would probably be a trial lawyer. "She met him here, don't you remember? The night we all got bombed and stayed up all night at Marilyn's house playing Pictionary?"

"Don't you love Pictionary, by the way?"

"I don't know," said Phoebe.

"Oh, whoa," said Kate and Serena. Phoebe could see that their world had bobbled along on its own current at a great rate since she last saw them. So had hers, on a rapid but diverging current. The river was wider than she used to dream.

Pictionary. The last time she was with them, they didn't play games in mixed groups. They went shopping. Or when the stores closed, they read through *Vogue* and *W,* planning the perfect $10,000 wardrobe for each other. Then the perfect $20,000 one. ("I'll add that St. Laurent mink trenchcoat." "I want the Geoffrey Beene." "With the ruching?" "No, the taffeta.")

"Did he rape her that night?"

"No, they went out a few times."

"How did it happen?"

"She says he was high."

"But, where were they and stuff? What time was it? What did he do?"

"Her living room."

"He raped her in her own *living* room?"

A pause.

"He must have been on the moon."

"He seemed so cute. . . ."

"I saw her bruises. She had to be examined by a doctor, and he confirmed that it was rape."

"God, how *gross.* Can you imagine some doctor pawing around in there when you've just been raped?"

"Did she press charges?"

"No. Her parents decided she shouldn't. They thought she'd been through enough."

"She says she *hates* men now. She says the thought of being touched makes her throw up."

"I've heard that if you're raped, normally you become a lesbian."

"God," said Phoebe.

The waiter came over, and they decided they better order some more Surfers. At this time of night it would take forever for the waiter to get back through the crowd to their table.

"So what happened to him?"

"Phil?"

"Paul," said Phoebe.

"I don't think anything. I saw him in here last week."

"God," they all said again.

"But in her own house? He must have been absolutely in the zone. What was he taking? Where did he get it?"

"Coke. Crack. Heroin. Pills . . . could have been anything. She said his eyes were *weird*."

"But where would he get it?" Phoebe asked again.

Kate and Serena both looked at her. "Here," they exclaimed together. As if everyone knew that.

"Oh," said Phoebe. After a minute Kate asked, "How do you like Cropp and Thatcher?"

There had been an immense cloudburst at midnight, but now the moon was up and the night was full of mist. Phoebe and Jack had entered the park at the Metropolitan, skirting around past the Temple of Dendur. They walked through the warm silvery air, holding hands.

"I worked there one Christmas," said Jack, meaning the Met. "At the Degas exhibit. Putting those Acousti-guide things on people, the recorded tour. It was a great job. There were all these cute little small old people who don't have their own walkpersons. You have to explain to them about the stop button and the rewind. They get all anxious."

"Did you like the exhibit?"

"I did. I usually hate museums. I usually have to have a nap after about a half hour in one. My mom used to drag me through them every weekend when I was little. She denies it, but she did. I think now I'm allergic to them."

"Me too! Exactly. I get just overcome, I think I'm going to pass out right on my feet!" They looked at each other, smiling. As with any two people in love, the world seemed full of proofs that they were perfect for each other.

Serena and Kate had decided it was too romantic, Phoebe having this boyfriend, and too sad that they had so much trouble getting to see each other. Also, they wanted to meet him.

"Why don't you tell your dad you're spending the night with me?" said Serena. So Phoebe had called her father to say she was spending the night with Serena. Then she had called Jack to have him meet her at the Beach Club. When he got there, Serena and Kate had given Jack their stamp of approval and advised him and Phoebe to run along. Serena and Kate had joined a table full of jubilant young people attempting to make spoons hang from their noses, and Jack and Phoebe left hand in hand.

When they were outside, Jack said, "Guess who I passed on Crosby Street on the way to the subway?"

"Who?"

"Your father."

They both whooped with laughter.

"He must have streaked downtown the minute he heard you were out for the night."

"You don't mean you left the two of them there without a chaperone?"

"Fred's in charge."

"Did Daddy see you?"

"No."

"Good, good. They're not overbright, the Big People, but we still shouldn't draw them a road map." Phoebe and Jack stopped to kiss in the shadow of a tree, and a breeze showered them with water from still-drenched leaves. They discovered you can kiss and laugh at the same time.

Since Phoebe had gone to live with Charlie, she and Jack were keenly aware that the love affair between their parents was changed. Charlie couldn't spend the whole night at Martha's anymore and leave Phoebe alone. ("Well, he *could,*" Phoebe said. "I keep telling him I don't care, but you know. He thinks I'm six or something. He thinks I'll light my hair on fire. Or have an orgy.") But more than once she'd heard him creeping in at ungodly hours, like six in the morning. She thought about how hard it must be to drag yourself out of a deep sleep and a warm bed and away from the sweet body of someone who loves you.

Martha sometimes, rarely, left Jack in charge of baby Fred and came uptown to have dinner with Phoebe and Charlie, but you could see she felt guilty about it, to be making motherly conversation with Phoebe while her own children were home alone. On those evenings Phoebe left her father and Martha alone as much as she could, but once she'd caught them necking by complete mistake, she had just popped out of her room to go to the kitchen, and after that she thought they hardly even held hands when she was around. They just listened to music and talked, and then Charlie went downstairs with Martha to put her in a taxi, where no doubt their good-night completely embarrassed and mortified the doorman. Martha and Charlie didn't go out on dates by themselves very often anymore, because that would leave Jack and Phoebe unchaperoned with too many bedrooms at their disposal. On the now-frequent nights Charlie and Martha were apart, Phoebe's friends complained they could never get her on the phone because Martha and Charlie talked for hours.

"I got him one of those hourglass egg timers and we agreed he could turn it over three times and then it was my turn to use the phone, but he cheated," said Phoebe.

"Of course," said Jack. "Wouldn't you, if you were talking to me?" She would, of course.

Jack was worried about what was happening to their parents. They had seemed so happy in the beginning, and it had been a relief to him not to worry if his mother was lonely, or out with some scumbag, or missing him if he was out with his friends. But more than once in the past weeks, lifting the receiver to see if the line was finally free so he could call Phoebe, Jack had heard not the sweet hum of pillow talk, but tension and pain in his mother's voice, or Charlie's.

"They're full of raging hormones. All this frustration is bad for them."

"Next they'll develop acne," said Phoebe. "Do you think they're fighting?"

"I don't think they're happy. . . ."

"Do you think it's true that there's one perfect person in the world for everyone?"

"Do you mean them? Or us?"

"Maybe all of us," said Phoebe. "Your mom. My dad. Maybe we were all a family in another life or something." The night was full of stars. Anything seemed possible.

"I don't know," said Jack.

"When I was younger I used to ride my bike around this cemetery near our house in the country. Some of the stones had people's pictures on them. Photographs, set in the tombstones some way. I found one with this picture of a really handsome boy . . . he looked my age but he died in like 1943. I kept thinking, What if there's one perfect person for me in the whole universe, and he already died?"

"Sad. Poor you," said Jack.

"Poor me." They were both smiling broadly.

"I don't think there's a plan in the universe, though," said Jack. "If there was, everything would have a point. There's no point to my father dying." They walked, holding each other. They decided to walk all the way downtown and watch the sunrise from the Brooklyn Bridge.

Connie slept on the couch in Sophie's living room in a pair of Sophie's shortie pajamas and a sleeping bag. She was dead to the world when Sophie slipped out in the half-light of morning, carrying her shoes in her hand. The living room of the little apartment was filled with the minty smell of adult sleep.

Connie was exhausted by tears, exhausted by anger, exhausted by fear. From time to time during the morning she would swim almost to consciousness, like a trout rising to a mayfly. Then she would feel the rough tweed of the upholstery against her arm, feel the dry hot stiffness of tear-swollen eyelids, and dive again. This was not a world she wanted to wake up to. From time to time in the night she had wept in her sleep.

It had seemed simple yesterday. She was going to save her own life. She would end her marriage and protect her children. But starting today, lasting for years, nothing would be simple again. If you save yourself by leaving your children, haven't you wrecked yourself and them after all? Her children needed her, and she wasn't there. She wanted to hold William. She wanted to stroke his hair and explain that it would be all right. That she would make it all right. But how, exactly, when today she couldn't even get out of bed?

What would happen to the girls? Would they be angry at her for leaving? Would they blame her for destroying the family, for not making their father happy, for not keeping them safe? Would their view of the lives of women be warped forever? Their mother had failed. Their mother had tried to do the one thing to which women seem dedicated by anatomy and history, and failed. It wasn't anything complicated, pioneering, it wasn't that she had tried to be an astronaut or a leveraged buy-out queen or a firewoman. She had tried to marry one man and raise his children, and she had failed.

The future seemed like a wasteland before her. Ruined children, ruined hopes. Where would it end?

It was noon. She was awake. She didn't want to be, but she was. Sophie's cat was in the hall doing his business in the litterbox. A box of tissues was on the end table beside the couch, and used ones lay on the floor where she had thrown them in the night. The wastebasket was across the room. From where she lay on the couch, she could see balls of dust behind the television stand. Sophie had a maid who spoke only Tagalog, who came to work on Thursday afternoons. Sophie had seen her when she hired her two years ago and hadn't laid eyes on her since. Well, tomorrow was Thursday. Connie would be able to give Sophie a full report on the maid, and explain to her about moving things so you can dust behind them. If she was still here.

And where else would she be?

Connie wiggled out of the sleeping bag with a motion something like that employed by a seal climbing a tide rock. (The sleeping bag zipper was struck. Sophie had apologized.) Connie made her way into the bathroom where she was confronted with the sight of herself in a pink camisole with matching bloomers, sort of like the things they used to wear to play field hockey. Is this what all single women wore to sleep in? Would she have to, now? Her knees were horrible looking. Since when did her knees look like a matched pair of basset hounds? She needed a pedicure. She needed to lose ten pounds. She needed fresh clothes to put on, but she didn't have any, and Sophie was smaller and much slimmer than she.

She decided to take a bath.

The phone rang while she was in the tub. At home, if she was in the tub and the phone rang, it would be early morning, or evening, and there would be a stampede of Ruth and Molly to answer it. Here, just as she climbed out of the hot water and got a fresh towel soaking wet, she heard the call answered by a machine. She got back into the tub and listened through the door; it seemed that the caller had hung up without giving a message. She finished her bath, dried and dressed herself in the clothes in which she'd fled last night. Since she didn't have any fresh underwater, she decided not to wear any. Being a houseguest was horrible; she'd forgotten. She was always the one with the house. Other people were guests.

In the kitchen, trying to make herself breakfast at one in the afternoon, she discovered that her sister didn't seem to eat breakfast, at least not at home. There was no cereal, hot or cold. There was no juice. There was milk, but not much and it was skim—blue milk, Ruth called it. There were tea bags, nasty antique-looking ones, a supermarket brand. But no teapot. There were plenty of expensive coffee filters, and about seven little brown bags of different blends of coffee in the refrigerator, but Connie couldn't drink coffee in the morning; it made her stomach hurt. She was afraid she had an ulcer. At last she made a cup of tea by dangling a tea bag in a mug of hot water. The mug had a teddy bear on it, wearing a bow tie.

Connie was drinking her tea and reading the *TV Guide,* the only magazine she could find, when the phone rang again. Her stomach tightened. Dave. It would be Dave. She didn't want to talk to him, she didn't want to deal with his apology, his bewilderment, she didn't want to start over again. She picked up the phone.

"You're there," said Sophie. "I called before. . . ." Connie burst into tears.

Sophie was calling to see if Connie wanted to meet her for lunch. Connie explained that she was trying to eat breakfast, and Sophie told her where she kept the juice oranges and the juicer. Making fresh juice doesn't occur to people who have to get a husband and three children out of bed by seven-thirty and out the door by eight-ten every morning. Sophie said that they could still meet for lunch, and Connie said that she wasn't wearing any underwear. Sophie recommended that Connie finish breakfast and go straight to Bloomingdale's and choose a whole new wardrobe, and charge it to Dave.

"Do you think I should call him? To arrange about getting my things?"

"No," said Sophie. "That's what he expects. You're always the conciliator. This time, let him stew in his own juice, so he'll know it's really different. He'll call you. He's a baby, Connie. He won't be able to manage on his own . . . believe me. He'll call you. He needs you a lot more than you ever knew. And a lot more than you need him. Let him find that out; then it would be time to talk."

Connie agreed, and by the end of the conversation was actually looking forward to going shopping. Sophie promised that if Connie were hit by a bus and rushed to the hospital before she got to Bloomingdale's, Sophie would follow at once and explain about the underwear to the staff of the emergency room, and to their mother.

Charlie and Martha sat at Charlie's dinner table in the candlelight. The meal was cleared away and Phoebe had excused herself to go back to writing her Wordsworth paper. It was April, and the evenings were getting longer; outside the window there were streaks of mauve and blue against the deepening night. Outside in the distance, now that it was weather for open windows, New York wailed. Sirens howled, horns honked, radios played. It was nice, this interlude before the heat forced windows shut again, and air-conditioning blotted out the street sounds.

Charlie and Martha talked softly of this and that. It hardly mattered to them what, since the real point was the soft interweaving of their voices, making a fabric of their shared life. What mattered was flesh against flesh, the sight and sound of each other.

Martha reported that she was doing a still life in oil for a book jacket. It was a long time since she had worked in oil, and she was enjoying it. But she kept coming home and finding that Jack or Fred had eaten the grapes out of the arrangement.

Charlie said he was bogged down in a case that should have been settled weeks before, that now looked as if it would go to court. He was depressed about it, since he hated litigating.

"Albert loves it," Charlie said. "He loves the tension and the drama, he loves thinking on his feet, he loves manipulating the jury. I'm awful at it. I flop around like a smelt." Martha smiled and rubbed his neck.

Charlie's case was on contingency, which annoyed his partners. It was a product liability case, not the kind of thing the plaintiff usually wins. But the client was the daughter of one of the doormen in Charlie's building. She was an art teacher in Queens who dreamed of showing her fiber art in Manhattan galleries. Instead, she had lost years of her life fighting a rare form of blood cancer caused by the fabric dye she used. Which the company had labeled FOR HOME AND SCHOOL. NON-TOXIC. ALL NATURAL.

Martha was incensed and proud of Charlie for taking the case. But Charlie's partners had been surprisingly unsympathetic.

"You should have heard Steve and Albert when we were in law school," said Charlie, trying to sort it out. "Steve's parents were old left-ies. We were all going to open storefront law firms and do pro bono work at least half the time."

"I wish I'd known you then."

"Oh don't. You'll make me sad."

"I love you so much and we missed all those years."

"We only have about forty more to be together, and then we'll be dead." They kissed.

"How did you wind up with a firm on Fifth Avenue?" Martha asked. "Instead of a storefront?"

"Well, *I* got married. You should have seen Patsy's face when I told her I'd had an offer from Millbank Tweed, but Steve and I were going to go to work in the East Village instead. Starting salaries on Wall Street those days were about forty thousand dollars. She didn't know whether to shit or go blind."

Martha laughed. She traced with her finger the veins on the inside of his wrist.

"Steve *did* work as a public defender for four or five years. He had one client who blew away a bus driver on the Madison Avenue line because 'The guy was in my face, man.' His client felt that was a full defense.

"He got to know a lot of dealers, and a lot of whores. In the meantime his own babies were being raised by keepers who either didn't speak English or spent all day watching soap operas, because his wife had to work."

"Did his wife want him to quit?"

"Marilyn? No, she didn't. Although it worried her some when her daughter's first words were in Spanish. But she's tough. She believed in the way we thought it would be—that Steve would be defending poor street kids who'd been harassed by racist cops, or keeping helpless welfare mothers from being evicted. But Steve got tired of the junkies and the hookers, and he got tired of driving a Nash Rambler when his classmates were bitching about how the Jag was always in the shop. And we wanted to work together. So. Next you turn around and you have an office on Fifth Avenue."

"Steve must understand why you took this case."

"He does. But he's got a point, too. Even if I win, which I won't, they'll appeal and drag me along for months. And we have rent and salaries to pay, and maintenance contracts to keep up, and leases on the copy machines, and while I'm in court making an ass of myself, someone has to tend my other clients."

"Daddy," Phoebe wailed from the master bedroom where she was writing her paper on Charlie's computer. Charlie hesitated a beat.

"Yes, Phoebe."

"How do I run the spell checker?"

"Honey, don't yell across the house, come in here and talk to us."

Charlie and Martha stopped holding hands and straightened up as Phoebe's chair scraped and she plodded across the hall and into the dining room.

"Excuse me," said Phoebe, "how do I run the spell checker?"

"You have to exit the program, and then type SPELL at the DOS prompt."

Phoebe looked nervous. "Is that the way I did it before?"

"No, on your mother's computer you can run it from inside the program, but mine doesn't have enough memory."

"Why not?"

"Because your mother's computer is better."

"Why? She never uses it."

"Such is life," said Charlie, and then thought he ought to try not to sound snide. "She felt she needed a big powerful one because she was going to do graphic design on it. Remember? She and Aida were going to start a business?"

"Sort of," said Phoebe. There *had* been a month or two when Patsy's dining-room table was covered with all sorts of fancy letter paper and announcements and invitations and business cards, and Patsy and Aida sat around criticizing them and talked about developing "a look."

"Do you understand how to save all your work and exit to the DOS prompt?"

"Could you help me?"

Charlie said, "Sure."

He followed Phoebe out, and Martha went to the kitchen to finish washing up. There the phone rang.

"Honey, do you mind?" Charlie called. Martha answered.

The woman on the phone was startled. "Hello?" A beat. "Is Charlie Leveque there?"

"He is. May I tell him who's calling?"

"Is this Martha?" The woman had a warm pleasant voice.

"Yes, it is."

"Martha, it's Sophie Curry."

"Oh, hello. It's nice to meet you. Sort of meet you."

They both laughed. Sort of. Why was Sophie calling him? Did she call often?

"Well," said Martha. "Charlie's helping Phoebe sort out the computer. Can you hold on?"

"Sure. Thanks."

Charlie looked a little reluctant when she brought him the message. He finished with Phoebe, then came to the kitchen. He stood in his shirtsleeves leaning against the doorjamb and holding the phone against his ear with his shoulder. Reflexively, he picked up a pencil stub and a memo pad. Martha stopped putting dishes away; she sat down at the counter and began refilling the salt and pepper shakers. She watched him.

"Of course you're not. It's fine," said Charlie. Then a pause, while he listened.

"She left the house?" said Charlie.

Pause.

"How is she?"

Pause.

"I'm sorry. Tell her I'm sorry."

A longer pause.

"Ummm. Well. That wouldn't be my advice. I think she should go back to the house tomorrow while Dave's at work, and have the locks changed."

Pause. Charlie was writing on his piece of paper.

"Maybe. Advice is worth what you pay for it, but that's what I'd tell her."

There was a longer pause then. Charlie looked over at Martha and smiled, apologetic.

"Sophie. It's okay. Look, call me tomorrow, or have Connie call me if you need to know how to go about it. There are a few other things she should do, about joint bank accounts and so on." He mimed to Martha, Sorry . . . and made a winding motion with his hand, meaning he was trying to wind it up.

Another pause.

"I do know. All too well. I wouldn't wish it on anybody."

And another.

"If she and Dave have any joint accounts, checking or savings, or brokerage accounts, she should empty them, and close them, and put the money in another bank that she's never used before."

Pause. Charlie rolled his eyes. Martha watched, grave. At last he said to the phone, "Soph, I've got to go. Please have Connie call me in the morning, or have her come see me."

Pause.

"You don't have to thank me."

He hung up. On Eighty-ninth Street, Sophie hung up and turned to her sister.

And on Seventy-fifth Street, Charlie, in his kitchen, took Martha in his arms and gave her a long kiss. She returned it but then still holding him she asked, "Was it you who told Raymond to clean out our bank accounts?"

They looked at each other for a long moment.

"No. He'd already done it when he came to me."

"Oh," said Martha. And with an effort, she let the shadow that had moved between them dissolve, and turned to washing the wineglasses from dinner. Charlie explained the situation with Sophie's sister, although Martha had inferred most of it.

"I guess when things start to fall apart they really fall apart. How's her daughter?" she asked. It was more than a month since Jack and Phoebe had found Molly Justice in the park, and since then she'd thought of Molly often, and of her mother, to whom she had spoken once.

"Molly seems to be fine," said Charlie. "She was back in school after three days. She won't talk about that night at all. But physically she's all right."

"I'm glad," said Martha. "Jack will want to know."

But between them, although this time Charlie didn't see it, there now moved another shadow.

Molly is fine, she was back in school after three days. How often did he talk to Sophie? And why?

So many times Raymond had cheated. So many times he had been where he shouldn't have been, known what he shouldn't have known. So many times she'd wished not to have noticed. But she had learned to notice, because underneath Raymond had wanted her to. It excited him to cheat people and then let them know it.

She thought, I know Charlie is a completely different man. I would never think of this, to be suspicious of Sophie, it wouldn't enter my mind, if Charlie and I could sleep in each other's arms and wake up together.

Inside herself, Martha wanted to change the subject. "Would you like to go for a walk?" she asked Charlie.

"I'd *love* to."

They smiled at each other and stopped in mid-kitchen for a long hug. Perfect. They could be alone a little. Ramble and natter. Smell the sky. Neck in the park.

"Daddy . . . ," Phoebe called from the bedroom.

They stood holding each other.

Finally Charlie called, "Please don't yell across the house at us. We're in the kitchen." And they broke apart and waited. Phoebe appeared. Phoebe had grown, and thinned out. Her eyes had interesting hollows, and she was wearing a big red crew shirt over T-shirt and tights. She looked very gamine. Martha liked it.

"Daddy, what does it mean when the NumLock light comes on and the screen freezes?"

Martha and Charlie looked at each other. It didn't mean anything good.

"Were you using the number pad?"

"No. I was just typing and the screen froze."

"How long ago did you save?"

Phoebe looked upset. Was this important? "I don't know. Not very recently."

"And you've written a lot since then?"

"Well . . . yeah."

"Shit," said Charlie.

They all piled into the bedroom where the computer glowed, large and green, on a desk in the corner. Charlie pushed various things on the keyboard but nothing happened. Phoebe looked more and more unhappy.

"It's hung up," said Charlie.

"Does that mean I lose everything?"

"We have to reboot. You lose everything since you last saved."

Mentally, both Charlie and Martha braced for a tantrum. But Phoebe just rolled her eyes.

"Oh, great. Girl Computer Nerd destroys the system with touch alone."

"It's not your fault, honey. The machine screwed up."

"I finally got this paper right, and the computer ate it! This is grotesque." She was being a good sport, but she looked exhausted. Suddenly Martha had a flash of seeing what drew Jack to her.

"Honey," said Charlie, "I'm terribly sorry."

"Does the paper have to be done tomorrow?" Martha asked.

"Yes. I already had an extension. It's for Mr. Kelley." Mr. Kelley seemed to be someone the kids wanted to work for. Phoebe had talked more and more about his class lately.

"Don't you think he'd understand, if you asked for one more day?"

"I'm sure he would, but it's really my fault that it's already late. I mean, I wasn't swamped with work or anything. I just felt like putting it off until after the weekend. I told him I'd do it tonight and I think I should."

Martha and Charlie touched each other's hands briefly. Hello, what's this? Is this our own little house shrew?

Charlie smiled at her, proud. "Okay, kiddo. Do you think you can reconstruct what you've lost?"

A pause. "I think so."

"Do you want to copy down what you have on the screen, before you reboot? Then you just have to retype it."

"That's a good idea," said Phoebe, looking as if what she really wanted to do was go to bed and cry.

"Honey," said Charlie, "we were just going out for a short walk. Do you know how to do this by yourself? Press Control, Alt, Delete?"

Phoebe looked miserable. "I think so. But what if it comes up still frozen or something?"

Martha said to Charlie, "You better stay with her. I'll go on home and see how the boys are getting along. Jack has a paper due, too, I think."

"No, he finished his," said Phoebe. "But he has a take-home French exam."

"Oh," said Martha. "Thanks." They smiled at each other. Phoebe saw more of Jack than she did. She wished she saw Charlie like that every day.

Charlie went down to the street with Martha to put her in a cab; at least they could neck in the elevator. It was agony saying good-bye. And yet, once alone in the taxi, she was eager to be home, to hear in Jack's own rollicking kid patois what was going on in his world, to give Freddy a hug and smell his sweet skin, to pay a couple of bills she hadn't gotten to, and write a letter to Raymond's mother. All things that could have been part of normal domestic pleasures, if Charlie were in the next room and they shared a life. But since they did not, they were pleasures partly spoiled because they meant she and Charlie had to part.

When she got home, Jack and Jaywalk were shooting pool. There was a stale greasy smell in the air.

"Hi, Mom," said Jack.

"Hi, Mom," said Jaywalk.

"Hello, little boys," said Martha.

"We decided to work on our French exams together."

"So I see," said Martha.

"No, but Mom, we had to wait for you because we couldn't understand something. Wait a minute, I'll get it." In a flash he was back with the exam. "We're all done except for the sight translation, but look, it doesn't make any sense. See, here it says very clearly, the hat of my grandmother is full of pigs. . . ." The boys started giggling. "No, not *chapeau, château*," said Jaywalk, "the castle of my grandmother is full of pigs. . . ." They had clearly been in fits of mirth for hours.

Martha looked at the passage, and indeed, someone who spoke no French had done the typing of it. It was riddled with mistakes.

"Madame whatshername should have proofread this . . . ," she said, annoyed.

"No, but really, the hat might be full of pigs, it could be right, these people are French. . . ." The boys were off again. Martha took the paragraph into the kitchen, where she could sort it through in quiet. But in the kitchen, she found the source of the odor in the air.

"Jack, what the hell is this in the broiler?"

"Oh, we were going to tell you about that. That's the steak."

What Martha could see was a charred acrid lump, covered by about a pound of what looked like flour. There was a good deal of it on the floor as well, though attempts had been made at sweeping.

"The broiler caught fire," said Martha.

"It was quite exciting. First we heard something, then I opened the door and these flames shot up to here." Martha winced, thinking of dish towels on fire, children's clothes in flames, the whole kitchen burning.

"You're all all right? Is Fred?"

"Yes. Jaywalk held him while I tried to find baking soda, but I couldn't find it and we decided powdered sugar would work as well. I thought you'd be quite annoyed if I let the house burn down."

"Good boys. You knew not to use water?"

"Oh yes. We know these things."

"But why did that happen? The broiler was clean."

"No, I made bacon in it this afternoon."

"You did? When?"

"When you were out picking up Fred."

"Oh."

"Is that what made it happen?"

"I would think. Grease catches fire, so you should trim meat and keep the broiler clean."

"I didn't know that."

"No. How much bacon did you cook?"

"Only about a pound."

Martha laughed. How could anyone eat a pound of bacon and want a steak three hours later? Boys were amazing. She felt a terrible mixture of relief and fear at what could have happened.

"What did you have for supper then?"

"Cheerios."

"Oh, sweetheart." To make up for leaving Jack and Fred she'd bought a really good steak and asparagus and potatoes.

"It was fine. We love Cheerios."

She stood for a moment, with the garbled exam in her hand and the ruined dinner at her feet. Then she shook her head and gave Jack a hug. He hugged her back strongly. He was glad she was home. She went off to have a quick look at baby Fred, to be sure he was breathing.

Connie *sat alone* in her car in the driveway at Arden Forest and stared at her house. She'd been gone for thirty-six hours.

The shade was still drawn in William's bedroom. Connie always raised it when she went in to get him up for school. The roses Dave had brought her were in the vase she had thrown at him. Someone had picked them up and rearranged them and put the vase on the piano. She could see them through the window of the living room. A bicycle—Ruth's—had been left leaning against the side porch. She must remember to take it into the garage, and to scold Ruth about it when she got home.

It took a long time for Connie to make herself get out of the car. Once she heard an engine start in the next yard behind the box hedge, and then in the rearview mirror she saw her neighbor, Joan Board, pull out in her Suburban and drive away. Across the road, the Heindells' boxer was sleeping in the sun in the middle of his front walk. Connie couldn't analyze the cold reluctance she felt to get out of her isolation bubble and set foot into this tranquil scene and become part of it. Instead she sat in silence hovering, by a tire's half-radius, above the earth, looking, and remembering.

There was the spot where Dave fell off William's skateboard and into the juniper bush. ("And I didn't even break the glass," he roared, recounting the story about a hundred times.) It had been a cocktail party stunt, their midsummer barbecue.

There was the lawn where Dave had played endless games of horsey, with the girls taking turns on his back, and where later Ruth had played horsey with William, since Dave couldn't be bothered. There was the tail of Ruth's kite that got caught in the oak tree. They had pulled the kite down by the string, at last, but the tail was still caught there after . . . how many years? You could barely see it, you had to know it was there.

Over there was the spot they put the wading pool every summer. Beside it, in the shade, Connie used to read to the children *Uncle Wiggily* and *Dr. Doolittle* for half an hour after lunch every afternoon, so they wouldn't get cramps swimming too soon after eating and drown in five inches of tepid water. On cool days or after rain, she'd run the hose in through the kitchen window and fill the pool for them with hot water from the kitchen sink. The children loved it, though it made Dave roar about the fuel bill. We were ahead of our time, Connie thought. We invented the hot tub.

Connie's rhododendrons were nearly past, and the forsythia was long gone. Down the hill she had stopped to admire the Munns' magnolia trees. She loved magnolias. She had worked so hard on the rhodos and on the tulips and daffodils. The next delight of the season would be the honeysuckle. There was a bank of it around behind the house. There she had taught the girls, and William in turn, how to pull the stamen of the flower down through the tiny neck of the blossom and to capture on the tongue the fragrant drop of nectar that pulled out along with it.

Dave had taught the girls how to make whistles with a blade of grass held between the thumbs, and had led all the local children in games of Sardines and Kick the Can and Capture the Flag. They had had fun here. Other things too, but fun, certainly.

She realized how long she'd been sitting when Joan Board drove back up the hill in her big Suburban and back into her driveway, with her backseat full of sacks of lawn food. Connie decided she better do what she'd come to do.

She got out of the car and walked to the front door. She never used the front door—nobody did except guests. But this seemed a formal occasion. She was about to hijack the house. And perhaps after that, go on to a life of other crimes against the life this family had led.

The doormat was rather a disgrace. She'd have to change it. And the fan light over the door needed washing. That was hard to do alone; it was best done with Dave on a ladder on the outside and Connie on the inside, both washing. That way you could tell each other where the streaks were—on your side or his—and get it all done in a few minutes. But she would manage alone. She would manage many things alone from now on.

She reached for the doorknob. It wouldn't turn. She tried again and put a little weight into it; this door was never locked. But it wouldn't open. She fished for her keys.

Her front-door key went in but wouldn't turn. She tried it again and again, with mounting panic.

She went to the back door and tried there. Locked—again, her key didn't work. She hurried through a mulch of leaves that should have been raked last fall, toward the side porch. But she knew what she would find. Dave had already had the locks changed. Had he talked to a lawyer, too? Or was he that big a son of a bitch all by himself?

Well, she knew it didn't make great moral sense to feel this outrage at him for doing what she'd been about to do to him, but if he'd walked up the driveway at this minute, and if she had a gun, she'd have plugged him through the heart, kicked gravel at the corpse, and worn red to his funeral. Her anger was towering, blinding. Dave was a bastard, a cold-hearted, cheating, mean-spirited son of a bitch. And Sophie was a stupid witless prune for telling her to wait for him to call, and she, she was the biggest, stupidest, sorriest ass of all for leaving the house, for letting this happen, for exercising no cunning whatsoever even though she was now in the fight of her life. She shouldn't have gone to New York. But once again she was a day late and a dollar short. Once again, she'd been out-maneuvered, out-thought, out-done, lollygagging around the lingerie floor at Bloomingdale's while her husband locked her out of her life. She wanted to kill somebody and she wanted to die and she cried and cried and cried.

Fortunately, she was around in the shadow of the side porch where none of the neighbors was likely to see her. When she stopped sobbing and slowly began to think again, she realized that there was still a great deal to do. She thought of breaking into the house and calling another locksmith. (Which one had Dave called? This could soon reach the level of farce.) But, she realized that if she retook the house that way, she'd never have an easy moment. She'd never know when she was going to come back from the market, or wake up in the dark, and find that Dave or somebody hired by him was breaking in, in retaliation.

She realized, too, that she had to get to the bank.

Connie parked her car in the lot behind the bank. She had to sit still for a moment before getting out because she was shaking. Suddenly, a shadow darkened her window. She looked up.

There was Margaret Wickwire, perky as always. Her buckteeth gleamed, as she motioned Connie to roll down her window. Which Connie did, and as she did, her own face assumed the sort of demented Junior League smile with which she had greeted unwanted interruptions in this perky little village for twenty years. You couldn't live here if you weren't prepared to treat the village center as if it were a big common living room, and every friend and acquaintance was welcome to greet you as a member of your own family. That's what village life was about. If you wanted privacy, if you thought people should think twice before intruding on your personal space, you could move to New York.

"Good morning!" screamed Margaret, brightly. "You must be so proud!" She was wearing a puke green polo shirt with a little polo player on her left boob, and Connie thought she looked like a hockey coach. Why the hell do you wear men's clothes, she wanted to say to her, with all your money? What would you say if your husband ran around town in a tennis dress?

"We were *all* so proud of Molly! I was sorry you couldn't be there, but wow, she's becoming quite the athlete!"

Connie beamed back at her. Why don't I just close the window on her hand, she thought.

"Look, while I've got you," said Margaret, leaning in. "The girls have an away game this Thursday, and I'm signed up to drive, but we need one more mom. Are you free?"

"I don't know," Connie smiled and smiled. "I'll have to check my book."

"Oh, I *know*," said Margaret, who knew nothing, nothing, nothing.

"I'll call you, why don't I?" said Connie.

"That'll be fine. I'll let you go. You look great, by the way." And Margaret burbled off in her Nikes to her Mercedes station wagon. Connie wondered if Margaret owned a dress. What were people thinking of, what had *she* been thinking of for twenty years, sticking their stupid perky smiles into people's faces? Didn't it occur to anyone that people were leading real lives here? That not everyone was having a nice day? She felt vicious, utterly homicidal. She wanted to peel out of the parking lot and run over the first stranger she saw. Splat! Screeching tires! Squirting blood! Crunch of bone and gristle! Sirens! Tragedy! Mess and destruction! Reporters pushing through the crowd! Police dragging her off in handcuffs! It sounded wonderful. But instead, she had to take a deep breath, climb out of her stupid car, and walk in the blaring sunlight into the bank.

She pushed her check across under the teller's cage, and with it her banking card. She had made the check for $1,200, which she figured would leave about $40 in the account, just to keep it open. Without the master checkbook, which was in Dave's desk at home, she couldn't guess the exact balance, and she didn't want to overdraw.

"I'm sorry," said the horrible, pewling, pimply high school drop-out behind the grill. "This account is closed."

Connie stood for a moment, feeling her heart pause, then lurch, ka-boom. A red and black fuzzy ringing swarmed around the outside of her vision. She had fainted once in her life, and this is what it had been like just before.

But the red and black receded, and she was still standing here looking at this item holding her check and refusing to give her her money.

"That can't be right," said Connie firmly, nicely. "I just made a deposit Friday. There's at least fourteen hundred dollars in it." She had no idea if that was right, but she didn't want this person to imagine she was someone of no substance.

"There must be a mistake, then," said the teller. Such a bright, helpful girl she seemed. Of course there was a mistake. Her name tag said she was Betty.

"My little machine is showing me this code. See?" Betty showed the little electronic screen to Connie. Where her account balance should have been, there were these stupid brackets with the number 39 between them.

"The machine's probably down again," said Betty. "I'll use someone else's."

She trotted away to the manager's office. Connie stood there, aware of a growing line of people behind her, and hoped no one she knew would come in.

Soon Betty was back with the manager, a Mr. Krupa. He was in shirt-sleeves, probably because he was so fat. Fat people were always hot. Both Betty and the manager were looking grave.

"Mrs. Justice? I'm sorry, your checking account has been closed."

God, he was a fat boorish man. Connie happened to know that people who wound up managing provincial branches of great metropolitan banks were going nowhere. Ever. They'd been sidetracked, forever, to this backwater. Maybe she should tell him that.

"I don't understand," said Connie pleasantly. "It's a joint account."

"Either you or your husband could make withdrawals at any time. Apparently your husband withdrew the funds and closed the account."

"But it was a joint account. Don't you have to *ask* me?" Her voice was rising a little. Mr. Krupa, like many grossly fat people, was covered with a gleam of sweat. Why did people use fruity words like "funds" when they meant money? Why did people say "I'm an attorney," when they meant lawyer? She bet that Mr. Krupa and his wife talked about their "accommodations" when they meant their motel room.

God, you're a bitch, Connie, she thought.

"What about our savings account?" she said mildly, to Mr. Krupa.

"Do you have your passbook?"

"No, I'm sorry." It's at home, locked inside my house, by my vicious mad-dog husband, how the hell do you expect me to have my passbook?

"Never mind. I can access the information for you. Why don't you come with me?" He opened the door that led to the officers' area, and held it for her. Gratefully, she allowed herself to be led away from the public floor.

He was trying to be nice. He was truly trying to be nice. Why couldn't she ignore the fact that he said things like "I'll access it for you" instead of talking like a normal human being?

He showed her to a chair in his office. It was a sort of purple chair in some nubby wool with wooden arms and legs. On the wall were horrible matched prints with different bright geometric shapes of purple, blue, and yellow. Connie crossed her ankles and composed her face in a smile.

Mr. Krupa heaved himself into his own chair and turned to his computer. He typed some things on the keyboard, then he waited. He put her bank card, which he still held, into the little electronic gizmo on his desk, which normally told you your account balance. He grunted, then typed some more things on the computer.

"I'm sorry," he said, and she believed he meant it. "That account is closed, too."

A long pause. "I see," said Connie. Apparently Mr. Krupa saw, too.

"I'm sorry," he said again.

"It's all right. I understand." And she rose and left. She hoped he would forgive her, when she realized she had not shaken hands or said good-bye.

On the sidewalk, she tried to think what she should do. She was almost too upset to speak. She certainly didn't want to drive. She thought she should speak to Sophie's friend, the lawyer. Charlie. But where could she use a telephone?

At last, she decided to go into Nina's Place, a paper placemat sort of lunch place where she hoped she wouldn't meet anyone she knew. The club made more sense, but that was impossible. She wanted to be invisible.

Nina's had a phone booth in the back. The phone booth stank of cigarette smoke and the odor of disinfectant from the rest rooms. There she called Sophie's office. Sophie was out to lunch, but her assistant gave Connie Charlie's office number and told her how to spell Leveque. She called that number and learned that he too was out to lunch. "He should be back in twenty minutes," said the girl. Connie thanked her, and left her name and said she'd call back.

She took a booth at the back of the room with her back to the street. She could get in her car and drive to New York, but that would take over an hour. She wanted to talk to Charlie. She wanted to stop being the person she'd been all morning. She ordered a glass of wine, and an egg salad sandwich.

She ate very slowly. The wine made her feel calmer, and by tiny increments she began to digest what had happened along with her lunch. She was out of the house, she had no cash. She had a brokerage account at Merrill Lynch in her own name. It had in it stocks given her as presents by her parents, and sometimes by Dave. She had to find out if Dave could get at that . . . and if he would. It was he who always made the investment decisions. The broker knew Dave, not her. Still . . . it was hers. Her name alone. (He hadn't cosigned in any way, had he?) She had to talk to a lawyer.

The house was in both their names. Her parents had made the down payment, Dave had paid the mortgage every month. The children . . . the children. She longed to see them. But what was she going to do? Wait for them outside school? Yes, maybe. Go back to the house at three o'clock? And risk meeting Dave? No, he'd never be there. She was sure. She was almost sure. But what if he'd arranged a sitter, or told the neighbors some lie and sent the kids home with someone else? (Connie is drunk, Connie is unstable, Connie is out of town . . . could William come to you after school for a while? Oh, and if his mother tries to see him . . . better not let her, she just upsets him.) It sounded farfetched. But who could have imagined what had happened already?

The waitress appeared. "Coffee, hon?"

"Yes," said Connie, gratefully. Yes. And thanks for calling me that. I need all the human kindness I can get. The waitress came with coffee in a thick white mug, and brought the bill.

When the coffee was gone, Connie left her credit card with the bill, and went back to the phone booth. She tapped the number of Charlie's office into the phone, and then her calling card number. She waited. The phone beeped and booped. She hoped, hoped, that Charlie would be back from lunch. She needed an ally. She needed help.

"I'm sorry," said a recorded voice, "your charge did not go through. If you need further assistance, please stay on the line."

She stayed on the line. Her rage was back. And panic. What the hell was this, now?

"This is Miss Podder [or something that sounded like that], how can I help you?"

"I'm trying to call New York, but the charge didn't go through."

"I'm sorry. What was the charge number?" She didn't sound sorry. Why were these people trained to say utterly false things? She could hear Miss Podder doing things to the computer.

"Yes," said Miss Podder, "that account has been canceled."

"That's ridiculous. I used it forty minutes ago. From this very phone."

"That account has been canceled as of this morning, ma'am. Sometimes it takes a little time for the order to go through."

"Well then, charge the call to my home phone. It's an emergency, I must get through."

"What is your home phone number, ma'am?"

Connie told her. The same as the charge number of course, minus the final code digits.

"And the number you're calling?"

Connie told her. There was keyboard tapping. Connie felt a wave of relief; in a minute she would hear Charlie's voice. She would have an ally, and things would begin to be all right.

"Ma'am, I'm sorry, but the number you gave me has been disconnected."

Connie felt her stomach drop to her shoes. She thought she might be sick. Disconnected? That was their *number*. The children lived there, at that number. How was she going to call them? Or were they all gone? This was a nightmare.

"I see," said Connie, and hung up. She leaned against the wall of the booth for a moment, trying not to faint or be sick. The wall was cool. It felt good on her hot face.

Finally, she picked up the phone again, and dialed Information.

"Please, in Arden Forest, the number for David Justice, on Bathgate." Almost at once, a recorded voice came on and gave her her own familiar number. So she hung up, found a quarter, and dialed it. After two rings, a recorded voice said, "The number you have called has been disconnected at the customer's request. Repeat . . ." And it repeated it. Connie dialed Information again.

"Operator, please, will you see if you have a new listing in Arden Forest for David Justice? Bathgate Road?" After a minute the operator answered, "I'm sorry. That is an unpublished number."

After a pause, Connie said, "Thank you" and hung up.

She went back to her booth. She sank into it, feeling utterly beaten. The kind waitress came back to her, and Connie said, near tears, "Could I have another cup of coffee?"

The waitress said, "Hon, do you have another credit card? That one didn't go through."

"What do you mean?"

"It didn't go through. Do you have another? MasterCard? VISA? We don't take American Express."

"Oh," said Connie, dazed. "Sorry." And she looked in her wallet for another card. "Let me have that one back."

"I can't do that, hon. The card's been canceled. The company told me to cut it in half."

Connie felt the killer rage flush. "And you did it already?" After all, she'd used the phone card this morning, maybe this card would work somewhere else.

"Yeah."

Connie, cold with anger, stopped looking for another credit card. She couldn't sit there while this monster cut them in half, one after the other. She looked in her wallet for cash. She had $7.60. And she needed gas and toll money to get back to New York.

"Will you take a check?"

"Is it local?"

"Yes."

"Sure, if you've got ID."

She wrote the waitress a check on Mr. Krupa's bank. On the back she wrote, Sorry. And she was. But when it bounced they wouldn't know where to reach her. Dave could fucking deal with it.

Gillis Burnham had never been highly verbal. When he listened to music, he preferred massive, chordal music like Brahms or Bruckner. When he wrote music it was structural, volumetric, an edifice of sound and color tones that you could live in like a house. He used orchestration to make floors, walls, and arching space out of melody; you could sit inside the string section and feel how far overhead the piccolos were. He had no sympathy for music like Mozart's, where the lines were so much like language, where the variations interlocked with the rhythm of sentences, making jokes and comments on the original thesis.

So it took him a good while, several months, to figure out the word for the way he felt nowadays. It wasn't a feeling that he recognized from the past. If he had been a reader, a student of the human condition, he might have hit on it faster. But he didn't read much, and when he did he preferred to read French novels in the original with a Larousse at his side, so it was more like doing a puzzle than like reading. His wife, Valeria, had always said his taste in literature made perfect sense; that his emotional system was so abstract that he used even English as a second language.

Nevertheless, he found himself, in the forty-sixth year of his life, wanting very much to put a word to the feeling that filled him now when he walked into his loft in the evening after rehearsal and stood in the dark and silence for a moment before flipping the light switch. Or when he walked out to Prince Street in the morning, when the streets were washed and clean and the light looked somehow like Paris, to buy a cup of coffee and a bagel and the *New York Times*. Or when he sat at the piano during his workday and looked out the window at the sky, or into the windows of the buildings across the street. On the floor below him and to the left, he could see into a sweatshop with rows of Asian women hunched over sewing machines. On the next floor opposite him, there was a dance studio where men and women in brilliant spandex formed into rows and leaped around to some unheard (no doubt hideous) music until they ran with sweat. Above him was a half-loft where a family lived, a family he studied. The wife was quite beautiful, the husband, black, was a painter. They had a baby daughter whom he'd been watching now for a year; she was finished nursing and was almost ready to walk. In addition to caring for the baby, the wife had a row of spectacular plants, trees almost, that she tended near the window.

Eventually the name for the feeling occurred to him. He was lonely.

Gillis had spent his whole life shaking off the hands that reached to cling to him. His mother's, his sisters', who seemed always to be all over him, in his room, mussing his music, making a racket, wanting him to play with them and carry them and lift them up to reach things, and love them. Even as a boy, he didn't talk much, he didn't complain, he just shut them out of his head and wished they would go away. Of all people in the world, Valeria had been the strangest choice of wife for him, since she was noisy and self-absorbed and demanded complete attention when she was home. But then, people do make strange choices of mate when they marry young, and especially when they marry the first person they sleep with, never knowing that they've fallen in love with sex, not with a person. And of course people often marry what's familiar, even though it's what they hate.

Probably the reason the marriage lasted so long was that Valeria wasn't home that much. And yet, to tell the truth, Gillis had been fascinated by his wife's very self-absorption, as if she acted out something he couldn't do for himself. Gillis's sole theory about himself was that he was one to whom needy women were always clinging, and his idea of needy was one who wanted human contact more than once every forty-eight hours. He was the one trying to get needy women to leave him alone.

Now, finally he had achieved that, and for very long stretches it had satisfied him deeply and he expected that state to last forever. When music is your life, your language, your emotional world, then silence is your indispensable medium, the state in which your art can begin. But he found after a time, that just having said all his life that he wanted to be alone, didn't make it true. At least, it didn't make it all he wanted. And now that he understood that he was lonely, he studied it, the way he would have worked at a harmonic problem in a concerto, until it came to him. What he would like would be to talk to Martha.

Gillis and Martha saw each other from time to time. They would meet on the street, or less often make a date for lunch. Once in a while he'd visit Crosby Street to see the boys. He loved them both in his abstracted way; he didn't like to be needed, but he did love. Many of his friends, and Martha's, thought it very odd that Gillis was content to have a relationship with his own son that was like that of a casual friend, but it never occurred to him that it was odd. He didn't think about relationships or what was considered normal in them, any more than he thought about his own feelings. He had never wanted children, he had made that clear. Martha had made her own choice and she was a woman who kept her bargains. Fred was her son, just as Jack was. As such, Jack interested and amused him, and Fred was beginning to as well. Gillis wasn't playful, so he hadn't much idea what to do with babies. But Fred would someday reach the age where he could be taught things, and Gillis would like that. He was a natural didact.

When he and Martha talked, it was about the boys or about work or about common friends. Gillis had never talked much about himself. He thought now maybe he'd like to. He remembered things Martha used to say to him, about growing together, about missing him when he was home reveling in silence, not missing her . . . and he began to think he'd like her to talk to him again. To see if he'd understand this time. Besides, it was April and Gillis, the least romantic human being in the world, remembered somehow that it was in April that he and Martha had first met. It was their anniversary of sorts. He thought about how he had felt with her, a night four years ago when they had talked about Mahler at Fanelli's, and he was falling in love.

Martha was just finishing work on the still life she was painting, when the buzzer sounded. It was late afternoon. She was surprised when the voice on the intercom said, "It's Gillis." She pushed the button to unlock the door and listened to him climb the stairs.

"I'm sorry I didn't call," Gillis said, kissing her. "It was an impulse."

"How fascinating. You're not impulsive."

"It's the new me."

"Well, I'm glad to see you." One of the interesting things about Gillis was that he was spectacularly handsome and didn't know it. It always struck Martha afresh, when she saw him after an absence. Lucky Fred, who looked like him, was going to be very beautiful.

"Are the boys here?"

"Fred will be home in a minute. Annie brings him on Thursdays. Heaven knows where Jack is. How are you?"

"I'm fine. I just finished a sonata for a competition, and I thought how nice it used to be when you'd make tea in the afternoon."

Martha smiled. "Are those thoughts connected?"

"Oh, sorry. I meant, it was nice to sit over tea, and tell you about my workday. Especially when I finished something."

"Would you like some tea, Gillis?"

"Why Martha, what a nice idea."

She set about getting out the tea things. It *had* been a nice ritual, their tea in the afternoons. Sometimes they would have spent the day quietly working in opposite ends of his loft, sometimes she'd work at home and he'd come to her when he finished his work, as he had today.

"How are your parents?" Gillis asked, as they waited for the water to boil.

"They're fine. Daddy will be eighty next month. Mother is still insufferable to Charlie."

"How's he taking it?"

"Luckily they never see each other. Though there will be the big party for Daddy, and I'm sure she'll call him Gillis the whole time, and all that."

"What's the theme for the party?"

"Guess."

"Scotland."

"How *did* you know."

"I can see it. Bagpipes?"

"Waiters in kilts . . . the boys reciting doggerel in Scottish accents. She wanted me to sing a song she wrote to the tune of 'Auld Lang Syne,' but I drew the line."

"It sounds wonderful."

"Great, you can go."

The tea tray was ready. They carried it to the corner of the loft where Martha's studio was, since the former living room was full of pool table. There they were chatting and discussing Martha's painting—Gillis thought the background should be grayed down some, to set off the colors of the fruit, and Martha thought he was probably right—when Annie arrived with Fred and her own daughter Lara.

"Gillis!" said Annie. She kissed him.

"Gillis!" said Fred, and Gillis picked him up and hugged him.

"Have some tea," both Martha and Gillis urged Annie. Gillis put Fred down, and he and Lara were disappearing toward Fred's room.

"Is there anything in there they can destroy or put up their noses or anything?"

"No."

"Then I'd love some."

Annie stayed to chat for some time. She was glad to see Gillis, and she thought the background of Martha's book jacket was fine but that the grapes were too green.

"Why not make them . . . oh, black. I love black, don't you?" Martha laughed. "Black grapes," said Annie fervently. Annie's gift was that she thought the real world unbelievably droll.

"It's not that kind of book," Martha said, with regret. Gillis told Annie about the sonata he had just finished. And Annie told them both about a wedding she had been to in Phoenix, where the bride insisted on singing with the band at the reception. Finally, Annie gathered up Lara and said good-bye.

Fred emerged from his room carrying a book and the ancient bald bear his grandfather had given him. He climbed into Gillis's lap and handed him the book. Martha took the tea things into the kitchen and washed and put them away. She smiled to herself, listening to Fred and Gillis laughing. This hadn't happened before.

When she was done she came back to them. "I'd invite you to stay to supper, but there isn't any food. I could go out to the corner market, though."

"Shall I stay to have supper with you, Fred? Is that a good idea?"

Fred said it was.

Martha asked, "What would you like to eat?"

"Or you could come to my house for supper," said Gillis. "I can make spaghetti. And you could hear my sonata. And you could see where I live, Freddy. You've never seen where I live."

"I hate to go when I don't know what Jack's up to. Let me see if I can find him."

She called Jaywalk's house and Jack was there. He and Jaywalk and Pia and Jenny Krass were planning the seniors' graduation party. Jack said if it was all right with her, he'd probably spend the night. So it was decided: they would go home with Gillis.

No one would have called Gillis a good cook. He was not deeply sensitive to creature comforts, and he could eat Ritz crackers and cream cheese for dinner night after night without feeling particularly deprived. So when he said spaghetti, he meant spaghetti with red sauce from a jar and a nice big salad of iceberg lettuce, and peanut butter and jelly on crackers for dessert. Fred loved it. He sat on telephone books to eat, and got spaghetti sauce all over his face. After dinner, and after being mopped up, he toured the loft with Gillis. Gillis gave him an electronic metronome to play with that ticked and blinked; Fred thought it was wonderful.

"Where do your children sleep?" asked Fred.

Martha looked at Gillis, but he held his attention on Fred.

"I don't have any children except you."

"You *don't?*"

"No. Isn't that sad?"

Fred nodded.

"But if *you* wanted to sleep here, we would make this couch open up and turn into a bed."

"We would?"

"Want to see?"

Fred did.

Gillis did the trick with the bed, and Fred climbed on it and bounced and found it good.

"Would you like to spend the night here?"

Martha looked at Gillis and at Fred. She was completely surprised at this development, and happy, and a little jealous. Fred knew that Jack used to go and sleep at *his* father's house, and apparently he assumed that would happen to him sooner or later, too. But Martha always thought Gillis would sooner fill his house with slime.

Gillis looked at Martha. Is this okay? She smiled back and shrugged. Fred looked from one to the other.

"Why don't I play my sonata for you, and you think about it." They both assented and settled down to listen. Fred was getting sleepy, and he had a surprising amount of natural repose for such a little boy . . . Gillis's genes, perhaps. He snuggled into Martha's lap and listened quietly while Gillis played.

"I love the adagio," said Martha, when the piece was through.

"I thought you would." Gillis realized, as he played, that that thought had been in his mind when he wrote it. Martha would love this. Martha will love this. They talked a little more about the technical problems of the piece, what he was trying to do with it.

There was a silence. They were both smiling. Fred seemed half asleep, content in his mother's arms.

"This is nice," said Martha.

"This *is* nice," said Gillis.

Then they both felt embarrassed.

"So, Mr. Fred. Do you want to stay? Have a sleepover?"

"Do you really want to do that?" Martha whispered to Gillis.

Fred nodded gravely. Yes, he wanted to stay. His eyes were wide.

"Yes," said Gillis to Martha. "I do. Why don't you have a night to yourself?"

Martha's heart leaped—a night off! She could spend the night with Charlie!

"Thank you. That's really nice of you." He shrugged, embarrassed again. "What an adventure, Fred! A sleepover! Are you sure?" Fred was. "He gets up early," Martha warned Gillis.

"That's okay, I do too."

That was true, Martha thought. Gillis might even like not being the only one awake at dawn.

At the door Fred, in his father's arms, looked suddenly tentative.

"What, dearie?"

Fred couldn't say what.

"Do you not want me to go?"

Fred look distressed but indicated that wasn't it.

"Do you want to come with me after all?"

He shook his head no. For a moment there was an impasse, as Gillis looked helpless and Martha thought.

"Do you want Mr. Bear?"

Relief. That was it. Fred nodded solemnly.

"Of course you do. He probably wonders where you are, too. I'll go bring him to you."

She hurried off, filled with joy. She felt so light with happiness that she ran part of the way home. This was the first night . . . could this be right? Yes. It was, the first night in almost three years, the first night since she brought the baby home from the hospital, that she had been alone, completely free, with no one needing her. And on top of it, what Gillis had done was something she had dreamed of. She had never asked for it, she thought it would be like asking a rhinoceros to jump through a hoop, but she had dreamed that one day Gillis would look at little Fred, and see that he was a dear, responsive, bright, beautiful boy, and want to be a person in his life.

How amazing. Maybe people could change. How amazing.

The evening air was full of the scent of green leaves. Somewhere someone was grilling on a rooftop . . . she could smell the sizzling meat. It was a wonderful evening, a wonderful world, a wonderful life. She was going to spend the night with Charlie.

* * *

The line was busy. Phoebe, no doubt. Martha went to change her clothes. She decided—this would make him smile—she decided to get dressed up the way she had the first night she went to Charlie's for dinner. First date. It had been so long since they had a gift of time like this, she almost felt it *was* a first date.

When she was dressed—garter belt, high heels, lipstick, the whole thing—she tried to call once more. Still busy. She was almost glad . . . now she was looking forward to surprising him. She went downstairs and a cab rolled right to her feet. It was that kind of night. She swung by Gillis's building and delivered Mr. Bear to Gillis, with more thanks. Then all the way uptown, she was singing to herself, having an imaginary conversation with Charlie in her head. Oh this was fun, this was going to be fun.

"Hello, Pete," she said to the doorman. She loved the way this lobby smelled. It meant she was going to see Charlie. In the elevator she combed her hair. At his door, she actually had to stop and take a deep breath. Where would he be? In the kitchen? In the living room? At the computer? How would he look when he turned and saw her? Oh, she loved his smile. Oh, she was smiling.

She unlocked the door and walked softly in, keeping her heels from making a racket in the hall. She could hear Charlie's voice in the living room. Talking to Phoebe? Or on the phone. She was at the door.

And her heart nearly stopped, for there on the couch was Charlie, thigh to thigh and holding hands with a small blonde woman she'd never seen before in her life.

The woman saw Martha first. Charlie saw the change in Sophie's face and looked toward the door.

"Martha!" Charlie leaped to his feet and started toward her, then stopped when he saw the way she was staring at him.

"I'm sorry," Martha said, feeling her lungs might collapse. "I tried to call."

"Honey, this is Sophie Curry."

"Martha," said Sophie. She got up and crossed the room to Martha and offered her hand. Martha shook it. She felt as if she'd wandered into an asylum.

"Sophie's sister has had the most terrible day . . ."

Martha stared. "Is she here, too?" she finally asked.

"Well, no. . . ."

"I gave her a Valium and made her go to bed," Sophie said.

Martha looked from one to the other, waiting to hear how this fact was related to Charlie on the couch, looking into Sophie's eyes and holding her hand.

"Sophie put her to bed. So she could sleep. I asked Sophie to come here and tell me what happened so we could work out a game plan for her. To have something to give her hope when she wakes up. She thinks she's lost her children and everything. . . ."

Martha said, "I see." What she meant was, I want to go home and die.

"Martha . . . you look wonderful. Where are the boys?"

"They're both out for the night."

"What? That's great!"

"Uh . . . Charlie? I'm going home now. You finish what you were doing, and we'll talk some other time."

Sophie looked upset, but she did nothing to stop Martha. When she had nearly reached the door, Charlie caught up with her. "Honey. . . ." He put a hand on her arm. "Please . . . stay. I can talk to Sophie in the morning."

"I have to go, Charlie."

"Call me when you get home."

"No." She barely knew what she was saying. She was more and more upset the longer she stood there, with Charlie's hand on her bare skin and Sophie watching. All she wanted was to get out of there before she started to cry. And before Charlie started making excuses.

The doorman put her in a cab. She didn't really remember getting home, but after a while she was there in her silent, empty house, with nobody else breathing in it but her. She got into bed, though the last light of evening was still in the sky, and after that it was a long night. Sometimes, awake for hours while her thoughts ran the whole gamut from I'm being silly, he was just comforting her to How long has this been going on, she thought, Charlie will come. He'll get in a cab, he'll come through the door, he'll peel off his clothes and slip into bed and explain to me why it's all right.

But he didn't.

∞

Charlie *spent four* hours, until two in the morning, staring at the phone. Ring, he said to it in his head. Ring. Ring. Please, ring. Martha, call me.

When he wasn't saying that, he was calling Martha, in his head. Martha, please. Martha, let me explain. Martha, please, tell me what I can say to change the expression in your eyes as you stared at me.

He read volumes in those eyes as she had stood at the living-room door. He knew what he was seeing. He knew when he fell in love with Martha that it might take years of his loving her faithfully, being absolutely trustworthy, before she would believe that all men were not Raymond, that he was one who would keep his promises, be where he was supposed to be, never ever give her cause to doubt his word. He had wanted to make it up to her, about Raymond and all that pain. He was the one who was going to make everything all right.

And now he felt paralyzed. He felt as if he were coming apart. He had never in his life given Patsy cause to mistrust him, and he loved Martha ten times as much. So what the hell had he done?

He pictured himself explaining to Martha. "See, Sophie was frightened and upset because her sister is having a bad divorce. Her husband, Dave, you don't know him but he's just the kind of husband who's going to fight dirty to prove what a man he is." Oh, god. How could he of all people say that to Martha? "I was holding hands with my ex-girlfriend because her sister's husband is going to do to her what I helped Raymond do to you"?

He couldn't pick up the phone. He couldn't stand the thought of hearing himself say, "Oh, hey, I was holding hands with my ex-girlfriend and cuddling her a little, but you know it didn't *mean* anything. . . ."

Martha, call me. Martha, tell me you understand me even though I don't understand myself. Martha, forgive me, Martha, I need you, Martha, read my lips, read my mind. I love you this minute, I loved you every minute I was with Sophie, I was just feeling sorry for her because I fell in love with you, not her. . . .

You're a slow learner, Charlie, he thought, over and over. What right do you have to learn so slowly. All the rules apply to you, life isn't simple just because you want it to be, not everything you feel like doing is all right just because you feel yourself to be a good person. He thought, but fought against, feelings of anger toward Sophie, for needing him and missing him and leading him to do what he should not have done. The one thing he didn't think of doing was going to Martha.

By morning, Martha was a wreck and Charlie was no closer to knowing what to say. "I'm sorry" was pretty much all he could come up with. He rejected "It was nothing, it wasn't what it looked like." It was exactly what it had looked like. It was a breach of trust when perfect trust is perhaps the most precious thing lovers have. So he said into the phone, standing in his shorts unshaven in the kitchen as early as he thought he could call, "I'm sorry."

Martha was up and dressed, so tired and sad that she wanted to go back to bed.

"Is that all?" she said, finally.

"No. I'm sorry and I love you."

Another pause.

"Is *that* all?"

"Yes."

Another pause. "I'd like to see you," said Charlie, and Martha had to struggle to keep from crying. It had been such a long night.

The buzzer rang.

"I have to go," said Martha.

"Martha . . . please don't hang up. I'll wait."

"Fred's home. I have to go."

And Charlie, miserable, accepted this.

"Good-bye," said Martha, and hung up, and Charlie said good-bye and hung up, too. Charlie went to shower and begin a day with so heavy a heart that all day was going to feel like dragging a coffin through Mardi Gras. Martha went to buzz in Gillis and Fred.

Fred had had a wonderful time. He'd sat on a stool and eaten croissants and jelly while Gillis drank espresso and read the paper. He'd been introduced to several of Gillis's friends on the sidewalk in the sun, and together they had made friends with a huge dog called Boris.

Gillis looked at Martha closely.

"You look tired."

She nodded. "Bad night."

"I'm sorry." Gillis looked as if he wanted to know more.

She carried Fred to the door to say good-bye.

"Say thank you to Gillis," she said.

"Thank you, Gillis."

"You're welcome, Fred. We'll do it again sometime."

"Thank you again," she said to him softly.

"It was fun. I really liked it."

For a moment she wanted to ask him to stay and talk to her. But she didn't speak, and the moment passed, and Gillis turned and went down the stairs. Martha and Fred went to the window to watch him emerge onto the street. He crossed the street so they could see him, and he looked up and waved. Looking down from their window, they waved back.

Martha and Charlie met warily, when they met again, and they met on neutral ground. Martha had come uptown to meet him for lunch. They were both dressed rather formally; Charlie had chosen a chic restaurant new to them both, much talked about in the press, in the hope of a special occasion, a fresh start.

"This is rather grand," said Martha, to break the silence between them when the waiter had stopped hovering.

"You look beautiful," said Charlie.

"I feel half dead," said Martha.

"I'm sorry."

She nodded. She knew he was sorry. She didn't believe she looked beautiful, though he looked beautiful to her. She believed he loved her. She wanted to stop feeling separated from him; she missed him horribly. After the first conversation, there had been no others about Sophie. What they had said instead, in a most gingerly way, to avoid accusation or blame, was how sorry they were they had missed a night together.

"I hope we like this place," said Charlie now, to break the silence between them. The restaurant was packed and noisy and very jolly. Martha nodded. And yawned.

Charlie said, "Am I keeping you up?"

"I don't do very well without you," she said.

He reached for her hand.

"I *love* you, Martha. I don't want to be away from you."

"Would you like to hear our specials?" cried a waiter who had appeared at their elbows.

"Give us a minute," said Charlie, after a beat.

"No problem. Can I bring you a couple of Frozen Rosas while you decide?"

"What are they?" asked Charlie.

"Yes, bring them," said Martha.

"*Very* good," said the waiter, and he spun off.

They held hands for a moment. Charlie was trying to think how to say what he wanted to say.

"You're my heart," he said at last. "I want to be with you."

"But I don't know how we solve this," said Martha miserably. She'd thought of this night and day, the last two days. It was too hard to be so in love, and so little together. There would be more and more disappointments; there would be more mistrust. For the first time, she was afraid they wouldn't survive it. "We can't live together, with the children in each other's pockets, it's too much for them, they're too young for it . . ."

"But it's wrong for us to be apart."

"Here we are," cried the waiter, whizzing to their sides. Proudly he set down tall glasses full of something orange with cream and mint all over the top. "Are we ready to hear the specials?" he asked with excitement.

Martha and Charlie both gazed at him, their eyes imploring him to go away and stay away.

"Give us a minute," said Charlie.

"*Very* good. I tell you what, I'll just bring you a basket of our garlic pizza bread." And he whirled off.

"We've tried being apart and it's too hard. Let's try being together," said Charlie.

"We can't. How can we?"

"Let's try a weekend all together. Let's all go to the country together this weekend."

Martha looked doubtful. She was so tired she could hardly remember why it was she couldn't just fall into his arms and go to sleep. *Why* couldn't they just tell the children to behave themselves? Think of the pleasure of cooking breakfast together for all three children, of going to bed together two nights in a row, of going to the supermarket together and deciding together what to cook, of taking a walk together without having to arrange baby-sitters or take three subways to get to each other to do it. Think of sitting together in lamplight after dinner, reading and looking forward to going upstairs to bed together, instead of looking forward to going out in the rain, getting in a cab, and going sixty blocks to sleep alone.

"It's a suicide pact," trilled the waiter, as he whipped a basket under their noses. "You'll both reek of garlic, but these are to die for. Just be sure you both eat some."

They looked up at him.

"Thank you," said Charlie, at last.

"Our soup today is a cream of leek with hazelnut croutons, the fish of the day is salmon in parchment, and if you're thinking about the rabbit paillards, tell me now because I think we only have one order left." He beamed at them and flourished his order pad. They looked at each other and back at him, then opened their menus.

"Give us a minute," they said.

The drive to Ashfield Friday evening was wonderful, after the long week apart. Martha had packed a picnic for them to eat on the way. Fred went to sleep almost at once, so Martha and Charlie had a delicious hour to hold hands and talk in the front seat, while Phoebe and Jack sat in back, playing chess on a traveling chess board. They were both beginners at the game, and there was a lot of giggling. When it got too dark for chess, they all played Twenty Questions and Botticelli.

They arrived at Charlie's house about ten. The first order of business was to get Fred to bed, but he wanted to see the koala posters he remembered from Phoebe's room. Phoebe carried him to her room, where they went from picture to picture, giving the animals names. When Martha went to see what had become of them, she found Phoebe holding Fred on her hip. They were telling each other a story about a red fox in a picture Phoebe had cut out of her *Ranger Rick* magazine when she was ten.

Martha, watching this scene from the doorway, felt a rush of affection for Phoebe. How she had changed this year. What a difference a little time makes when you're that age. How important to remember, everything changes.

"It's time for bed, little Fred," said Martha.

"But we're telling a story!" He was very sleepy.

"We are," said Phoebe to Fred, "but we can finish it in the morning. And you know what? Tomorrow it will be a whole new day here, but in the picture it will still be Fox's birthday!" Fred looked intrigued and consoled by this. He consented to be handed over to Martha.

When she had gotten Fred into his jammies, teeth brushed, face washed, she put him into bed in the guest room, which he was sharing with Jack.

"What shall we read?" she asked. "*Uncle Wiggily? Bartholomew and the Oobleck?*" Fred studied the pile of books she'd brought from home, books that had first been Jack's. He chose *The King's Stilts*.

As soon as Martha began to read, Jack and then Phoebe appeared, and came in to listen. They settled down on the floor. Charlie came upstairs, having filled the woodbox and laid the fire, and stretched out on the other bed. At the end of the story, when the king leaps onto his stilts again, everybody in the room cried in unison, "Patrooool cats!"

After Fred's lights were turned out, Charlie lit the fire in the living room, and the four played Scrabble. Charlie started out with a score of about a gazillion by spelling "magneto," using all seven letters on the triple word score square in the center.

"What's a magneto?" Phoebe asked.

"It's a dingus in an internal combustion engine," said Charlie. "I think."

"You don't have to know what it means?"

"No, you just have to use a real word."

Phoebe thought for a while and then spelled "blart." "Nine, I got a double letter score."

There was a silence.

"What does that mean?" Charlie asked.

"You don't have to know what it means, you just have to be able to use it in a sentence," she said.

"Okay, use it in a sentence," said Martha.

"There was a loud blart, and then the house blew up."

Jack began to laugh.

"I don't see anything wrong with that," said Charlie. Martha wrote nine on the score pad. After that the game degenerated rapidly. At the end, there were very few words on the board that were recognizably English, and Charlie claimed to have a score of two million and five, and the children had laughed until they cried.

"I think you guys should go to bed," said Charlie. "It's late, and if you don't you'll sleep all morning, and we'd like to get up and do things."

"Like what?"

"Maybe pack a picnic and ride bikes to the river."

"Can we do the rock slides?" asked Phoebe, excited.

"What's that?" Jack asked.

"It's this place up the gorge where the water has worn a slide in the rocks, and you can ride it down like sliding a waterfall."

"That sounds great!"

"Daddy, we haven't done the slide in so long! Can we?"

The truth was, they hadn't done it since Charlie and Patsy separated. It wasn't the kind of thing you do if there are only two of you.

"It'll be freezing, but you can if you want to. If you go to bed now."

She was excited, and so was Jack. They got up at once and carried their glasses and pretzel bowl back to the kitchen.

"Goodnight, Daddy, goodnight, Martha."

"Goodnight, Momski, goodnight, Charlie."

And they went upstairs. Charlie and Martha looked at each other.

"They go to bed the first time they're asked?"

"They carried their crud to the kitchen without being asked?"

"I call this a class-B miracle," said Charlie. He got up to stoke the fire and brought them each a glass of wine. They settled down in the quiet and the firelight, snuggling against each other. They listened for the footsteps overhead.

Phoebe's footsteps went into her room. Soon they could hear water running in her bathroom. Jack went into the guest room, then down the hall the other way to the bathroom. Phoebe's water was turned off. Jack's water was turned off. Jack's footsteps sounded down the hall, past the guest room to Phoebe's room. Silence. After about five minutes Charlie said, "I think I'll go up and say goodnight."

He wasn't gone long, and he came back smiling.

"They were discussing Phoebe's collection of *Oz* books. She's got some Jack never read."

"I would have said that was impossible."

"He was deciding which one to borrow."

They heard footsteps go from Phoebe's room to the guest room. Then, silence.

Downstairs, sitting cuddled together, they watched the fire. Finally Charlie said, "I may have been happier at some moment in my life, but if so I can't remember when."

Martha picked up his hand and kissed it. She nodded, wordless.

In the meantime, Patsy didn't like the way things were going at all.

For instance, her friend Aida. At one point she and Aida were supposed to start this business, a graphic design business. Patsy was the one who schlepped around shopping for computers and buying books on design and meeting with Charlie's accountant; all that time Aida was supposed to be lining up accounts. But then right when everything was ready to go, Patsy got some horrible flu or something, just horrible, she felt like a zombie, and things had to be on hold for a couple of weeks. And just when she was feeling better, Aida called her, all excited and said Guess what, she'd just been offered a job with The Silver Spoon, the catering business, wasn't that great?

Well, what the hell was Patsy supposed to say? It was true Aida had paid her share of the expenses, and their major commitment to the business—except for the computer, which Charlie had paid for because it was for Phoebe, too—consisted of going out to lunch together and talking about it, but still. What was she supposed to be, happy about it? And the thing was, Aida wasn't even that great a cook! If they wanted a cook, they should try Patsy's grapefruit cake! Well, as Aida explained later, they didn't actually want another cook, they wanted a manager, someone to meet with the clients, plan menus with them, hire the freelance waiters for big parties, keep track of the cambros and the china and linen rentals, kind of thing. Just what Patsy herself would be brilliant at. She'd chaired the benefit tea dance for Phoebe's school four years ago, and people said they had never seen a better-run event, never. And these were people who went to a lot of top-ticket benefits.

Never mind. A friend was a friend. Patsy could never stay mad for long, that's why people found it so easy to take advantage of her. Patsy gave up the graphic design idea and took this great-sounding job with her friend Bella Magee, who ran a PR company. Bella Magee was a girl who in college they all called Dribblyjaws, there was something so mournful about her. The whole class was just amazed that Bella had turned up running this fabulous little company.

Bella had an idea for a new kind of service, and she thought Patsy would be perfect to handle it. The idea was, celebrities come to town to promote a book or a new perfume, and they don't know how to get a cab in the rain in the West Sixties, or how long it takes to get from the Westbury Hotel to Channel 9 at seven in the morning. Instead of hiring a limo, Bella's idea was, why not hire a sort of adjunct PR person who would function as a guide and companion and driver, someone bright and presentable, someone like Patsy. She wasn't planning to pay too much, but then Patsy would learn a lot and she'd get to meet all these glamorous people.

It turned out to be harder than it sounded. Patsy's first celebrity was a cookbook author from Denver. She was flying TWA into Kennedy, and naturally Patsy went to the domestic arrivals building to meet her. She was running a teeny bit late because she'd had trouble locating Bella's car. But she had prepared such a delightful little speech about the Saarinen architecture with which to amuse the client, she thought it would be all right. ("Do you think it looks like a womb? Or a mushroom?") How was she to know that TWA would route the stupid plane into the international arrivals terminal? Denver was not exactly European. Anyway, there she was at the terminal, and the flight she was meeting wasn't listed on the monitors, and it was supposed to be on the ground five minutes ago, and a busload of Japanese tourists had just arrived to check in, so she had to be positively rude to get one second of an agent's time to learn where she was supposed to be.

By the time she got to the right gate, the passengers were gone.

There was no one waiting for her at the luggage carousel, and she called Bella to admit she had lost the client altogether, and she learned the client had taken a taxi direct to the cable TV station where she was at that moment giving her first interview.

Bella pointed out gently that knowing exactly when and where the plane was coming in was part of her job description, but she was nice about it. Patsy apologized prettily, and managed to get back into town in time to take the woman to her hotel, and for a while after that things seemed to go all right.

Patsy felt that if *she* were on the road far from home she would appreciate a friendly attitude, so she worked very hard to make conversation, flattering the clients, asking them questions, relentlessly telling them how exciting it was for her, a mere Manhattan housewife, to meet the likes of them. But it seemed not everyone was pleased by these attentions, since more than one of the clients called Bella and said that after weeks of giving interviews, they didn't want to make any more new best friends and would really prefer a non-English-speaking driver next time.

There were one or two other little mistakes. For instance, she told the author of a series of mystery novels that he would be telephoned in his hotel room to give a live radio interview at 9:00 A.M. She was dead sure that was the time the airhead at the station told her. But the call came through at 8:00 A.M. when apparently the client was in the can in the middle of—well, never mind. He got to the phone and was giving the interview, not that it was very pleasant to be virtually naked and trying not to finish your private business on the floor while someone is asking you something like "Where do you get your ideas for your books?" But then, room service arrived with his breakfast and kept knocking and ringing the doorbell to his suite all during the interview, so he actually had to interrupt his host on live radio and excuse himself to let in the waiter. He was not very pleased, this client, and not at all polite to Patsy when she came to take him to NBC, even though she told him it wasn't her fault and tried to point out that from one point of view it was rather funny.

"Fine," he said, "let me know when *you* take a crap, and I'll have Geraldo show up with a camera crew."

Patsy had read one of this client's books and didn't think it was very good, but she couldn't get Bella to see that that made any difference. But even that wasn't the last straw. And the last thing truly wasn't Patsy's fault in any way.

She was escorting a couple who had written a book entitled *How to Live to Be 170*, with lots of juicy subtitles about better sex, better dreams, and an end to dentistry as we know it if only you would follow their harebrained diet. Well for starters, they were two of the mangiest, most unhealthy-looking specimens Patsy had ever seen, and for seconds, they were only about thirty-two themselves with no medical background of any kind, so how the hell did *they* know how long they were going to live? And they were bossy and unpleasant and full of themselves because their book had sold about 150,000 copies and looked like making them billionaires. The worst thing though was the diet. It consisted of carrot juice, goat's milk, and brewer's yeast, and a lot of other horrible things that this pair was willing to sell you by mail order for about twenty dollars for a two-day supply. (If you did live to 170 on this diet, you'd spend about 150 of those years in the poorhouse, Patsy figured.) Anyway, since this drool was all that they would eat, they carried great jugs of it with them everywhere, and at one point in the middle of midtown traffic they decided they felt peckish. The wife was passing a big cup over the backseat to her husband when a taxi cut Patsy off and she put on the brakes, and about a quart of goo went all over the car. For weeks afterward the car reeked of sour milk and yeast, in spite of having been cleaned professionally twice. Subsequent clients kept asking if someone had recently been carsick, and when Bella's husband refused to ride in the car with Bella to a wedding in Short Hills, insisting on hiring a taxi at about eighty dollars, Bella decided to turn the car in for a new BMW and to get out of the celebrity-escort business.

There were other things that were not going so well for Patsy either. The breakup with George was shocking to her. She had thought that if she had some time to work on him, without feeling pulled between him and Phoebe, she would get him back. They could take a nice trip together, or stay up all night and sleep late and make love in odd parts of the apartment. It was true he had left her before, and there had been long periods of dramatic misery, during which she had talked on the phone and written volumes in her diary and gone out on pointless dates with other people, but in the end he had always come back. And it was perfectly clear that undeneath it all, what kept driving him away was Phoebe. She was tired of trying to balance her duties as a mother and her needs as a woman. George had said ugly things the night he left, but he didn't mean them. Patsy didn't believe in taking things like that too seriously. What mattered was, she was Patsy and she needed love and what she needed she should get.

She left George alone for a week or two as she negotiated the transfer of Phoebe to Charlie's apartment, and adjusted herself to having no one to cook for or shop for or talk to. She was doing fine, though. She was pleased with the way she had stuck things to Charlie. She had a plan too, a good one. Aida said so, even Charlie said so. She was going to get her license and sell real estate. She would be perfect at that. She would sell the six- and seven-figure co-ops on the Upper East Side; those were her kind of people, and she already had the wardrobe.

When she felt ready, she called George at the office. When she reached him, he was wary but polite. Very polite. He asked her to hold on while he closed the door of his office. (Oh good, she thought. It's going to be intimate, he doesn't want his girl to overhear.) But then he only listened politely as she described the changes she had made in her life. She waited for him to say, What a goof, why don't I pick you up after class some evening. She waited for him to say Can I come over tonight? But all he said was "You sound fine. Thank you for calling." When she found herself with the dead phone in her hand, she felt lost. Come on, George, she wanted to say, stop playing dead, I know you're breathing. I'm alone, the house is all ours, it's what we've been waiting for.

Her real estate course was turning out to be quite hard, and she was surprised at the first exam to find that several tough-looking, hard-eyed young women, one of whom actually chewed gum, scored much higher than she did. She set up a preliminary interview at Sotheby's real estate division, and learned to her dismay that selling million-dollar apartments to leveraged buy-out kings was what every realtor in New York had in mind. And the territory was pretty much covered by a couple of very successful agents who gave fabulous dinners for all the right people and in that way got all the best business first. Oh.

Patsy was in no position to give fabulous dinners. She had room at her dining table for eight at the most, but two of them had to sit on the piano bench. Also, she didn't know all the right people. She knew a few of them to say hello to at parents' meetings at Phoebe's old school, but that wouldn't help much. What opportunities there were in real estate right now were in commercial. And even there, as with most things in New York these days, there was no free ride because of your social graces. The agencies wanted rainmakers. They didn't *mind* if you had a string of good pearls and a boarding school accent, but if you couldn't close the deal, they'd rather have a hard-eyed little killer from Kew Gardens.

A week later, she had called George again, at home. Again he was sympathetic, soft voiced, polite. This time she left him no room to evade. So he answered, softly, that he had meant what he said. He didn't care for being yelled at. She couldn't undo that, he was permanently changed toward her, that was it, good-bye. And he hung up.

Patsy was stunned. Everybody yelled when they were provoked enough . . . didn't they? What did he mean?

Patsy had a long stretch of time in which she took a good hard look at herself. She called Phoebe and didn't blame her when she wanted to talk about her Shakespeare paper instead of mothering her mother. Patsy was sick of her own selfishness and her tears and her dependence on feeling loved—and by whom, a sadist like George? If she had known what it would be like, all alone out here without the fortress of family belonging around her, she never would have left Charlie and Phoebe. She hadn't known.

Without anyone at home to lean on, she didn't know how to say who she was or what she was worth, if anything. When she left Charlie, she thought there would be a sad period of adjustment, and then some wonderful man who thrilled her and understood her perfectly would materialize. But it hadn't worked out like that at all. Total strangers who aren't married to you don't have to understand that you're noisy sometimes because your mother was difficult, or that you're distracted sometimes because your child is on your mind. They don't have to make any allowance for you at all. They can look you over and say no, thank you. Full stop, end of explanation. No, thank you.

It was bad luck to have married a man like Charlie when she was so young. A man who listened, a man who was kind, a man who could trust. She hadn't known it was rare. She thought probably most men came with that equipment, and then had other great stuff on top of it.

World-beating cleverness at business. Directorships on ballet or museum boards, so they would go to benefit balls all the time and have their pictures in the paper. Great big trust funds.

Time passed. Patsy refused to believe that this emptiness was all the future held for her. She worked hard at her real estate course and waited for her luck to turn. One Friday she was elated to learn that she'd gotten one of the top grades in her class on a final exam. Her happiness ballooned inside her and buoyed her up all through the evening. It was that sort of manic happiness in which you have conversations with people who aren't there, and you laugh and nod, and then catch yourself and laugh at yourself and feel glad that no one saw you. She slept fitfully, too happy really to let go of the day. The next morning, Saturday, she did what she'd been waiting to do, knowing she would do it sooner or later, waiting for the moment when she felt she couldn't be denied. She dialed George's number.

"Hello," his voice boomed. He was full of joy too! She could hear it! Oh, this was going to be fine.

"Hello," she said, carelessly.

"You're up early, darling." She could hear the smile in his voice.

"Yes, I am," she said. "I was up and I felt too good not to call."

There was a silence.

"Who is this?" said George.

Patsy felt a terrible coldness, but she fought it down. "It's Patsy, of course." She kept it light. Again . . . oh, shit . . . a silence.

"Who were you expecting?" she said. She was still trying to keep her voice full of merriment.

"Patsy," said George, "I'm sorry. This isn't really a good time to talk."

"Isn't it? Why not? You seemed awfully happy when you answered the phone."

"I know. I am."

"Well . . . I'm glad. But I think that makes it a good time to talk." She waited, but he didn't say anything. "I have so much to tell you . . . and George, dear, there's so much still unfinished between us. Don't you think it's time?"

She knew that sudden change of gears, that disarming reference to their passion, would soften him. Could he resist her, when she took that tone?

"Patsy," he said at last, "I'm getting married this afternoon."

She got through the rest of the conversation somehow, with a few shreds of pride intact. She wished him joy. She got off the phone and sat for a while in silence, and then she began to cry.

Charlie *was happy* with Martha. He was happy with Jack, he was happy with Fred. He watched with quiet joy, during their Saturday at the rock slides, how Phoebe took to Martha and trusted her. He liked it when, at lunch, he and Jack found themselves declaiming that dead languages were for dead people, while Martha and Phoebe, full of scorn, thought they were boneheads not to love Latin. He liked having Martha defend Phoebe when he was inclined to patronize her; he liked seeing his daughter through Martha's eyes. And he liked Martha's boys. He loved having a toddler around; he had always wanted more children. It had been a day of laughter and peace, and he was a deeply happy man. He had a family.

The water was so cold in the ravine that Martha said just putting her foot into it made her leg ache all the way up to the shin. But Jack and Phoebe spent an hour riding the rapids down over moss-slippery rocks, to a pool where they landed, splashing. Martha and Charlie laughed out loud, watching them and listening to their shrieks. Martha took a whole film roll of pictures. She was proud of the physical courage Jack and Phoebe showed. They were ordered out of the water when their lips turned blue and it took a long while in the sun, in dry clothes, before their teeth stopped chattering.

They ate the picnic lunch Martha and Phoebe had packed. Wicked Phoebe, who didn't like spicy food, had suggested they make a special deviled egg for Charlie, who bragged that no food was too hot for him. Martha and Phoebe dosed one egg with Tabasco sauce such that when Charlie bit into it, his eyes bugged and watered and his nose began to run. He ate the whole thing and said how sorry he was there wasn't another just like it, while Martha and Phoebe had to look away from each other to keep from laughing.

After lunch they lay around reading and chatting while Fred had his rest. Jack, rambling around exploring, came upon a mystery. A pair of young birds, pretty things, were lying at the base of a rock wall, dead. Jack called Charlie to come and look.

"They're little quails," said Charlie. He touched one gingerly. "Their necks are broken."

"What happened? Did they fly into the rock? A kamikaze mission?"

"I don't know. They may have been thrown against it by wind. They haven't been dead long." They were both quiet, contemplating.

"I'd like to bury them," said Jack.

"I would, too. But I don't think we can without a shovel."

Jack decided to make a burial mound for them. Using sticks to move them, he nestled them together. The head of the slightly smaller bird lay against the neck of its companion. Then he gathered fragrant pine brush and arranged it over them, gently, so that the branches wove into each other and made a little house around the bodies.

"Good," said Charlie.

They went back to the others, but neither of them mentioned what they had found. If either had been asked, they would have said they didn't want to make Fred sad.

At Phoebe's request, they drove home and got bicycles and rode them into town for ice-cream cones. Charlie could carry Fred, because his bike still had Phoebe's baby seat on it.

"Daddy keeps it that way because he *really* wishes I were four years old still, don't you, Daddy?" said Phoebe.

"Not at all," said Charlie. "I keep it because I can carry home groceries in it." But they all knew that he had loved having Phoebe little and uncomplicated. Martha, by contrast, rather reveled in the utter confusion of adolescence. She liked things multilayered and elaborate. She had once said to an anxious mother of a younger child, "Don't believe what you hear about adolescence, it's wonderful fun," and Jack, aged fifteen, had said with surprise, "I'm glad *you're* enjoying it."

In town with their ice-cream cones, Jack and Charlie watched Phoebe and Martha buying nail polish together at the five-and-ten, both astonished, for different reasons, to learn that either one knew anything about the subject. Jack was thinking that it was fun to have two parents. He hadn't thought he spent much time worrying about his mother, but now he knew it was an ache you didn't recognize until it stopped. She and Charlie could worry about each other. He and Phoebe could be kids.

Charlie was thinking that his happiness of the night before had grown tenfold. He had a family. Martha made him feel valuable and loved, as if she saw him whole and was absolutely on his side; and he gave her a security and happiness that let her blossom. It's such an effort to be your best self when you're not loved. Martha made him feel that with her he could be who he was supposed to be, give the best he had to give. And watching her walk ahead down the street in the sunshine, giggling with his daughter, he believed that she felt that way with him.

They stopped in at the video store and chose a Monty Python movie to watch together. They bought a steak and corn for dinner and rode home together. They put their bikes away and established in what order they would take their showers, so as not to run out of hot water. Baby Fred went up for a nap; Charlie went off to marinate the steak. Martha was taking the first shower, and Phoebe answered the phone.

At first Phoebe couldn't understand what was going on. She said "Hello" several times, and she could hear that there was someone on the other end. After a bit, she realized that what she was hearing was sobs. She said "Hello" again, and waited. Then there was a sort of wail, and in one second everything altered. The person sobbing on the phone was her mother.

Charlie had come to the kitchen door to see if the call was for him. He saw his daughter standing, looking puzzled, listening. Then he saw her face change.

"Mom?"

"I'm sorry, I'm sorry, I'm sorry," Patsy sobbed, and then cried again without being able to speak.

"Mom, what's wrong?" There was panic in Phoebe's voice. Someone had died. Someone was hurt. Someone had mugged her or raped her. She pictured Patsy's apartment in ruins, her clothes torn, her face bruised and broken.

"Oh, honey. . . ." More sobs. "I've been trying to find you. I've been calling all day."

"Mom, I'm here. I'm right here . . . tell me what's wrong." Phoebe was growing terrified. And Charlie was watching.

"Phoebe . . . Phoebe . . . I just feel so lost! I miss you, I miss your father, I've fucked up everything . . . I want to die. . . ." Long, wrenching, terrible sobs. Phoebe listened. She felt her father's eyes on her, but she wouldn't look at him. Her mother wanted to die. And it was her fault, Phoebe had left her and been pissy to her, and closed her out. And today, she'd been thinking of how much fun life could be with Daddy and Martha.

"I want to die, and I can't stop crying. Phoebe . . . oh, honey, I'm so sorry, I'm so sorry to do this to you. But I'm frightened. I don't have anyone else to call and I can't stop crying."

"Do you want me to come home?" This time Phoebe looked at her father. He was staring at her.

"Just talk to me. I just have to get a hold of myself."

"But, Mom . . ." Phoebe had heard her, she'd said it twice. She wanted to die.

The conversation went on for some time. Patsy didn't say much of substance beyond lacerating herself and apologizing, though she did tell Phoebe about George getting married. She grew calmer as they talked, and she insisted that she didn't want Phoebe to come home that minute. Phoebe tried every way she could to assure her mother that things would be all right, that she was a good person, that Charlie cared for her, too. "I'll come straight there tomorrow, as soon as we get back," Phoebe said.

"Sweetheart. Yes, call me right away when you get back to town." Actually Patsy was invited to Aida's to a dinner party the next night, and now that she was feeling calmer she thought really that going would be the best thing for her, if she could make herself do it.

"Are you sure you'll be all right tonight?"

"Yes, honey. I'll have a hot bath and get into bed. I'll be all right."

"Promise."

"I promise. Is everything all right up there?"

"Yes, fine," said Phoebe, a little surprised.

"What are you all doing?"

"Well, we went to the rock slides this morning."

"Really. Oh, we used to love that," she said, neatly reminding her daughter that this had once been her paradise, and now she was closed out of it, home alone in tears. "That sounds wonderful, darling." Pause. "But it must have been awfully cold. It's so early."

"It was."

"But you went in?"

Phoebe wondered why her mother wanted to pursue this.

"Yes," she said finally.

"Alone?"

"No. Jack did, too."

"Uh huh. With Jack." A pause, in which Phoebe feared she could hear another storm of tears gathering.

"But it wasn't just the two of you?" Patsy persisted.

"No. We were all together."

A long pause. "Well that sounds lovely, honey. I'm glad." Phoebe doubted this profoundly, but she was grateful that her mother wasn't going to fall apart all over again.

Patsy had grown calmer during the conversation, because as so often happens in close relationships she had managed to transfer a great portion of her anguish to her daughter. Her emotions were as real as peas on a plate, and they hadn't just gone up in smoke; Patsy had squeezed a great lump of pain and fear into the phone line, across the miles, and right into her daughter's ear.

"What was that all about?" Charlie asked, coldly, when Phoebe finally hung up the phone. He could see how unstrung Phoebe was. Goddamn Patsy, he had been thinking, throughout this conversation. Goddamn her. They had been looking forward to such a happy night. And now goddamn Patsy had shown up like a ghost that won't die, and thrown her mess and self-drama like a bag of dirt onto the middle of the floor.

"Oh, *Daddy!*" Phoebe was near tears. "She just cried and cried. She kept saying she had lost us . . . you and me . . . that it was her fault, and she ruins everything, and then she said she wanted to die." Phoebe's voice was tiny, pinched by fear, at the end of this sentence.

Martha came in, clean and pink from the bath, with her hair wet. She saw their faces and came to them. But she didn't say anything; she just looked from one to the other.

"Dammit, Phoebe. This isn't fair. It isn't fair of her to call up and upset you."

Phoebe was shocked. "Daddy! She was desperate! She said she wanted to die! I can't believe this, she was your wife. She's my mother! I think we should all go home. Or you should call her at least. She kept crying and crying, Daddy, and saying how it was her fault that she had lost you. . . ."

"Time for Patsy to grow up."

"What do you *mean*?" Phoebe's eyes flashed. She was appalled that her father was being so hard and angry, when her mother was talking about killing herself.

"She didn't lose me, she left me. I'm sorry if she regrets it now, but come on, Phoebe. Actions have consequences. Anyway, she doesn't regret it, she's just bored again and she wants an audience, and I'm angry that she chose you. It's not fair to you, it's not fair to any of us."

"I can't believe you're being like this. How can you say she's *bored*? How are you going to feel if she kills herself?"

"She's not going to kill herself," he said, disgusted. "She's tough as old boots. Come on, tell me what happened. This isn't some existential crisis, she had a fight with her boyfriend or something. Didn't she?"

Charlie and Phoebe glared at each other. Phoebe couldn't exactly answer the question directly, given that her mother's boyfriend did happen to be getting married just that minute, so she went on the attack.

"You didn't *hear* her!"

"I've heard her before. Come on, Phoebe. We were going to have such a nice evening. I'm sorry your mother's upset, but I want you to calm down and pull yourself together. We're going to have dinner together and watch a movie."

"Oh fuck you, Daddy," Phoebe yelled. "You think I'm some little twerp that you can tell me how to feel. Pat me on the head and say 'Now, calm down, dear.'"

"You do *not* use that language to me, young lady, and you do not use that language in front of Martha!" Charlie was furious.

"Oh, *sorry*. I'm sure she doesn't know what it means." Her tone was pure nastiness, full of implication. Charlie lunged for her and spanked her hard across the bottom. Phoebe's face was scarlet and tears welled in her eyes, but she wouldn't cry. She just glared at him as if she'd like to spit.

"Let me go."

"Apologize to Martha!"

"*She* doesn't have to apologize, Charlie." Martha spoke at last, and Charlie was so surprised at the anger in her voice that he dropped Phoebe's arm. Phoebe burst into tears and ran. As she went she mumbled, "I'm sorry, Martha." And now there were tears in Martha's eyes.

"What do you mean, *she* doesn't have to apologize?"

"She doesn't have to apologize, you do. What the hell do you mean, attacking her like that?"

Charlie felt as if he were going mad. "What do you mean, I attacked her?"

"You patronized her, Charlie! You do it over and over! She's right, you don't want her to grow up, you don't want to take her feelings seriously, and you don't realize that it's mortally insulting . . . people need to be seen, Charlie, they need to be seen as they are! If you don't see her, and don't take her seriously, then how can she believe you love her? Who is she supposed to think you love?"

"But it's nonsense! It's so maddening, her mother following us here. . . ."

"It may be nonsense, but if it is, Phoebe doesn't know it, and that's what you should have been talking about. Phoebe, not Patsy."

They stared at each other, angry and miserable.

"I don't get it. I think everyone's gone nuts," said Charlie. And he turned and left the room, and then the house. As the kitchen door slammed, Jack came down. He looked bewildered. "What's going on?"

Martha sank down on the couch.

"Phoebe's in her room with the door locked." Martha nodded. Jack sat down, too. He waited for his mother to speak, and after a moment to collect herself she told him what had happened.

"Bummer," said Jack after a while, and Martha laughed.

"I'll say. Look, honey, I'd like to catch up with Charlie. Will you stay here until the baby wakes up?"

"Sure. Do I need to do anything about dinner? Start the coals or anything?"

"I think not, till we figure out what happens next."

Charlie was standing at the bottom of the meadow, throwing rocks into the woods. He didn't look around when Martha joined him.

"Sorry," she said. He turned and put his arms around her.

"I don't like it when you tell me what I'm doing wrong and what I *should* do instead. Should, should. I hate it."

"I don't blame you." They kissed.

"It was so perfect today, Martha. I felt as if everything would work out, we were just making it seem more complicated than it had to be." Martha nodded, her head against his shoulder. He smelled of sweat and pine needles and the sunwarmed cotton of his shirt.

"I was so disappointed," he said.

She nodded again. "Me, too. I loved last night. And today."

"Goddamn Patsy." Martha nodded again.

"And poor Phoebe," he added. Martha kissed him. "I shouldn't have hit her."

"No. But she'll forgive you."

"Will she?"

"Yes. She has her mother's manners sometimes, but she has your heart."

Charlie smiled. "Thanks. I love you."

Martha smiled. "Thanks. I know."

"But I would have said she takes after you," said Charlie.

"Don't I wish." And she did. She wished very much that she and Charlie had met twenty years before and that all three children were theirs.

"Let's go see if we can salvage this evening." Arms around each other, they walked back toward the house.

The evening, however, was as Charlie had feared. Phoebe wouldn't come out of her room. Jack was quiet; he tried to make conversation at dinner, but he was hampered by the fact that his loyalty lay with Phoebe. Mostly all three of them made much of baby Fred, as being the most neutral course of action. When the dishes were washed, and Fred was asleep, Charlie said, "Well. Shall we watch our movie?"

"I think I'll go up and read," said Jack.

"Oh. Okay." When he had gone, Charlie said to Martha, "What about you?"

"I think I'd like to just sit here by the fire with you, if that's okay."

"Sure," said Charlie. He built up the fire, and Martha found her book and his reading glasses, and they settled down. After a while Charlie said, "I think I'll try talking to Phoebe again." He went up and knocked on her door, but she wouldn't answer him. He reported this to Martha. Martha didn't say anything. She thought it was bad form of Phoebe not to let her father apologize, but she thought too that she'd done enough of taking sides and announcing what everyone should be doing differently. So she just stroked Charlie's neck, and felt his restlessness, and said "Good idea" when soon after he suggested they pack it in and go to bed.

Somehow, no matter how badly they wanted everything to be as it had been, there was a distance between Charlie and Martha that night. He didn't like being criticized, any more than anyone else does, and it took some time for him to shed his resentment about it. And he was very disappointed about the ruin of their evening. And preoccupied with Phoebe.

Martha too was disappointed that the evening had gone wrong. She felt sorry that she wasn't Phoebe's mother, she wasn't Charlie's wife. She felt sorry that Jack didn't have a father. She felt sorry that even though it looked at times and felt as if they were a family, they weren't. And it didn't take much to show it.

Martha and Charlie made love as usual, but it was disappointing. They lay wrapped around each other, knowing that in their hearts they were apart, that probably the experiment was over.

Charlie woke up at three in the morning. The house was silent. Martha seemed to be asleep. He lay listening to the night, trying to guess what had awakened him. Nothing stood out. There were cricket noises. All the birds were asleep.

He got up. Martha, too sad to sleep, opened her eyes and watched him go, but he didn't see this. He'd have been surprised to learn that, awake in the night, prey to the harpies, Martha had been lying there reliving the moment she'd walked in and found Charlie with Sophie.

Charlie went quietly into the hall and stopped at the guest room door. He opened it softly. Baby Fred was asleep, completely out of the covers as usual, with his arm around his bald bear. Jack's bed was empty.

Charlie went in and covered Fred. Then he went out again and closed the door.

He went down the hall to Phoebe's room. The door was shut, as it had been when he tried to talk to her before going to bed. He hesitated . . . he was not in the habit of intruding in his daughter's room un-invited. He knocked softly. He didn't want to wake her at three in the morning, but even less did he want to walk in on something it would drive him wild to see.

There was no answer. He tried the knob; it turned. He turned it so the latch was all the way open, and then pushed. It was unlocked.

He stepped in. The room was empty. He stood in the room, quite light with moonlight, and stared at the rumpled bedspread. She had never gotten into bed.

He closed the door behind him and went down to the kitchen. The whole downstairs was dark. He went from room to room, softly, but no one was there. He went back up to Martha. He was angry. At Phoebe, certainly, mad as hell at Jack, and at the moment he even felt irrationally angry at Martha.

She was sitting up, waiting for him.

"Jack and Phoebe are gone."

Having listened to him patrol the house, she wasn't completely sur-prised.

"Is the car here?"

"Yes."

"Well. Good. At least they're safe."

"I don't think they're safe, Martha."

They looked at each other. He was mad, for the second time that day.

"I meant, they're not dead on a highway somewhere."

"Jack should know better, even if Phoebe doesn't, than to do this un-der my own roof."

"Now, wait a minute. All you know is, Phoebe was upset, and you could expect she'd want to talk to Jack."

"I know that if they just wanted to talk there's no reason for them to leave the house."

"There could be. Look at the sky. It's beautiful." She was trying not to flare at his blaming Jack.

"And look at the thermometer! It's freezing out there, Martha."

"Then maybe they've gone jogging."

"At three in the morning. That's probably it."

They sat in silence for a while. Charlie reached for Martha's hand. They sat together, each full of painful thoughts.

"Charlie. They're old enough to be married without permission."

"Where? West Virginia? Maybe they ran off to get married."

"All I mean is, they're not babies. They can make their own decisions, and that's the only way they'll learn anything."

"Fine. I agree. They should decide for themselves what courses to take and where they want to go to college. But they shouldn't make decisions that are irrevocable, that have consequences they can't imagine."

"I would have said most decisions were like that."

"You know what I mean," said Charlie.

"Honey. We know they care a great deal about each other. We know neither one is promiscuous. We know they know about birth control."

"How the hell do we know that?"

"I know Jack does, because his father talked to him. I believe Phoebe does, because it's taught in schools and because her mother probably talked to her, and failing all that, it's what girls' magazines are full of."

"I'll cancel her subscriptions."

"We know neither one of them would use another human being for sex. That's an improvement, anyway, from when we were sixteen."

"Nobody had sex when we were sixteen. Boys just pretended they did. So what if they *know* about birth control. Do you think Jack's wallet is full of condoms or something?"

"I think it probably is. Wasn't yours, when you were that age?"

"You seem to think this is funny," said Charlie.

"I certainly don't. I think it's impossible. I think it means we have to stop seeing each other." They stared at each other, horrified at what she had said.

"Oh *shit!*" said Charlie. He suddenly felt tears coming. He stifled them somehow.

"I do think they're much too young to have a full-blown love affair under Mommy and Daddy's roof, with everybody beaming approval," said Martha, wishing he would say she was wrong. "Don't you?"

"I think they're too young to cross the street by themselves."

It was nearly four in the morning when Phoebe and Jack made their way up the meadow by the light of the setting moon. They had taken blankets with them. Jack carried one, and the other was wrapped around them both. They had to match each other step for step, to move as one, and they looked like a little walking tipi moving over the ground. Their breath showed in the cold predawn air. They had had quite a night: lots of tears, lots of talk, a little sleep—a night neither of them would forget. The more so, when they came around the corner of the house and saw that the kitchen lights were ablaze. Through the window they could see Charlie sitting at the kitchen table, waiting.

"Oh shit," said Jack.

Phoebe, guessing what was coming, didn't say anything.

Connie was emerging from the worst depression of her life. She hadn't known, in all her years had not imagined, that a human being could feel such pain for so long, without relief, and live. She felt far from herself, far from Dave, far from the children, far from God. She wept for days at a time, and slept, and wept more; she could, through this, still sometimes think with some corner of her brain as if she were perfectly rational, and she often thought it was a wonder she didn't perish from dehydration after all those tears. You wouldn't have thought there was so much salt water in one human body.

Sophie hadn't wanted to leave her but there was not much she could do for her. The day after Connie's trip to Arden Forest, the day she fell apart, Sophie took her to a psychiatrist; her boss arranged an emergency appointment with his own shrink when Sophie described what was going on. The psychiatrist asked Connie gentle questions and watched her cry for fifty minutes. Then he asked Sophie to come in. He said that little, if any, therapeutic learning could take place when a patient was either in crisis or in love. He felt certain that Connie's maternal instincts were too strong to allow her to kill herself. ("I'm glad *he's* so sure," Sophie said to a friend, when evening after evening she arrived home terrified that she'd find her sister in a state of rigor mortis.) The doctor prescribed a course of "chemical intervention" ("Tranquilizers, to you," said Sophie) and told Sophie to take her sister home and wait it out. He would be more than happy to begin a talking cure with her when she was calmer, he felt her case was not uncommon, and he was sure he could help.

So for almost three weeks, Sophie left her sister in tears, and came home to find her still in tears. Connie wasn't taking much to the chemical intervention, which annoyed the psychiatrist, but turned out to be lucky, as the particular pills he favored were within the year discovered to be highly addictive and more dangerous than the symptoms they were meant to cure.

Connie went from crying on the kitchen floor, to prone on the couch, to sitting up in chairs, and by the third week, she began to function a little better each day. Once she called Sophie at work, and they had a small laugh over this triumph, since, in the depths of her depression Connie had become phobic about the telephone. She wouldn't answer it, and she certainly wouldn't make a call. She just lay in the apartment weeping and listening to messages come in on the machine. (Most of them were from Sophie, calling her, telling her it would be all right, asking her please, please, to pick up the phone and tell her she was alive.) "I meant to," said Connie. "I hated frightening you like that. It just all seemed so pathetic and sad, and the phone always seemed so far away and heavy, and somehow instead of getting around to answering it I'd hate myself for being such a failure and a mess, and start to cry again."

By the end of the third week, she was beginning to believe that she was going to live. She took an interest in things around her; she wanted Sophie to tell her news of the office and what was going on in her life. She didn't feel ready to talk about her own situation or to discuss what her next move should be, because she was terrified of falling apart again.

Sophie told her about the night she went to see Charlie, about Martha walking in.

"How long ago was that?"

"Three weeks," said Sophie. To Connie it could have been three days or three months.

"It sounds as if he still cares a lot for you," said Connie, hopeful.

"I know he does, but he doesn't love me. I could see the difference the minute she came in."

Connie reached to touch her sister's hand. Sophie smiled, sad.

"Have you talked to him since then?"

"Only about you. He called Dave to make sure he was compos mentis and that the kids were all right."

"And are they?" Her voice sounded strangled. This question had been booming in her head day and night through this whole terrible time. It was so terrible to her that her fear of the answer had helped to keep her paralyzed.

"They seem to be. They're going to school and everything. He isn't going to leave the jurisdiction."

Connie nodded. The floor beneath her seemed a little more solid. The livid shimmer of depression that had surrounded her, bathing the walls for weeks, receded farther. For the first time in an eternity she could see they were not curtains of depression, but simply walls made of Sheetrock. Of course the kids would be all right. They'd take care of each other.

"But I don't have to ask how he feels about me," Sophie was saying. "From the moment she walked out the door, he wanted me gone. You could feel it. She was all he could think about."

"Don't you think you should call him?"

"I'll call when . . . now, don't cry. I'll call when it's time for you to de-cide what to do next. You'll need a divorce lawyer."

A pause. Connie didn't cry. "Should it be Charlie?"

"Up to you. Are you ready to talk about it to someone?"

Connie took a deep breath. It was ragged, but again she didn't cry. "Yes," she said.

"Do you want me to call him now?"

"Yes," said Connie.

Sophie smiled at her. They were sitting at the tiny kitchen table, hav-ing finished supper.

"Okay," said Sophie. She touched her sister's shoulder as she left the room. Connie, moving as if she were made of glass, got up to do the dishes, and quietly prayed for strength. Lord, help me to do what I have to do. Lord, don't let me fall apart again; if that happens again I won't survive. She hadn't prayed at all during her time of tears, and she thought that to be able to pray again was in itself an answered prayer.

Sophie was gone quite a while. Connie sat in the living room waiting for her. At last she came out and sat down.

"He was a mess," Sophie said.

"Charlie? Why?"

"He and Martha have broken up." Connie sat up straight.

"For good?"

"He thinks so."

"What happened?"

"Too much baggage, he said. The right love at the wrong time, he kept saying." Sophie sat silent for a minute. Charlie had been fighting not to cry throughout the conversation, and it had been painful to listen to. He certainly never cried for her. Also, she loved him, and his pain hurt her heart.

Connie reach for Sophie's hand. "Does he want to see you?"

"It sounds as if he doesn't want to see anybody ever again."

"That will pass," said Connie. Sophie nodded. She knew that was true. Sooner or later, it would pass. Would he want to see her then? Should she hope? Would she ever have him? Would she ever get over him?

The phone rang. Sophie jumped.

"Charlie," said Connie. Sophie thought it might be. She stared at the ringing phone.

"You answer it," she said to Connie. Connie, feeling that this show of bravery was the least she owed Sophie, did so.

"Hello . . . ," said the voice on the phone, and Connie's heart lurched. Lord, don't let me cry. I wasn't ready for this, sweet Lord, please let me pass this test.

"Hello? Mummy?" said Ruth, her voice very small, and uncertain, and surprised.

"Sweetheart." God in heaven, she had missed Ruth so much. Grave quiet Ruth. Molly. William.

"Mummy . . . I was calling Sophie to see if she knew where you were."

"I'm here, darling. I've been here all the time."

"Why didn't you call us?"

Ruth's voice was full of pain. Molly and Ruth, as the days passed, debated and debated. Mummy has left us. Mummy would call us though, if she was all right. Maybe not, maybe she's gone really far, like to Australia. Maybe she's mad at us, and that's why she left. Maybe she's not all right. Maybe she's dead. Maybe she's never coming back. Once, on a particularly bad night, Ruth had looked across the table at her father's handsome, fleshy face and wondered if he had killed her.

"I couldn't call, honey."

"Why not?"

How to explain this. Connie did not believe in lying to children, but she didn't want to scare them. Nor, it suddenly occurred to her, did she dare exactly tell the truth. In case they repeated it to their father, and he used it to keep her from them.

"I had trouble. I couldn't use the telephone."

"Why not?"

"It's hard to explain. I'm sorry, though. I'm terribly sorry. And I missed you."

"Oh." A pause. "Can you hold on a minute?" And Connie heard, though Ruth put her hand on the receiver, that Ruth was explaining something to Molly.

"Well, are you all right now?" Ruth came on the line.

"Yes, I think so. I think I'm fine."

"Why didn't Aunt Sophie call?"

Connie paused to think. "I guess because she felt it was up to me, and she was right. I'm sorry that you had to be worried so long. So is she. And honey, you know, your father changed the phone number."

"And he didn't give it to you?"

"Of course he didn't give it to me. Did he tell you he did?" Goddamn Dave. Of course that's what he'd tell them. She glanced at Sophie. Sophie frowned and shook her head.

"Just a minute," said Ruth, and again there was a conference with Molly. When she came back on the line, Connie could feel, without having to be told, that the children did not want to hear her bashing their father, whatever they might decide among themselves. She had never done that to them during the marriage, and she would try not to begin now.

"How long are you going to stay at Sophie's?"

"I don't know exactly, sweetheart. There are a lot of things to work out. But Ruth, I want to see you. All of you."

Ruth was plenty smart enough to know that if Mummy didn't have the phone number, she didn't have the key either. And yet she knew her father wanted Connie to come home. All he did, now, was come home and cook them dinner, and then sit in the living room and drink and cry. They were all afraid to talk to him.

"We could come down on the train," said Ruth.

Connie held her breath. Oh, to see them. Oh. To hold them, one after another. To hold them all at once.

"How will you get to the train station?"

"We can walk there from school."

"You could catch the three-fifty."

"Yes. Molly will have to skip softball." In the background Connie heard Molly say, "That's all right."

"Do you have money for the tickets?"

"Yes, I do. I can lend Molly."

"I'll pay you back when you get here. Can you come tomorrow?"

"Yes."

"I'll meet you at the station."

"Oh. Okay. Okay, we'll see you at the station at four forty-five or whatever it is."

"All right, darling. I'll see you then. You were right to call, Ruth. I'm proud of you."

They hung up then, and Connie cried, but she didn't come unraveled again. She cried tears of happiness at the thought of her children, and then she stopped.

Connie stood at the top of the ramp at Grand Central at track 32. The dark platform smelled of steel. She was there at 4:30, waiting, and by the time the train pulled in at 4:52, she thought her heart would burst.

She saw Ruth first, of course, Ruth the tallest. But they were all together. She was determined to wait for them like a sane person, not to charge down the ramp, but it was they who ran to her. William started it. He gave a shout when he saw her. They came together laughing and hugging; it was a sweet moment, the first for Connie in many weeks. Then they all talked at once. The children were giddy with relief to actually see her, to see for themselves that she was all right, that she looked the same, that she still loved them. Then came the problem of what to do next.

Connie had meant to take them to Chinatown, but now she didn't want to waste a minute of her time with them in traveling, or shouting to be heard over the shriek of the subway. Besides, Chinatown had been a rare but favorite Sunday outing for them all, with Dave. She thought it would be better after all to go somewhere new to them all. They wandered out into the sunlight and ended up in an Irish bar near the station. There was a back room, nearly empty at this hour, where they wouldn't hear the chatter of the television mounted above the ranks of bottles.

She wanted to know everything that had been going on. They started with school. William had gotten a *D* in shop, which Mrs. Colonna found shocking. She had asked a lot of intrusive questions, too, about where Mrs. Justice was and when she could come in for a meeting. (Nosy old trout, Connie thought. She wanted to savage anyone who had made this time harder for the children.) Ruth had had a big start in softball this spring, but then she stove her finger and quit the team. "See?" She held it to out to show her mother. The joint of her middle finger was still swollen like a sausage, and blue.

"Ow," said Connie. But Ruth was nonchalant about it. She liked anything that excused her from PE.

Molly was playing shortstop and batting well. Her grades were better than last term, too. Ruth's grades were mostly *A*'s. (They had just gotten report cards two days ago.)

Their food came. Connie wanted to know what they'd been eating since she had gone. Spaghetti, and a lot of frozen dinners, it sounded like. Ruth and Molly cooked about half the time. They could cook hamburgers. And Daddy had discovered some frozen ravioli and frozen sauce that they all now knew how to cook. Breakfast and lunch went all right, they said. When there was no milk for cereal they ate bagels from the freezer. Daddy couldn't seem to remember to keep enough sandwich stuff in the house, so he'd arranged for them all to take hot lunch at school, which Molly and William liked, and Ruth hated. "I wish I could drive so I could do the shopping," she said. Connie nodded. (And privately thought, Well fuck you, Jack, to Dave, who had argued for years that hot lunch was too expensive and he didn't see why it was so much trouble for Connie to make lunch at home.)

Then Ruth handed her an envelope. All three children watched silently as she opened it. It contained a key, and a piece of paper that read, in Ruth's handwriting,

Our Number. 555-5424.

Connie looked at it quietly.

This was what she needed. The information, the method, and most of all, the message. The children wanted her to come home.

She looked at Ruth. "Thank you." Ruth ducked her head and nodded.

"Can I have another Coke?" asked William. Connie said of course, and signaled the waiter. The girls, though, waited to hear what their mother would say.

Connie felt that she had been gathering strength from the moment her children came into sight, as if their presence was a necessary part of the air she had to breathe. Their needing her was her strength, and she could feel it growing.

"Daddy isn't doing very well," said Molly.

"He's waiting for you to call," said Ruth.

"How could he be? How does he expect me to call if he changed the number?"

They shrugged. They knew their father wasn't being completely rational, and it scared them, and they didn't want to talk about it.

"What makes you think he wants me to call?"

"He keeps telling us you're coming back. He tells everyone that. He keeps telling people nothing's wrong, you're visiting a friend, and you'll be back any day. Then he sits in the living room and cries."

All three faces were gazing at her. For the first time since she saw the children coming toward her, she remembered the bottomless pit of tears. She thought of Dave, all noisy braggadocio in public, like a little boy, crying by himself with no one to comfort him. Oh Dave. Poor hurt Dave. She had been there to comfort him for so many years. It was cruel to let him finally feel the pain he'd been hiding from himself, by raging at her. It was cruel. He wasn't strong enough. She wondered if he could survive it. She wondered what seeing it was doing to the children. She wondered if he had felt enough pain now to make him finally able to change.

She wondered if she was out of her mind to be thinking this way. She had just been through something so bad she had almost lost her mind. Did she need more proof that she had to protect herself at last or die?

She could see that the girls at least understood exactly what was going on.

"Does he know where you are tonight?" she asked.

"We left him a note," said Ruth.

"What did it say?"

"It said 'We're going to see Mummy. We'll be back by bedtime.'"

She frowned. They should be home by dark, come to think of it. She should get them to the train. They should call Dave from the station, but if he wasn't at home or in shape to drive, she didn't want them walking in the dark. There was no taxi in town.

She hoped Dave wouldn't punish them for coming to her. Rage at them.

"What do you think I should do?" she finally asked.

"Come home," they said.

When Connie told Sophie what she was going to do, Sophie just stared at her. The next morning, she telephoned the psychiatrist from work.

"My sister's gone back to her husband," she told him. He was disgusted.

"Well, that's it. I can't help her. She doesn't need a psychiatrist, she needs AA."

"I don't understand," said Sophie, panicking.

"This is not an interesting problem. She's simply an addict," said the psychiatrist. "She's addicted to a terrible marriage."

"But would you see her, if I can arrange it?"

"No," he said. "I'm not kidding. She doesn't need me, she needs AA." He was still annoyed that Connie hadn't taken the pills he'd given her.

Sophie called Charlie, theoretically for advice. To her joy, he suggested they have dinner.

Sophie dressed carefully and arrived at the restaurant first. She wanted to see Charlie before he saw her; it was a superstition of hers. She sat at their table toward the back of the room, facing the entrance, and waited for the first sight of him, remembering what a rush it always gave her. She loved his walk, the pitch of his head, the way his hair curled. She loved him.

And he didn't love her. When she saw him this night, for a moment she was shocked. Charlie had lost weight, his face was drawn and pale, and he moved in a tentative way, like someone who's not sure where the next punch is coming from.

They kissed each other.

"You look . . . are you all right?" she asked.

"That good, huh?" He signaled for the waiter.

"A bottle of Orvieto, please. Oh, sorry . . . is that all right with you?" Sophie nodded. It was what they always used to drink when they came to this restaurant, but a lot had happened since those days.

Sophie described to Charlie her sister's horrifying depression, the tears, and then her infuriating decision to go home. Charlie was particularly interested in the tears.

"It's just what everyone's afraid of, isn't it," he said, "that you'll start to cry and never stop."

Sophie looked at him. The Charlie she knew didn't say things like that. The Charlie she knew didn't cry and didn't have theories about what everyone was afraid of.

"You've lost some weight," she said.

"Uh . . . yes."

"Do you want to tell me?"

"No. Yes. Do you want to hear?"

"Yes."

"God, you lie. Oh, Soph. You are a dear friend. You are."

She smiled. "Thanks." Well, it was something. She could be his sister. She wanted to be somebody's sister, and her own sister seemed to have lost her mind.

Charlie talked. He said Martha was the love of his life. He said that he thought she felt the same way.

"Doesn't sound like a problem," said Sophie.

"Wait for it," said Charlie. He described the tension, the frustration of the weeks they'd spent apart, talking on the phone, rarely together, rarely alone, never able to spend the night, always having to get up and go home.

"It was bad. We both want family, a normal peaceful life, we want that a lot. We missed each other, we'd try so hard to be good sports and pretend we didn't mind . . . it was just because we wanted to be together so much. We felt frustrated and bad and tried to pretend we didn't, and that didn't work."

"How about the children? What was happening with them?"

"Remember your first crush?" Charlie asked.

"Sure."

"Tell me about it."

"Johnny Lerner. Ninth grade. We used to leave each other secret notes in the Latin-English dictionary on the shelf of the study hall. He brought me a yellow heart-shaped box of candy at the Valentine's Day dance. I nearly died."

"Have you ever felt anything stronger than that in your life?"

They both smiled. "Not really."

"Where is he now?"

"I have no idea." They laughed.

"The point is," said Charlie, "what if you were in the grip of all that . . ."

"Lust," said Sophie.

"Right. And your parents decide that Johnny Lerner should move in and live in the same house. And whatever happened between you would happen right under their noses, and when it was over you wouldn't be able to get away from each other. You'd be meeting each other going in and out of the bathroom for the rest of your lives."

"Oh, god," said Sophie.

"Well, yes. I mean, I know things have changed, but I don't think anyone is going to change *that* much."

"So . . . ," said Sophie after a long pause, in which Charlie looked sad and lost in thought and seemed to have forgotten she was there.

"Well. There was the wonderful night you know about." Yes. She didn't need to hear again about the night Martha walked in when she was there.

Charlie described the pain he felt at having betrayed Martha (and Sophie for the first time felt truly ashamed of being part of it). He said they both felt, he and Martha, after that night that they couldn't go on with that half-life. It was worse than nothing; they would grow to distrust and resent each other. He told her about the plan of the weekend in the country.

"I take it it didn't work out."

He laughed, bitterly.

"What happened?"

"Let's order dinner." That gave him a rest. Oh, how he didn't want to live through that weekend again. And yet, couldn't stop.

When the waiter had gone, he described it all. He described the phone call from Patsy, and his fight with Phoebe, and then with Martha.

"I don't get it," said Sophie. "I don't see what was wrong with you telling Phoebe to snap out of it."

"I'm not explaining it well. Martha was right, I just wanted it to be simple. I just wanted to give everyone orders in my simple manly way, who to be, what to feel. No wonder everybody was pissed."

He told her then about the evening and the night, and the way it ended.

"So . . . can't you just go back to the way things were before? I know it was hard, but it wouldn't have been forever."

"Uh, well. I haven't exactly told you about my hour of glory."

"Oh."

"After I finished yelling at the kids and reducing everyone to tears, I had another fight with Martha."

"Oh."

He was silent for a moment. His eyes were clouded, as if he'd gone to sleep in a world full of clarity and awakened in a maze.

"I was mad at her. She's always saying things I don't want to hear. She's always saying I don't want Phoebe to grow up, and she's right. I don't. I loved it when she was little and I'd come home and listen to her burble about her bug collection. Who wouldn't? Why doesn't Martha just love me the way I am?"

"You say she does love you the way you are."

"I know. She does. But I want her to find me perfect." He smiled, but it was sad.

"Do you find her perfect?"

"No."

A long pause.

"But you love *her*."

He'd seen this coming.

"Yes, but see, she's perfect for *me*." They both laughed. Their food arrived, and they ate in affectionate silence for a while.

"Anyway," said Sophie, "you had another fight."

Charlie nodded. "I'd been hard on Jack when the kids came in.

Martha says I was, and I guess I was. Both kids were pretty shattered by the time I was through with them. So they went upstairs, and then Martha said it wasn't fair to put so much of the blame on Jack. She said it was true he was older, but not by much, and that I was saying that boys are always more responsible and girls are lesser beings morally, and I just tore her head off. I said—" He stopped. "I can't tell you what I said. I can't stand to think about it. But I was so sick of being told I was wrong and that I couldn't have anything I wanted. She just stood there looking at me, with this terrible hurt expression on her face—" He stopped again. Sophie took his hand.

"It was late. You were exhausted. It's so unlike you . . . she'll forgive you."

He shook his head. "That's not even the end of it. Jack came down the stairs again and watched me standing there yelling at his mother. And he said, 'Charlie, please don't. It's my fault.' And I turned on him and told him that he'd caused enough trouble in my life and couldn't he leave us alone. I didn't put it as nicely as that either. Well, at least I wasn't treating his mother as a morally inferior being." Sophie smiled.

"Martha looked at me . . . we were staring at each other, trying to figure out how the hell this could be happening. Then she went to Jack and said, 'Thank you, honey.' Not like she thought he was right, or that she needed the protection, but just that she thought he was brave to try." He paused. "And he was," Charlie said. "He's such a good boy." He had to stop talking again for a moment.

"I looked at them there together and I realized that if push came to shove, she was closer to Jack than to any human being in the world, including me. And I had just given her the shove. She didn't look at me again. She touched Jack on the shoulder and then went past him up the stairs and began to pack. As soon as the baby was awake, we loaded the car and left. The whole way home no one spoke, except to Fred. And when we got to their door—Sunday morning, bright sun, deserted street—she got out and took her stuff and Jack carried the baby, and when it was all on the sidewalk she came to the car and looked me in the eye and said, 'Good-bye.'"

"Just like that? No discussion? Are you going to write or call each other?"

"Just 'good-bye.' And Phoebe suddenly jumped out of the car and went to hug Martha. Then they were gone, and Phoebe got back in and cried all the way uptown."

There was a long silence between them, during which the waiter cleared their plates. Charlie had barely eaten.

"Sophie . . . I'm sorry. I didn't mean to do this. I just needed someone I could trust."

"Thank you."

"But I shouldn't have done this."

She took his hand. "It's all right. How about Phoebe?"

"Oh, poor Phoebe. She cried saying good-bye to Martha, and then the next thing was she had to tell me she wanted to go to her mother's . . . she didn't know what kind of storm that was going to cause, but she did it. And then she called Patsy. I think she expected she was going to move back, I mean at the least, that her mother wanted her to move back, after her performance on the phone. And instead Patsy said, no, no, that Phoebe should come for lunch but after that Patsy had things to do because she was going out to a dinner party."

"Oh, no."

"Oh, yes. So it was pretty much a clean sweep. Phoebe lost Jack, she lost Martha, she lost her mother again, and she was so afraid of me she didn't dare talk to me about any of it. She went to her room at three in the afternoon, and I don't think she spoke to a living soul until she got to school the next morning."

"Poor little thing."

"And I didn't have such a great time myself for the next few days."

"Jack and Phoebe will see each other at school, won't they?"

"Yes, but I can't imagine there are going to be a lot of phone calls flying back and forth. Hi Charlie, it's Jack, may I talk to Phoebe? I don't quite picture."

"You'll be lucky if they don't elope."

"I'd be lucky if they did elope. Then I could set them up in their own apartment and go beg Martha to take me back."

Sophie laughed.

"I'll be lucky if any of them ever speaks to me again. I picture myself at Phoebe's college graduation. 'Yes, dean, I'm Phoebe's father. I love her very much so I follow her around, hoping she'll forget who I am and speak to me by mistake.'"

They drank espresso together, and after dinner took a long walk home in the spring evening. For Sophie it was both comforting and very sad. She knew now that the moment when she and Charlie might have chosen a life together had irrevocably passed. On the other hand, tonight had begun a different kind of closeness. Not what she had wanted, but much better than nothing, love being love.

They tried walking with their arms around each other, and remembered it didn't work. She was too short, their strides were different lengths, her arm around his waist began to ache because it was at an uncomfortable angle. They stopped trying, and Sophie took Charlie's arm instead, and they walked up a quiet, empty Fifth Avenue the way an usher escorts the mother of the bride up the aisle of a church.

Charlie walked her to the door of her building. She didn't even think of asking him to come up. He held her for a long warm time, then kissed her cheek.

"Thank you."

"You're welcome," she said. "Thanks for dinner."

"I'll call you tomorrow."

"Good," she said. And they parted.

Gillis *was having* dinner at Crosby Street again. He was there now most nights, when he wasn't working. At first, he came as a sort of uncle to the boys, very shy of imposing on Martha, very circumspect about her privacy. He knew something had gone wrong between her and Charlie. He knew she was sad and that she didn't want to talk about it. He understood that; he never wanted to talk about anything either. But he'd drop by at hours when he knew she was busy with Fred. They'd have tea.

One afternoon, although Martha had determined never to ask Gillis to assume parental duties, she called him and asked if he could pick up Fred from nursery school; she had to go to the dentist. Gillis was pleased, and to make an event of it he decided to bring Fred home by way of the new exotic food emporium on Broadway that people kept talking to him about. He found it to be a giant space coated with dazzling white tile and equipped with a great sound system. Gillis hadn't known there were musical grocery stores. They were playing the Brahms *Requiem* when he walked in. Gillis had been there for several minutes before he noticed they were also selling food.

They were, though. There were tables heaped with fruits he'd never seen before and amazing newborn vegetables, racks and racks of imported pastas and biscuits and jams and spices, and oh, then the Brahms ended and they began Bach's *French Suites*. Gillis found himself at the fish counter, where a man was buying mussels from New Zealand with huge green shells. Fred was agog, and so was Gillis. He'd lately learned a new recipe from the newspaper that featured canned salmon and water chestnuts and he had thought *that* was exotic.

Fred noticed a counter full of cakes and cookies and tarts and then heaps of ruggalah and candied orange slices dipped in chocolate. Gillis bought Fred a gingerbread man, and himself a chocolate truffle, which he thought was going to be one of those things they use pigs to dig up in France, but it was candy. But this piqued his spirit of adventure. He decided to buy a bagful of things he'd never heard of and take them home to Martha and see if she could make dinner out of them.

"You've been to Dean and Deluca!" she said, when she came home and saw the shopping bags.

"Yes," said Gillis. "My first time."

"What did you get?"

"Surprises," said Fred.

"He doesn't know the half of it," said Gillis.

Smiling, Martha started to unpack.

"The meat's in the refrigerator."

"What is it?"

"It was this thing that looked sort of like a xylophone, but it's made of lamb chops."

"Gillis . . . that costs a fortune."

"Everything costs a fortune there, I thought that was supposed to be part of the fun."

She shook her head, smiling, and went on unwrapping things. There was a kind of pasta called orzo that looked just like rice, and some black squid-ink fettucine that they'd bought because Fred hoped it would be licorice. There was some fruit crossed between an apple and a pear, and some berries also from New Zealand that cost about a dollar apiece. There was Devonshire cream, and a package of crumpets, and a jar of lemon curd from Scotland, and then some fresh herbs, sorrel and coriander, and some baby golden beets.

"This is lovely of you, Gillis."

"May I stay for dinner?"

She smiled. "Yes."

They had a feast that night, and after that Gillis would often take Fred shopping, and then Martha would cook whatever they brought home.

She did realize that Gillis was courting her. She didn't take it very seriously at first. At first, nothing seemed very real to her except missing Charlie. It was like a sharp ache that was with her day and night—the nights were terrible. Dreams, the worst. She could keep from calling him . . . just. But she couldn't keep him out of her dreams.

It was a bad time for her. It was a time in which she accepted a view of a diminished life for herself, and the acceptance cost her a great deal. It had been hubris, she thought, to expect her life to have a happy ending. Why should it? She didn't deserve it; nobody did. Think of poor Raymond, all his schemes in ashes. She had hoped for too much. Wanted it too much. Mistake.

Her work, which she had always loved, messing about with pencils and charcoals and paints, keeping her Rapidographs in perfect order, creating illusions of shape and volume and light, became a torture because she worked alone. When she had company she could function. Alone, it was so hard not to be paralyzed with missing Charlie.

She'd look across the table now in the evenings at Gillis, holding Fred, and feel grateful to him for being there. She saw how much Fred resembled him, both with their bright blond hair and long eyelashes and long delicate fingers. Fred was teaching Gillis how to make a carnation with a Kleenex and a bobby pin, which he had learned at nursery school that day. Gillis was terrible at it. Fred thought that was very funny.

One night when Martha was cooking, Gillis answered the phone.

"Who was that?" she asked, when he came back to the kitchen.

"Charlie Leveque."

Her heart nearly stopped.

"Didn't he want to talk to me?"

"He said not to bother you, he'd call another time."

But he didn't. For several nights Martha barely slept, picturing what Charlie must have felt, finding the courage to call and then getting a man on the phone. But she fought it. It had hurt enough to leave Charlie once. She couldn't bear being in touch with him and having to begin the separation all over again.

Jack was often not with them. He and Jaywalk were studying for SAT's and they spent a lot of time at Jaywalk's. Whatever was going on now between him and Phoebe, Martha suspected that it was oppressive to Jack to be around the house too much. She didn't blame him. Though she missed him.

Madelaine called almost daily these days to discuss the eightieth birthday party she was giving for Martha's father.

"I've decided against the haggis," she announced one morning. "I understand it smells rather horrible. And the caterer thought there would be a problem getting enough sheep stomachs."

"I think that's just as well."

"It makes it difficult, though, to know what to put in its place. The caterer seems rather at a loss, confined to Scottish cuisine. Especially since so few people really care for mackerel. We're having these exquisite marmalade tarts, though, did I tell you?"

"Yes, they sound wonderful," said Martha.

"Your father's no help at all. I asked him what his favorite food is, and he said chocolate chip cookie dough. We never really get over our childhoods, do we? That cook of his mother's would never let him in the kitchen to lick the spoons when she was baking."

"Neither would Bessie, Mother."

"Oh really? I didn't know that. I thought you were all out there making angel food cakes the whole time."

"No."

"Now what have you decided about having the boys in kilts?"

"Jack feels a little resistant to wearing a skirt."

"Oh, how silly. You know your great-uncle Rowland used to wear skirts whenever the mercury went above eighty. He said they were far more comfortable than trousers. The Scottish cousins will wear them, of course. And the bagpipers."

The Scottish cousins were several times removed, and all in their seventies. "Still, I think he'd rather not. It's enough that he's letting me buy him a suit."

"Oh, all right. Well. Now, you know the boys can share their usual room, but with your brothers home I don't know where we're going to put your friend Charlie."

"I'm not seeing Charlie anymore, Mother."

"Oh!" There was a pause. "When did that happen?"

"About a month ago."

Another pause. "Well, then you can bring Gillis," she said brightly.

"Mother."

"You know, as a friend. We're all so fond of him, and that way you'll have someone to walk with in the parade of children."

"The what?"

"Oh, didn't I tell you? To begin the party the pipers will play, and all the children and spouses and grandchildren are going to march across the lawn two by two and then form a group around your father for pictures, while the caterers serve milk punch."

Martha was silent for a moment. She couldn't tell which was more horrifying, the parade or the milk punch.

"If I bring Gillis, where will you put *him*?"

"Oh, we'll figure something out. He's family," said her mother happily.

"I tell you what, Mother. *You* invite him."

So Madelaine did.

"Your mother sent me an invitation to the great birthday party," Gillis said to Martha over dinner. For once, they were not at home eating pumpkin ravioli. Jack was home studying for finals, and so could baby-sit Fred. Gillis had taken Martha out to dinner.

"Do you want me to come?"

Martha smiled. "Thank you for asking." She was silent again, because she felt so sad. Fortunately, Gillis was not uncomfortable with silences.

"Yes, I'd like you to come," she said at last.

"Good," said Gillis.

It seemed like some kind of commitment, though neither of them knew what kind.

Connie *let herself* into the house and stood in the front hall in silence, listening to the house breathe. She had far from gotten over the experience of coming home and being barred, like going to a beloved friend for an embrace and instead being knocked down. She felt now as if the house might offer invisible resistance. With each step, she would be asking permission to penetrate further.

There was a glass standing empty on the front hall table. She picked it up. There was a white ring on the mahogany.

She sniffed the glass. No smell. It had been there for days. It could have held Coke, Scotch, anything. She walked, carrying it, to the living room opposite the front stairs.

She had expected the living room to look as if a homeless person had set up camp there. Usually by the time Dave had watched half a football game, there were glasses, newspapers, and empty ice-cream bowls standing wherever he had finished with them. But the room was quite neat. All the papers were put away; there was only an open copy of Dave's college alumni magazine beside his chair. She picked it up and read the page where it lay open: the obits. A classmate of Dave's, Rick Lazar, had died. She didn't recognize the name and wondered if Dave had known him. The obituary didn't mention a cause. Did that mean he killed himself? She always wondered. She turned to the notes for Dave's class and saw that one of Dave's roommates, Ralph Brown, whom they all called Buster, had remarried. His new wife was an associate at the same law firm as Buster in San Francisco. Dave had been an usher at Buster's first wedding. They hadn't known that Buster and Margo were divorced.

She went through the dining room into the kitchen. The breakfast dishes were in the sink. There was a milk carton on the counter, but at least it was empty. Usually the empty ones were in the icebox and the full ones stood on the counter going sour.

On the pad by the phone, in Ruth's writing, was a list of groceries they needed. Connie turned the page back; there was another note:

Daddy:
We've gone to see Mummy. We'll be home before bedtime. Don't worry.

Connie wondered, how did Dave feel when he stood on this spot reading that?

Quietly, but with growing confidence, she went from room to room. The house did not resist her, and by the time she was finished with her tour, her sense that she was intruding had disappeared. She changed her clothes, made the beds, and went out to the garden to cut flowers for the dining-room table.

When Ruth and William got home from school, they burst into the kitchen with cries of joy. William leaped into her arms and she staggered, laughing, as she hugged him. She put him down and gave Ruth a long, quiet embrace.

Neither child wanted to let her out of their sight. They followed her around the house as she set things to rights and started dinner. By the time Molly got home from softball practice, the house was full of the smell of cooking. William ran out to the driveway when she arrived, shouting, "Molly! Mummy's home!" Molly glowed as she ran to her mother. She hadn't looked so truly happy since before the night in Washington Square.

They chattered excitedly to each other until finally they heard Dave's car drive in. Then silence fell. Connie watched out the kitchen window as he stood in the driveway staring at her car. Then he looked toward the house, and stood there. Slowly, he approached. He looked pale and tired. He looked wasted and handsome. Connie, watching from the window, felt her palms sweat, and her heart seemed to jerk around as she waited for him to come in the door.

When he did, Dave found his wife, flanked by three children, staring at him. He closed the door carefully behind him, and then stood just inside it, holding his briefcase and *The Wall Street Journal*. He looked as if he were trying to frame a sentence in a language he hadn't spoken for decades. After what seemed an eternity, he set down his briefcase and laid his paper on the table. Then he went to Connie, wrapped his arms around her, and buried his face in her neck.

It was a joyous evening. Connie had gotten a rib roast and made a Yorkshire pudding. (She'd had to borrow a hundred dollars from Sophie before she left, as she had no source of cash whatsoever.) She set the table in the dining room with the good china, and Dave said grace as he usually did only on holidays. The children laughed more than they had in weeks, and Dave told all the jokes he had learned at the office since Connie left. (There were always new ones; salesmen had to be entertaining. It was a family tradition to milk the new jokes out of Daddy at least once a week.)

After dinner everyone made Connie sit while they did the dishes. She followed their every move with hungry eyes, as if she would never get enough of simply looking at them all, all together. For her the best moment came when the dishes were in the dishwasher, and the pots were all washed and dried, and the children were finally told to go do their homework. Dave turned to Ruth and gave her a bear hug and a kiss. He didn't say anything, but they all knew what it was for.

Dave and Connie sat at the kitchen table talking until the children's bedtime. Dave told her about his troubles at the office . . . she told him nothing of her three weeks in tears, but spoke of Sophie and Charlie and of New York. William came down in pajamas and asked Connie to read to him. Instead of making a fuss about whether he was too old to be read to, Dave came up to sit on William's bed and listen. Then they said goodnight to the girls and went upstairs. Still without having said a word about anything that had happened between them, they went to bed and made love, amazing love. Afterward, as they lay in each other's arms, Connie touched his face and whispered his name. For a long minute he didn't respond; then he turned to her and kissed her, and said, "I was saying my prayers."

In the middle of the night, they found themselves awake, and made love again. In the morning, Dave kissed Connie and told her to sleep; he would get the children off to school. So she slept in her own bed, feeling deeply filled, until well past nine o'clock.

∞

It *was Park* Day at Cropp and Thatcher. On Park Day, the lower and middle school kids were taken to Prospect Park for sack races and things. Since many members of the high school faculty were dragooned into helping at the games, things were a little irregular even for the juniors and seniors, and most of the hip ones cut school. The corridors echoed and the whole building had the feeling of summer recess, which in fact would arrive soon enough.

The juniors had finished their SAT's. There were a few advanced placement exams to face, and of course, final exams. Mr. Kelley's classes were all writing long term papers. You could either write a research paper on one of the authors the class had studied, or you could retell a well-known story in the style of a different writer. *Ethan Frome* in the style of J. D. Salinger, for example, or *The Exorcist* in the style of Annie Dillard.

On top of that, there was the annual play-writing festival. Six years in the last ten, the citywide Young Playwrights competition had been won by a student from Cropp and Thatcher, and everyone involved with the English and drama departments took the tradition very seriously.

Jaywalk had started a play about a white boy who wants to be a rap artist, but abandoned it. Jack had started his play late and was not going to have time for a complete staging; he hoped to cast and direct a reading. No one's material deviated far from autobiography, and no one expected it to, although there had been one year when the hit of the festival—a comedy about a girl whose mother wandered around in curlers, chain-smoking and writing letters to the president—caused such hard feelings that the playwright temporarily had to go live with her father.

Jack's play was about a boy who won't make plans, or go anywhere, or even get on with growing up, because he's waiting for his father, whom his friends and the audience come to realize is never coming back. Phoebe was not writing a play, but to her surprise she had been asked to act in three of the student productions.

"I guess they really liked me in *The Three Musketeers,*" she said, shyly, when she told Jack.

"No, they're just pretending because you're like so pitiful. What did you think all that stamping and yelling was about?"

"I don't know."

"You're a silly person," said Jack. Jack, who had been the lead in two productions the year before, had this year only been asked to do one small role. He said he didn't have time to do more, but that wasn't really the point, and Phoebe knew it hurt.

Phoebe was doing the part of somebody's mother in Jenny Krass's play, and somebody's best friend in a play written by a senior boy whom she hadn't even thought knew her name. But the biggest part, and the most demanding, was in Bernie's play. Bernie, who couldn't talk with his mouth, could talk with his hands in more ways than one. It turned out, he wrote like an angel. It was as if the frustration of being unable to speak clearly was a machine he had learned to use, to crush and grind away any obstacles or infelicities in his written prose; his language flowed like liquid. The play had an oddly mature flavor to it, too, since Bernie couldn't hear the locutions of his own generation. He could read lips, but the language he was in love with was written, not spoken.

He had written a play about a deaf girl and a boy who falls in love with her. The boy is a beauty and an athlete. The girl teaches him sign language, and he finds, speaking to her in her silent language, that he recognizes and can express things about himself he couldn't in speech, especially that his own feelings about his own worth and other people's are based on physical perfection. He comes to admire the daily heroism of living with a handicap as more remarkable than completing the touchdown pass—there are no awards, and no applause, and it's never over.

Bernie had thought about casting Jaywalk to play the boy opposite Phoebe, but Jaywalk was so absurdly storklike. Bernie wanted a real jock, and he also wanted someone really to be learning sign language in the course of the play. He decided to ask a boy called Joe Brockett, tall and beautiful, a young professional actor who had already starred in a PBS play on television. He was pretty full of himself, Brockett, and had turned down other chances to try out for school plays, let alone to help in the play-writing festival. Everyone was surprised when Bernie reported that Joe Brockett had said yes. Bernie wasn't surprised though, since he was hopelessly in love with Phoebe himself.

* * *

On Montague Street, Bernie's rehearsal had adjourned to the Fortune Garden for fried rice. The morning had gone well, and Jaywalk and Phoebe and Bernie were relieved and surprised at what a nice guy Joe Brockett was turning out to be. The talk over lunch was getting-to-know-you, as they decided to settle in and become a company.

"How come you decided to come to Crapp and Thrasher?" Phoebe asked Joe.

"My dad wanted me to go to boarding school."

"Why?"

"I don't know. Because he's a snob. The school I went to stops after eighth grade. My sister's school goes to twelfth."

"Where is she?"

"Replogle."

"That's where I went! What's her name?"

"Rochelle."

"Oh, Rochelle. Brockett, sure. I know which one she is. Braces, right?"

"Right. And the motor mouth."

Bernie decided to speak. He did that sometimes, when he felt comfortable with people, and they didn't know how to sign.

"Where did you go after eighth grade?"

There was a pause.

"I'm sorry," said Joe. "What?"

Bernie repeated his question. There was a longer pause.

"I'm sorry, I still didn't get it."

"Where did you go after eighth grade?"

"Oh. Where did I go after eighth grade?"

Bernie nodded. He never minded when people couldn't understand him. For him the nightmare was people who pretended they could, who nodded and smiled and then turned to talk to somebody else.

"I did go to boarding school," said Joe. "For one year."

They all looked at him, wanting to know more, but he didn't make it easy to ask.

"Why did you leave Replogle?" Joe asked Phoebe.

"I got kicked out. For smoking pot in the girls' room. And then I called the principal an asshole."

Everyone laughed. Phoebe looked pained.

"Where do you live?" he asked her, suddenly sorry that he hadn't been more forthcoming about what had happened to him.

"I live with my dad." She told him the address. It turned out to be two blocks from where Joe lived.

"We must take the same train every day!" he said. They did, though on comparing schedules they discovered that Joe always had to be at school an hour earlier than Phoebe, and they finished at the same time only on Thursdays.

The waiter arrived to ask if they were finished. When they said they were, he came back with oranges and fortune cookies. Joe read his fortune first.

"'Now is the time to try something new.'"

"In bed," said Jaywalk. And they all laughed. Joe blushed.

"They're much better if you read them that way," said Jaywalk.

Bernie handed his to Jaywalk, smiling. Jaywalk read, "'You may attend a party where strange customs prevail.'"

"In bed," said Joe and Phoebe. Bernie took back the slip of paper, dipped it in tea, and applied it to his forehead.

Phoebe opened hers, read it, and said, "Oh no."

"Come on, come on."

She read: "'Avoid flirting with a casual acquaintance. It could lead to an embarrassing situation.'"

The others took the addendum as read, and laughed.

Jaywalk's was: "'New career ideas are worth pursuing.' In bed. How dull."

They paid the bill and walked, or in Bernie's case, rolled, back toward school in the sunlight. Bernie went ahead, as there was no way for him either to read lips or talk with his hands while traveling.

"I went to Choate for a year," said Joe, suddenly, "but I came home because I was homesick."

"Really," said Phoebe. Jaywalk looked at him, sympathetic.

"I don't blame you, man, I'd hate it."

"My father was furious. Embarrassed, I think," said Joe, "but my mom wanted me home, so they let me come back."

∞

Gillis *and Jack* were packed and waiting for Martha. She had gone to rent a car to take them all to Massachusetts for the great event, her father's birthday party. Jack was telling Gillis about the play he wrote for the festival.

"My father died when I was ten," said Gillis.

Jack had known that, but he'd never known Gillis to talk about it.

They were drinking iced tea out of cans in the kitchen of the loft, Jack having just slaughtered Gillis at nine-ball.

"Was it sudden?" Jack asked.

"Sort of. He killed himself."

"Jesus," said Jack. Did his mother know that? Had he been told it but forgotten?

"The worst thing," said Gillis, "was, my mother wouldn't let me go to the funeral."

"She wouldn't? Why not?"

"Because I cried when they told me he was dead. She said if I couldn't control myself, I couldn't go to the funeral."

"So what happened? You sat home by yourself?"

"Yes. I remember how quiet the house was after they left. My little sisters—everybody. I remember just sitting in the living room, waiting for them all to come back. There was a shaft of light coming in the top of the window, and if I sat at one angle I could see a cobweb in the corner of the room, up by the molding. It was summer and the doors were open, so when the air moved I could see the web move, like a curtain waving. Then, if I moved my head just a little bit, it changed the way the light caught the web, and it would disappear. It seemed like I sat there for a year. I was wearing these little gray shorts, and a clip-on necktie, and my Sunday school jacket. Then everyone came back from church. All my mother's family. My father had one brother, Uncle Neville, but he just came in for a minute to say good-bye to me. Then they all had lunch. I remember everything on that plate. Cold ham, and bean salad, and white rolls that felt like you were biting into a paper napkin, and Jell-O salad with green grapes and little marshmallows in it on a piece of lettuce. They sat there eating that, and my father was dead. I stared at the plate they gave me till I memorized it."

"God," said Jack.

"Yeah. Well, speaking of God, I had a lot of questions for him that year. That was the year I stopped playing the violin and took up the piano. It made my mother furious—she thought I was Paganini or something. But the violin can only play one line at a time. I thought playing the piano would be like playing every instrument in the orchestra, holding whole worlds of music in my head and hands at once. And if I could do that, maybe I could understand what God thought he was doing when he made a world my father couldn't live in." He paused. "At least, I thought that would be the way to pose the question."

"I know what you mean," said Jack, after a silence.

"I thought you would."

"Did you find an answer?"

"Oh, I think so. My father was an eighth note, or a thirty-second rest or something, that had to be taken out of the music. We all are. It happens all the time when I'm composing. God is the music."

"My father didn't have a funeral," said Jack after a while. Gillis nodded.

"He didn't want one. He put it in his will."

Gillis nodded again. "So you know how I felt, watching the cobweb."

Jack nodded.

"If you were going to make a funeral service for him, what would it be?"

"I think he'd have liked a Viking funeral pyre," said Jack, and Gillis laughed. "Me and my friends could have painted ourselves blue and marched along the shore playing Black Uhuru on our boom boxes while he blazed out to sea."

"Look, if *I* should be gathered soon, I want you to do that for me," said Gillis.

"Okay. Black Uhuru? Or would you like the Wild Tchoupitoulas?"

"How about Men Without Hats?" They both laughed. They had always shared a taste for music that Martha couldn't be in the same room with.

"I'd like to read your play," said Gillis.

"Would you like to come see the reading?"

"Yes, I would. When is it?"

"Next week. Thursday."

"Great. Thanks."

The doorbell rang.

"We're downstairs," said Martha through the intercom. Jack and Gillis collected the suitcases and baby gear and began loading it onto the elevator.

In the car, Jack said to his mother, "Charlie called." They were on the FDR Drive. Martha, driving, hoped she wouldn't pass out and crash the car, hearing his name like that, so suddenly.

"He did?" She was amazed that her voice sounded calm.

"He said to wish Grandpa a happy birthday."

"That was nice."

"Yes. I told him I wanted to go teach riflery at camp with Jaywalk this summer and he said that was fine."

"Did he? Good. Did you tell him what the salary was?"

"Yes. He said it didn't matter, he could keep up my allowance."

"Oh. Good," said Martha.

They crossed the Willis Avenue Bridge. Well, then, she thought. No need to call him about that. Or excuse to. Another week without hearing his voice.

She asked, "Did he say anything else?"

"He said to tell you to drive carefully."

Martha didn't reply. Gillis studied her face in profile as she drove. In the backseat with Fred, Jack put on the earphones to his Walkman, and was lost to them.

"Oh *isn't* this lovely," cried Madelaine as she swept out onto the driveway to greet them. It was dusk; she had had her bath and was wearing a long velveteen hostess gown, and her face smelled of the orange-scented face cream she had been using since Martha was a child. She had in her hand the latest of the supposedly idiot-proof cameras her husband had given her. There were about fourteen of these already gathering dust in the playroom. Last year Martha had found a Brownie box camera at the back of the shelf with film still in it; she took it to be developed and back came three pictures of herself, aged seven, wearing a pink tutu with gauze wings attached to her shoulders.

There were also disk cameras, a Polaroid, several disposables, a narrow pocket camera, and some odder-shaped ones that used kinds of film you could no longer buy. Every other Christmas or so, some salesman would convince Martha's father that the technology was now so simple that all you had to do was push a button, and Dr. Forbes would buy his wife a camera. On Christmas morning they would all exclaim with joy over it, and Dr. Forbes would say, in his deliberate way, as if the thought had never occurred to him before, that it would be so nice to have an album full of family pictures like other families, and Madelaine would exclaim that that was so true. She would then shoot a half roll of pictures of children and grandchildren opening their stockings and at dinner wearing the paper hats that came out of their Christmas poppers. Then by summer she would have forgotten which button to push, and the Christmas following, someone would catch Dr. Forbes doing his holiday shopping and sell him a new camera.

This evening Madelaine had appeared in the kitchen with last year's camera, and one of the caterer's boys had shown her how to use it.

"Isn't this *lovely*," she cried as Martha and Gillis and Jack and Fred struggled out of the car, stiff from the drive. "Now just a minute, stand right there by the car." She snapped several pictures, facing directly into the setting sun. "There!" she said, and went to kiss Martha, then Gillis, then the boys.

The driveway was nearly impassable because it was full of trucks. One was delivering tables and chairs, another held china, linen, and glassware, and a third, full of ropes and pegs and mauls and gay yellow and white canvas, looked as if it were setting up for a circus.

"You see how busy we are," she said happily. "Isn't it fun! But I'm so glad you're here. Gillis, you can tell the men where to set up for the orchestra. They're moving the piano outside tonight, so it can be tuned in the morning. I think it should be right in the middle of the tent, but the man wants to put it at the end."

She led Gillis away, around the corner of the house, and Jack and Martha unloaded the car and carried the bags into the front hall. Then they went out to the back lawn, where the party was to be. The tent was up and the dance floor was being put in place. Gillis, standing with Madelaine in the middle of the tent, was directing the men to put the piano where Madelaine wanted it. Beyond the tent was the hill covered with dune grass and beach roses, stretching away to the sea.

They all had dinner together outdoors on the terrace.

"I thought we'd better stay out of Bessie's way," said Madelaine. "She's in a temper about the caterers as it is." They were eating jellied consommé with a thin slice of lemon and a leaf of parsley on top. "How is your mother, Gillis?"

"She's fine, thank you for asking." Gillis's mother was in a retirement home in Florida and Gillis had as little contact with her as possible, so in fact he had no idea if she was fine. Her nurses could be beating her senseless daily and he wouldn't know it, and might have sympathized with them if they had. Gillis's mother had had a mild stroke and then gone precipitously deaf in her early fifties, a phenomenon that puzzled her doctors. She'd had an operation that was supposed to improve the condition in 98 percent of such cases, but had no effect in hers, nor did she seem to be helped by her hearing aids. Gillis had never been able to shake a feeling that she'd gone deaf in order to avoid hearing his music.

But it was Madelaine's fancy that everyone she liked enjoyed a rich and stable family life, as she did. So she always asked fondly after Gillis's mother, and she was always pleased with the answer she got.

Gillis asked Dr. Forbes about his golf game, and they arranged to play a match in the morning. Madelaine beamed. Madelaine told at length about everyone's arrival plans throughout the next day. It appeared that Martha was expected to spend a good deal of the day driving back and forth to the airport.

"Dick and Gina will rent a car," she said, "and they'll be in the guest room, because you know there's only a shower in the boys' room and Gina likes a tub. So Gillis, I've put you in the boys' old room with Jack and Fred. Matthew and Sally are going to stay at the club, which is fine because really those children are so noisy. Jack, you and Fred can bring the cousins over to play in the afternoon. And Uncle Bud and Aunt Rhoda are staying with the Chaplins, but I said you'd drive them, Martha, because they're dying to see you." As Aunt Rhoda was a third wife whom Martha barely knew, and Uncle Bud not an uncle at all but a college classmate of her father's, she doubted this, but she agreed to act as jitney, if her mother would tell her where the Chaplins lived. Her mother could never absorb the fact that Martha was not familiar with all that had gone on in Alewife since she left, though she had lived there for fifteen years and been gone for twenty-five.

After dinner, Gillis and Martha decided to walk to the beach.

"Oh what a good idea," Madelaine said. "But wear white socks, and tuck your pants into them, that's what we all do now, and when you come in check for deer ticks. Bessie's husband has Lyme disease, and it's no fun. And take a flashlight."

Madelaine watched, highly satisfied, as they walked off across the lawn together toward the sea.

Martha and Gillis walked in peaceful silence in the last evening light. This was her favorite time of the year in Alewife, and she was glad to have an evening of quiet before the day and night of hoopla to come. The only problem was how not to think about Charlie, how they had walked here together and talked about June, and the honeysuckle.

"I'm sorry the cousins aren't going to stay here," said Gillis. "Is Carol . . . twelve?"

"Fourteen. They were here at Christmas and they got Daddy addicted to Nintendo. Mother was furious."

"I'll bet."

"Sally says Matthew is hooked, too . . . that sometimes she'll wake up in the middle of the night and find that he's downstairs in his bathrobe playing Super Mario Brothers."

"I wish I'd been here. At Christmas."

"You do?" Martha was astonished. The disappointment that had ended their relationship had been over Christmas. Martha loved a houseful of her brothers and their families, and Gillis hated everything about Christmas. He went into a black depression about the tenth of December, and resented shopping, resented the idea of people shopping for him, said he hated secular Christmas music and was going to punch somebody if he once more had to walk into a store and hear some ass singing "Oh my gosh my golly, it's time for mistletoe and holly." He wouldn't explain or examine his mood, and when Martha pressed him he grew rude and angry and said he had important work to do and couldn't be interrupted. So Martha, six months' pregnant, had celebrated Christmas without him, with plenty of time to think about what kind of family man he would be, and Gillis, who had probably been considering the same thing, insisted he was extremely glad to have spent the day playing the piano and eating tuna fish alone.

"I like your brothers. I think it sounds like fun."

"Oh," said Martha, and looked at him in the fading light. He smiled and shrugged. Curious, thought Martha.

"Jack invited me to come see his play at school next week," Gillis added.

"Oh. Are you coming?"

"Yes, I'd like to, if it's all right with you."

"Yes. It is."

"Good."

They walked on in silence until they came to the lip of the hill, where a steep dune of soft sand sloped down to the beach.

"Shall we go down?" asked Martha. "Or sit?"

"Let's sit." The moon was just rising and though it was only three-quarters full, it cast a silver path across the water. To say it was beautiful seemed hardly to state the case.

They sat down on the dune grass side by side, and Gillis put his arm around Martha. She settled against him. They didn't talk for a while, and then he kissed her, their first kiss in almost three years. After that, they sat in silence again for a time. Martha felt as if her attention and intelligence had been closed down like an aperture, to the place where she had no history and no curiosity; she was completely flooded by the moment. The world was a silver and blue vision of moon across the water, and she was a dark, warm body, beside another.

"I've been thinking," said Gillis.

Martha nodded. She had begun to wonder in the past weeks if he was ever going to touch her again.

"Well?"

But Gillis, feeling unequal to the task of expressing in words what he'd been thinking, turned to kiss her again.

After a while, Martha said, "Let's walk," and they got up and brushed away sand. Gillis took the flashlight and went first, holding the light between them to illuminate the path down the dunes. On the beach they walked with their arms around each other.

"I like your family," said Gillis.

Martha nodded. "They like you."

"I know." Most people found Gillis easy to be around, because he was handsome and because he said so little. It was easy to imagine a whole Gillis that bore small resemblance to the stubborn reality inside him, and never suspect that the Gillis you were so fond of was perfect because you had invented him. Certainly that was Madelaine's relationship with him, and certainly he knew it. It amused him, although when he thought too long about what people would think of him if they really knew him, that was usually the moment he decided he should go home for a week or two and lock the door.

What more was he going to say? He liked her family. He desired her. He had learned, in his few forays after leaving her, that making love could be a lot more work and a lot less thrilling than it had been with them, even with someone who wants you. He was a truly passionate man, but his passion for isolation was as great as his passion for physical love, and those two were not particularly compatible in a world where girls who might sleep with you also seemed to expect to be taken to dinner and talked to on the phone and so forth.

What he wanted was to change nothing about himself or his life, and yet be loved and desired and free from loneliness. Arguably, what everyone wants.

He stopped walking and turned himself and Martha to face the sea. He looked at the moon and the sea and he thought about being dead. (He often thought about being dead. Or more accurately, saw an image of his body, dead, being looked at by strangers. Before he could feel anything, he stopped thinking altogether, and instead found his brain swamped with music.)

The wind riffled their hair. Gillis said to Martha, without looking at her, "I want to marry you."

She stood very still. She wanted to make love with him. She also liked him very much, and she wanted her children to have a father. Mostly, at that moment, she wanted to make love with him.

When she didn't speak, he turned to her.

"The wrong thing to say?"

She smiled, and looked away from him.

"Let's walk," he said, and they started back toward home.

Gillis let her have her silence as they walked. Certainly the night and the sweetness of being near someone who simply knows you was enough for him. So they walked, soaking in the night sky and the sea. Gillis kept his arm around Martha like a protecting wing.

When they got back to the house, it was nearly eleven, and it seemed that everyone was asleep. Dr. Forbes had left the hall lights on for them, but from the lawn outside they could see that even Jack's bedroom light was out. Without discussion, they went softly up the stairs and down the hall to Martha's room.

Martha's room looked very much as it had when she had left it to go away to school. Her diaries from sixth grade were on the bookshelf, her box of trading cards was on the mantelpiece, her dancing school jewelry case, full of poppet pearls and pins in the shape of animals, was on her dresser. This made it an odd place to make love. But Martha could appreciate Gillis's choosing it. Let's begin again, as if there hadn't been the first marriages, as if we hadn't already disappointed each other, as if the false starts are erased, and we are young and unmarked, and choosing each other seemed to be the point of it. They made love in the dark, in the room where long ago she'd had so many dreams, waking and sleeping, and it was intensely sweet. Gillis was gifted in his passion, his concentration in it. Making love became the whole world to him when he was doing it, as music did when he was hearing it, and it was a world in which he was as utterly giving as in other areas of life he was withholding.

Afterward, as they lay together, Gillis said, "Martha, will you marry me?"

And Martha said, "Yes."

When Gillis had gathered his clothes and slipped off down the hall to go to bed, Martha turned on the light. She lay there, looking at the ceiling and thinking about the way the sea had looked as they walked. What would happen now? Would Gillis move in with her? Would he keep his loft? Would they find someplace new together? If they did, what would he do when he wanted to draw away from them and close everyone out?

And what would Charlie say? Where was he, right this minute? Did he know she was leaving him? For a moment she thought she would cry, and for another long mad moment of struggle, she thought she would go to the phone and finally call him. Charlie, I'm moving on, I'm going to stop loving you. Charlie, I left you so we could get on with our lives, and it's happening. I'm going.

She looked out the window at the moon and felt a longing, intense to the point of pain. If Charlie knew, what would he do? Cry? Rush up here and demand that she marry him right now, tonight? And what good would that do?

No. He would wish her joy. And her heart would break, and his heart would break. And they would go on doing what they were doing already, which was sleeping in beds sixty blocks apart for the rest of their lives.

She got up and sat by the window for another hour, watching the moon begin to set and trying to say good-bye to Charlie. She wondered how many months, she prayed not years, it would be before this feeling of grief at the thought of him would leave her. She thought of him at that moment, asleep. Trusting her. His dark eyelashes, his arm stretched across the empty place in bed where she should be. His glasses would be on the night table on top of whatever he was reading. He would still be marking things in the margins of magazines to show her, even though he was never going to see her again. He would be trusting that even though they were never going to see each other again, she was his, he was hers, they had already married each other. She could see the moon, he could see the same one if he were awake. She wished she could see his face right now, just for a minute. Just once more.

Finally she got back into bed and wrapped the thought of Gillis around her. Of Gillis, a dear and decent man, and of a life of affection and shared domestic pleasures. Toward morning, she managed to go to sleep.

Gillis and Martha took the subway to Brooklyn Heights the night Jack's play was on in the play-writing festival. Their subway car was nearly empty, except for a dirty man asleep on one seat, who seemed to live there. The car floor was strewn with pages from a dismantled newspaper. They didn't try to talk on the train, because on subways Gillis wore earplugs to protect his hearing from the screech of the train wheels.

Walking up the street to Cropp and Thatcher, Gillis took Martha's hand. He remembered a time three years ago when (still in bed after making love, still with his declarations of love in her ears) she had asked him to come with her to school to a performance in which Jack was singing, and he had refused. He hadn't had much of a reason; Jack wasn't his son, she wasn't his wife, he didn't have to go, and he didn't feel like it. He'd taken the afternoon off to make love, and he felt like going home and going back to work. What he had said at the time was he wouldn't go because they were singing Vaughan Williams and he didn't like Vaughan Williams. He remembered that it had hurt her, and apparently disappointed Jack. At the time he couldn't understand why. If he were giving a performance and she didn't come to it, it wouldn't have upset him; but when he told her that, it hurt her more. The whole thing had annoyed him.

It looked different to him now. He wondered, as they walked into school, if she was remembering it.

Martha nearly jumped when Gillis asked her what she was thinking.

"I was thinking about Raymond," she said.

Oh, Gillis thought. Well, that makes sense. It never failed to amaze him how often he thought he and Martha would be thinking about the same thing, and how rarely it turned out that they were.

"Have you read Jack's play?" Gillis asked.

"No. He said it wasn't finished."

"Do you know how long it is?"

"I think it ran about twenty minutes in rehearsal."

They gave their names at the door of the theater, and the girl checked the reservation list. Then they found seats in the rapidly filling hall and settled down.

"A lot of people," said Gillis, automatically counting the house.

"Yes. They usually *are* full. Jack's been here every night of the festival, and he said last night was standing room only."

Just then, Martha's heart nearly stopped. Charlie was walking down the aisle, looking for seats. He was holding Sophie's arm. He hadn't seen

Martha. As she watched him signal to someone to ask if seats were taken, watched them climb into the second row and sit down, she thought for a moment that she was going to stop breathing.

She busied herself with her program. There were five plays being presented. Jack's was untitled and would be read by Jack, Pia, Toby, and Nick. It was scheduled third. The first play was by Jack's friend Bernie Goldring. In it were Phoebe, Jaywalk, and a boy named Joe Brockett.

Gillis pointed to Phoebe's name in the program.

"Is that Charlie's daughter?"

Martha nodded. Then she said, "Charlie's here, in fact."

"He is?" Gillis looked surprised. For her part, Martha was astounded that she had uttered those words as if they were not freighted, as if it were a normal thing to say.

"Where?"

She pointed him out. From where they were sitting you could see Charlie's profile and the back of Sophie's head. Martha half expected Gillis to gasp, My god, he's the handsomest man I ever saw, I give up, but Gillis appeared to find Charlie unremarkable looking.

"Do you know who he's with?"

"Yes. His previous incumbent girlfriend, Sophie Curry."

"Sophie Curry. I know that name."

"You do?"

"Yes, now let me think. Sophie Curry . . . it was a friend of mine, a bassoonist, who kept talking about her. I always remembered her name because I like curries."

The lights went down, and the plays began. Martha barely absorbed anything of Bernie's play. She was trying not to stare at Charlie, not to have a stroke, not to cry. She hadn't thought the sight of him would affect her so much. But she followed the play enough to be impressed by Phoebe. The boy playing with her, Joe Brockett, was very handsome. Jaywalk was adorable. Very funny.

Phoebe, whose part was played with body language and hand signs, got a thunderous applause. She and Joe Brockett took their bows together, holding hands. Martha thought it was gracious of her; Phoebe could have taken most of the thunder for herself. Then Bernie rolled out, in response to shouts for the author. During his applause, Martha found herself in tears.

The second play was very macho and noisy and Martha didn't know any of the kids in it, though she was interested that the part of a police captain was taken by the famous Mr. Kelley.

Jack's play undid her. Nick Jardine read the part of the boy who is waiting for his father; Pia played his girlfriend, who leaves him for someone else because he seems paralyzed and she can't help him. Jack played Nick's best friend, who keeps trying to trick him into getting on with his life by making bets with him on everything. The small ambivalent triumph at the end of the play took the form of Nick agreeing to play a hand of poker. Take a chance. If you don't play you can't win. Play the hand you're dealt.

Martha had to sit for a minute, recovering, before she could speak, as the lights came up for intermission.

"Do you want to stretch?" Gillis asked her, finally.

"Do you?"

"I think I better. My leg's asleep."

Martha stood up, and found Charlie coming up the aisle. He had already seen her. She could hardly bear the expression in his eyes. He looked at her with perfect calm. She searched his face for a message that was only for her, but there was nothing. Was this an act? If so, how was he doing it?

They met in the aisle.

"Hello, Charlie. Hello, Sophie. This is my friend Gillis Burnham."

"Hello, Martha, you're looking well. Nice to meet you, Gillis." Charlie shook hands firmly with Gillis. And then went on looking at him. Well, he'd heard enough about him.

"I think we have a friend in common," said Gillis to Sophie, "Stanislaus Korbet?"

"Oh, do you know Stanley? I haven't seen him in years."

"You broke his heart, I think," said Gillis, smiling.

Sophie looked genuinely surprised. "I don't see how I could have. We were just in a cooking class together."

Gillis laughed. Apparently to get the joke, you had to know Stanislaus. Stanley.

"I thought Phoebe was wonderful," said Martha to Charlie.

"Yes. She's getting very serious about acting. She won an internship at Circle Rep this summer."

"Really! That's wonderful. Please tell her . . . tell her I thought she was great."

"I will." Martha waited for Charlie to say something more, but he just looked at her pleasantly. If he missed her, if she had hurt him, it was obvious he'd decided never to let her see his guard down again.

Gillis and Sophie had finished what they had to say about Stanley and fell silent too, waiting for their next cues.

Martha, feeling she was going mad, turned away from Charlie. She said, "How is your sister, Sophie?"

"She's just fine. She went back to her husband."

That got Martha's attention.

"She went back?"

"Yes, the children convinced her to, and it seems to be working out. I guess it was just one of those bad spots in a long marriage that has to be gotten over."

"And how's Molly?"

"Molly? She's all recovered. Thank you for asking."

"I'm glad it worked out. Well, we have to walk around, Gillis's leg is falling off."

"Oh, yes, ha ha, the chairs are awfully hard. Maybe we'll see you after."

"Maybe," said Martha, smiling. Downstairs, she said to Gillis that as they didn't know anyone in the second half of the program, why didn't they go home. So they did.

Jack and Phoebe were out on the fire escape. It was after the intermission; they had seen both plays that made up the second half on earlier evenings. Phoebe was wearing Jack's jacket, and someone had given them the tail end of a bottle of Old English 800, which they were sharing in celebration of their evening's work.

"Your father's staying for the second half?" Jack asked.

"Yes, I told him he'd like the last play."

"Mom went home."

"Because of Daddy?"

"I think so."

"Shit."

The night was cool and smelled like rain. Jack put his arms around Phoebe and they watched fast-moving clouds blank the moon.

"Gillis is very handsome," said Phoebe.

"He's droll. I like him a lot."

"You had fun on the trip to Alewife?" (They hadn't seen each other much in the last week except running past each other backstage.)

"The party was boring beyond belief . . . like a wedding. Except for the bagpipes. How did they *ever* think of an instrument like that?"

"Weren't they originally made out of sheep bladders or something?"

"I think so. I guess if that's all you have to work with, you can see why the Scots didn't come up with reggae. Or twelve-bar blues."

Phoebe laughed.

"There was one great thing at the party; on this table, where they had huge plates of shrimp and things, my grandmother put big silver bowls of chocolate chip cookie dough. Here were these octogenarians standing around eating chocolate chip cookie dough with silver spoons. It was very cute."

"Were your cousins all there?"

"The Nintendo addicts? Yes. That was fun, except we couldn't all fit in the same house."

There was a silence.

"Is your dad very serious about Sophie?"

"I don't think so. I think they're basically friends. He seems sort of flattened. I'm glad he has someone to go out with. *Two* depressed parents is hard to take."

"Your mother still upset?"

"She is definitely not psyched. She feels like a failure at everything. I have these depressing lunches with her. For a while she wanted me to move back with her, and I really didn't want to. I mean, I couldn't tell which of them needed me more. But now she's very excited about my acting and everything, and she's talking about going to drama school herself." They both howled.

"Perfect," said Jack.

Then Phoebe asked, "Is Martha very serious about Gillis?"

Jack sighed. He'd been dreading telling her this. "Well yeah, apparently. We haven't really talked about the details, but Mom said they're thinking about getting married."

"Oh *shit*," said Phoebe, sitting up and turning to look at him. Inside, they could hear the applause as a play finished. "Thinking about it? What does that mean?"

"Well, planning to. Over the weekend, he asked her to marry him, and she said yes."

"But . . . it's only been a month or something. . . ."

"They've known each other for years. He *is* Fred's father."

"This is all wrong," said Phoebe. She was upset. "Why don't they just live together and see if it works out?"

Jack laughed. "Shacking up isn't really Mom's style."

"But is she *happy* with him? I thought you said he was odd."

"He *is* odd, but so is everybody. I'm odd. You're odd. I don't think she's very happy right now, period, but I think she's happy with him. Fred's *very* happy."

"I'm completely opposed. I don't believe in this. I think there are a few people who are really made for each other and a lot of people who just really don't want to be alone."

"Which are we?"

"Shut up. I mean my parents, when I look at them. They don't belong together at *all*. There they were, just trying to be themselves, which they each had a perfect right to do, but they made each other miserable."

"Boy, you're tough."

"I'm not. I'm a complete romantic. I think there are people who are perfect for each other, but most of them don't find each other because they can't stand to be alone long enough to wait for each other. My dad was just so . . . *happy* when he was with Martha. I've never seen him like that with Mother. Or with Sophie. And so was Martha. Admit it."

"I admit it, I just don't know what to do about it."

"I think they're being dumb," said Phoebe fiercely. She stood up.

"Well, don't be made at *me*," Jack said.

"I'm not, I'm just mad. I felt safe when they were together. I thought that things made sense."

Jack laughed. "Phoebe Beebe. Nothing makes sense. You're never safe."

"Yes, you are! You're safe when good people love you! You're safe when people are what they seem!" Phoebe glared down at Jack, who was still sitting. He laughed again.

"I'm pissed! Don't laugh!"

"I can see you're pissed, but you're dreaming. You're not safe just because you want to be."

"Why are you being so cynical?"

"I'm not. I just don't want to believe things that aren't true. Why are we fighting about this?"

"We're not fighting," said Phoebe, and she flounced off.

Jack sat on the fire escape alone a little longer. He thought maybe she would come back. But she didn't. When he went in he found her talking to Bernie. He asked if she wanted him to ride home with her on the subway. But she said no, she could go with Joe Brockett. She went back to talking with Bernie.

Dave came home one night with a huge box, gift wrapped. He put it on the kitchen table. Connie was cooking. The twins were sitting at the breakfast counter, nattering with their mother, when he came in.

"Daddy! What's that? Who's it for?"

"It's for your mother." He looked pleased with himself and went to make a drink.

"It's for me?" Connie put down her whisk and turned to him, smiling. "What is it?"

"Well, you'll have to open it, won't you?"

"But it's not my birthday!" She made all the right noises, as she came to gawk at the package. "Did you go buy wrapping paper and everything?" She could guess the answer pretty readily. Dave was not an experienced gift wrapper. Connie was more touched by the lumpy folds at the corners than she would have been by any professional wrapping job.

"Shall I open it now?"

"Yes! Yes!" the girls weighed in. This was completely unprecedented behavior for their father, and they were eager to see what it meant.

"I thought you might wait till after dinner," Dave said.

"Oh! I don't know if I can!"

"Well. It's your choice, it's your present." Dave's good humor embraced them all. He was going to enjoy this no matter how it unfolded.

William wandered in and saw the box as if it were the only thing in the room. "What's *that?*"

"A present! From Daddy! For Mummy!"

"Why?"

"Yes, why, Daddy?"

"I don't know. Your mother will have to tell you when she opens it."

Connie had dried her hands and taken off her apron, and she was ready. She sat down and began to untie the ribbon.

The box turned out to be like a surprise ball. Inside was a mass of tissue paper wrapped around something. The something proved to be a large, square gold box.

"A basketball!" cried William.

When she opened the gold box, she found a mass of shredded paper. (Everyone was laughing and commenting as the kitchen began to be strewn with packing litter that looked as if it wouldn't have fit in a box three times the size of the original.) From the shredded paper emerged a long flat box.

"A necktie!" said Ruth.

"Just what I wanted!" Connie opened the box. Inside that was some more tissue paper, and inside that, an envelope sealed with a sticker of Snoopy dancing in ecstasy. And inside the envelope were airline tickets.

Connie was properly mystified and thrilled, as she opened one. "Mrs. David Justice . . . June 2d . . . Bermuda! Dave!" She put her hand over her heart. Dave was beaming.

"The other ticket's for me, I'm going too," he said. And everybody laughed. The children burbled, Bermuda, gosh, how great, Bermuda. They wondered, if their parents were going away, what was going to happen to them.

"Oh, *Dave,*" said Connie.

"We went to Bermuda on our honeymoon," Dave explained to the children. "And we have an anniversary coming up."

"Oh, *honey,*" said Connie, and she got up and gave him a big hug and a kiss. He laughed, happy and pleased with himself.

"Sophie's going to come out and stay with the kids," he said. "Everything's set. All you have to do is pack."

* * *

Bermuda was windy. Dave had booked them into the same hotel where they had stayed nineteen years before. There was one other honey-mooning couple, obvious newlyweds; the groom had a painful sunburn, and the bride always came to breakfast in a T-shirt that read EXPENSIVE, BUT WORTH IT. The rest of the hotel was booked solid by a convention of California dentists and their spouses.

The afternoon of their arrival, Dave suggested they take a nap, his euphemism for sex during daylight. For those first hours in Bermuda, they felt a euphoria, almost a folie à deux, in which twenty years had rolled away, and they were each ten pounds lighter, and they had every-thing ahead of them. They made love *and* had a nap.

"This is bliss," said Connie, as she fell asleep, and Dave nodded and stroked her hair.

Later, they took turns in the shower and dressed carefully for dinner. On the first night of their honeymoon nineteen years ago, they had ap-peared shyly, hand in hand, at the door of the room the hotel called the salon. They had been shown to a table by the window overlooking the veranda and the beach and the sea. There was a gardenia tree nearby, in full flower, and its perfume was hypnotic. The captain brought them champagne cocktails in tall fragile flutes, with a smile and the compli-ments of the management. It was a magic evening; somewhere below, a steel drum played.

Tonight, they appeared at the door of the salon. Connie wore a new flowered silk dress, and Dave wore green pants. The room was a wall of babble and absolutely full of people.

"I am so sorry," the captain said, waving his hand. The dentists had taken over the room for a wine tasting and seminar on "The Wine Cellar, Pleasure and Investment." All around the room were long white-draped tables on which stood ranks of bottles of chardonnays, sauvignon blancs, zinfandels, and pinot noirs, and all the tables were crowded with dentists, swirling wine in their mouths, looking thought-ful, spitting the wine into white cardboard buckets, and holding their glasses out for more. The air was filled with voices saying things like "too much tannin," and "good fruit," and "disappointing nose."

"I can offer you a table on the veranda," said the captain, looking re-gretful. Dave and Connie looked at each other, each privately dismayed, each trying not to look too disappointed.

The wind on the veranda was such that the candle, flickering in a glass chimney on their table, first kept splattering the leeward side of the chimney with hot wax, and then blew out before the drinks could arrive. Connie wrapped her tiny cashmere sweater around her bare shoulders, and said what a pretty evening it was. When Dave picked up his planter's punch to take a drink, the cocktail napkin under the glass blew away. By the time the waiter came to see if they were ready for another round, Connie's lips were turning blue.

They had their second drink in the dining room. It was quiet and nearly empty. Connie began to thaw out and Dave loosened his tie.

"Do you remember," Connie asked, "playing golf the first day?"

"And you hit a hole in two?" They both smiled at the memory.

"A hole in one, be fair." What had happened was she whiffed the ball on her drive and it rolled eight feet from the tee. On the second stroke, she hit it into the hole. Unfortunately, there were witnesses to the tee-off.

"And remember playing croquet with that old couple from England?"

"Who cheated," said Dave.

"Well, he did. She was sweet."

"Let's play golf tomorrow."

"Great. Unless it really pours, then we'll go to Hamilton on the ferry and shop."

"Let's rent motorbikes."

"And go out to the end of the island, where we found the private beach." They had found a deserted beach, which they pretended they would come back and own someday. They had made love outdoors, feeling very daring. They had made jokes the rest of the stay about how they would explain their arrest for lewd public behavior, should they have been discovered.

Dave took Connie's hand. "You're beautiful, you know that?"

Connie blushed and shook her head.

"I'm not kidding. You are. I bet nobody walking in this room would guess you had a sixteen-year-old at home."

"Two of them."

"Two of them. I remember when I first met your mother, I said, 'This is it. This gal is going to age well.' And you have."

"You look great, too."

They were gazing at each other.

"Naw. You're a real prize. I don't know how I got so lucky." He leaned over and kissed her cheek. Connie raised his hand, which she held in hers, and kissed it. She was about to ask him how he pictured them in another twenty years, where they would be, how they would look, when the doors opened and the dentists crashed in.

From then on, all speech had to be conducted at the top of the voice. The dining-room staff sprang into action, but overtaxed by having the entire hotel appear for dinner at once, the kitchen took nearly two hours to produce Dave and Connie's dinner, and by then they were almost too tired and full of planter's punch to eat.

In bed that night they began to make love, and it started well enough. But midway along it became apparent that Dave's most essential contribution to the proceedings was not going to be forthcoming. After this there was an awkward passage during which both tried to convey the impression that a little heavy petting was all that had been wanted anyway. Then Dave fell asleep, and then Connie. In the middle of the night Dave got up and spent quite a while in the bathroom. Connie heard him go but pretended to be asleep when he came back to bed.

They played golf in the morning. It was windy and bright. Dave wore white zinc cream on his nose, and Connie bought a sun visor that said BERMUDA on it in pink. As they walked around the course they talked companionably, about practical things, daily things. Ruth's PSAT's, Molly's desire to play rugby. William's Cub Scout meeting, at which Dave was supposed to teach the boys how to make a genuine Indian drum. After golf they decided to have lunch at the pool.

Dave got into a jolly chat with a group at the bar. When he returned to their beach chairs carrying two cold beers, he said to Connie, "Guess what! Some of these dentists are popsies!"

"Are what?"

"Those two couples I was talking to? It's the gal in the green hat who's the dentist. The guy is her husband. He's an almond farmer."

Connie felt a flush of anger at him. So dentists can be women, women can be dentists, so what, Dave? Do you have to call them belittling names to keep from being threatened? Wake up and smell the coffee.

But she suppressed it. The question was not really Dave, was it.

Well, it was, but the point was, if her self-esteem was so fragile that remarks like that made her want to call her husband a pig, then she should do something about it. Actually, until the moment Dave spoke, she too had assumed that the men were all dentists and the women were wives. But the world was full of women who were editors and executives and doctors and dentists, as she had had plenty of time to think while she lay in tears on her sister's floor feeling like a bag of dirt. If she felt so angry about being dependent on Dave to make her feel or even seem like a valued member of society, maybe it was time to think about a career.

But a second honeymoon was not the time to discuss it. Dave had made it so clear from the moment she got home that all he wanted in the world was for nothing to change, for everything to be exactly as it had been.

So instead of calling Dave a pig, she said, "Let's take a nap after lunch." But it turned out Dave had made a date for them to go windsurfing with the almond farmer and the popsy dentist.

The almond farmer, born and raised in Modesto, had never seen a Windsurfer before, but Dave said he could teach him. Connie and Elaine the dentist stood looking at the whitecaps on the water and said why didn't the boys just rent two Windsurfers, and they would all take turns. Dave and Bucky agreed to go first.

At first, Bucky fell off every time he got up, and Dave patiently shouted confusing instructions, though the wind carried away his words. Then Dave decided to teach by example. He got to his feet on the surfboard, pulled the sail up and filled it, and zoomed away. Bucky pulled his board onto the shore and all three watched Dave's progress from dry land.

"What happens when he wants to come back?" asked Bucky. Dave seemed to be getting dangerously far out and making no attempt to come about. In fact, though he was quickly becoming a distant speck, Connie had the distinct impression that Dave was frozen in place, feet planted, arms locked, heading at about eighteen knots straight for the coast of North Africa.

Down by the boat dock owned by the Windsurfer concession, two strapping young men in tiny bathing suits began to watch the disappearing surfboard, and point. Then one got into a motorboat and peeled off toward open sea. The group on the beach watched as the motorboat reached Dave, and Dave dropped his sail and fell off his board into the water and allowed himself to be hauled on board the boat by the kid in the tiny bathing suit. He was brought back, sitting stiff-backed in the passenger seat, and covered with goose pimples, while the Windsurfer bobbed along, cleated to the stern.

"Honey . . . ," said Connie as he approached. But the look on his face stopped her finishing the sentence. Dave stomped off to the bar without looking at any of them. After a while, Bucky turned to the girls and said, "Anybody else want to try?"

That night Dave and Connie found the salon free, because the dentists had taken over the dining room for a luau. The dining tables were gone. Instead, there were thatched lanais, with picnic benches and grass mats on the floor. Down the middle of the room, chefs and waiters dressed in grass skirts were poised to serve roasted pig, and poi, and pineapples and heaps of other island comestibles. (The luau had been scheduled for the beach, but the wind was too strong and the temperature too cold.) Steel guitars played hula music, while the room seethed and swayed with flower-draped dentists. One man took the mike and sang one extremely creditable verse of "Hawaiian Love Song." After that he forgot the words.

"I am sorry," said the dining-room captain when Dave and Connie presented themselves, hoping for dinner. He shrugged as if to say, What can I do? "We are not serving tonight. I am sure if you'd like to try a restaurant in Hamilton, the concierge would call you a taxi. . . ."

Just then Bucky and Elaine floated by, wearing flower leis and evidently full of whatever is drunk in the islands.

"Dave!" they cried. "Connie!" Nothing would do but Connie and Dave should join them. So they spent the second night of their second honeymoon sitting on grass mats surrounded by a crowd of new best friends. That afternoon, the dentists who were not, like Elaine and Bucky, playing hooky had apparently heard a terrific presentation about tax shelters. A lot of dentists had been burned, they learned that night, investing in shopping malls. Dave, being in real estate, could talk a fairly good shopping mall game, but altogether by the end of the evening Connie and Dave were too tired to speak, and they undressed in silence and went straight to a dreamless sleep.

On the third and last day of their second honeymoon, the wind died and the rains came. Dave and Connie took the ferry into Hamilton and trekked around under dripping umbrellas, buying presents for the children. They got Bermuda shorts for the girls, and a sweater for William at the House of Scotland and a Liberty scarf for Sophie. While Dave was looking over a collection of antique Scottish weapons, Connie secretly bought him a cashmere muffler in fire engine red, from Edinburgh, to give him at Christmas and remind him of their trip.

They spent the afternoon playing Bingo at the poolside casino with the dentists. It was rather fun. Dave played four cards at once. Connie won on the second game, but since she split the pot with six other people she only got twenty-five dollars.

The rain stopped around sundown. They had a romantic walk arm in arm along quiet lanes. The trees dripped rain whenever the leaves rustled, and the flowers, their blossoms full, seemed glistening and drunk. The soft air smelled of earth and hibiscus.

Back at the hotel, they had cocktails in the salon, and a quiet orderly dinner, as the dentists were at the casino having a slide show. The night was sweet and everything a honeymoon should be, except that once again their sex life misfired. Later, Connie woke up in the middle of the night to find Dave having a nightmare. His jaw was clenched and he was mumbling in a voice that sounded frightened. At last he shouted and woke himself up. She rubbed his back until he fell back to sleep. But she herself didn't sleep again until dawn. The night was filled with panics that seemed huge and jumbled all out of proportion, as always at that hour. A conviction that she'd left an iron on in the sewing room at home seemed as real and terrible and degrading to her sense of competence as the fear that Dave's nonperformance meant that he once again—or still—had another lover. Or worse, that at bottom, he just plain hated her.

On the plane on the way home, Connie said to Dave that she hadn't made up her mind, she was just throwing this out to see how it sounded, but what would he think about her going to law school.

Dave, sitting beside her, strapped into a tiny chair at thirty thousand feet, stared at the upholstery on the seat in front of him. He uncrossed his legs, swallowed and cleared his throat, and narrowed his eyes.

"Where?" he asked, finally.

"Well, I don't know," she said, surprised. She hadn't in fact thought about that. She'd thought more about who would shop for groceries if she were busy and couldn't, or about how Dave would feel if he wanted to go to a movie or something and she was tied up on a case.

"I'd commute into the city, I guess."

"Oh. Well. Why not. Sure, if you want to."

He picked up the magazine he had been reading. He thought she'd been about to say she wanted to go away for three years and only come home on weekends.

Connie knew he hadn't exactly given the most heartfelt endorsement anybody ever heard, but she was surprised by a rush of excitement and gratitude. He said yes! She could actually do it! When she got home, she could start phoning around for application forms, and find out about taking the law boards, and enroll in one of those cram courses that prepares you. She'd be a student again! She'd have textbooks and homework, like the children! It would be fun! Sometimes they'd all have to eat microwave dinners because Mummy had an exam, but no one would mind because they'd all be so proud of her!

She turned impulsively to give Dave a kiss. It surprised him. He wasn't crazy about public demonstrations of affection. Besides, he was reading.

They had been home from Bermuda for a week, and already Connie had received in the mail law school catalogs from Columbia, City College, NYU, and Brooklyn College. She'd talked to the dean of admissions, or their secretaries, in each of these places. She had called her old college for transcripts and discovered that she had three letters of recommendation on file from professors who had taught her as an undergraduate. Her college had insisted, on the theory that she might want to go to graduate school some time in the future when her teachers had forgotten her, retired, or died. Connie had thought graduate school so unlikely at the time that she'd forgotten she had done it.

Of all the children, Ruth was the one who really lit up when her mother told them her plans. Ruth would sit with her mother poring over course offerings and curriculum requirements. Connie was excited at the idea of family law, while Ruth thought criminal law would be best, litigating if possible. She saw her mother at the bar, in her Princess Di hairdo, defending the rights of some poor downtrodden murder suspect.

"Maybe I'll be a lawyer, too! And we'll call our firm . . ."

"Justice and Justice!" they cried together.

"We've got to do it! How can we miss?" cried Ruth. Connie put her arm around Ruth and hugged her, and Ruth blushed and laughed. She was quite serious.

Dave wandered into the kitchen. "What are you gals up to?" he asked absently. Since the kitchen table was piled with law school catalogs, it was not all that hard to figure out. He went to the refrigerator and took out a Popsicle.

William came in to ask what time they were having dinner. Connie looked at the clock.

"Oh dear. I'm afraid it's going to be late, honey. Are you very hungry?" William shrugged.

"I'll start it in a minute," said Connie, loath however to do so.

"Hey, pal," said Dave. "Let's shoot some baskets." William's face lit up. Connie watched them go out. She thought, Well well. Maybe this is what I should have done all along. Maybe if I have a life and get out of the way, Dave will discover he has a son, without me in the middle between them all the time.

Ruth said, "Mummy, if you go to NYU, what courses will you take your first year? I think you should take constitutional law. You'll probably be a judge someday, they need women judges." Happily, the two settled down to argue the merits of this course plan over that one.

After a time, Connie became aware of the slam of the basketball against the backboard mounted on the garage. And of Dave's voice.

"Okay, tiger, try to get around me. Try to get around me—oops, he intercepts, he goes for the shot, and swish! It's in! One for me! Okay, tiger, here you go. Here you go, take it easy, that's right, oh, he shoots and he misses! The big guy has the ball, and it's swish! Two for me!"

"Two to nothing, okay, Big Will, here you go. . . ."

Connie listened as this went on and on. Finally she put down her pen and went to the window.

Dave was red faced and excited, beating the socks off a ten-year-old.

He'd pass William the ball. He'd feint and dart around him, guarding the basket. William, looking tense and determined, would start to dribble, drop the ball, and Dave would crow, grab it, and shoot. Then he'd yell the score, now up to about 24–0. He'd pass William the ball, William would dribble and try to shoot. Dave, about three feet taller than his son, would rise up and bat the ball down, bounce, turn and shoot, and all the while, he was noisily doing the play by play, announcing his complete rout, his son's complete failure.

Connie went outside.

"That's enough, Dave," she said.

"Don't be silly, we're having a great time," said Dave, sweating. He shot again and sank another. "Aren't we, tiger. You should watch, see the old man show his stuff, what a score we've racked up here. . . ."

"It's enough. William, why don't you go in and help Ruth with the salad. I need you to start the charcoal, Dave." William trotted off into the house without a backward look at his father, like someone released from purgatory. Connie and Dave stood in the driveway staring at each other.

"Now what the *fuck* was that all about?" said Dave at last. His face was red and dripping with sweat. "That's what you told me to do, isn't it? Haven't you been telling me that you want me to play with the little twerp? I was playing with him."

"I don't know what you thought you were doing, but you weren't playing with him! You were humiliating him! A forty-two-year-old man doesn't play his hardest against a ten-year-old!"

"Why the hell not? *You* coddle him all the time, and it's made a namby little toad out of him! Maybe being treated with some respect will make a man of him!"

"Treating him with respect? Is that what you were doing?" Their voices were rising. "He isn't a man, he's a boy! You're supposed to be the man! A man doesn't get his rocks off humiliating children!"

"I'm *supposed* to be the man? What does that mean?" Dave advanced on her, his face purple with anger. Connie took a step backward.

"Don't you touch me," she said.

"Touch you? What makes you think I want to touch you?"

Again, they faced off, staring at each other. Suddenly, like an over-tense coil coming unsprung, Dave yelled, "Goddamn it, I am *sick* of being the butt around here!" And with the sibilant, his open hand hit Connie in the face, so hard that she reeled backward and fell down.

"You *bastard,*" she said quietly, amazed. He stood over her, near tears, and then, unable to take back what he'd done or go forward in any way that wouldn't make it worse, he kicked at her, spraying gravel in her face.

Then he turned, walked majestically to his car, and climbed in. He discovered he didn't have his keys, so he climbed out again, strode to the kitchen where he kept a spare set, strode out again past Connie, climbed back into the car, and drove off.

Dave didn't come back until the next evening. When he came, he had an armful of flowers. But of course, by that time Connie had had the locks changed and the bank accounts canceled. She had sent the children to a neighbor's to spend the night. Connie sat inside the house, listening to Dave hammer on the door, howling threats, begging to be let in, pleading to be forgiven. Finally she saw him stand in the middle of the lawn, with tulips and snapdragons scattered on the ground around him, his whole body shaking with sobs. Inside, she had to block her ears, like an ancient sailor resisting the calls of the sirens. Dave called to her powerfully, with a power that was almost magical. But she sat still, behind the curtain. And she wept as he did, bitterly, but that was the last she saw of him until they met in his lawyer's office.

Patsy's *ob-gyn* was a small man, very round. He reminded Patsy of "The Little King," a comic strip of her youth. He was called Dr. Lowen, and the only thing she didn't like about him was that he allowed smoking in his waiting room, because he smoked himself. She thought it shocking to sit with immensely pregnant women, who often brought their toddlers with them to appointments, in a room where someone was puffing blue smoke and dropping ashes on the table with the magazines.

Other than that, he was ideal. Harvard degree and Columbia Med School, and a copy of *Our Bodies, Ourselves* prominently displayed along with his *Physician's Desk Reference*. He had read it, too. He was respectful and patient about answering questions, and he always ran the speculum under warm water before using it instead of sticking this frigid piece of metal into you and making you jump out of your skin.

Today, as he examined her, they chatted about a novel Dr. Lowen was reading and a diet he was on. He finished with the pelvic exam, peeled off his gloves, and did his breast exam, all the while talking, which Patsy liked because it distracted them both from the realization that he was a man and she was a woman and he was briskly doing something to her body that resembled milking a goat.

"How old is your daughter now?" he asked absently. "I really should remember."

"Phoebe's sixteen."

"Oh, good lord." Dr. Lowen had delivered her. "Did you nurse her?"

"I didn't." Patsy had been brought up to feel that nursing was for peasants, and also that it would misshape her breasts.

Dr. Lowen was washing his hands. "Well. Get dressed, and I'll see you in my office." Patsy appreciated that he didn't expect to have a conversation of moment with her when he was fully dressed and upright, and she was wrapped in a paper sheet with her private parts full of K-Y Jelly, in the most undignified position ever conceived by man.

Restored to her attractive suit and her Belgian walking shoes, Patsy seated herself in Dr. Lowen's office. He sat, as so often before, at his desk facing her with her file before him. There were new pictures of his daughters on the bookshelf; evidently Shauna had had a Bat Mitzvah.

"You have a small lump in your left breast," he said, looking through his glasses at her records.

Patsy felt nothing for a moment, and then a surprising rush of terror that for a brief time seemed to fill her from the pit of her stomach right up to the middle of her field of vision. Her ears were filled with a sound like rushing water.

When the black shriek receded, she said, "Really."

"Yes. Very small. It's here. . . ." And he handed across the desk to her a Xeroxed form of a line drawing of a female torso, front view and two side views. He had marked an X on the drawing's left breast, near the outside of the ribcage. "You haven't felt it, when you did your own breast exam?"

"No." Actually, she rarely remembered to do the self-exam. She was never sure she was doing it right.

"Well, it's very small. It could be a cyst, or a tiny fibroid. When was your last mammogram?"

"I've never had one."

He raised his eyebrows. "How did we miss that?"

"I don't know." In fact, he had said when she passed her fortieth birthday that a mammogram was a good idea, but she didn't know that meant she *had* to.

"Well. Let's fix it." He buzzed on his intercom. "Jean, would you call Whitney Memorial, please, and set up a mammogram for Mrs. Leveque." He got off the phone. "When you go out, Jean will explain exactly what you do. Everything else looks fine. I see you have a history of breast disease in the family."

"Only my maternal grandmother . . ."

"Your mother, no?"

"No."

"But your other grandmother died when she was thirty-six."

Well, that was true.

"Why did you ask me about nursing Phoebe?"

'There's some evidence that nursing provides some protection against breast cancer."

"Why didn't you tell me that?" she asked, knowing perfectly well it wouldn't have affected her decision in the slightest.

"Let's just see what we're dealing with, shall we?"

Patsy had had Phoebe at Whitney Memorial, and the day was with her like a flashback as she walked back into the hospital sixteen years later. Phoebe was now taller than Patsy was. The baby she had been was gone except in memory. And the only other person on earth who remembered that baby and those long, sweet, exhausting days of early parenthood, filled with the smells of baby oil, and Pampers, and cries of delight over her first tooth, her first word, was gone from her, too.

Patsy presented herself to the appropriate desk of computers, and was eventually located on the green screen, loaded into the records, and sent to the radiology department. This hospital was a place of life as well as death, she kept telling herself as she tried to follow instructions, traversing a confusing lane of stairs and corridors that took her from one building to another, all with no windows as if she were underground. She felt cold with fright.

Having found Radiology, she sat down as she was told, to wait in a corridor with about a dozen others, most of them in-hospital patients. There was an old man with an immense blackish growth on the side of his neck, like the bole of a tree trunk. She could barely look at him without her gorge rising. How could you look in the mirror year after year at a thing like that and not say, Gee, I wonder if that's supposed to be there.

There was a frail lady in paper slippers and a hospital gown, incompletely closed in the back. She arrived on crutches accompanied by a nurse, at whom she smiled her thanks as she sat down in an orange plastic chair against the wall. The nurse smiled back and left her. There was a young man in a wheelchair. He had been very handsome once. He was now grotesquely thin, and slumped over, asleep or unconscious. He was drooling slightly. Patsy couldn't look at him either, not only because his condition was so piteous and frightening but also because she felt so sickened that anyone would leave him in that state in a public corridor to be stared at by strangers. Presently an orderly arrived with another young man on a gurney. This one, too, was horribly thin; his arm was attached to an IV bottle, dangling from a rack above the gurney. He was awake. The attendant walked away from him without a look or a word and left him lying in the hall staring at the ceiling.

Patsy stared at a page of the *People* magazine she had brought with her. It seemed incredible that somewhere in this building at this moment, younger women were giving birth.

Charlie was at the office reading something called *The Tobacco Litigation Reporter*. It was boring and he had to keep starting the article over again. Almost everyone had gone home, but he had nothing to go home to, and his lawsuit against Quality Foods, which owned the dye company that had poisoned his client, was going to trial in a week. He was reading everything he could about other product liability cases. Asbestos, tobacco, Dalkon shields. The more he knew about the field, the more deranged it seemed to him that corporations could impose mortal risks on people that absolutely would result in a certain number of maimed bodies, ruined lives, and deaths per thousands of units sold, and that the individual humans who sat in boardrooms and decided that those statistics were acceptable in light of the profit to be made were effectively immune to legal sanctions. The companies might have to pay a financial penalty should a suit succeed against them, but no human had to pay a personal penalty, although it was individual humans who suffered the dangers and deaths. Wonderful.

He had become quite rabid on the subject. It was good to have a cause. He hardly thought about Martha at all.

The phone rang. He answered. "C.B.," said Patsy. Charlie smiled. She had called him that through law school, part of a joke about how he was going to become a famous jurist in a ten-piece suit and rule the world. He'd forgotten.

"What's up?" he said.

"I tried you at home."

"Good luck. I'm never there. I have a case going to trial."

"So Phoebe told me. Anyway . . ."

And suddenly her voice caught, and there was a long pause.

"Is something wrong?" Charlie asked. It seemed like a stupid question, but then you never knew with Patsy. She could make you think her best friend must have died, and then it would turn out that she'd had a bad haircut.

"Well," she said finally, "I've had better days. I know you're busy, but actually I could use a friend, just at the minute, Charlie."

Charlie looked at the journal in his hand. Boring.

"I could get away for an hour or two. Have you had dinner?"

"No," said Patsy, surprised and grateful. They arranged to meet at a steak joint halfway between her apartment and his.

"You look fine," said Charlie, kindly, when they had ordered drinks. She did, too. She took good care of herself, and it showed. She had beautiful hands, always perfectly manicured. He no longer desired her; in fact, he could no longer remember a time when he ever had; but he knew objectively that she was a handsome woman.

"Thank you." Patsy smiled. There was a silence.

"Guess who I saw last week," said Patsy. "Chuck and Stephanie."

"You did? Where?"

"I ran into them on the street."

Chuck and Stephanie had been neighbors in their first apartment building, before Phoebe was born. Charlie and Patsy could hear their fights through the thin Sheetrock walls. But when they met in the hall-way they always seemed like the perfect couple. The four had become friends in a casual way, and Charlie was amazed to learn that they were still married and in fact had three children. "They live in Knoxville now, they were just in town to go to the theater. Funny coincidence."

"She was from the South, wasn't she?"

"They both were."

"What do they look like?"

Patsy told him. It was the kind of thing she was clever at.

They talked about Phoebe. Charlie was not feeling very pro-Phoebe at the moment. Somehow the press of the play-writing festival and of fi-nal exams had brought to the fore her qualities that Charlie found hard-est to like—a selfishness, a stubbornness, an inclination to find fault with everything and everyone except herself. Like an unwelcome reap-pearance of the girl who had gotten kicked out of Replogle.

"She'll bitch all through dinner to me about how unfair it was of Mr. Kelley to give a ten-page paper just when he knew they were studying for finals. Never once a word of, How was *your* day, Daddy. None of that. And then instead of writing *or* studying, she spends two hours on the phone."

Patsy knew the pattern well. "It was the mess in her room that always got to me. She never had anything to wear, but when I'd suggest that that was because her entire wardrobe was on the floor, she'd say, 'Okay *fine,* if you want me to do laundry instead of getting to bed at a decent hour or something.'" Patsy did a really wicked imitation of Phoebe in her it's-not-fair mode.

Charlie laughed and shook his head. "Jesus. When I was in high school . . ." He stopped. But he did feel surprised to have raised a child who felt hard done by to have to put her own clothes in the hamper.

Patsy said, "Just remember that it passes. She's always a little beast when she's under pressure, but it passes."

"Thanks. You're right," said Charlie.

"Oh, well. It's easy for me to say. You're the one who has to live with it."

They smiled at each other, the smiles speaking volumes.

"It's the shamelessness of her selfishness that always surprises me," said Charlie after a bit. Actually it didn't just surprise him, it frightened him. What was she going to be like when she grew up?

"She's an only child. You weren't. And you were raised by two consistent parents who were a team. She was raised by two needy single parents. It's different."

"You're right," said Charlie again. He thought of Jack, suddenly. Jack was raised by two single parents, too, but Charlie had to admit that he never showed the relentless self-absorption Phoebe did. He missed Jack. His sunny disposition, his tenderness with Fred.

As if she could read his mind—and maybe she could, it was one of the things that had most annoyed him about being married to her—Patsy changed the subject.

"How is Martha?" she asked. She asked it gently, as if she really cared.

"I guess she's fine. Phoebe tells me she's planning to get married."

"Oh . . . Charlie." She said it with real compassion. And touched his hand. "I thought you'd get back together in the end."

"I did, too, Patsy. I did, too."

They were silent for a long moment.

"What does she say? Have you talked to her?"

"No. I don't know what to say. If she's happy with Gillis, I don't want to upset her. She doesn't owe me an explanation."

"But . . . you seemed so happy together."

Charlie was touched. So even Patsy could see that.

"I thought so. We had problems, but I thought they weren't inside us. I thought they were external things that would change or could be changed. In ourselves, I thought we were as happy as two people can be."

"I envy you," said Patsy quietly.

"Yeah. Thanks. I'm not sure I envy myself. It's not going to be easy going through my whole life without that. Having had it. Could we change the subject?"

Fortunately, the waiter appeared.

After they had given their order, Charlie said, "You weren't very happy when you called. What's going on with you?"

"Oh, dear. This isn't going to brighten the conversation." She told him about Dr. Lowen finding the lump and about the hospital. She would know the results of the mammogram on Friday. It had hurt too; they squeezed your breasts hard between freezing plates when they took the pictures. But that was nothing, compared to the fear. Of being disfigured, of dying, of having done nothing with her life that seemed to mean anything. Except having Phoebe.

"I mean, the point of the exercise is to be some use on this planet, isn't it?"

Certainly Charlie thought so. It was news to him that Patsy did, but she was earnest. She spoke softly, though, without melodrama. She'd been thinking calmly, and it seemed like a new woman speaking to him. Patsy, grown up. She was asking herself some very hard questions. He began, for the first time in a great many years, to remember what he had liked about her when they met. The vision he had had of the woman that glamorous girl might grow up to be.

Charlie listened. He was moved. He asked hard questions too, about the medical prognosis. The possibilities ranged from no problem, to a highly dubious future. Dr. Lowen was not giving odds.

"I feel like making deals with the devil at this point," said Patsy. "I'd try God, but I understand he doesn't make deals."

"I don't know about that. Read the Old Testament."

Patsy smiled. "I was just trying not to blaspheme. Anyway. I find myself talking to God—or the devil—making promises. And it *seems* blasphemous to me, not to use the life God gave you. To think it belongs to you, instead of being something that belongs to God, that was entrusted to you. To me, I mean. I'm ashamed to have done so little. I'm secure, I had a good education, I had love, I had my health, and what did I do with it?" There was a long pause.

"It's hard for you to say this," said Charlie. "I know. Especially to me."

"No. You're the one I should say it to."

They looked at each other and smiled. Their dinners arrived.

They ate and talked of neutral things. There were silences. Both had much to think of.

When their plates had been taken away, Patsy said, "Charlie. I want to say something . . . I just want you to think about it. I didn't call you with this in mind . . . and maybe I'll change my mind. But let me just say this out loud."

Charlie assented. She sat for a bit, collecting her thoughts.

"I've lived my whole life . . ." She had to stop. "Sorry." She laughed. "For some reason, *this* is hard to say. I guess the notion that I've already lived my whole life." Another pause. "Let me try again. I've lived my whole life trying to keep my options open. I don't think I knew it at the time, or if I did I didn't know that not everybody did that. But when I married you, you were totally committed and I wasn't. I thought, This is great for now, but it's probably not all there is. There's probably something *perfect* out there, but this will do until I find it."

Charlie looked at the tablecloth. Hearing her say it made him want to cry. It was certainly what the marriage had felt like.

"I could see that you were utterly committed to me. I thought, Fine, that's how men are, but that's not me and I should be the way I am. I saw that you were utterly committed to Phoebe. That you absolutely loved her, even when you didn't like her. I didn't, always. Sometimes she'd piss me off, and I'd close my heart against her. I'd think, This isn't perfect. She's not perfect, she's not *exactly* what I had in mind. As if it wasn't my real life, as if my real *perfect* life was still out there somewhere, waiting for me."

There was a long pause. "You had great happiness, and you lost it. I don't know why. I guess you don't really know why." Charlie realized she meant with Martha, not their own marriage. Although he had been very happy with her for a long time. It was her unhappiness that had ended the marriage, not his.

"I had great happiness, too. With you. I see now that I was so young and so spoiled when you married me that instead of being grateful for your steadiness and your goodness and your loyalty, I thought, Well, this is easy. Forget what I've got . . . what am I missing?

"I guess you can see where I'm going. I destroyed something that was very, very good, because it wasn't perfect. Only to find out that nothing is perfect. And very good is very rare in itself. And you may be looking at a future in which you say no to what isn't perfect, because you had something almost perfect once. And you could wind up with nothing, too."

She stopped. She fooled with a butter knife. She gave a little laugh, embarrassed to go on. But Charlie listened quietly. This was the moment to stop her if he was going to, and he didn't.

"I see now, that for me our marriage and raising Phoebe with you was the best time of my life. I know that a lot has happened since then. And please, please, don't answer this now. But I wonder if we couldn't think about . . . trying again together. I'm different. You may be, too—God knows, we're older. And I'm sure that together we'd be better parents than we've been apart. I'll shut up now. Don't answer."

Charlie nodded. They sat in silence for quite a while, but it was charged, fully loaded. Then the waiter brought coffee, and they deliberately, and by tacit agreement, made the effort to resume more normal conversation.

Outside on the street, Charlie hailed a cab for her. He opened the door, but before they parted, they stood looking at each other. Then Patsy said, "Thank you for dinner."

Charlie said, "I'll think about it." And she got into the taxi. He closed the door for her and watched her, down the street and around the corner.

"I *want one* thing clear," said Martha. "I'm not going on anything that turns you upside down."

It was Jack's birthday, and the next to last day before he left for New Hampshire. Gillis and Martha and Fred and Jack and Phoebe were on their way to Great America.

"Fred will come with me, won't you, Fred?"

"He will not."

"I'll go," said Phoebe, not sounding very sure.

Phoebe had never been to Great America, and baby Fred had never been to any amusement park. Gillis had borrowed a car to take them, and the day had dawned cloudless and hot.

Phoebe had arrived in time for Jack's birthday breakfast, looking fresh and pretty. She brought Jack two presents wrapped in aluminum foil and red ribbon. The first was a T-shirt with a picture of Jack on it.

The camera had caught him about four feet off the ground, shouting, and Jack loved it.

"Yo, this is *chill!*" he said, pulling it on over what he was already wearing.

"Phoebe, how wonderful!" said Martha.

"It's my jumping series. I took all these pictures of my friends, jumping over things and off of things."

"How did you get the picture onto the shirt?" Gillis asked, peering at it.

"Silkscreen."

"You your own self with your little paws?"

"Yes. We have a graphics studio at school." She was pleased that everyone was so pleased.

Her second present was a steel pocketknife with Jack's initials on it. Raymond had always carried such a knife and Jack had wanted it, but they hadn't found it among his things. He must have been carrying it when he died. Jack had told Phoebe, and she had remembered.

"That's your real present," she said shyly.

"They're both pretty real," said Jack. His smile was wonderful.

Amid the breakfast plates covered with scraps of bacon and pancakes and sticky with maple syrup, he opened the rest of his presents. Gillis gave him a beautiful pool cue with a carrying case. Fred had drawn him a picture of a boat. Martha had been stymied. She had always given him a lot of little presents to unwrap, and then she and Raymond together gave him one big present that he really wanted. After a lot of thought, and after months of not hearing his voice, she had called Charlie.

The call went like this. "Martha," Charlie had said, the moment she said hello, as if he had been expecting her and no one else. Her heart nearly went through the floor.

"Yes."

Pause.

"How are you?"

"Fine, thank you."

A pause. She felt a hot flush, like fever.

"Your case goes to trial this week, I know," she said.

"Yes."

"Good luck."

"Thank you."

Pause.

"I hear you're getting married," he said.

"Yes."

"He's a lucky man."

"Thank you for saying so."

A long pause, in which they could hear each other breathing.

"Jack's birthday is coming up," said Martha.

"I know."

"He's been taking a photography course this term."

"I know," Charlie said again. He asked Phoebe everything he could about Jack, hoping he'd learn something, anything, about Martha.

"I'd like to buy him a good camera."

"That sounds like a good idea."

"I can't really afford the one he wants. It's the sort of thing Raymond and I would have shared."

"Buy him a Pentax. Send me the bill."

Long pause.

"Thank you."

Another pause.

"Everything else okay with you?" Charlie asked.

"Yes. Fine."

"I'm glad. I'd like to send Jack a small present from me, too. If you don't mind."

"Of course I don't mind. I'm sure it would please him."

"Good—" An interruption on his end, then, "Martha, sorry. I'm due in a meeting."

She felt rebuffed. "Yes. Take care."

"You too."

He really did have a meeting, though at that moment he'd have given anything to keep her on the phone, and for about five minutes after the connection was broken, he felt sick. Then he shook off the thought of her and her fiancé planning Jack's birthday, and went out to join his partner in the conference room.

So Martha had given Jack a new Frisbee, and a box of razor-point pens with green ink, and a new bathing suit, and a Pentax camera. Jack was amazed and excited.

"But Mom," he kept sputtering. "But *Mom,* it's a Pentax! But this is the best camera in the *world!*"

"So I'm told." She was very pleased that it was really what he wanted.

"But you can't afford a *Pentax,* get serious!"

"It's from your father and me."

He sat for a minute, just looking at the camera. Then he got up, not going to cry after all, and gave his mother a kiss.

"Thank you, Momski."

"You're welcome, young hoodlum."

There was one more present, from Charlie. It was a camera bag, full of film, and with a flash attachment for the Pentax.

"Oh, this is *great.* This is just great! Phoebe Beebe, tell him I love it. I mean naturally I'll be getting right to my thank-you notes, with my green pens, but in case it takes me a day or two to find a stamp or something . . ."

"I'll tell him," said Phoebe.

Gillis was quiet as he drove them down the New Jersey Turnpike. At least Martha thought he was. She tried a couple of times to get him to play a car game with her and Fred, while Jack and Phoebe chattered about school and Phoebe's summer job and the evening games of Ultimate Frisbee their crowd had been playing in various parks. But Gillis didn't want to play. They listened to Jack wax rhapsodic about a new killer roller coaster at Great America that sounded as if it were designed to shake you around until everything came loose, and then hang you upside down until your guts fell out.

"How do you know all about this horrible thing?" Martha asked.

"They show it on television. Some of our little friends went on it, and they said a girl in the car in front of them actually threw up," he reported joyfully.

"Oh, good."

Another silence. Glancing at Phoebe in the rearview mirror, it seemed to Martha that her affection for Jack might be about to be tested to the limit.

Jack fell to playing with his camera. He hadn't put any film in it yet, so he could snap the shutter endlessly and look at everything through the viewfinder. Phoebe from an inch away, baby Fred's hair, the car's dome light. It all fascinated him.

"How is your mother, Phoebe?" Martha asked.

"Did you hear what happened to her?"

"No, what?"

"She has to have an operation. She has a lump in her breast."

"Oh, Phoebe! I'm sorry . . ."

"They're going to do a biopsy tomorrow."

Martha had turned around in her seat so she could talk to Phoebe. "She must be terribly frightened."

"She's being pretty good, actually." Phoebe was surprised at this herself. Her mother had been quite calm and quiet, telling Phoebe the news, with a minimum of self-pity and drama, and an emphasis on the positive. "It's almost like I'm more scared than she is."

"Dearie. I don't blame you. When did she find out?"

"About two weeks ago. At first she was just going to have it monitored every month or something. But then she got a second opinion and they convinced her it was too risky."

Martha took a deep breath. Horrible subject. She felt for Patsy, and she felt for Phoebe.

"It's hard on you too, she doesn't really have anyone but you to turn to, does she?"

"Well . . . Daddy."

"I know, but that's different. She's not really his responsibility anymore. It's a lot for you to have to take on." Martha was trying to get Phoebe to accept the sympathy, and in doing so missed Phoebe's drift.

Phoebe was thoughtful for a moment. Then she said, "No, I mean she's been spending a lot of time with Daddy since she found out. I'm not sure, I think they're thinking about getting back together or something."

Martha hoped her jaw didn't drop. Her stomach did. She was speechless for a moment. Why she should be, she didn't know. If she were going to marry Gillis it shouldn't matter to her if Charlie was dating Sophie or marrying his wife or working his way through the Dallas Cowgirls. But it did, it did.

She tried to think of something more to say to Phoebe, but she couldn't think of anything that wouldn't be false. At some other point, she'd have a nice composed chat with Phoebe about whether this prospect made her happy, but for the moment she thought she'd just turn back around in her seat and stare out the window.

Once they were in the amusement park, they rode the merry-go-round all together, and some flying saucers, with Phoebe and Jack in one saucer and Gillis and Martha and Fred in the other. Fred's howls of joy, and the smiles on the others' faces, made it worth it, but Martha felt queasy. Happily, at that point they decided to separate.

"Phoebe and I will go ride the Killer before the lines get too long, and you can do the baby rides, and we'll meet you for lunch." They parted.

As soon as Martha was alone with Gillis and Fred, it became clear that Gillis was indeed in a monumental black funk. He walked beside her in silence, responding neither to her or to Fred, until she just stopped still and said, "All right. What is it?"

He took a deep breath.

"That business with the camera."

She had to keep asking for a few minutes before he would say exactly what he meant. He was hurt and angry and had been stewing for two hours in the car, and by this time couldn't believe she couldn't read his mind.

"We're supposed to be a family! We planned Jack's birthday together, I borrowed the car, I'm giving my whole day to this because I'm supposed to be Jack's stepfather, and then it turns out that you give him this great big fancy present *with Charlie!*"

"Gillis . . . I didn't! I gave him a present with the help of Raymond's estate, if you want to get technical."

"Which is Charlie! At least to Jack. And then he gives this present to go with yours—what did you do, go shopping together?"

She was silent. She began to see how it looked to him, and she could see why it hurt. She knew Gillis was sensitive about his place in Jack's life. It had taken him so long to commit himself to wanting a family; now he was very jumpy about it, as if he wanted it too much.

And that wasn't all. "Then you nearly fell apart in the car when Phoebe talked about Charlie. You're in love with him, Martha, and it hurts. It hurts, and I'm mad."

"I *was* in love with him. It takes some time to go away."

"Did you love him more than you love me?"

"Gillis . . . stop this. Comparisons are odious."

"*Odious?* What kind of word is that?"

"It's a quote. Sorry."

"From who?"

"I forget."

"Charlie would have known that, wouldn't he?"

"Gillis!"

Fred was getting very distressed, and they were both in pain. Now was not the time to try to bottle this up and pretend nothing had happened, nor could they carry on this way with their son between them.

"This was a very important day for me, Martha. We planned it together. It was . . . " He didn't have to finish. She could see now what it was to him, though she hadn't before. To her it had been Jack's day. To him, it had been their day to begin to be parents together, his first day as the father.

They were facing each other. Gillis had been carrying Fred, but now Fred made it clear he wanted to go to Martha. Gillis handed him over. Their eyes were locked.

"I don't know what to say. I'm sorry, Gillis."

"I'm sorry, too," he said coldly. They both understood that he meant that he was sorry the day was spoiled. That it was serious, and not all right.

That was the end of the subject for the time. They had reached the section of the park with the rides for little people, and it was time to be tilted and whirled.

Meanwhile, in another part of the park, Jack and Phoebe were in tears. By private agreement, this was to be their last day together as anything but friends.

They had been fighting off and on, stupid little brushfires that kept erupting between them ever since the weekend in the country had ended in such unhappiness. There had once been a time when it had seemed as if they were twins. When one spoke, the other felt ah, *exactly.* Now, it kept happening that one would speak and the other would think, What? What do you mean, how can you say that? It was like the building of the Tower of Babel. One minute they understood each other perfectly, and the next they looked at each other with wonder, because each felt the other had begun speaking in tongues.

They fought about Jaywalk. Phoebe was jealous that he and Jack were going off together for the summer, and she thought teaching riflery sounded stupid. Jack couldn't understand. He loved little kids, he thought playing with guns all summer sounded def, he loved Jaywalk, who continued to speak his language perfectly, who had been his best friend since they were twelve. Jack and Jaywalk had probably clocked in 15,000 hours together over the years. When they were twelve, they used to do their homework on the phone together, sometimes going for ten and twenty minutes at a stretch without speaking. They just liked having the connection open, hearing each other breathe.

Jack and Jaywalk would fall into dialogue routines they had been doing for years, and end up rolling on the floor, weeping with laughter. Jack and Jaywalk liked to stay up all night together because they loved the spacy euphoria exhaustion brought. Phoebe felt left out and privately thought they should, like, grow up.

Phoebe had needed a defender badly when she first came to Cropp and Thatcher. She had made a colossal mess, in her own terms and everybody else's, and she didn't even know why. She was cut off from her old friends, her parents didn't understand *anything,* and she was mad at everybody. But nurse relationships change when the patient gets well. Phoebe had begun to find her own ground with her success in *The Three Musketeers.* Though she was far from finished trying on faces and hats, she had found a more constructive and rewarding way of doing it than being rude or getting thrown out of school. And she had learned to talk the cant of drama classes, more every day, which made Jack privately want to say Oh puhleease, are we kidding here? (She kept saying things like "it worked for me," and talking pretentiously about the growth of a performance, seemingly forgetting she was talking about moments and relationships from which Jack was excluded.) An acting company was a family. First there had been the casts of the three festival plays, and now that she had started her summer job she belonged more and more to the world of her rep company, even though what she did there so far was mostly sweep the floor and make the coffee.

The real break had come one night during exam period when Jack brought up the question of whether they would be faithful to each other over the summer.

Instead of answering, Phoebe got an annoyed look on her face, one that her parents knew well but which was new to Jack. Jack knew in the moment of her hesitation what the answer was, but of course they had to play out the whole thing.

"What do you mean?"

"I mean are we going to wait for each other and not see other people?"

"Okay, I know, but what do you mean by 'see other people'? I mean, does that mean not going out for coffee with someone, or just not falling in love, or what?"

Jack had been amazed. He had met Patsy once, when Phoebe asked him to come with her to her mother's apartment. Patsy had been quite hoity-toity with him, and Phoebe had apologized afterward. Now suddenly he heard Patsy's voice coming out of Phoebe's mouth.

"Beebe. I didn't think it was a hard question."

"I just want to know what you mean. I mean, do you want me to be like a nun or something?"

"Nuns are actually very sociable, I understand."

Phoebe made a face at him, meaning "cute."

"I'm not putting you on the spot. We're not engaged. I just think we should have the same understanding. Do you want me to write to you?"

"Yes."

"Will you write to me?"

"Yes."

"If I meet someone I like while I'm away, do you want me to say no? Or do whatever I want as long as I tell you about it? Or not tell you about it?"

Phoebe was silent. She had been thinking more in terms of *her* being interested in someone else.

"What do you want to do?" she asked.

"It depends on what you want to do."

"Oh great, that's helpful."

"Phoebe, you don't have to get mad. It *does* depend on what you want to do."

"I don't see why we have to talk about it."

"You don't?"

"No. Why don't we just take things as they come?"

"I think you've answered the question."

Phoebe, who hated to be understood when she didn't intend to be, had gone ballistic. She yelled that Jack was always criticizing her and trying to pin her down, and he countered that that was ridiculous, she just wanted to have her cake and eat it, too. She yelled that he wasn't being fair, and he did the thing he had sworn to himself he wouldn't do, which was to blurt out that he thought she was flirting with Joe Brockett. They had a long, painful, and unproductive set-to about whether she was or wasn't and whether it was any of his business. Then they didn't speak for a day, then they apologized and tried to start over again and ended up having the same fight with minor variations. And after that, they both decided it was time to stop.

"It's not that I don't love you," said Phoebe.

"I know that, it's not that I don't love you."

"I know."

"But we seem to fight all the time."

"I know."

"If we keep fighting, we'll end up hating each other." Like our parents, they both were thinking.

"We should stop now, so we can be real friends."

"Forever."

"And maybe in the fall, or someday . . ."

"No," said Jack. "If we're going to stop, let's stop. If we're going to keep each other and be friends forever, we have to be clean. No talking about old times, no teasing each other about starting up again. It just hurts."

Phoebe reluctantly agreed. After that, they had to decide how to handle it. They decided to be absolutely with each other and for each other for as much time as they had left, and then to part at the end of Jack's birthday, and be really apart the whole summer, and when they met again in the fall they would be different. There remained only to decide what to tell people.

"I don't want to tell anyone," said Phoebe, beginning to cry. "It's so sad." Jack put his arms around her. He too felt bereft.

"I want to tell Jaywalk."

"But wait. Please. Wait till you're both away. I don't want to answer any questions or anything."

"He wouldn't make you."

"I know. But please wait."

Jack said he would. "Aren't you going to tell anybody?"

She shook her head. Now that the words had all been spoken, she was filled with missing him in advance and fear that it was a mistake. "It's too sad," she said again.

So they had ridden the killer roller coaster, and Jack had screamed with joy, and Phoebe with horror, and when they got off they were giddy and laughed and laughed, and now they were in tears. They knew each other so well, they would miss each other so much, they had so much fun. All the annoyance was gone and all the sweetness was left, and in many ways they knew this would rank as one of the most excruciating days of their lives.

"Remember the day at the water slides?" Phoebe asked, and took out a Kleenex.

"Come on, Beebe, don't. We agreed."

"I know, but it was such a great day . . ."

"You know what I never told you?" Jack described the two birds with their broken necks.

Phoebe was impressed.

"It scared me to death," Jack said. "It scared Charlie, too. I could tell."

"I wonder if that had anything to do with him being such a shit that night."

"It could have. It was like a warning that it was all going to go wrong."

"But with us. Instead it turned out to be them."

Talking had made them calmer.

"Do you want some popcorn or something? A Coke?"

"In a minute."

He put his arm around her and they sat on a bench and watched people go by.

"What do you think about your dad and Patsy getting together?"

"I don't know. Two months ago I'd have said it was the stupidest thing

I ever heard, but now I don't know. She's changed. They've both changed." She sat in thought for a minute.

"I guess if they do get back together, it will take me a long time to trust it." Jack nodded. He kissed her cheek.

"Are you scared about her operation?"

"Yes. No. It's probably nothing."

They watched a toddler go by pushing her own stroller. She had bright red curly hair and little fat legs such that you could hardly tell where the knees were.

"No little blond babies for us," said Phoebe. Jack shook his head. "No reading *Babar* aloud to them and teaching them how to talk ob-language."

"We'll still do that together. I'll be Uncle Jack. I'll be the godfather."

"And I'll be Fat Auntie Phoebe. Will you have a lot of kids?"

"Six. Will you?"

"It depends. I want to start a career first. I think I'll start having babies when I'm thirty-two."

"That sounds good."

"Where will we be in twenty years? Will you be in New York?"

"Wherever I am, I'll be your brother."

That started the tears again.

"Oh shit," said Phoebe, searching for more Kleenex.

"I know," said Jack, crying too. "Let's ride the Killer again."

"I *hope* you are kidding," said Phoebe.

Later, when they met Martha and Gillis and Fred, they told about all the rides they'd done and what a wonderful time they were having.

When *Patsy woke* up from the anesthetic she was back in her hospital room, and Charlie was there. He was looking down at her, and when her eyes opened and stayed open, he smiled. She thought it was the sweetest smile she'd ever seen.

"I thought I was going to the recovery room first."

"You did."

"I did? Were you there?"

"Don't you remember telling me about the ducks?"

"Oh, no." She closed her eyes. "This is so embarrassing." She lay still for a minute, and the warm confusing dream world was right there behind her eyes. She opened them again. Charlie was before her, stable and solid, still smiling.

"Anything else?" she asked.

"There was something about an umbrella."

"I don't want to know." She searched his face. They both knew what she really wanted to know. But she couldn't bring herself to ask. She could be lying there minus a breast at that minute. She knew something hurt like hell there.

"Okay. Tell me," she said.

"Benign," said Charlie.

It was like a door opening in a tiny tight room, letting in the light. She felt as if she'd been holding her breath for three weeks. She inhaled. She smiled. Charlie smiled back.

"Dr. Lowen's been here. He said he'd be back."

"Did he say anything else?"

"He said you should think about giving up caffeine, and other than that, congratulations."

"I feel like I just won the lottery."

"Me too," said Charlie. "Me too."

"Does Phoebe know?"

"Yes, I called her. She'll be here in about a half hour."

"Good. She's been scared, hasn't she?"

"I think so."

Patsy reached out her hand to Charlie, and he held it.

"How do you feel?" Charlie asked.

"Great."

"I mean, does it hurt?"

"Oh, yes, it's horrible."

"Apparently you can go home tomorrow, if you promise to be quiet. You won't be able to shower for a while, though."

"I don't care. I want to go home. I remember from being here when we had Phoebe, everything they give you to eat is white. I don't know why the patients don't all die of malnutrition. White bread, white macaroni, white Cream of Wheat, white milk . . ."

"Are you hungry?"

"God, no. But if I'm going to live, I have to plan ahead."

"When you go home, do you want to go to your apartment? Or mine?"

She thought a bit. Their time together in the past few weeks had been like a honeymoon. No, not even that, like a first courtship. They had been tender with each other, presuming nothing, getting to know each other as if it were all new. And as with new courtships, it had been sweet to come together, and also sweet to close the door and be home alone in your own familiar place at the end of an evening.

"Mine, I think. I'm not a very good patient, and if I'm going to be washing my hair in the sink and things I probably should be at home."

"Are you sure? Don't you want someone to bring you beef tea and toast?"

"No. I want to get used to being me again. Still intact."

"After all these years."

Phoebe arrived. She had bought Patsy a copy of a glossy new magazine for women over forty, and a Dick Francis novel newly out in paperback. She came in smiling and sat on her mother's bed. She was wearing an orange miniskirt, and her hair hung loose to her shoulders.

Charlie went to sit down in the chair across the room, and from there he watched his wife and daughter talk to each other. It was something he hadn't really seen for years. Phoebe glowed with relief to see her mother awake. Patsy was more touched than she could say that self-centered Phoebe had spent her own money to bring her presents; it was like a visit from a grown friend. Phoebe's hair slanted in a shining curtain down from her forehead as she talked. From time to time, she'd toss her chin to throw it back. Charlie watched them look at each other, smile at each other. The profiles were the same, though Phoebe's face had a slightly blurred, unfinished look, while the lines of Patsy's nose and cheekbones and jaw were sharp and clear.

Charlie listened to the ripple of their words, rather than their meaning, and saw that Phoebe, now rattling on about her indecision over which magazine to buy, made her mother laugh. They had the same sense of humor. He hadn't really realized that. Phoebe had grown into a young lady as Patsy had faded from his life. Now there Phoebe sat, with Patsy's eyes and Patsy's laugh, and his blond hair and strong square hands. Suddenly both Patsy and Phoebe turned to Charlie, smiling, expectant. The same eyes looking at him from two different faces, it was amazing.

"Sorry, what?" he said. "I was thinking of something else." Phoebe and Patsy laughed. So like Daddy.

After a week, Patsy was glad that she had decided to go home to her own apartment. She felt restless and irritable and dirty, unable to take a bath, which she really preferred to showers. Also, the painkillers they gave her didn't do all that much good, and the constant pain in her side made her feel snappish. And if she took extra painkillers, like the old Percodan left over in the medicine cupboard from a root canal she had last year, or some really ancient Demerol someone had once prescribed for Charlie, she felt groggy and hung over, and then edgy as hell when it wore off. Anyway, by now she'd taken all the drugs she could find in the apartment, including some aspirin with codeine that Aida always brought back from England by the tub.

She spent the mornings in bed writing in her journal, and the afternoons watching television. It was a long time since she'd done that, and she found there was one soap opera that came on right after lunch that was really quite engaging. One day Aida had come over to see Patsy, bringing a picnic for the two of them to share, and it had been great, great fun to see her and it was terribly sweet of her to take such a long lunch hour, but Patsy had felt really restless the whole rest of the day and evening and annoyed to have missed what happened that day on her show.

Charlie called her a couple of times a day, and Patsy loved that. She kept the remote control thing in her bathrobe pocket so she could turn down the TV sound when he called, so he wouldn't hear what she was watching. And Phoebe would call every evening when she got off work, and stop for whatever Patsy needed from the store, and then come to have supper with her. Phoebe was getting to be a not-bad cook. She could roast a chicken and make pesto—it seemed Martha had taught her that. Several times Charlie would join them for dinner and then Phoebe would go home with him afterward. It was really very nice. She had a loving family, and they called and visited her and brought presents and flowers, and then they went home.

It was getting to be high time Patsy got back to normal. She was supposed to be taking moderate exercise and so forth and there was really no reason she shouldn't go back to what she had been doing before the terrible visit to Dr. Lowen, which was, planning the rest of her life. There was Charlie now, of course, and that brought her a measure of comfort and safety that she had lost and feared never to find again. But now that she was not in imminent fear of dying—and it was like a horrible pain whose dimensions are understood only when it stops, how frightened she had been, how the fear had invaded her waking and sleeping, how much energy it had taken to behave normally, even bravely. . . . She felt as if she had carried a huge boulder across a tiny swaying bridge over a terrible chasm. No wonder she was exhausted. No wonder all she really wanted to do was sleep and drift.

Charlie, she could see, was very happy these evenings when they were all together. She could see that it was fun for him, acting as sous-chef for Phoebe, who knew in this kitchen where the spoons and mixing bowls were. She knew—and this was just Charlie—that he was always happy when he had someone to take care of. He liked nursing her, he liked bringing her little presents, clippings from *The Wall Street Journal* he thought would interest her, a box of giant paper clips in Day-Glo colors that he'd bought her while he happened to be in a stationery store, just so she'd know he'd been thinking of her.

The weird thing was—and she knew this wasn't good, she didn't like herself for it—instead of making her feel loved and happy, Charlie's attentions, his own happiness even, seemed to annoy her. She felt . . . what? Churlish, yes, but that wasn't what she was trying to identify. She felt crowded by his happiness, as if there were only so much happiness in a pie chart for Patsy and Charlie to share, and if he was happier than she was, he had taken some of her share. She didn't really think that was reasonable, but on the other hand it was really the way she *felt*. And she didn't feel this way with other people, it was just between her and Charlie. The way brothers and sisters will still be getting into snits with each other when they're fifty and no one else can see what on earth is going on between them.

And Charlie's kindness, his little presents, the way he took care of her. She knew, she *knew* that he was just being himself. Generous, giving, loving. But that's not the way it *felt* to her. The way she felt was, he's trying to own me. If he gives me all these little presents and I take them, then I won't have the right to say But I don't *feel* like cooking dinner, or I don't want to go to the partners' cookout with you, it's boring, or I want to paint the bedroom peach and hang lace curtains, and if you don't like it, screw you. She felt he was beating her to the punch all the time, demonstrating This is the way I am, this is how to be Charlie, instead of letting her be Patsy. She wasn't the type to give someone little presents all the time or go to the partners' cookout if she didn't feel like it. Oh, why did these examples always seem so petty? But anyway, she was feeling like that. Struggling with an irrational annoyance with Charlie because once again, just as he always had, he was being ebullient and positive and loving, and not noticing that she was somewhere else.

One morning, as she was feeling particularly fretful because she couldn't figure out what to do with her life and she couldn't even figure out what to do with her day, the telephone rang.

"Baby," said the deep familiar voice she had expected never to hear again.

"George," said Patsy.

Suddenly, for the first time since she got home from the hospital, something besides *The Young and the Restless* had her full attention.

"How are you doing?" said the voice. Full of weariness.

"Do you want the long answer or the short answer?"

There was a pause. Actually, he didn't care, he hadn't called for the answer to that question.

"How are *you*, George?" asked Patsy. She felt her voice held the proper amount of dry cynicism, that he was calling her at all and that he was, unbeknownst to himself, playing games with a woman who had been under the knife.

"My wife just left me," he said.

"What do you mean?" said Patsy. She didn't really mean that she couldn't understand the sentence, she meant, Your wife just went out the door and you can still feel the draught? Or she left last week and you just thought of me?

"Baby," said George, beginning to cry. "I don't have anyone to talk to. I've never felt like this in my life. I'm scared." He sobbed. She listened.

"You can talk to me, George," she said gently, at last.

Oh, what the hell, was what that meant. Climb aboard, fasten your seat belts. Where someone else might be listening desperately for a still small voice of calm, she felt a dirty little thrill.

Summer *was dragging* on. Charlie's case had been postponed for a month, leaving him with a sickening feeling of emptiness, of being all dressed up with no place to go. This was made much worse by the fact that his former wife had begun dating again, just as he was beginning to plan a life around her.

"I feel like a sap," he said to Sophie, when he told her that Patsy had asked if they could put their reconciliation "on spiritual hold" while she worked something out. "How many times am I going to fall for the same thing? It's not like I don't know the woman."

"We're all saps about something," said Sophie.

Charlie and Sophie hadn't seen each other for weeks. He had been busy preparing his case, and also preoccupied with Patsy. Sophie had been spending part of each week out in the Hamptons, where she had a client who wanted an $800,000 studio apartment created in the remains of a chicken coop. (When asked why he didn't tear it down and start over, he had said that he didn't want to alter the character of the neighborhood.)

"I know what you need," Sophie said. "Let's get out of town. Let's go see Connie."

So they had called Connie, who sounded delighted, and made a date to go up to Arden Forest for the weekend. Charlie, though he had sworn off divorce cases, was handling Connie's. He felt that even if he never saw her again, it was one last thing he could do for Martha, to defend a nice woman from a husband whose tactics were, thanks to Raymond, now all too familiar to him.

"Will you bring Phoebe?" Sophie asked Charlie.

"No, she's been invited to a house party in Millbrook. By that boy from the play she was in. Joe Brockett."

Sophie wondered what that meant about Phoebe and Jack, but she decided not to mention it. Charlie hadn't spoken of Martha for some time and she thought it was better to let sleeping dogs lie. He seemed torn up enough about Patsy at the moment, without her making it seem like a losing streak.

They took the train up the Hudson, and Connie and William met them at the station. Sophie kissed her sister.

"You're just beautiful," said Sophie.

"Thanks. I feel great. I'm taking Jazzercise classes."

She had lost some weight and she moved with a bounce that Sophie envied. What was going on here?

"You must be Ruth," said Charlie, shaking hands with William. William giggled and wriggled and got all shy, all the while looking into Charlie's eyes.

"The way I know is, I met Molly a long time ago so I know you're not Molly."

"I'm *Will*iam," he cried, delighted.

"Oh, *William!* Oh I *see!* Oh, then you're the one who can't run any faster than a rowboat."

"Yes, I can." William was fascinated but wary.

"Tell you what . . . I'll race you to the end of the parking lot. Ready, set, go." Charlie dropped his overnight bag and ran off.

"Hey!" yelled William, and took off after him. Charlie began to run in a lurching pigeon-toed style, panting and waving his arms in huge circles. William was laughing as he ran past him.

"My friend the goofball," said Sophie to Connie as they watched.

William yelled, "I beat you!" and Charlie fell down on the finish line. William fell on top of him, burbling with hilarity. Connie could see from fifty paces that this was the start of a serious friendship.

"He's really quite a good lawyer," said Sophie.

Molly had no memory of ever seeing Charlie before, and Charlie didn't remind her. He just studied her carefully when they met. She had a suntan now, and her hair was short and shiny; she'd cut it because she was swimming for the club team, she told him. He told her about the time he'd swum breaststroke for his college and the coach had made all the boys on the varsity shave their legs. She giggled shyly.

They sat outside in the cool shade of early evening. Connie had two huge arching oak trees in her backyard. It would still be sweltering in the city, and the rich green smell of the trees and the lawn reminded Charlie of the smell, and the noontime hum of locusts in Richmond, when he took his nap in summer, when he was a very little boy.

"It's awfully pretty here," he said, looking at Connie. She was wearing a white caftan and sandals, and was looking cool and fresh. Her toenails were painted pink. They were drinking cold beer and eating guacamole.

"Did you ever think of moving out of the city?"

"No. I grew up in suburbs and I always thought that was enough of that. But this is really nice."

"Thank you. It's been good for the kids."

They talked a little about Connie's current situation with Dave, but they had to do it in little bites, dropping it whenever one of the children swam into hearing. He was living in the city, Connie said, and he came out on Sunday afternoons. Connie vacated for the duration so he could spend time with the children in the house. He didn't have room for them to stay with him, real estate prices in Manhattan being what they are, and she didn't want him to be one of those Sunday fathers you always see at playgrounds and zoos.

"He asked me to sign an agreement that we could each behave as if we were single, and there wouldn't be any penalty in the terms of the settlement. He thought it would panic me. The day after I signed it, he called up in a rage and called me a slut." Connie and Sophie both laughed. Typical.

And yet, Sophie thought, it was amazing that Connie could laugh. She looked at her sister. She was a completely changed creature from the one who had had a nervous breakdown on her floor such a short time ago. It was as if, after being completely taken apart by grief and pain, Connie had put herself back together differently. She was sleeker; the soft spots were gone. It was a little frightening. It was attractive. Sophie wondered if she had ever felt as much pain in her life as she had watched Connie suffer. And if not, why not.

Connie and Charlie discussed law schools. They discussed the effect of divorce on children. Charlie tended the charcoal and cooked the steaks, while the sisters sat together talking of Sophie's work, Connie's diet. The children were called, and they all ate together under the trees.

William wanted to sit beside Charlie. He looked as if he'd really like to sit on his lap. Ruth wanted to know all about being a lawyer. Was law school hard? Did they have a moot court competition? Did he win? Had he done any criminal law? How much money did he make?

Molly wanted to know if Charlie liked Billy Joel. He said he didn't, much. Then they all wanted to know what he did like.

"Brahms."

"No, no. You know. Regular music."

"I like what my daughter calls Linda Ronstadt rock."

"What's that mean?"

"I think it means country," said Sophie.

Molly and Ruth looked disappointed.

"Well, what did you used to like?" Molly asked. She didn't say "when you were our age," and Charlie suspected she was afraid they didn't have records then, or something.

"Beatles. Elvis. The Band. The Stones."

"That's just like Mummy! Mummy, tell him what else you liked."

"Mamas and Papas. Joni Mitchell."

"You can't *dance* to Joni Mitchell."

"Oh, are we talking about dance music?"

"We didn't actually dance," said Charlie, "except for the minuet."

Sophie said, "Connie, remember that blue vinyl box you had for carrying forty-fives?"

"That Alison George gave me for my birthday and you always wanted it?"

"Tell me you still have it."

"Of course."

The upshot was, after supper Connie found the record box in the toy closet. It had a picture on it of a bobby soxer, like something from an Archie comic, dancing in a poodle skirt, and the twins were convulsed that their mother had possessed, even treasured, something so fifties. They carried the box out onto the wide porch off the living room. The three adults pored over the contents while the children watched and listened.

"'Poor Little Fool'!"

"'Silhouettes on the Shade'!"

"'Wake Up, Little Susie'!"

"'Mr. Blue' . . . my absolute favorite," said Charlie, with his hand on his heart.

"Me too," said Connie.

"'To Know Him Is to Love Him,'" Sophie exclaimed.

"By the Teddy Bears," said Charlie, not even having to look.

"Remember when I had such a crush on Mr. Weaver, and you and Sally used to sing that every time his name was mentioned?" said Sophie. "God, you were horrible to me."

"Was she horrible to you?" Charlie asked Sophie.

"She was. She used to have slumber parties in our very own house and I wasn't allowed to go to them."

"All *right*. Chubby Checker!" cried Charlie.

"See?" said Sophie. "She's having the same effect on you. I'm in the middle of telling you this sad story and you're not even listening. Being a little sister is hell."

"I was the absolute king of the twist," said Charlie solemnly. "I don't like to brag, but I must tell you that I was the best. In the interest of full disclosure."

"That's because you're so old," said Sophie. "My generation did not do the twist. You can probably even jitterbug."

"Mummy can do the twist!"

"Can you?"

"Certainly," said Connie. "I am also extremely accomplished with the Hula-Hoop."

Ruth and Molly had taken the Chubby Checker record from Charlie and rushed inside to the stereo. They had some trouble getting the middle thing to fit into the big hole, though their father had once shown them how to do it. But soon they had the window open and the music on and they rushed back outside. "Let's twist again . . . like we did last summer," bawled the record, and Charlie and Connie, after a moment's acute shame, began to dance.

The children fell about laughing. Connie was adequate, but Charlie was inspired, and even Sophie was roaring with laughter by the time it ended.

"Again!" William wanted more. He wasn't used to grown-ups making fools of themselves. Or to dinner parties where he was included.

"No. You have to wait another twenty years before we do that again."

Ruth dashed inside, and in a moment, there was Ricky Nelson's voice and a rockabillly beat. The girls stood expectantly.

"Come on!"

Charlie looked at Connie.

She held out her hands to him. They did a passable jitterbug, and the girls were overjoyed.

"Show us! Show us!" So they put on the record again, and Charlie danced with Ruth and Connie danced with Molly. The girls loved the part where they got twirled around and ended up dancing back to front, and then were suddenly twirled again. They had never done the kind of dancing where you touch your partner.

"Sophie, come dance, too."

"I can't," she said with dignity. "In my day, we only did the frug."

There were cries of joy until suitable music was found for a demonstration. It turned out Charlie could do that too, although he claimed they had called it something else, and soon they were all up, jerking and bumping.

"William has found his calling," said Ruth.

"Speaking of calling," said Connie as the phone rang. She returned to the porch to say that the neighbors wondered if they could turn the noise down. With regret they moved inside, and it was discovered to be long past William's bedtime.

Charlie slept in a room on the third floor that had been the cook's, in another era. He dreamed about Martha. He dreamed they were buying a house together on a cliff overlooking the surf, in a town called Reliance, Maine. He woke feeling logy with sadness, and when he came down to breakfast he asked Connie for a map so he could see if there was such a town. She produced a handsome leather-bound atlas that Dave's best man had given them for a wedding present. CC and DJ and a date in summer nineteen years ago were engraved on the cover in gold. Charlie searched the map of Maine, but it seemed there was no Reliance.

Connie made waffles for breakfast, and afterward they all went to church together. They made a handsome group, walking in, and they knew it. William held Charlie's hand as they walked up the aisle, and sat beside him until after the children's homily, when he was sent off with the other young ones to Sunday school in the basement. After church, Connie and Sophie and Charlie waited for Dave at home. As he drove in the driveway, they drove out. Dave kept his eyes fixed forward as he passed them, as if he would turn to stone if he should see Connie enjoying herself, or worse, people enjoying, supporting, defending Connie. In the rearview mirror, Charlie watched the reunion between father and children. The girls both rose from the kitchen steps and walked to the car to kiss him on the cheek.

Connie, Sophie, and Charlie carried a picnic and went for a long walk in Pocantico Hills. The open rolling land was at its peak of beauty, green and golden and fragrant in the summer sun. Sophie carried field glasses and watched the birds.

At the end of the afternoon, Charlie and Sophie urged Connie to come into town with them to have supper and see a movie. But she said she would be fine, she would have dinner with a friend.

"Some lady," said Charlie to Sophie on the train back to New York. They were watching the early evening sun on the Hudson, as the train rattled south.

"Yes," said Sophie.

"Thank you for taking me," said Charlie. "That was just what the doctor ordered."

"Yes," said Sophie again. He looked at her, and thought she was about to cry.

"You're sad," he said after a bit.

She nodded.

"Why?"

It took her some time to say, "I want a family."

"Oh. That." He thought it would make her laugh, but it didn't, and he realized he didn't feel much like laughing himself. He sighed deeply and put his arm around her.

"Don't we all," he said softly, and she nodded. The light was silver on the river.

∞

*C*harlie's case went to trial at last, and suddenly he was too busy to think, to talk, practically to breathe. Quality Foods used every trick in the book. They had avoided for months giving him documents he had subpoenaed; now suddenly they swamped him with boxloads of stuff, all of which had to be assessed, though most of it was junk. He had to pull paralegals and associates off other work and ask them to stay practically around the clock at the office, which greatly annoyed his partners. He found himself balked over and over, trying to get officers of the parent company to New York to testify in person. Instead he was forced to travel to Des Moines to take testimony on videotape. No matter what he got, he knew it would have little force. No matter how the witnesses lied or evaded in Des Moines, the jury in New York would subconsciously feel that what they were watching was not real people under oath, but television.

Every night he would go over the testimony of the day before. The transcriptions were costing him a fortune and he was paying for them out of pocket. He felt he was battling not only a Goliath, but almost more difficult, his own sense of hopelessness. Even if he won a jury verdict, the other side would appeal and neither he nor his client could afford much more of a fight. He knew that what he was really fighting for was a tiny victory here and there in what evidence was admitted to the record, in the hope that the next team to take on a suit like this would push a little farther until somebody somewhere won one.

At night, when he finally let himself into his apartment, he was usually too tired to speak. Sometimes Phoebe was there, watching the tube or already asleep. Often she was out with Serena and Kate and Joe, or spending the night at Patsy's. He would listen to his messages, take notes, open a beer, and sit in the silence, trying to clear his brain of the cacophony of testimony and jargon that swam in it waking and sleeping. He was sure that he talked in his sleep these days and that what he said was all a jumble of objections and citations.

It was one of the loneliest times he could remember in his life. Usually he had a thrice-weekly squash game with Wick Brainard, but now there was no time. He was feeling soft and out of sorts; he had trouble sleeping and he was gaining weight. Phoebe was sulky with him because she had had a small speaking part in a Circle Rep production, which she said was, like, unheard of for a first-year intern, to do anything except walk-ons and shit work, and on the night she had house seats for him, he forgot and went home and went to sleep.

Sophie had left messages on his machine at home a couple of times since the trial began, but when he didn't return them, she stopped calling. Charlie kept meaning to call Patsy to talk to her about Phoebe's curfew, which seemed to him to have become unilaterally nonexistent, and to see what Patsy knew about Phoebe's relationship with Joe Brockett, but somehow he just couldn't face talking to Patsy. He read briefs and ate pizza with Lenore, his associate on the case, and felt as if he hadn't seen the sky for weeks, and as if the New York summer had become one long steaming dirty fluorescent-lit tunnel.

Charlie was aware that from the time Jack left New York, there had seemed to be no letters between him and Phoebe and as far as he knew, no phone calls. When he asked Phoebe, she stared at him and said, "Everything's fine."

When he said, "But are things the same between you?" her face assumed the cold, congested look he knew well.

"Things are fine, Daddy, okay? He's fine, I'm fine, everything is just the way we want it. May I be excused?" And she got up, cleared her plates and Diet Coke can from the table, and left the room.

He kept wishing that someday he'd pick up the phone and it would be Jack on the end of the line, and he could chat with him and then say, casually, "How's Martha?" just for the pleasure of saying her name. He missed her, he just missed her, he wanted to know where she was and how she was, even though the answer was probably Fine, she got married last week.

One night just before Labor Day, his case very suddenly went to the jury. It was almost as if the opposing team had controlled the timing so the verdict would come out over the holiday weekend with as little press coverage as possible. Did that mean they thought they might lose it? Charlie thought he had done them some damage. He felt a curious mixture of hope and despair. Hope because his take on the other counsel table was, they were nervous. Despair because suddenly he was facing a long empty weekend with nothing to do.

He left the courthouse in the late afternoon and went to a restaurant across the square where lawyers and reporters hung out. Usually it was packed, but not on this Friday. He went to the pay phone to call home, to see if Phoebe would like to meet him for dinner. He got his own voice on the answering machine.

Next, he called Sophie. He got *her* voice on an answering machine. She had recorded a new message, in fact. Was it that long since he'd called her? Anyway, she was probably out in the Hamptons or something. Charlie had a feeling the chicken coop client was courting Sophie.

Next he tried Wick Brainard, to see if by any chance he was in town and up for a double date of any kind. Wick's girlfriends always seemed to have friends. He'd like somebody to talk to who hadn't been to law school. Many of Wick Brainard's girls seemed not to have finished high school, and tonight Charlie was in the mood for that.

But Wick's number didn't answer. Charlie had no idea what that meant; Wick was the sort who always had a machine on and called in for his messages three times a day with a beeper. Maybe he had moved. Or died. Charlie decided to go home and go running.

Central Park was warm but not sweltering; there had been rain earlier in the day. Charlie ran hard for about two miles and then slowed to a race walk; he was drenched in sweat and his heart was pounding. He didn't want to have a heart attack and die while the jury was out.

The park was full, with an air of fiesta. Lots of families from the sorts of neighborhoods where people didn't have houses in the Hamptons were in the park with grills and ice chests and bags of groceries, cooking dinner. There were families playing Frisbee and softball, and flying kites. There were people of every imaginable color and Charlie loved that. His favorite New York day was the Puerto Rican Day parade in the spring, because one year right outside their apartment building on this fancy block of the East Eighties, the marchers had lit an old car on fire and roasted a goat. Patsy of course had gone critical, but Charlie thought it was very festive, and he pointed out, after going downstairs to talk to the attendant policeman, that it was after all their own car they were burning.

This evening things were similarly gay and as he walked and ran, walked and ran, he watched the picnic and parties and people jogging and babies wheeling before them in three-wheeled strollers, and roller skaters and skate boarders, and it made him feel lonely. And back in his own apartment, having showered, he felt even more alone. He thought about having a can of lentil soup for the fifth time that week, and decided he couldn't bear it. He called to see if there was news of the jury; they had retired for the night. He made one last attempt to reach Wick, then Sophie. Then he gave up and got dressed.

Charlie had never liked going to restaurants alone. He didn't like the feeling that everyone knew he was hungry for company. He didn't like having girls try to pick him up, although he realized that their assumption was perfectly natural. But tonight he wanted to be around people. He decided to go to Turino, where at least he could have steak frites at the bar and talk to the bartender.

He was relatively early for the Turino crowd. It was cool inside and there were huge vases of flowers on the bar. He ordered a beer and sat, content, listening to two men down the bar, evidently old friends, talk about their wives.

After a while, gazing into the mirror behind the bartender, he became taken with a couple at a table near the back of the room, who were leaning toward each other, talking and smiling. The woman had a way of moving her head when she laughed that reminded him of Sophie. She laughed frequently; she was happy and the couple was holding hands.

The thing was, he began to realize that the woman not only reminded him of Sophie, it *was* Sophie. He put on his glasses and looked again. Absolutely Sophie, looking like two million bucks, and the man she was holding hands with was . . . Gillis Burnham.

Charlie turned around to look at them straight on, without reflection. Definitely Sophie, definitely Gillis. Gazing into each other's eyes and smiling. Lord, he was a handsome man, and Sophie Curry had never looked prettier in her life. Charlie put money on the bar to pay for his drink, and went to them.

He reached the table before either of them saw him, and then they both looked up at once.

"Charlie!" cried Sophie, with joy.

Gillis rose and put out his hand. His smile was as welcoming as Sophie's.

"Who let you out of your cage?" Sophie asked.

Charlie explained about the case going to the jury and then stood looking from one to the other.

"Can you join us?" Gillis asked.

"Yes, please," said Sophie.

"I don't want to interrupt . . ."

Neither denied that three would be a crowd in the long run, the way they were feeling.

"Just have a drink with us."

"Thank you. I'd love to."

He sat down. They all looked at each other, then Sophie and Gillis began to laugh the way people do when they've been in love for about seven and a half minutes. It was infectious.

"Well," said Charlie, "I don't want to pry but, um? . . ." He made a motion with his hands, meaning, come on, tell.

"I invited Sophie to a concert, to meet a friend of mine."

"Well, to meet him again. We had a cooking class together."

"I remember. Stanley."

"Right." This made them laugh, it was so delightful that someone else remembered the very moment they first met.

"It was a chamber group, playing one of Gillis's pieces," said Sophie, looking starstruck.

"And Stanley . . . poor Stanley . . ." Both Gillis and Sophie giggled. Once again, it seemed you had to know Stanley to quite understand what had happened next.

The waiter brought a round of drinks and Charlie seized his beer. Suddenly his adrenaline was pumping like to take his head off.

"Do you mind my asking," he said after a bit, "how long has this been going on?"

"That's a song, isn't it?"

"Please, no cheap music," said Gillis.

"The concert was two weeks ago," Sophie said.

Charlie took a deep breath. The two looked at him, seemed to agree by mental telepathy that they really must try to act normal, and Sophie said, "Now tell us about you. I tried to call you."

"I know. I haven't talked to anybody except lawyers since the trial began."

"And how is it going? Oh sorry." (She remembered she'd just been told it was over.) "I mean, how do you think—I mean, can you tell?"

"Not a clue."

"Do you know how long the jury will be out?"

"Not really. The longer they're out, the better it is for me."

"Well, *good* luck," said Sophie warmly, and Gillis echoed it.

"Thanks. Um, listen, do you mind my asking? Gillis, I thought you were . . . engaged."

"No," he said shortly. Then felt he'd been too short and amended. "It was brief, I mean." He clearly didn't want to say any more, and Charlie didn't blame him.

There was a pause in which Sophie and Gillis took each other's hand under the table. Time for Charlie to go.

He knocked back the rest of his beer. "I've thought a lot about Connie since that nice weekend," he said, rising. "How is she?"

"Terrific. She's in love with her jazz dance instructor."

Charlie couldn't help laughing. He'd suspected something like that. "Good for her."

"That's what I say," said Sophie. "He's twenty-eight."

Charlie whistled. Then he leaned over to kiss Sophie good-bye, and Gillis rose to shake his hand.

"Well, this has been a particular treat," Charlie said.

"Yes, what luck," cried Sophie and Gillis, delighted with the world, but ready to be alone again. He left them.

Charlie spent the night in turmoil. What did it mean that Martha was free and hadn't called him? Maybe she really didn't want to see him. Maybe she had forgotten him. Maybe she'd left Gillis for somebody else. At three in the morning, he suddenly remembered the beginning of the summer. Maybe Phoebe had told Martha about him and Patsy. Hadn't that been right around Jack's birthday, that all that happened? He got up and checked his date book. Yes. Patsy's operation was the day after Jack's birthday. And then Jack and Phoebe parted, and Martha would have had no more news of him. He actually got up and went to Phoebe's room thinking to ask her. (What, wake her up and ask her? No, just try to read her sleeping brain from the doorway.) But it was a moot question, whether he would have wakened her, as it turned out the little beast wasn't home and had left him no word of any kind about where she was going.

He called Patsy, and she turned out to be the only person in Manhattan who was at home without her answering machine on.

"Hello?" she answered on the second ring.

"Patsy, it's me. I'm sorry to call so late. Do you know where Phoebe is?"

There was a beat in which Charlie, who knew her so well, understood that she was awake waiting for a call, but not this one.

"Oh, Jesus, didn't she tell you?" Patsy asked wearily. "She went to Serena's country house for the weekend."

"Where is that?"

"Sagaponack or something. I have the number."

"Will you give it to me?"

"You're not going to call at this hour."

"No, but in the morning."

"I'm sorry she didn't tell you. I told her to . . . I think I told her to."

"Never mind. You shouldn't have to tell her. I'm sorry if I woke you."

"No. You didn't, actually."

A beat. Was Charlie going to ask her why she was up? No, he wasn't. He knew her well enough, and he could guess.

"Well. Thank you. I'll call her in the morning."

"Okay then."

They said goodnight.

Charlie *made himself* wait until nine o'clock in the morning before he dialed Martha's number. He got an answering machine. He left no message.

The morning was bright and clear and the streets below were nearly empty. Of course she was out of town, but where? She could be anywhere. He tried calling Annie, but there was no answer. Damn. If Martha was out of town, it was pointless anyway—he had to wait here for the jury to come in.

He called the number in Sagaponack where Phoebe was supposed to be. After a lot of rings, he got the drunk-sounding voice of a teenaged boy.

"Hullo?"

"Hello, this is Mr. Leveque. Is Phoebe there, please?"

There were some inarticulate mumblings; he realized the boy was drunk with sleep. He could hear some conversation with several other male voices in the room, then the first voice, somewhat more awake and aware, said, "Nobody's really like awake yet. Could you call back later?"

"Who is this, please?"

"This is Evan," said the voice, sounding puzzled.

"Do you mind telling me, is Phoebe Leveque *there?*"

"Uh . . . oh, yeah, she's here somewhere. At least she was last night."

Charlie took a deep breath. He was trying to picture the scene he was talking to.

"Is Mr. or Mrs. Rosen there?"

"I don't know. What time is it?"

"About nine-twenty."

Evan groaned and there was groggy laughter in the room behind him.

"I'm trying to find out if there are chaperones there."

"Oh. Oh, yeah. Oh yeah, they're like here and everything, but I don't know, maybe they're already gone or something. I was asleep."

"I gathered that. I'm sorry to disturb you, but would you please have Phoebe call me as soon as possible? This is her father, and I'm at home."

He sat for a while, fuming and missing Martha. Where was she, where *was* she? She would know what to do. She would love him even though his life was a shambles and his daughter was a self-centered lit-tle beast. The desire just to hear Martha's voice seemed to rise in him like a wave that would crest over him and drown him. It *did* keep crest-ing over him, and yet somehow he kept breathing air and continued to live. Where had that *been* all these months? How had he lived, some-how not knowing that in a room in his brain he'd tried to lock and seal, that huge love was unchanged?

He had known it, of course. He had known it every moment, waking and sleeping.

At eleven-thirty the phone rang, and Charlie jumped for it, imagin-ing for a split second that through some magic it would be Martha.

"Hello, Daddy," said Phoebe's sour voice, clearly indicating that she was struggling to be patient.

"Phoebe."

"Look, I really do *not* appreciate you calling up at the crack of dawn and asking some person you don't even know if there are like chaperones here. I *told* Mother where I was going."

"You didn't tell me. You left town for the weekend without calling, without leaving a message, without leaving a note."

"I left a message at your office."

"You did?"

"Yes," she almost shouted, very indignant and aggrieved, "I *did*."

"I haven't been back to the office for two days. Couldn't you have left word here? I was worried."

"Look, Daddy. This is so stupid. It really makes me mad. You act like I'm some baby you can't trust to do anything right."

"Phoebe, I can't trust you to put your own dishes in the dishwasher. You are not grown up, you are sixteen, and we have rules."

"Look, Daddy. I really cannot get into this on the phone. I just want you to know that I am really annoyed, and I think that this is just not working out. I'm right where I said I would be, Serena's parents are here, we're all having a good time playing go fish and pin the tail on the donkey."

"Don't be snide, Phoebe. I was right to be worried. Would you rather be lying dead in a ditch somewhere and have your father take a week to notice you weren't in your room?"

"Daddy, I hate to say this, I know this is going to hurt you, but I really think I should go back and live with Mother. This is just not working out."

There was a silence. She was right; it did hurt him. He was also so annoyed by her tone that he wished he could tell her how much she hurt him, but he didn't. The silence lengthened.

At last Phoebe said, "Look, I have to go now. Serena wants the phone, and we're going out to play tennis or something."

"All right. I'll see you Monday night, I guess."

Phoebe slammed down the phone. Charlie put his face in his hands. There is nothing quite like having someone you love hang up on you.

The empty afternoon seemed endless. He went down to the courthouse, but that was pointless. The jury was working, they had asked for some exhibits from the defense and some transcripts of his depositions. There was no way of telling what it meant or how long they would take.

He went to the Metropolitan and spent the afternoon in Renaissance Paintings. It was cool there and jammed with tourists. He thought it impossible to be in a place with so many other people and not run into anyone he knew, although it was true that the great majority of those here seemed to be from Japan.

He met no one he knew. At least four times he started, thinking a figure in the distance was Martha. But it never was. At the end of the day he walked slowly down Fifth Avenue. He stopped at a pay phone; the jury, he learned, was on its dinner break. He went home and called again; they were back at work. He looked in the paper and tried to choose a movie to see. Nothing appealed; he hated going to movies alone. He didn't want to see anything but Martha.

He called her number again and got the machine. He called Annie, and to his amazement Annie's husband answered. He could hear the sounds of a dinner party.

"It's Charlie Leveque," he said.

"Oh, Charlie. Yes. How have you been?"

"Fine thanks. Busy."

"Look, we're right in the middle of dinner . . ."

"Sorry. Could you just tell me, do you happen to know where Martha is?" His heart was in his mouth. He prayed he was going to say, Yes, she's right here.

"Oh, gee. I hope this isn't an emergency."

"No, no."

Al called, "Annie, do you know for sure where Martha is?"

There was a conversation Charlie couldn't hear.

"Charlie, she went up to Alewife for the week."

"Oh. I see. Thanks very much."

"You're welcome, nice to talk to you." Click.

Charlie felt sunk. He wanted to see Martha, to hear her voice, to talk to her. He wanted to be with her, giving a dinner party, or going to one. He wanted to be with her doing anything.

He didn't much want to talk to her dragon lady of a mother in Alewife. What if Martha had told her family she didn't want to talk to him? One thing about Martha, she did not like pain. It was one of the many ways she differed from Patsy. When Martha decided to stop the pain, she stopped it. She didn't call, she didn't write, she didn't say oh let's just play with it again until it starts to hurt. She could easily have told her family she didn't want to talk to Charlie, or see him.

He spent a frustrated night and woke with nothing resolved. He drank a pot of tea and read the Sunday paper. He called to learn that the jury was back at work and they looked settled in for the day. He did the crossword puzzle and had just decided to go to church when the phone rang. The jury was coming in.

A half hour later he was downtown in the courtroom, and two minutes after that it was all over. His only thought was Now I can leave.

The drive to Alewife took four hours. When he arrived at the house, he was shaking and could barely make himself get out of the car. What if she wasn't here? What if she was here with a date? What if the mother wouldn't let him see her?

He walked to the door, wondering if his knees were going to give way. That would be good. Martha, he could hear Madelaine calling, that divorce lawyer friend of yours is here lying in the driveway . . .

He stood at the screen door and looked into the front hall. He could see through the house to the back garden, and he could hear voices. He rang the bell. Martha, I'm here. Martha, dear love, please come here before my heart stops.

Across the hall, he saw the door open from the garden and Fred came in, holding his grandfather's hand.

"Let's see who's at the door, Fred. You answer it, all right?"

Fred came to the door and opened it, and when he saw Charlie he broke out in smiles.

"Hello, Fred. Hello, Dr. Forbes." He and Martha's father shook hands. He dropped down. "Can I have a hug, Fred?" Fred wholeheartedly hugged him.

"I was hoping to see Martha," he said, standing, trying to sound casual.

"She's not here, is she, Fred?"

Fred shook his head.

"You tell him where she is."

"She's playing golf," said Fred.

"Aha," said Charlie, surprised. He didn't know she played golf.

"You could come in and wait," said Dr. Forbes. "Mother's out here on the back terrace."

"Do you think Martha would mind if I went and joined her?"

"Not a bit. I don't think they're playing for money."

"Thanks. I'll see you later, Fred." He waved as he started back to the car. I hope I will, I hope I'll see you later.

He got lost only once on the way to the club. The golf course, where he had once played with Dr. Forbes, was very rough and beautiful, on a bluff above the sea. The soil was sandy and the greens were a mess, but Dr. Forbes loved it because it hadn't changed since his father was a boy. In a changing world, there were not many places a man of eighty could go and see things exactly as they had been when he was eight.

Charlie checked in at the pro shop, a shed where you could sign for soft drinks and golf balls. They. Dr. Forbes had said "they." Who was she playing with? What was he going to do if she was with a new love? Fall on his sword, he supposed, in the middle of the fairway.

"I'm looking for Martha Forbes; can you give me a guess where she'd be?"

"I think they teed off about three—I imagine they'll be on about the fifth about now."

"That's this way, isn't it?" Charlie pointed.

The boy behind the counter grunted.

Charlie made his way across the wide fourth fairway, expecting at any moment to be brained by somebody's drive. Standing on the ridge above the fifth green, he saw Martha. She was standing with a handsome man of about fifty, with graying hair and, Charlie could see as he got closer, brilliant blue eyes. They were waiting for an elderly pair to finish putting.

Charlie wasn't sure when exactly Martha saw him. She didn't move; at a point, he realized she was just standing, watching him approach.

Finally, he was standing before her. Her eyes, blue-gray, looked wary. She looked tired, but to his eyes, utterly beautiful. He had no idea what he looked like to her.

"Hello," he said.

The man with Martha was looking very curious.

"Hello. Matthew, this is Charlie Leveque. Charlie, this is my brother."

The two shook hands.

"I'm sorry to interrupt."

"That's all right. I'm losing."

"I'd like to talk to you."

"Oh." She looked at Matthew.

"Go ahead," said Matthew. He was too discreet to reveal any curiosity about this turn of events. "I'll play the next hole and meet you on the seventh."

Martha nodded. She handed her club to Matthew, who was evidently sharing his golf bag with her. Matthew chipped his ball onto the green and went off to putt, and Martha went on standing there as if paralyzed.

"I'm surprised to see you."

"Yes. I imagine so."

"Were you in the neighborhood?"

"No. God, it's wonderful to see you."

"Is it?" For the first time, she smiled.

"Yes. Look, I ran into Sophie the other night. She was with Gillis."

"Was she?" Martha thought about it and then smiled again. "Well, that's nice. That's very nice."

"I thought you were going to marry him."

"Yes. Well. I changed my mind."

"*You* did."

"Yes."

"Will you tell me why?"

"Will you tell me what you're doing here?"

"I came to ask you to marry me."

"I thought you were marrying your wife."

"No."

"Oh," she said. She looked surprised.

Charlie got down on his knees. He thought he saw Martha stifle a smile.

"Martha. Please. You are my heart. I love you, I will love you for the rest of my life, and probably after I'm dead. Will you please marry me?"

Martha gazed at him, her expression hard to read. Then she knelt down too so they were looking into each other's eyes.

"Do you remember what you said to me, the first night you told me you loved me?" she asked.

"About how frightening it is to be in love?"

"Yes."

He remembered.

> "'They have most power to hurt us
> whom we love
> We lay our sleeping lives down
> in their arms.'"

She looked at him, grave. "I will love you for the rest of my life," she said, "and probably after I'm dead."

"I bet I loved you before I was born," said Charlie. "Will you marry me?"

"Yes, I will," she said, and he gave a whoop and kissed her.

"Are you sure?" he asked. "My daughter's a horror and I just lost the biggest case of my career. And I snore."

"You do not."

On the fifth tee, a foursome stared down the fairway at them. "What's going on down there?" asked an ancient man in plaid pants.

"I can't quite make out," said another. "Somebody must have lost a contact lens."

"I adore you," said Martha.

"I thought you stopped."

"No. Never."

"Good. But you weren't going to tell me you loved me or ever come back to me?"

"No. Not if we couldn't be together. I was just going to wander around missing you for the rest of my life."

"God, I love you."

"Let's go tell Matthew."

"Will he be glad?"

"Very."

"All right, then. Then can we go somewhere and neck?"

"Yes."

"Oh, look," said the man in the plaid pants. "They must have found it." And when he was sure Martha and Charlie were in the clear, he stepped up to address his ball with his mashie.

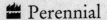 Perennial

Books by Beth Gutcheon:

MORE THAN YOU KNOW
ISBN 0-06-095935-5

In a small town on the coast of Maine, Hannah Gray begins her story: "Somebody said 'true love is like ghosts, which everyone talks about, and few have seen.' I've seen both, and I don't know how to tell you which is worse."

"An exceptional novel—thrilling, taut, austere: this is extraordinary writing of a tense, crytalline beauty." —*Shirley Hazzard*

FIVE FORTUNES
ISBN 0-06-092995-2

A warm and witty story of five unforgettable women and the unexpected friendships forged over a transforming week at the "Fat Chance" spa.

"[Beth Gutcheon] has absolutely perfect pitch when it comes to capturing the lives of these remarkable women."—Anne Rivers Siddons

SAYING GRACE
ISBN 0-06-092727-5

This "deliciously readable" *(San Francisco Chronicle)* story focuses on Rue Shaw, a woman who has it all – a great child, a solid marriage, and a job she loves – and wants to keep it that way, despite the changing world around her. Funny, rich in detail and finally stunning, *Saying Grace* is "by turns heartwarming and heartrending" *(Boston Globe)*.

DOMESTIC PLEASURES
ISBN 0-06-093476-X

Charlie and Martha, two divorced parents of teenagers from two very different worlds, are thrown together by drastic circumstances and suddenly find themselves falling in love . . . life is about to become more complicated than ever.

"[A] witty and often moving tale of love among the moderns."—*Washington Post Book World*

STILL MISSING
ISBN 0-06-097703-5

When six-year-old Alex Selky doesn't come home from school, his mother begins a desperate vigil that lasts through months of false leads and the desertions of friends and allies. The basis for the feature film *Without a Trace*.

"Haunting, harrowing, and highly effective . . . a stunning shocker of an ending. . . . It strings out the suspense to the almost unendurable."—*Publishers Weekly*

THE NEW GIRLS
ISBN 0-06-097702-7

A resonant, engrossing novel about five girls in prep school during the '60s, into whose protected reality marches the Vietnam War, the woman's movement, and the sexual revolution – and changes their lives forever.

"Funny without sacrificing intelligence, intelligent without being pretentious. It's all-around good reading."—*Boston Globe*

Available wherever books are sold, or call 1-800-331-3761 to order.